The present disappeared, and she was once again Philadelphia, vibrant and spirited . . . in a lush meadow, in a colonial America before the war . . . in the arms of the man she would always love.

He laughed quickly, and I was so enraged at this, I gave him a quick hard slap. The next moment I was in his arms, not as I had been before, but differently. He was holding me close, not tenderly at all, not at all like a brother or a father. For the second time in three days, I was kissed by a man, and I kissed him back with as much enthusiasm as I had showed before, and—I must confess it—a great deal more of energy and passion. I know not why unless it were the aftermath of anger and great emotion, but I kissed Bram with far more fervor and fierceness than the man who I have intended for years to be my lover. Bram, the calm, the steady, the dependable, was none of these things when he kissed me. A veritable tiger he was, and in his arms I became someone I did not know. . .

It is past my understanding that I could love one man and revel so much in the arms and kisses of another. . .

Books by Jacqueline Marten

Loving Longest
An Unforgotten Love
Kiss Me, Catriona
To Pluck a Rose
Glory in the Flower
Forevermore
Bryarly

Published by POCKET BOOKS

Bryarly
Jacqueline Marten

Previously titled <u>Nightmare in Red</u>

POCKET BOOKS

New York   London   Toronto   Sydney   Tokyo

Acknowledgments: To the numerous nameless hostesses of Sleepy Hollow Restorations, Westchester County, New York; and the incredibly helpful and knowledgeable staff at Valley Forge National Park, with a special mention for Drum Major Tom McGuire, Jinny Atkinson, and Supervisory Park Historian Louis J. Venuto. To Al, for stories of a Coney Island boyhood; Marylou Meister of Larchmont, for the loan of her accident; Nancy Loewenberg, for the loan of her profession; Caleb, for the loan of himself. And not least, Ruzell Browning, who gives me time to write.

Note: Spelling in the eighteenth century, even among the educated, was likely to be individual, inconsistent, and occasionally incomprehensible, including the lavish use of capitals.

POCKET BOOKS, a division of Simon & Schuster Inc.
1230 Avenue of the Americas, New York, N.Y. 10020

Published by arrangement with the author

ISBN: 0-671-63522-0

First Pocket Books printing October 1988

10 9 8 7 6 5 4 3 2 1

POCKET and colophon are trademarks of
Simon & Schuster Inc.

Printed in the U.S.A.

For
Albert E. Marten
My sword and my shield, my best friend, too;
Our sons
Richard, Jonathan, Seth, Ethan
and
Nancy, the first of our daughters

When Golda Meir was prime minister of Israel, a serious outbreak of night attacks on women took place in Tel Aviv. One cabinet member's solution to the problem was a curfew. Women, he suggested, should not be allowed out at night after a certain hour.

"But, Minister," Golda Meir is said to have turned to him swiftly and retorted, "it is the women who are being attacked by men. If there is to be a curfew, let the men stay at home."

There was no curfew.

Deborah Sampson is the only woman known to have fought in the American Revolution—disguised as a man.

This is not her story.

PROLOGUE

A naked Venus knelt at the center of the fountain with a trio of toga-draped goddesses ringed around her. The girl standing at the fountain's rim in a gown of white lace and chiffon stayed motionless as any one of them.

"Aren't you wasting the music and the moonlight out here in the garden by yourself, honey?"

The girl wheeled around. "Oh—it's you, Hank."

"My, my. Don't get carried away with enthusiasm." He stepped nearer to her; his hand, lightly caressing, touched her neck and lifted her chin. "I must say, Miss Lee Allen, you don't look overly bright and bushy-tailed for the vestal virgin of Ambruster, Georgia, the girl who got herself crowned senior prom princess and engaged to Randolph Jefferson Ambruster the Fourth all in the same month."

"The engagement's off."

He glanced down at her clasped hands. "You're still wearing his ring."

"The damn thing's too tight. I'll need to use soap to get it off." She waved her hand half mockingly. "My fingers aren't as slender as his great-grandmother's."

"Who decided, you or he?"

"The announcement in the newspaper usually says 'by mutual consent.' It was very, very mutually consented to."

"Poor pretty little princess," he said lightly. "We all wondered if you'd ever feel the pea under the mattress."

She reached up suddenly and yanked off the silver crown that had been placed on her shining hair an hour before. A shower of bobby pins fell into the fountain as she held it out to him.

"Look, just tinsel and cardboard."

With an overhead toss, she sent the crown into the center of the fountain, watching with satisfaction as it turned into a sodden lump and sank below the water.

Smiling, she looked back at him. "You're confusing your princesses. I'm the one who just awoke from a long dream. A *bad* dream."

"Dance with me, Sleeping Beauty?"

She moved into his outstretched arms, and they stood together, swaying slowly in time to the distant music.

"Only I'm not asleep," she murmured as his cheek rubbed against hers and his hands moved down to the unbelted waist, and he whirled her round and round the fountain. "I'm awake for the first time in years."

"No more princess, no more engagement, no more vestal virgin?"

"No more any of them."

The music stopped, and they came to a breathless halt. She bent over the fountain, trailing her hands in the water, then touched cool, dripping fingers to her heated cheeks.

"Lee?"

"Mm?"

"You don't want to see Randy again tonight, do you?"

"I surely do not."

"What I mean is, honey, why don't we cut out and go back to the frat house for a party of our own? I'll pick up some of the other girls and guys. If you wait in the parking lot, you won't have to worry about running into Randy."

"I was going to go home . . ."

"It's not even ten o'clock. Think of all the explanations if you go home so early."

"I'll have to tell them sooner or later."

"But not tonight," he whispered, his hands gentling her shoulders. "I think you need comforting tonight. I think you need a party. We've got some champagne at the frat house."

She released her lower lip from between her teeth. In the moonlight her face was pale, but her smile was wide and reckless.

"Stay me with flagons, comfort me with apples," she murmured, *"for I am sick of love.* All right. Why not? I do need a party. I would rather explain tomorrow."

There were four of them in the car with her, Hank and Webb Carlin, George Hunnicutt, and a sharp-faced straw-haired boy she had never met before.

"Meet Drake Tanner," Hank said before he shoved her into the car between himself and George.

Webb and Drake got in behind, and one of them leaned across the front seat to offer her a half-full bottle of champagne.

She tilted the bottle to her lips. A very little went down her throat and more down the front of her dress. George patted her dry with his handkerchief. It was an accident, she thought hazily, that his hands lingered over her breasts.

"Where are the other girls?" she asked vaguely, twisting at her third finger. It was wet and sticky with champagne, and the ring seemed to be getting looser.

"They're coming in another car."

"Oh."

It didn't sound quite right, but she was too busy struggling with the ring, and they kept giving her sips of champagne.

Just as they pulled her laughingly out of the car, she gave a final tug and the ring came off.

"Look." She held it out. "It's off. It's official. I'm unengaged."

"You're available," said Webb Carlin.

"I'm available," she agreed.

3

As they went up the front steps, her footsteps lagged. "There aren't any lights. Where's the party?"

"We're the party, honey," Hank told her.

"But, the other girls—"

"They'll be along any minute now."

"But—"

"No buts, princess. Remember, it's your party. We're all here to hate Randy Ambruster and comfort you. You want to be comforted, don't you, honey?"

She remembered his arms when they danced, and the soft reassurance of his voice.

"Oh, yes, yes, I do."

Hank took her arm as they went into the darkened hallway, and someone switched on the light.

There was a low curse, and Webb said, "Turn off the light, you fool. Wait till we get her upstairs."

"I don't want to go upstairs." She turned to run too late; someone latched onto her other arm and the one Hank was holding was wrenched behind her so viciously, she felt as though it were being torn from the socket.

Unbelievable that Hank's voice should still be that soft, caressing purr in her ear. "You've changed your mind, haven't you, Lee honey? You do want to go upstairs?"

"Please," she whispered. "Oh, please."

"Say it, honey. Say you want to go upstairs with us."

She cried out as he doubled her arm farther back, and he did it one more time before she whimpered, "I want to go upstairs with you."

"Now, that's an invitation if ever I heard one," Webb Carlin said gleefully; and in the darkness, as they half propelled, half dragged her along the steps, one of them cupped his hand over her bottom, cursing the layers of chiffon that got in his way.

After the long, curving staircase, there was a hallway to be stumbled along before they let go of her arms and pushed her through another door.

"Pull down the shades." Hank was still in command. "And close the door."

There was a rustle and a slam. "Okay. Now let there be light."

The overhead light went on, and she stood in its glare, blinking and trembling. The new boy, Drake, had his back against the door. The other three circled her pantherlike, eyes glistening, hungry animals preparing to attack a tethered goat.

"Why—Don't d-do this. Hank—we—I'm—I thought —friends."

"Friends, Miss Snooty Nose. And you too uppity for anyone less important than Randy Ambruster? Well, Randy Ambruster doesn't want you anymore. He sat in this very room last night, moaning in his cups about Miss Prunes-and-Prisms fooling us one and all, chiefly him. Someone had plucked her little cherry before old Randy got to it."

"No, please, it's not true. You can't. I'll tell. I'll—"

"Don't look for support from old Randy, princess. He's not about to care what happens to some other guy's leavings. And what's the difference to you? You told me yourself, you ain't no vestal. Take off that dress."

The sick trembling spread downward from her stomach to her legs. She could only shake her head wordlessly, pressing her quivering thighs together, trying to suppress the warm tickle sliding down the sides of her legs.

"Drake?" Hank said softly, his cruel eyes never leaving her face.

"Yeah?"

"Got that Swiss knife of yours?"

"Yeah, in my desk, but you promised me no rough stuff. You said—"

"Give it here, boy."

Drake left his post by the door to rummage in the desk over near the window.

"Here it is, but remember, you said—"

"Shut up, Drake. There won't be any rough stuff unless Miss High-and-Mighty asks for it. Now, princess, it's your choice. I'm gonna count to three; then the dress comes off or I cut right down the middle. One, two, that's a good girl."

Her fingers were fumbling with the back zipper when Webb stepped behind her, and with a single powerful jerk zipped her gown open from the lacy top to the middle of her knees. Someone else tugged, and a swirl of chiffon lay about her feet.

She stood there in nothing but white nylon briefs, low-cut white lace bra, and open-toed white sandals, shaking and shivering, the tears that ran down her cheeks leaving dark mascara streaks.

When Hank stepped close to her with the knife held up, she flinched and half screamed, but the cold steel lingered only seconds against her breast and then sawed right through the lace of her brassiere. The two halves of the bra slid down her arms, and when she raised them instinctively to protect herself, pain forced the right arm down. Hank tossed the knife back to Drake and yanked down the left arm, too.

"Now, princess, why would you want to hide such a bee-yoo-tee-full pair of boobs?"

"I w-want to go home. Please, *please*. Don't do this. Let me go."

Drake, back at the door, avoided her pleading eyes. The other three just grinned at her, wide-mouthed toothy grins that reminded her of the skeleton's head in the biology lab.

"Of course you'll go home," Hank promised in the voice of deadly softness she had already learned to fear more than any threat.

"After we're through with you." Webb's grin grew wider.

"For God's sake, hurry up, Hank. My pants are like to bust," George complained; and against her will her eyes were drawn to him. Her body quaked in renewed terror and disgust at the sight of his bulging trousers.

Some unspoken signal must have passed between them, for the next moment she found herself pulled down onto the floor in the narrow space between the two bunk beds.

One of them used his fists to pin her shoulders to the floor. Hank held a merciless knee between her legs while he fumbled with the zipper of his fly.

"We stayed you with flagons of champagne, love, just like

6

you asked; now we'd comfort you with apples, if we had any. How about some nice hard bananas instead?" he asked and jammed himself right into her.

A hand over her mouth, fingers pinching the lips together, cut her scream in two. She went on screaming soundlessly in her head, throughout her body, until Hank collapsed onto her, the wetness spreading over and under and in her.

When Hank rolled over and George took his place, the pain of the battering was less because of the wetness, but when he was quickly done, his two hundred pounds of dead weight sprawled suffocatingly across her.

Webb kicked the inert body. "Hey, sleep it off somewhere else. My turn."

He aimed a few more kicks, and one of them landed on her shins. She wept desperately, helplessly, as George slid away and Webb straddled her legs.

Webb was the worst of the three. He was bigger and more controlled, hammering into her, and then, just when he seemed about to give her release, hammering in again, harder than before. From the way his eyes glittered and he licked his lips, she knew he enjoyed cruelty for cruelty's sake.

When she closed her eyes, he made her open them by pinching her nipples with the edges of his fingernails, smiling when she sobbed.

They no longer held her mouth; her throat was too rasped to scream.

"You love it," Webb said, hammering away. "Go on, tell me you love it."

She looked at him with dead eyes, no longer begging, no longer expecting mercy.

His hand smashed across her face. "You hard of hearing, bitch? I said for you to tell me you love it, tell me you want it."

"I love—love it."

His hand smashed against the other side of her face.

"Beg me."

"I want it."

"Say please."

7

"Please, I—I—I want it."

He launched himself at her with renewed vigor, shouting out, "Timber!" during his last fierce thrusts, laughing aloud in triumph at the agonized arching of her body each time it was pierced, not heeding the sluggish seepage of blood from the ripped tissue.

There was a broad bright scarlet cummerbund around his waist. She fastened her wide-open eyes on it, and the world dissolved into those two separate agonies—the rhythmic flash of red before her eyes and the red-hot pain of his rhythmic entries in and out of her.

Seconds after his weight crushed her into the floor, while he grunted and groaned, he was up and away. "Come on, Drake. Let's see what the new member of the frat can do."

"Do you think we should?" came Drake's hesitating voice. "It's getting late; someone might come."

"You losing your nerve, boy?"

"Of course not, but—"

"You afraid to do a man's job?"

"No, I just—"

"Looks like he ain't got no balls."

"Now see here . . ."

"Maybe he can't get it up."

"Who you saying can't get it up? Get out of my way!"

He knelt over her. He leaned against her unresisting body. His face touched hers, and he whispered a steady stream of apologies and remorse into her disbelieving ears while he pumped away at her.

"I'm sorry, I'm really sorry. I don't want to do this, but you can see I have to. You see how it is, they'll think I'm chicken if I don't go along. I'm sorry, honestly, I'm sorry. I'm trying not to hurt you. I'll come as fast as I can. I'm not really hurting you, am I?"

"No," she whispered hoarsely through cracked, swollen lips.

"I'm almost there," he whispered encouragingly. "It's almost over."

"Thank you," she told him politely before she fainted.

When she came to, she was still lying on the floor, but

they'd turned her over on her side. Hank was zipping her back into the white chiffon gown, which she knew with dreary certainty she would never wear again. Webb knelt in front of her, slapping vigorously at her hands and wrists, while Drake sloshed a cold wet towel over her face and neck. Some drops of water dribbled over her mouth, and she lapped them up like a thirst-crazed animal.

"See, I told you she was all right, Drake. A little lovin' wouldn't get the princess down."

"I still think we should get her out of here."

"Aw, she was probably just shamming." Webb let go of her hands. He bent over her with a death's-head grin, slipped his hand under the lace, and squeezed her right breast hard. "You were just shamming, weren't you, cunt?" he taunted her.

Until the very moment that she spat full in his face, she had thought that her strength and spirit as well as her saliva were all dried up.

Her courage was short-lived. A sick trembling began in the pit of her stomach when she saw the slate eyes staring down at her and the slow, deliberate way he used his shirt sleeve to wipe his face.

It was Hank, surprisingly, who said, "C'mon, Webb, let it go. Drake's right; it's getting late. We better get out of here."

"In just a minute. One little old minute more. First this cunt's gotta be taught a lesson. She's gotta learn how to treat her betters."

As he shoved her onto her back, her thighs contracted instinctively; but to her surprise, when he knelt, he straddled her waist. Then, almost negligently, his cold eyes never leaving hers, he opened his fly, and the rigid, tumescent organ popped out at her face like a jack-in-the-box. She still didn't understand until the warm stream jetted across her trembling lips and up her nostrils. Then she was choking and crying out and swallowing and retching, her open mouth an added invitation for this ultimate, degrading invasion. When she jerked her head convulsively back and forth to evade him, he followed her movements, hosing her eyes and her forehead, and when she managed a heave that turned her face to the floor, he drenched her hair and the back of her neck.

When he finally jumped off her, she stayed with her face pressed against the floor until Drake came with the wet towel and sat her up and gently washed her face and neck.

"He shouldn't have done a thing like that," he told her, low-voiced. "He ought to be ashamed of himself."

Hank was suddenly in command again. "Webb, you made most of the mess; you stay here with George and do clean-up. Drake and I will get her home. We're liable to have company soon; it's almost midnight. The party's over."

There was too much pain for her to walk as fast as they wanted; they half carried her down the stairs and out to the car and pushed her into the back on the floor.

"Stay down," Hank ordered, and obediently she shrank down in the corner against the door, just where he had shoved her. Huddling there, jolted up and down, to and fro, jarring her spine, adding pain on pain to her burning insides, they seemed to be jouncing over every bump in the road. A sharp swerve was too much for her roiling stomach; she began to heave—all over the seat, all over the floor, all over the white lace and chiffon bought for a princess.

"She just up-chucked," she heard Drake say from far away.

"Bitch!" Hank swore. "I ought to rub her nose in it. Well, this is where she gets out."

He pulled over to the curb and came to a grinding halt that threw her sideways, slamming her face against the side of the door.

She sat, dazed, even after he had ordered curtly, "Get out!"

With a muttered curse, he jumped out of the car, took a swift look around, then pulled open the back door, took hold of her arm, and jerked her onto the sidewalk.

"You can use your own steam from here; it's only two blocks. And I'm warning you, if you know what's good for you, you'll keep your mouth shut. Just remember we can find you any time we want to, you hear? Remember something else—whatever you say, it's four against one. No one will believe you, princess. You came with us of your own free will. You asked for it."

He gave her one last shove in the direction of her house, then got back in the car, not bothering to watch her weaving and stumbling down the street.

She swayed as she walked, biting her lips against the pain of each step, then weeping because her mouth was already so sore.

The endless blocks were done; the white fence rails gleamed in the moonlight. She reached out, grasping for them, using them to drag herself along. In the broad driveway she fell, the pebbles grinding into her knees.

"Please, God," she whimpered meaninglessly. "Please, God."

She tried to call out, but nothing more than a croak could get past her throat. She crawled until she reached the broad steps and buckled over onto them.

"Please, God, please, God, please, God."

The front door was flung open. A blessed, familiar voice, the one she most wanted, called, "Who's that out there?"

She managed to raise her head again without being sick. She had already lost control of the rest of her body.

"Hattie, it's me."

"My God, my God."

"He wasn't listening, Hattie," she whispered. "He wasn't listening at all."

Arms supported her. The clean, starched, fresh-smelling uniform enfolded her.

"Let me help you up, Miss Lee. Hattie will take care of you. Just lean on me. Oh, sweet Lord of mercy, who done this to you?"

"Hattie," she sobbed out wildly as they both stumbled into the house, "I want a bath. I want a bath. I want a bath . . ."

The small waiting room and four examination cubicles of the emergency ward were crammed to capacity with the victims of prom night pranksters, accidents, and a three-car collision on the highway.

She sat on a low, backless stool set in the very back of the room, her lower lip clamped between her teeth and her eyes staring blankly ahead. The wall supported her back; Hattie stood beside her, holding onto her hand.

A score of eyes looked up with interest as a policeman pushed his way through the crowded doorway and strode up to the reception desk. The nurse smiled prettily up at him.

He took ten seconds to smile back at her. Then his voice boomed out in the suddenly quiet room, bouncing from wall to wall. "Evening, Sally. You got an alleged rape case for me, I hear. A Miss Lee Allen. I gotta take her testimony."

"Oh, yeah." She ruffled through a sheaf of cards. "That's her in the back, the pretty one with the black woman."

"You got a room where I can talk to her, sweetie?"

"The only place not being used is the dental office."

"That'll do." He raised his voice again. "Miss Allen, would you come up here, please?"

She sat, paralyzed, the dead white of her face breaking out in a flame of red.

"Miss Allen," he said again impatiently; and Hattie whispered to her, "We better go to him, Miss Lee. I'll help you, honey. Just lean on me."

Putting almost her full weight on Hattie, she pulled herself onto her feet. Ignoring the avid, curious stares, the eager, excited whispers, she walked slowly and painfully over to the policeman.

In the cubicle they were shown to, Hattie helped her up onto the big dentist's chair.

"I'm Sergeant Gorsey," the policeman said, uncapping a pen and turning the pages of his notebook. "Now, if you'll just tell me what happened."

With her own eyes closed to shut out the cold hard look of his, she told her story slowly, haltingly, not always coherently, but without tears, seemingly, thought the listening man, without emotion.

He made her repeat all the names, spelling them out carefully. "Webb Carlin? Any relation to Hubert Carlin of the Farmers' Loan Association?"

"His son."

"And this George Hunnicutt? Is he one of the—"

"Ambruster Hunnicutts? Yes. His uncle's head of pediatrics at this hospital."

"Good families, most of them," he said to himself, and then to her, "Now, you say you're engaged to Randy Ambruster?"

"Not anymore. We—we broke it off."

"Why?"

"It's personal," she whispered huskily.

"Nothing's personal when you're charging rape, Miss Allen. These fellows will have a right to defend themselves." He added casually, impersonally, "Did you have an orgasm?"

Her eyes flew open at the same moment that he stilled Hattie's murmur of protest with a curt wave of his hand.

"An—an—" Her teeth chattered. "D-don't you understand? There were *four* of them. There—they *forced* me. I—I—I w-wasn't having f-fun. They—they—it was rape." She lowered her head and wept into her hands. "Oh, God, they raped me! They did—things—"

"Now, calm down, Miss Allen. It's my job to ask these questions. You know, with some girls they cry rape when what's really happened is that they changed their minds afterwards or maybe Daddy came home too soon."

"I was raped. I was raped. I was raped."

"Then I guess we better have a medical exam."

"And about time, too," Hattie spoke up tartly. "That's what we brought her here for."

Sergeant Gorsey opened the door of the room and hollered down the hallway, "Hey, Sally, can you get me a doctor?"

He stood outside waiting till footsteps sounded along the hall. An irritated voice addressed him. "What's all the rush, Sergeant? I have some pretty banged-up people who need me."

In the dental office they could plainly hear the sergeant's snicker and then again his booming voice. "According to her, the girl I've got waiting in here for you got herself pretty well banged, too."

Belatedly their voices lowered. After a brief whispered exchange, Sergeant Gorsey returned with a plump blond nurse and a balding, tired-looking doctor in a bloodstained coat.

"If you'll lower the back, Nurse, and get her legs hooked over the chair arms, I expect we can manage here," the doctor said wearily. "You want anything besides semen tests, Sergeant Gorsey? The usual?"

"No!" It was more a wail than a scream.

They all looked at the girl in the chair. She shook her head. She kept on shaking it. She started to shake all over.

"There won't be . . . I took a bath," she whispered.

"You took a bath!" Sergeant Gorsey howled. "You destroyed the evidence, if there was any evidence. Why in hell," he demanded suspiciously, "would you take a bath before you saw the doctor and police?"

She sat tongue-tied and guilty-looking. If he had to ask, there was no answer he would ever understand.

The sergeant shrugged. "Well, I still need your report, Doctor. I'd appreciate getting it fast."

"So would I," the doctor snapped.

"You'll have to hike up your skirt, hon. Shall I help you off with your panties?" the nurse whispered.

"Not in front of him." She pointed a trembling finger at Sergeant Gorsey.

"If you'll just wait outside, Sergeant."

"By all means, we gotta protect the lady's modesty."

After he was gone, Hattie and the nurse helped her undress below the waist, and the doctor straddled the floor of the dentist's chair in front of her.

"Legs wider," he instructed brusquely.

"Please, it hurts . . ."

"For God's sake"—he wrenched her knees apart—"I have seriously injured people waiting for me."

Lying back in the chair, with her legs stretched apart and her eyes wide and staring at the ceiling, she began to scream.

* * *

They spoke very little during the two-hour drive to Atlanta. At the start her father had offered a few cheerful platitudes on the weather, the scenery, and the condition of the road. When he switched to her next year's college courses, she said quietly, "You don't have to make conversation for me, Daddy. Really. I'm all right."

After which they both lapsed thankfully into silence.

She was glad to be left alone in the hospital room, lying on crisp clean sheets. To be clean . . . and alone . . . nothing mattered more now.

Her father's final words, lightly brushing her cheeks with his lips, had seemed more of a threat than a promise. "Your stepmother's driving here in the morning; we'll both visit you tomorrow."

If only she wouldn't come . . . If only none of them would come . . . If she could just lie like this forever, clean and alone . . .

"Good morning," said a cheerful voice from the doorway, and she reluctantly turned her head and sat up. "My, but you're the prettiest patient I've seen this morning."

He advanced into the room, a tall, dark, ugly man with warm eyes and a pleasant smile.

"I'm Dr. Wingrett, floor resident," he told her. "And you—"

He was lifting her chart off the bed as he spoke, and she stiffened, waiting for his expression to change, for the pleasant smile to become a smirk and the warmth to turn cynical and knowing.

"You're Miss Lee Allen," he said, his face not changing at all. He touched her lightly on the shoulder. "You've had a pretty rough time, Lee. We'll try to help you out."

She stared at him disbelievingly for a moment, then slowly lowered her head and began to cry. He made a few inarticulate comforting sounds, which caused her to cry harder.

When he approached the bed and asked, "Would you like a shoulder, honey?" she could only nod.

He sat on the bed and she flung herself against him, weeping with abandon, convulsively clinging to him.

"Feel better?" he asked when she finally pushed away from him, wiping her face with the top of the sheet.

"I'm sorry, but it was just so unexpected . . ."

"What was, Lee?"

"You not acting like I was a leper or had done some dreadful thing . . . or become a circus freak. I think you'll believe me . . . I did get raped. Nobody else, even my family, except Hattie . . . and one nurse, she was kind . . . but the others . . ."

"Anyone gives you a hard time here," he said firmly, "you just send for me."

She didn't have to send for him two hours later. He happened by when a nurse and an intern were standing at her bedside.

He overheard the nurse ask her, "Are you the one who claims rape?" and bounded furiously into the room just as the intern joked, "Aw, c'mon, we all know a girl can run faster with her skirts up than a man with his pants down."

Dr. Wingrett's pleasant-ugly face contorted with anger. "You ignorant bastards! Get the hell out of here and don't come near her again."

She was shuddering and shaking, her face and forehead covered with sweat. "I told you," she said. "A circus freak . . . a leper . . . T-t-tell me, do they stare at c-cancer patients, too, l-like animals in a z-zoo?"

"No one will again. You're going to be all right, Lee." He barked some quick orders into the intercom over her bed. Then he took her hand. "I've ordered something mild to calm you and help you sleep. I promise you, no one on the staff of this hospital will harass you again."

He continued to hold her hand after she was given her shot. When he laid it gently on the bed, she murmured drowsily, "Don't leave me. I don't trust anyone but you."

"I have work to do, Lee, but I'll check up on you every hour. Sleep, little girl, sleep well."

She slept well, as instructed, for several hours and woke up from a nightmare, screaming. The nurse who brought her out of it sent for Dr. Wingrett and waited with her until he came.

She sat huddled in a bed jacket, shivering in the heat. "Nightmare, Lee?"

"I think—I'm going crazy."

He pulled a stool up to the bed and plunked himself down on it.

"I doubt that very much," he said matter-of-factly. "Want to tell me about it?"

"I dreamt about being raped . . ."

"It's not surprising you would relieve your experience in a nightmare."

"No, you don't understand." She pounded the mattress frantically with her fists. "I didn't dream about my rape, I dreamt about *hers!*"

"Hers?"

"There was this other girl . . . in another place . . . and it was happening to her just as horribly as it did to me. She wasn't me . . . I know she wasn't me, and yet I could feel her fear and pain and . . . and the degradation, as though —I know this sounds mad—but almost as though we inhabited the same body."

"It's not mad at all, Lee. It's just as you said: the remembered pain and fear are perhaps too much for you to bear, so you've chosen to transfer them in your dreams to another person."

She clutched eagerly at this straw. "Do you really think so?"

"Yes, I really think so."

After he was gone, she pounded the mattress again, this time in frustration.

"She had a name. If I could only remember it," she said out loud to the empty room. "Somehow, I know it's important. I have to remember her name."

She came up out of the mist and the fog of the anesthetic, helplessly whimpering, "It's red, it's red all over."

Someone was moaning; someone felt sick.

"Watch out, Doctor. I think she's going to throw up."

She did.

Mercifully, the groaning and heaving subsided. A cloth

scrubbed the bitterness from her mouth; a comforting hand wiped her face.

"Poor girl," said a sympathetic woman's voice. "She has such dreadful nightmares."

"Just one," she tried to say. "Just one dreadful nightmare." She wasn't strong enough to get the words out. She slipped away into sleep again, this time without dreams.

"But it was the same nightmare," she told Dr. Wingrett hours later, "and the same girl. I couldn't see the men's faces, but there were two of them in some kind of red uniform . . . and there was blood all over the ground . . . red . . . red all over . . ."

She closed her eyes, shuddering, as a nurse's aide entered the room, chirruping, "Just look at these lovely red roses somebody's sent you. Aren't they just gorgeous? Would you like to smell them?"

As she advanced to the bed, Lee reared back in panic. "No, no, take them away, please. Give them to someone." She met the aide's puzzled stare. "I'm—I'm allergic to roses," she lied lamely.

"Oh, what a shame. Well, Mrs. Blakely in six-oh-two would just love these, I'm sure. Here's your card, dear."

Lee twisted the gift card out of its envelope. "Randolph Jefferson Ambruster the Fourth," she read aloud and laughed, almost without bitterness. "My dear ex-fiancé. It's not like Randy to bestow roses without a reason—or return."

The reason became apparent within minutes, when Randy Ambruster followed his roses into the room.

He stopped short at sight of the doctor, now lounging at his ease in the one big armchair.

"You're looking very well, Lee. I hope you liked the roses." He glanced about for them.

"I gave your roses away. How I look is no longer your concern. Kindly cut the chit-chat. What do you want?"

"Well, as a matter of fact . . ." He gave an artificial cough. "If we could have a few minutes alone . . ."

"I have no secrets from Dr. Wingrett." She smiled mockingly. "Do open up your heart to both of us."

He shifted uncomfortably and cast her a look of dislike, then blurted out like a sullen schoolboy, "It's my great-grandmother's ring. Mom's raising hell because I forgot to get it back from you."

"Try the floor of your friends' fraternity room. I had it in my hand when they dragged me there. Maybe it rolled under the bed, maybe someone vacuumed it up; or perhaps one of your friends pawned it. I really don't care which. Good-by, Randy."

"But you're responsible," he blubbered. "You—"

Dr. Wingrett unfolded himself from the chair and stood up, looking a foot taller than usual. "She said good-by," he said gently.

"But—"

"You're upsetting my patient," the doctor said softly. "Out!"

Randolph Jefferson Ambruster IV left quietly.

Dr. Wingrett had just finished his rounds of the wards when one of the older nurses approached him. "Dr. Wingrett," she said, "your little protégée down the hall is receiving a lot of flak from her family right now because what happened to her got into the local paper."

He swore softly and changed direction, heading back the way he'd come. Outside her door he heard a high-pitched, elegant voice say disdainfully, "In my day we would never have mentioned such a thing aloud, let alone go to the police. Good heavens! The vulgarity of discussing such a matter with a policeman!"

"And to have it in the newspaper," an equally high-pitched but less elegant voice lamented. "How will we hold up our heads again?"

"You'll manage somehow, especially if you can blame it all on me," he heard Lee say. Her voice, however scornful, had a quiver that told him she was just about at breaking point.

He barged into the room and straight over to her bed, picking up one hand to feel her pulse.

She was flushed and feverish, her eyes imploring.

He looked around at the parrot-nosed grande dame in purple and pearls, the middle-aged woman with the young figure and irritated expression, and the pretty girl with the sullen mouth.

The pretty girl wailed as though he wasn't there, "I'm ashamed to face my friends. Everyone asks such questions. They want to know was she *really . . .?*"

The pulse under his fingers leaped convulsively.

"And do you defend me loyally and with vigor, Maggie Louise?" Lee asked with contempt.

"Mama!" whined the girl. "She's picking on me again."

"I thought the shoe was on the other foot."

"Lee Allen, there's no call for you to be nasty!" "Mama" defended.

"I will not tolerate this bickering," the grande dame proclaimed.

"Ladies!" Dr. Wingrett's thundered exclamation brought a half minute of total silence. When all attention was on him, he smilingly indicated the door. "This conversation is not an aid to convalescence. My patient needs rest, not strife. I'm afraid I must ask you to leave."

"Well, I never!" gasped Mama.

The grande dame inspected him microscopically. "This young man may be right," she said and stood up. "We will return later," she promised and went sailing out majestically.

Mama and the pretty girl flounced after her. There were, he noticed, neither kisses nor flowery good-bys.

"Thanks," Lee breathed.

"Your family?" he asked.

She shrugged. "So to speak. My grandmother, Miss Annabel, who transferred her dislike of my mother to me. My stepmother, whom I do not call Mama, a bone of contention, not that she really wants me to. Maggie Louise, my stepsister."

"Do you have anyone else?"

"Oh, my father . . . he went downstairs, supposedly to send up some magazines and flowers from the gift shop, but really, I think, to escape when his womenfolk lit into me."

She said with detachment, "He's not a very strong character."

"Your own mother died?"

She nodded. "When I was twelve. Don't look so sorry for me, Doctor. The early years are the important ones. It was wonderful till then."

An aide came in with a pot of violets and a stack of paperbacks. "Your father said he'll leave you to rest now and be with you tonight," she said, placing her load on the dresser.

"Thank you." Lee grinned at Dr. Wingrett. "I knew he wouldn't come back now."

"You're not allergic to other flowers, I see, just roses."

A red-hot blush crept over her face, and she put both hands to her cheeks, as though trying to control it.

"I'm not allergic to roses either," she admitted in a low shamed voice. "It was—the color."

"The color."

"Red. I'm so—so scared of red—ever since my nightmare—actually since the—the rape." Tears glittered in her eyes; her mouth quivered. "Dr. Wingrett, I'm a real mess, aren't I?"

"You are no such thing, dear girl. You just need a strong dose of TLC."

"TLC?"

"Tender loving care. A doctor's chief medical aid. Don't you have other family, friends, anyone who can give you some?"

When she didn't answer, he said briskly, "We'll talk more later. I want you to rest now."

"No drugs," she begged. "I think . . . I noticed the nightmare comes whenever I'm drugged." She slid down in bed. "I'm tired, and I'm not upset anymore, honestly. You've been so kind. I'll sleep without any trouble."

He drew the curtains to darken the room. Half an hour later, when he poked his head in the door, he found her asleep, curled up on her side, with her arms flung above her head. Quietly, he closed the door.

* * *

She came awake all at once, sensing the presence in her room. She sat straight up, wincing from the stab of her stitches.

She saw a tall woman in her thirties, handsome in spite of small pockmarks on her face. Her silky hair was swept back under a frilly organdy cap, and she wore a floor-length skirt of dark blue with a starched white apron. Her shoes were black, square-cut, with large steel buckles. There was a woolen shawl all around her.

"Who are you?" Lee breathed.

"Why, I'm cousin Lucretia," said the woman, as though wondering that she should ask. "He's right, you know, my dear."

"Who? What?"

"The doctor. You must find someone else to turn to. Someone who loves you."

"But there's no one—I *am* alone."

"Think back, remember how it used to be when your mother was alive, remember who was there."

She fell back against her pillows. She breathed, "Aunt Lucy." Then, "Joel."

The woman smiled lovingly. "Yes," she agreed, "they're the ones."

"But who are *you?* I don't—didn't have a cousin Lucretia."

The smile came again, the one that seemed to warm her frozen heart and make her feel that gentle, caring hands were holding onto her.

"You'll remember." Cousin Lucretia shook her head and laughed a merry little laugh. "Someday you'll remember," she said as her presence faded away.

The girl hunched over in the bed with her face in her arms and whispered over and over, "I'm awake. It wasn't a dream. She was here in the room with me."

As she lifted her head, a sudden flash of red seemed to appear before her eyes, gone as suddenly as it had come.

"I remember," she said out loud. "Oh, my God, I remember. Her name was Philadelphia."

CHAPTER
1

Craig Burden is my agent, my friend, and a man of a hundred voices for wheedling and dealing with writers. So it was no surprise to me that my first firm refusal, instead of meeting with resistance, induced from him a lavish spreading-on of butter.

"Jake, Jake, I know you love your daughter. It's what I respect most about you—fame, fortune, but basically you're still a family man, not like the usual no-talent prima donnas I deal with. Their sales go up, their writing goes down, and they work harder at getting their names into the gossip columns than in the book reviews. But you, Jake —where was I?" Craig paused for breath.

"Extolling my virtues as a family man. To prove your point, I think I'll stay on in England."

"Now, Jake, what's another five days? Sue Lin won't mind. Isn't—"

"Sue Lin," I bawled, turning the receiver away, "would you mind if I left today instead of Saturday?"

The prolonged wail from the kitchen was loud enough to reach from Lakenheath Air Force Base in England to the offices of Burden & Freitag, Madison Avenue, Manhattan.

"Oh, Daddy, *why?*"

My daughter came rushing into her husband David's study, as light on her feet as though a five-month belly weren't bouncing a bit ahead of the rest of her. All the telltale signs were there on her face; fluttering eyelashes, quivering nose, and pouting lips. Countdown: ten, nine, eight . . . the tears would fall before I got to three.

"Sue Lin would very definitely mind," I reported into the phone. "So would I. Send my regrets to Mr. Corbin. See you next—"

"Don't hang up. Now, listen to me, Jake." I waited for the switch and grinned as he launched right into it. "This is carrying family devotion too far. Your book came out a month ago and, as expected, it's doing well, but not so well you can afford to pass up an appearance on Wally Corbin's 'Wake Up, America' show, especially right now before Christmas. It could be good for a hundred thousand copies. Let me tell you, when I heard they wanted you to fill in for Breckenridge—did you hear he just got indicted?—I said three Hail Marys. Say, are you listening to me?"

"Every word."

"Hell, what's the use? Lemme speak to Sue Lin."

I passed the phone over wordlessly, watched her face cloud over and then grow brighter. And brighter and brighter. She passed the receiver back to me.

"You have got to be the world's greatest con artist," I said into it. "What did you promise her? A piece of the World Trade Center?"

"Just that you would come back with Nancy when the baby's born."

"At your expense?" I queried politely.

"Don't be a horse's ass. I can get you a TV appearance or a special newspaper assignment with your expenses covered, and you know damn well you'll be paying Nancy's way over. She'll want to be with big sister for the big event."

"It's so helpful I don't have to plan my life. I have you to do it for me. When is this appearance on Corbin's show?"

"Tomorrow. Sometime between seven and eight-thirty A.M. But you have to be at the studio by six, so call right away and get yourself booked on the Concorde; it's the only way you can be sure of making it back to New York on time."

"It hasn't escaped your notice, has it, that I was a very vocal anti-Concorde agitator?"

"I should forget even your more foolish goings-on. This is a good way to show you're open-minded. British Airways is ready to forgive you; you're willing to give their Concorde a try. Now, I've already reserved you a room at the Waldorf. Call me as soon as you hit town, no matter what time. Don't be afraid to wake me up."

"Don't worry. I won't be," I snapped. He was still laughing when I hung up.

Sue Lin, amazingly cheerful, helped me pack and gave me some breakfast, and I was on my way to London within the hour.

The trip across the Atlantic was smooth and easy. I accepted liberal doses of champagne, which I usually don't drink, and decided Craig was not only one hell of an agent but a pretty good fellow, too. That was until two-thirds of the way home, or a little over an hour out of New York, when our pilot, in the overly cheerful voice pilots adopt to announce disagreeable news, informed us a blizzard was raging over the city, Kennedy Airport was closed, and we were being diverted to Washington.

Normally, since I live in Washington, this would have been a piece of good luck. As it was I cursed Craig Burden with passionate if silent fluency for most of the five hours and forty minutes that I bounced and bumped on the bus provided at Dulles Airport for New York-bound passengers. I treated myself to the pleasure of cursing him aloud when I got him on the phone at the Waldorf.

Like most agents, Craig calms storms with the expertise of long practice. It wasn't till after I had fallen into bed, groaning with the joy of lying prone, that I realized the ot.”

Applause . . . My eyes were closing again . . . I must have
missed someone’s frantic signaling . . . there was a shove
from Craig, and I stumbled on stage. More applause.

Then I was shaking hands with Wally Corbin, hearing
how glad he was to have me there, followed by my gladness
to be there—reciprocal lies, appreciated equally.

Once we were seated, he got right down to business.

"**You**r last book, *An American Myth: We Love Our
Children* . . . Now, wasn’t that quite a change of pace for a
political reporter?”

He paused, smiled encouragingly, and I elaborated obediently: "I suppose so, if I considered myself solely a political reporter, which I don't. I write about the American scene, and child abuse, unfortunately, is a prevalent part of the American scene."

"The figures certainly are shocking, if true," he murmured.

"They're shocking because they *are* true."

He turned from me to face the cameras directly, explaining to the unseen thousands I was struggling to keep awake for, "After its great success as a book, *An American Myth* was turned into a TV documentary, which not only won three Emmy awards but had a theme song, *Rock-a-Bye Baby*, which went gold . . ."

To my intense embarrassment, he began to sing with rollicking good humor, *"Rock-a-bye baby, crying's a sin."* After a few bars, he gestured with his hand, and somewhere out of sight, a piano and horn chimed in.

> *"If you fret or fuss, I'll bash your head in.*
> *Whimper or wail or draw a loud breath*
> *And Daddy or I will beat you to death."*

Singer, piano, and horn finished in lusty chorus, the audience burst into another round of applause, I blushed for the first time in twenty years, and with hardly a change of expression, Wally Corbin switched from poetry to promotion. "And now to your new exposé."

He held up my book to the cameras so the jacket was clearly visible. *"And a Walnut Tree.* This is quite an unusual title, Jake. Perhaps you'd like to explain it to our viewers."

"It's taken from an old seventeenth-century proverb. 'A woman, a dog, and a walnut tree, the more you beat 'em, the better they be.' In some versions, it's 'a woman, an ass, and a walnut tree.' Whichever, the principle is the same," I finished flatly, "beating a woman is acceptable practice."

"Is this book a result of your discovery that wife beating, too, is pretty prevalent on the American scene?"

"Unfortunately, yes again, though I must admit I started out believing it was peculiarly British. Last year I was visiting my older daughter, who is married to a Jewish air force chaplain at Lakenheath Base in England. One day a local friend of hers came to tea with a swollen lip, a broken wrist, and a black eye, and all my theories—rather snobbish ones, I'm afraid—went down the drain. The husband, who had inflicted her injuries, was upper middle class, educated, a professional. I started to investigate, and the result was a newspaper series and TV bit on the battered wives of Britain. It caused enough of a stir to cross the ocean, where I still—snobbishly again—thought we were fairly immune to this particular disease. It was the huge volume of mail I got that convinced me otherwise. The theme of most of my letters was, 'Why so down on Britain, Jake? What about your own backyard?' *And a Walnut Tree* is the result of investigations into my own backyard."

"This is quite a horror story you unfold here." He thumped the book vigorously and turned it around to show my picture on the back of the jacket. "May I ask what you hoped to accomplish by writing it?"

"I hoped, in your own words, to horrify. Horrify people into understanding the existence and magnitude of the problem. Arouse compassion for the victims and explore the means to protect them. Invoke the law to seek preventive measures. Change attitudes. Both the police and the public must be made aware that when a man uses his fists on a woman or sends her to the hospital, it's gone far beyond a simple domestic dispute. It's—"

"And I'm sure we wish you every success with your endeavor," he cut in smoothly. "We'd like to hear more about it, but our time is up now. We certainly would welcome you back to discuss this problem again. And now an important announcement—"

Thankfully, I allowed myself to be shepherded off the set.

"Do you realize," I asked Craig as we went down in the elevator, "that I spent more than twelve hours of traveling time yesterday for that five-minute bit just now?"

"Do you realize," he countered smoothly, "what that five-minute bit can do for your royalties?"

I grinned reluctantly. "Okay, you win."

"We both win, buddy. Now listen, can you meet me at the Lorrimer Press offices at eleven? Mark Lorrimer and I want to discuss a new project we have in mind for you, and there's someone you have to meet."

"Who?"

"A possible collaborator."

"No dice, Craig. I write my own books."

"You'll write this one, too. This gal is just the researcher. She's got all the material lined up; it could save you months of work. She doesn't want a by-line and isn't too concerned about money."

"She sounds highly suspicious; much too good to be true. What's the subject?"

"Meet me at Lorrimer; you'll find out."

"Deal. You can buy me lunch afterwards, but then I go back to Washington. These old bones are weary. I want to rest them at home."

CHAPTER
2

I looked at my watch after Craig and I separated. Only eight-thirty in the morning. With luck I'd have time for a catnap before the eleven o'clock appointment. I walked over to Madison Avenue, optimistically expecting to flag down a cab.

It was beginning to snow again. Large flecks landed on my head and face and were melting down my neck. I wandered south, occasionally sinking into drifts higher than my half-boots. My socks and pants were soggy, and my toes were beginning to frost over.

I wound up walking all the way down to the Waldorf, by which time I was ravenous as well as an icicle. I changed out of my wet clothes and hurried downstairs to Oscar's.

There was a long line, on which I stood for just three minutes. Then I marched purposefully to the head of it, where a hostess barred my way.

"I'm looking for a friend," I said, hoping to God I would find one.

I studied the prospects at the tables for two that were occupied by one. A distinguished gray-haired man, unfortunately puffing on a cigar . . . A pleasant gray-haired lady, unfortunately stabbing the air with a cigarette while she studied the menu . . . A young woman with coal-black hair that shot off electric-blue sparks under the lighting just as Sue Lin's did, probably Oriental. She was sipping coffee and reading, head bent, but I noted with pleasure that the ashtray pushed to the rear of her table was empty. I stepped forward as she looked up, and our eyes met. I stopped short, and she looked down at her book again, but this time she was only pretending to read.

"Have you found your friend, sir?" asked the hostess.

"I have indeed," I said softly.

My legs felt strangely stiff as I walked over to her table. She stared up at me calmly when I stood over her, but the dragon-lady fingers of the hand that held the book were clutching it tight and tensely, whitening her knuckles.

"I'm afraid I told the hostess you were a friend," I said quite seriously. "I'm too hungry to wait on line. If I promise not to interrupt your reading, may I share your table?"

"Please sit down," she invited, and I quickly did. "I accept your promise, Mr. Ormont," she added gravely. "Naturally, an author doesn't want the reading of his book interrupted."

"You recognized me from the cover? Well, I'll be—" I coughed, continuing smoothly, "Even my family didn't. I think the photographer used an aerial angle and a special lens to give me that six-foot look, and it must be obvious that in person I do *not* resemble James Bond."

She looked me over, a small smile playing around her mouth. "You do fall two or three inches short," she agreed.

"Four."

"I beg your pardon."

"Four inches short of six feet."

"An honest man, I see."

"No, merely a cunning one. I saw you making your own estimate."

She laughed out loud, a delightful sound. "Never mind, Mr. Ormont, you've got a six-foot-tall voice, and I never did think James Bond would be good to have around the house. He's strictly a wide-screen or paperback hero. Also, since we're being honest, I didn't recognize you from the book jacket. I saw you on TV this morning; I was watching 'Wake Up, America.'"

I smiled with the sheer joy I felt in her company, and my thoughts must have gotten through to her because she flushed and looked away, shifting uneasily.

A waitress offering coffee and a menu diverted me, and when I turned back to my tablemate, she had transferred my book from her right hand to her left. I stared at it, eyes narrowing, heart sinking.

"Wh-what's the matter?" she faltered.

"You're wearing a wedding ring," I stated baldly. "You're married?"

"I was."

My heart resumed its normal beat. "Divorced?"

"No, widowed."

"I'm sorry," I said. Then, "No, damn it, I'm glad. I mean," I floundered like an adolescent, "I'm sorry for any unhappiness you may have had, but I'm glad you're—hell, don't look at me like that, I'm going to say it because it's true—I'm glad you're not tied up with anyone."

The coral nails beat a nervous tattoo on the table. "I don't want to be tied up with anyone," she mumbled.

"That's a very unnatural wish for a girl your age."

"I'm not a girl, Mr. Ormont. I'm a woman of thirty-three, and I—I think you're going much too fast."

"I happen to be forty-three, Mrs.—?"

"Allerton," she supplied faintly.

"I don't have that much fooling-around time, Mrs. Allerton; and we did agree to honesty."

My omelette came, and I dived into it. When I looked up again, she was studying her plate, so I sat studying her. I doubted now that she was Oriental, despite the hair, but she had an exotic Oriental flavor that she obviously took pains to play up. The blue-black hair was brushed severely back from her forehead and fashioned into a braided chignon at the back of her neck. It was delicate penciling, not nature, that accented the slight upward tilt of her eyes and lengthened the winged swoop of her brows. Her skin was soft and smooth as an apricot and rouged to the same color. Her mouth was a pale orange.

She was beautiful, one of the most goddamned beautiful women I had ever seen, let alone had breakfast with, and yet somehow not real. I couldn't help wondering if just the shell was beautiful and not what was inside it. Then I knew I couldn't feel this way if the shell were empty. *What way, Jake?* I asked myself, and knew I needed time to get my feelings sorted out.

She looked up then, and my heart gave a great lurch because in the remote black eyes that met mine for just an instant I felt myself sinking ten fathoms deep into fear and loneliness. Then the eyes shifted, the moment passed, but not the sensation.

"What happened to your husband?" I asked softly.

"V-Viet N-Nam," she stammered.

I watched her body, not just her face, twitching hands, tapping foot. I listened, as a good reporter trains himself, to the sound of her voice, not just her words. "It w-was a long time ago," she added lamely. "I'm not still—bothered, if that's what you were thinking."

"Are you staying in the hotel?" I asked her presently.

"Yes, just for tonight."

Without regret, I jettisoned my plans to go home.

"I'm staying over, too. Will you have dinner with me tonight?"

"I have some business appointments," she said slowly.

"So do I. With my agent and my publisher. But I'm free after lunch except for needing a few hours' sleep. There's a Japanese restaurant downstairs—do you know it?—we can eat without leaving the hotel."

"Thank you, I'd like that." But she said it as though with great effort, *brave* effort, I found myself thinking.

As I finished the last bit of toast, the waitress hovered over us with the checks. I managed to secure both, ignoring the outstretched hand with the dragon-lady fingernails.

"Sorry," I apologized, grinning. "I try to be liberated, but—"

"You try to be no such thing. It's a matter of principle. You didn't invite me to breakfast. How would you like it if I grabbed the dinner check tonight?"

I pretended to consider. "I wouldn't object if it was necessary to your happiness. In fact, I might consider I'd had the best of the deal."

She choked indignantly, then started to laugh, shrugged, and gave up. "Shall we meet in the lobby?" she asked me.

"No, it's too big, I might lose you. Let's say the cocktail lounge of Inagiku's. Is seven too early for you?"

"No." For a moment she looked like a mischievous little girl. I couldn't figure out why. "Seven's not too early to meet. I'll see you then."

She walked away briskly while I stopped at the cashier's, but I noted that mine were not the only eyes to follow her. Her figure was definitely worth following, and it was set off, back as well as front, by her Chinese-style straight-line, side-slit, sapphire-blue wool dress.

CHAPTER
3

The doorman at the Waldorf managed to get me a cab, so I arrived at Lorrimer Press dry, on time, and in tearing spirits.

Craig, who finally seemed to be beginning to wilt, said disgustedly, "You some kind of manic, up down, up down?" He turned to Mark. "Say, let's get on with it. Where's Bryarly?"

Mark handed me a magazine, which I placed carefully on his nineteenth-century desk before I tilted back in my chair and put my feet up on it. "She'll be here any moment. Have you told Jake what we have in mind?"

"Nope. Left it to you."

Mark turned to me. "Rape," he said succinctly.

I came upright in the chair, feet on the floor. "No," I said just as succinctly.

They both spoke simultaneously. "No, just like that, no!" Craig squawked while Mark asked, "Why not?"

I shrugged. "It's been done and overdone. There's nothing new to be said. If there is, I don't want to be the one to say it." I shrugged again. "Maybe an article, but it just doesn't interest me a full book's worth."

Mark smiled blandly, almost as though I'd played into his hands. "Why not?" he said again.

"Because it's a—a—a woman's subject, a—a—" I wasn't doing too well and I knew it, but it didn't help to have Mark's broadening smile and Craig's uplifted eyes telling me so. I stopped floundering. "It just doesn't interest me," I finished crisply.

Mark rocked his swivel chair backward and studied the ceiling. "You know, Jake," he said, "there's a story about Golda Meir when she was prime minister of Israel. The whole cabinet had gotten together and was discussing the problem of attacks on women at night in Tel Aviv. One of those great statesmen came up with a brainstorm: he suggested a night curfew be instituted for women."

He paused for a long time. "So?" I prompted finally.

"So Golda said to him, 'But, Minister, it's the women who are being attacked by the men. If there is to be a curfew, let the men stay at home.'"

I knew him well. "Get to the point, Mark," I said wearily.

"I just made it, Jake. How can rape be a woman's subject when it's men who do the raping?"

Craig cut in enthusiastically, "Jake, if you could just see the files this girl has, the material, believe me, enough for a dozen books. And what material! It's dynamite. If you could hear her talk." He turned to Mark. "Shouldn't Bryarly be here by now? She could convince this skeptic a lot faster than you or me."

Mark spoke into his intercom. "Marge, would you please call and see if Bryarly's on her way?"

I murmured sardonically, "Who is Bryarly? What is she?"

Craig jumped right in. "She's helping to set up MART committees all over the country. M-A-R-T, for Men Against Rape Too. Believe me, she's a lucky break for you, Jake, if you take this on. All she wants out of it is a good book and a little money, a very little, and not for herself. Whatever we decide on would go to MART."

I turned to Mark. "Why do you think it would make a good book?"

"That would be up to you, wouldn't it? It's all in the writing, but a man's-eye-view of rape in this country is a damn good angle. I used to feel the way you do now, Jake, that it was a woman's question, but not anymore. Talking with Bryarly, I've gotten a whole new point of view. In two hundred years our laws and attitudes have changed about practically everything except this. Our country has been historically unfair to half its citizens, both before and after the fact, when it comes to protecting women from rape and the rapist."

It was a fairly impassioned speech for Mark, who prides himself on never losing his cool. I gathered a lot more from it than I think he intended and not just about rape.

"Where did you meet Bryarly?" I asked him.

He shifted a bit in his chair. "A—er—a mutual friend introduced us."

"During business hours?" I asked gently.

"At a cocktail party," he admitted, fumbling with his tie.

His phone rang just then, and he seized it thankfully, reporting to us ten seconds later, "Marge says she doesn't answer, so she must be on her way."

If she was, she had gotten derailed along the way. We waited an hour, all three of us. Then Craig had to leave, and Mark and I went to lunch. Luckily the food was good, because the conversation definitely lacked flavor. No matter what—families, politics, England, publishing—sooner or later it got back to: "I'm worried about Bryarly. This is not like her. Even if she was detained somewhere, she would have phoned."

A few days before, even yesterday, I might have polished my wit at his expense. But suddenly I was vulnerable, too, and I sat there during the periods of silence, stolidly chewing fillet of sole Véronique and salad while my mind's eye pictured blue-black hair and pansy-soft apricot skin, my senses recalled the laugh like the first half dozen notes of *Spring Song* and artistically penciled would-be almond eyes. Had I just imagined the moment when they had seemed full of fear and pain?

Mark was so anxious to hurry back to the office to start tracing the lost Bryarly, I waved him away and drank my coffee alone. He was touchingly pleased by my willingness to meet again at the same time next morning. I could hardly wait to get back to the Waldorf to sleep away the time till my evening date.

It seemed a lucky omen that I caught a cab in three minutes flat, so by way of celebration when I got to the hotel, I stopped in an overpriced lobby shop to buy the most sinfully expensive tie I had ever owned.

At 6:50 I was waiting in the cocktail lounge of Inagiku's, and at 7:10 I was still waiting. Also 7:15, 7:20, and 7:30.

At 7:40 I consulted with the host, who assured me courteously that he would hold Mrs. Allerton if she arrived, while I checked the lobby. When I returned alone, he lifted his palms deprecatingly to show that she had not.

Too nervous to sit in the lounge anymore, I paced back and forth in the entranceway. Occasionally, I encountered sympathetic glances from behind the reception desk and once a stifled giggle. Well, I couldn't blame her. At age forty-three to be stood up for a date—if that's what was happening—was a new experience for me!

In spite of her elaborate makeup, which indicated a fair amount of time given to dress, she hadn't struck me as someone who would play games. She hadn't struck me as bad-mannered either, but such lateness without phoning —it was now 8:15—was just as much bad manners as a stand-up.

At 8:30 I gave up, nodded my thanks to the host, and went upstairs to the lobby. I got the hotel operator on a house phone. "I'm sorry, sir," she trilled. "Mrs. Allerton has checked out."

No time for pride. I marched over to the registration desk, where a poker-faced clerk turned over records and reported impassively, "That's correct, sir. Mrs. Allerton checked out this afternoon."

I took the Tower elevator to my room and while I called

room service for a beer and sandwich, I unknotted my tie, resisting a childish impulse to throw it out the window.

I read until midnight but didn't fall asleep until past four in the morning, in spite of which I was on time for the morning appointment at Lorrimer Press.

Mark greeted me so cheerfully I knew he'd found his lost Bryarly. I should have been so lucky.

"You look like hell," he told me pleasantly. "Late night?"

I grunted. "Where's your girl? Let's get on with it."

"She's in the hospital, which means a longer delay. That's why I wanted to talk it out, Jake. If you're really dead set against the project, there's no point in waiting. You come up with something else, and I'll look around for someone else to work with Bryarly when she's able."

"What happened to her?" I asked curiously.

"She broke her ankle in three places, poor kid; slipped on the ice yesterday a block from the hotel just before she was due here. They operated last night; wired her tibia and put her entire leg in a cast."

Without knowing just why, suddenly I felt apprehensive. My voice came a little too loud. "What hotel?"

"The Waldorf, same as you. Craig made both your reservations at the same time. As a matter of fact, she lives in New York, but her apartment has been sublet for the last two months while she worked in Washington."

"What's Bryarly's last name?" I asked quietly.

"Allerton. Bryarly Allerton. Beautiful name, isn't it? It suits her. She's beautiful, too."

"What hospital?"

"New York. I was there last night, but it was just a few hours after the operation, she was pretty much out of it, poor girl. I didn't stay lo—Where are you going, Jake?"

"To New York Hospital," I said, halfway out the door, "to see Bryarly. I'll write your book, Mark, and yes, she's beautiful; I had breakfast with her yesterday at the Waldorf."

I was forty-three years old. I had been married, divorced, had an extremely successful career, rented a luxury apartment in Washington, owned a farm in Virginia, and was the father of one college-age daughter and one adopted pregnant daughter. Yet in the cab I sat like a tongue-tied schoolboy contemplating his first crush, while my heart pounded out the same rhythmic drumlike refrain: *She didn't stand me up, she didn't stand me up, she didn't stand me up.*

CHAPTER
4

"Mrs. Bryarly Allerton?" the receptionist parroted, flicking her index file. "Oh, she's in the next building. You go—"

I forced myself to attend to complicated directions that would get me to her faster. Then, when the moment finally came, I hesitated in the doorway of her room, my eyes on the mummylike white-sheeted figure in the bed with the masses of blue-black hair streaming untidily over her pillow.

She either felt the concentration of my stare or heard the pounding of my heart. The mummy did a slow quarter-turn; then her neck swiveled all the way around.

I said, "Good morning, Bryarly," and the beautiful Mrs. Allerton covered her face with her hands and unleashed a torrent of tears.

Which is how I got to hold her in my arms so soon.

I don't remember moving, walking across to her, or sitting down on the side of the bed and bending to her. But that's where I presently found myself, with Bryarly wrapped in my arms the way seconds before she had been in the sheet. My chin rested on the top of her head, her tapered fingers were pressed against my chest, and she wept against me with quiet abandon while I rocked her gently.

Once an orderly came by with flowers, retreating when I waved him away. Then a nurse came tapping in, saying briskly, "Dear me, you mustn't upset our patients like this."

"Go away," I said calmly. "It's doing her good."

Surprisingly, she went.

"Cry all you want to, sweetheart," I said, pressing kisses all around the damp forehead and hairline. And, when she obeyed, "Don't cry, sweetheart," I murmured fiercely into her hair.

In a few minutes the tears turned into a series of hiccuping little sobs; then there was a ragged sputter of laughter as she pulled away from my reluctant if aching arms and sank back against her pillow.

"I can't do both," she sniffled.

I stared down at her, puzzled.

"F-first you s-said to cry, then n-not to cry."

"I don't know what I'm saying. I'm so glad to be with you. I'm so glad I found you. I'm sorry about your leg, but I'm damn glad you didn't stand me up last night."

"Didn't you get my message? But I told the nurse—she promised to call—and my friend Terry left a message when she got my bags. Oh, Jake, Mr. Ormont," she wailed, "did you wait for me last night?"

"For an hour and a half. Then I checked with the hotel operator and the registration desk, and they both said you'd checked out." I passed her a box of tissues, and she blew her nose hard. "I spent a lot of time planning to wring your neck if we ever met again," I went on, "until I saw Mark Lorrimer this morning and connected the elusive Bryarly with the missing Mrs. Allerton."

"I'm so sorry, Mr. Ormont."

"Jake, Mrs. Allerton. I love you, Bryarly."

"You can't p-possibly love someone you've only had one breakfast with."

"You mean"—I smiled wryly—"without any night before?"

I felt her instinctive withdrawal but ignored it. "Maybe it's foolish of me to love you," I said slowly, "but it's equally foolish of you to tell me I can't do what I have already done."

She swallowed, looked away, and said in a little-girl voice, "I don't believe in love at first sight."

"Nor do I. How about love at instant recognition?"

"It's the same thing."

I stared down at the pale face on the pillow, puffy from crying. Without eye shadow, penciling, and mascara, the glowing black eyes, red-rimmed with tears, were less exotic but no less lovely. Her skin was more homogenized milk than apricot; her hair smelled of ether. Still, she was beautiful, with a wan, wistful, other-world beauty.

"It certainly is not, my dear," I contradicted her. "Sight has to do with looks. Admittedly, yours are remarkable —though not," I interjected politely, "at the moment. Recognition of affinity is something else entirely."

"Marriage doesn't interest me, and I'm not in the market for an affair."

"Then we'll be friends," I said equably.

"Are you as good-natured as you seem?"

"Absolutely not." I got up from the bed and drew a chair alongside it. "I can be sulky as a bear wakened from hibernation when I have a writing block, nasty when I don't get a meal on time, and I take rejection badly." I leaned back in the chair and watched her hands move restlessly against the sheet; her face had gone whiter. "Are you in pain?" I said quietly.

"Yes." It was almost a gasp.

"Are they giving you anything? Let me ring for the nurse."

As I got up to reach the bell, she gasped again, only this time she said, "No!"

"Bryarly, why not?" I sat down on the bed again, very careful not to knock against her, and took her hand.

"Don't like drugs." The words seemed wrenched out of her. Her face was flushed now and dewy with perspiration.

"It's just for a day or two to get you over the worst of it," I coaxed her. "The small doses they give you aren't addictive."

"I'm not worried about that." The words were spoken between gritted teeth. "It's the dreams. I—I dream when I'm drugged. D-dreadful nightmares."

"You won't have nightmares, darling." I leaned across her and gave the bell a mighty tug. "I'm going to sit right here with you and hold your hand and talk to you. All your dreams will be delicious."

She giggled at that, a little hysterically, and then closed her eyes and lay gnawing on her underlip while I sat and stroked her nearest hand and her cheek until a nurse came, following on the heels of an orderly with a lunch tray.

I made her needs known to the nurse, and Bryarly must have stated her lack of need for sustenance to the orderly because he was about to follow in the wake of the white uniform when I halted him with a simple command: "Whoa."

I wheeled out the tray table. "I'm hungry, if she's not. I hope that's fit for human consumption."

He grinned, slapping the tray down. "Not too bad, sir."

"Sure you're not hungry?" I asked Bryarly.

"I'm still queasy," she said simply.

I pushed the table over to the window so she wouldn't have to watch me. When I returned to the side of the bed, she said listlessly, "That was quick."

"I just ate the chicken and salad to keep me going through the hours of hand-holding and talking ahead."

"Will it be so hard for you?" She tried to smile, but it came out more like a grimace.

"My love, I propose to talk to you about myself. Could there be a more fascinating subject? To begin with"—I seated myself on her bed again—"I was born of poor but not poverty-stricken parents forty-three years ago last August. The name bestowed upon me, I greatly regret to tell you, was Gerard, which I myself shortened at the earliest possible moment to Jake. The Ormont part my grandfather had already shortened—if you want to call it that—from Goldberg."

"Goldberg?" She looked puzzled. "To Ormont? I don't get it."

"You must not speak French, then." I grinned. *"Or* means gold, *mont* is berg. Or-mont; simple, see?"

"But were your people French?"

"Not really. They stopped in France for a generation or so on the way from pogrom to pogrom."

"Then you're Jewish," she said.

"Yes. Do you mind?"

She said weakly, "If I didn't hurt so much, I'd smack you for that."

The nurse came back just then, brandishing a needle, and I retreated to the window, with my back turned to the proceedings. When we were alone again, with my chair pulled close to the bed and her hand held tightly between both of mine, she gave a little sigh, closed her eyes, and said dreamily, "Tell me more about yourself, Jake."

"I was born in Washington Heights, on Manhattan Island," I obliged, "but my parents moved to Coney Island when I was five, and I grew up there. I still think, if you take away the people and the garbage, it's the most goddamned beautiful place in the world."

"When did you become Jake, Gerard?" she asked provocatively.

"If *you* didn't hurt so much, I'd smack *you* for that," I told her cordially. "The answer is, when my mother sent me to school in a French beret. I not only changed my name, I learned to fight. It was that or be buried. Coney Island wasn't exactly a prep school, you know. Only the strong survived."

She opened her eyes a moment. "The biography on the book jacket said you married quite young but it didn't take."

"I married my high school girl when I was in college. We both went to Lincoln High, but she lived in the Manhattan Beach section, and her parents thought it was a comedown for her, which it undoubtedly was. She wanted to be a doctor, and she wound up a twenty-year-old mother instead. She loved our daughter, Nancy, and it wasn't that she couldn't cope—she didn't want to."

"Poor thing," Bryarly said drowsily.

"Yeah. I feel that way now. Of course, I didn't then. My senior thesis, enlarged, was my first best seller only one year out of college, when I was twenty-three. I thought she should be grateful for all the worldly goods I was heaping on her when what I really meant was: Here's one in the eye for you, dear in-laws."

"The—*The Criminal Class,*" she said thickly. "From Mark Twain's saying, 'The only criminal class we have in this c-country is Congress.'"

"You remember that?" I asked, pleased and surprised.

"St-studied up on you . . . wanted to see how you wrote—if—you . . . going to do . . . book together."

She was so quiet, I thought she had drifted off till I heard her whisper, "When did your marriage break up?"

I thought about it seriously. "It was a gradual thing, actually. We were living on the Virginia farm, and I was spending half my time rushing around the world on assignments. One time I came home long enough to talk with Melanie, really talk, and learned that she was miserably unhappy and couldn't go on. We got an apartment in Washington, and Melanie lived in it during the week and went to college. I got a healthy advance from my publisher, gave up my job, and lived in Virginia with Nancy and a couple who managed the farm."

I studied her still face and went on more softly in case she was asleep, "Weekends Melanie came home, and it was like dating all over again, which for a while had excitement and challenge. By the time she was in medical school and the visits were every other weekend, the glamour had begun to wear pretty thin. I wanted more than a four-day-a-month wife; she was beginning to find her doctor friends—one male, in particular—more exciting than a political writer. So we celebrated her first-year internship with a divorce. Nancy stayed with me by all-around consent, and I fixed up an apartment over the garage for Melanie and her new husband. They'd visit free weekends and whenever I had to go out of town. It worked out rather well, especially when I brought Sue Lin home from a Seoul orphanage in 1960."

Her eyes blinked open. "How did you do that?" she asked in sleepy surprise.

I laughed, playing with her fingers. "Strictly illegally, you may be sure. The mother superior of the orphanage had consulted me on the ethics of keeping the child, who was brought in by her grandmother after her mother was killed in the shelling. It seems she had a chain around her neck with a plain wedding band marked *Dav*, as well as a Star of David. When I smuggled her out, I promised to try to track down her family. I honestly tried, and by the time I realized it was no go, she and Nancy were inseparable. Melanie, my ex-wife, was the one to suggest, 'Adopt her yourself. It would be good for both girls.' "

Bryarly seemed to be struggling to speak, but no sounds came out of her mouth, and her eyes kept closing. "Shh," I advised her tenderly. "Go to sleep."

I went on with my story. "So I did adopt her, and we lived happily ever after—except for one thing." I leaned over to assess Bryarly's quiet breathing. She seemed to be asleep, but I finished anyhow. "I think I've finally found it, Bryarly. I've found you."

No answer, of course. Just her quiet breathing. The pain lines were gone from her face, and her nails no longer clawed my palms. Her hand lay limply between mine, and I was convinced she was asleep when once more the whispery voice addressed me. "Jake, you shouldn't have said that. Jake. Only other man . . . I ever cared about . . . Jewish."

"Your husband?"

She didn't answer, so I leaned forward and repeated close to her ear, "Your husband?"

"No, Benjy . . . must have heard of him . . . artist . . . Benjamin Heston . . . stepfather."

I continued to hold her right hand with my left while I fished out of my breast pocket the small notebook I am never without. On a clean page I scribbled *Benjamin*

Heston, artist. Then I sat studying her face, marveling that forty-eight hours before I had been in England and we had not met.

Suddenly her hand jerked out of mine, the still face on the pillow contorted, and she began writhing all over the bed.

She cried out so piercingly, "No, don't, don't!" that I got the door shut before I moved to comfort her. She was twisting about so among the sheets, I was afraid she would damage her cast. "Bryarly, everything's all right," I said quite loudly, but I had to pin her shoulders and repeat it three or four times to quiet her.

"Please, oh, please," she whimpered after a while; then in that shrill, fearful voice again, "Their coats are red. Oh, God, it's red all over."

I knelt with my arm across her, as a restraint as well as a support. I put my cheek against hers. "Bryarly," I whispered into her ear, "it's Jake. You're not alone. I'm here with you. Wake up, Bryarly. Stop dreaming. Whatever your nightmare is, it's over."

Presently the peaceful look came back to her face. Then she smiled quite joyfully. "Cousin Lucretia," she said in a soft clear voice. "I'm so glad you're back."

I sat down again, still holding onto her hand. Underneath *Benjamin Heston, artist,* I wrote, *Their coats are red. Oh, God, it's red all over,* and underneath that, *Cousin Lucretia, I'm so glad you're back.*

I called the *Washington Star* when I arrived at the Waldorf that night and got through to Barney Stapleton.

"Barney? Jake Ormont here. Listen, I need a favor. Would you get me any biographical info the morgue has on an artist named Benjamin Heston? I'm particularly interested in his marriage and a stepdaughter as well as anyone named Lucretia."

CHAPTER
5

On Christmas Day I walked into her hospital room with an armful of packages to find Bryarly's bed surrounded by women of assorted sizes and ages, ranging from an Alice-in-Wonderland blond teenager to a no-nonsense grandmotherly type.

They turned around in a group, and five pairs of eyes surveyed me and X-rayed me with such anatomical thoroughness, I braced myself for the invitation to bend over and cough.

Instead Bryarly murmured quick breathless introductions. Helen Donnelly. Marge Silverman. Megan Wallace. Terry Ramundo. Phyllis Browning. "Merry Christmas, ladies." I committed the names to memory as I dumped my packages onto the tray table.

"Merry Christmas, Bryarly."

Her cohorts parted like the Red Sea, making way for me to approach the bed where she sat wearing turquoise pajamas printed with Oriental figures, her blue-black hair roped

in a big knot on top of her head. She was in full war paint
again for the first time since our breakfast at Oscar's
—apricot rouge, coral lipstick, penciling to slant her eyes
and wing her brows. Beautiful, unrevealing, a mask for the
real Bryarly to hide behind.

Then she smiled at me, a bit shy in the presence of her
friends, blushed violently when I bent to kiss her forehead,
and cast an almost scared look about.

The grandmotherly one, Phyllis Browning, said briskly,
"It's been a lovely visit, Bryarly; family duty calls now. I'll
phone you tomorrow."

The others seconded Mrs. Browning with excuses and
good wishes, and a rapid exodus took place.

I raised my eyebrows at Bryarly when we were alone.

"Did I frighten them off?"

"You did look a bit alarming," she laughed, "but they had
to leave anyhow. They just organized a little party so I
wouldn't feel lonely being here today." She nodded toward
a miniature tree on the dresser circled by an assortment of
colognes, dusting powder, and books. "It was dear of them,
but actually I'm not too fond of the Christmas merry-
making. I usually avoid it by visiting my aunt in Florida."

"Were those friends or relatives who just left?" I asked
casually.

"Friends. Good friends. Most of them are working to
organize the New York MART."

I had brought my packages over to dump on the bed while
she was speaking.

"For *me?*"

"For you."

"Thank you, Jake." She ripped off the wrappings of the
smallest box and held up a glass paperweight with a snow
scene. "It's lovely. I'm sorry I have nothing for you."

"The way you look today is your present to me. No more
pain?"

"No more pain," she said happily, pulling apart the
second package and squinting to read the titles of her books.
"Oh, these will be fun when you're not here. Are you going
to Washington to spend the holidays with your daughter?"

"Nancy's in California with her mother. She and I will have a week together in February." I smiled broadly. "So you see, I'm quite free to be with you. If you're ready to start working on our book when you get out of here, I'll try to sublet an apartment in New York or find a cheaper hotel. The Waldorf is bankrupting me."

"Oh." She stopped unwrapping the third parcel to stare speculatively up at me. "Maybe I have a present for you, after all. Would you get me my pocketbook please, in the top drawer?"

When I came back with it, she was delightedly fanning herself with the lace-edged, flowered Spanish fan that had seemed to have her name on it when I saw it in the store window.

She rummaged in her bag and handed me a set of keys and a card with her name and a Central Park South address.

"It's my apartment," she explained. "The sublet was up the day before yesterday. Mark brought me the keys; my tenant was a friend of his. The doctor says I can't get out of here for another week or ten days, so someone else might as well have the use of it. Why don't you move in right away instead of staying on at the hotel?"

I took the keys she was holding out and her hand at the same time. "Sure?" I asked lightly.

"Very sure."

"Then, if you'll excuse me, I think I'll hop a cab and move out right now. Your lunch will be coming soon; you can eat and nap and be all ready for me when I come back."

"All right. Just wait till I get this last gift unwrapped. I saved the biggest for the last. I can—oooh . . ."

The box tilted sideways in her eagerness and the bright scarlet satin of the embroidered Chinese robe spilled across her lap. A look of absolute terror came over her face, and she reared back in bed like a startled horse. If she could have, I swear she would have been out of the bed, anywhere away from the shimmering red mass that she was pushing out of her lap with trembling hands. Her eyes were dilated; she was breathing like a runner in the last mile of the Boston Marathon.

51

I plucked the robe off her lap. "Shall I hang it up for you?" I asked quietly.

"Oh, please, yes, so it won't get crushed," she panted, her eyes turned away. "Thank you so much. It's—it's beautiful."

In the cab bound for the Waldorf, I took out my notebook and added the names of her friends—I could only remember four—to the growing list of notes on Bryarly.

Then I wrote, *afraid of a red robe,* with a big question mark and flipped back the pages till I found what I was looking for. *Their coats are red. Oh, God, it's red all over.*

Not the robe but the color . . . she was terrified of the color red.

The last thing I did before checking out of the Waldorf was to telephone Dan McCormack, Craig Burden's psychiatrist. After profuse apologies for my timing, I got straight to the point of my call. "Can you tell me, is there a phobia that has to do with fear of the color red?"

"E-r-y-t-h-r-o-phobia," he spelled out for me promptly. "Pronounced arithrophobia, morbid fear of blushing or the color red, an expression of social anxiety or social inhibitions. I've never come across it myself. Anything else?"

"Is there anything else?"

"Hold on." I heard the rustle of pages. "Here's a bit on it from Herman Furness's *Theory of Neurosis:* 'The neurotic personality, which manifests itself in erythrophobia, has social inhibitions consisting of general shyness and withdrawal; it hides its masturbation and longing, feeling ostracized and alone.' Is that enough?"

"More than," I answered a bit grimly, resisting the impulse to say what I was really thinking. *Crap!* "Thanks again, Dan. Sorry to have disturbed you."

That night at the hospital, a few minutes before the visitors' bell rang, I went over to the closet, took down the Chinese robe, and folded it into the gift box. I carried it over to the bed. "I'll change this for another color; is that all right with you?" I asked. "Or would you prefer something else?"

She said so faintly I had to strain to hear, "Another color, please," and then more faintly still, the color she was afraid of creeping into her cheeks, "I'm sorry."

"What are you apologizing for?" I asked brusquely. "I don't suppose you chose to be this way. Someday perhaps you'll trust me enough to tell me why."

She shook her head. "There isn't any specific reason."

I said coldly, "Lie number ninety-nine."

"Jake, don't make me into something I'm not. You'll only get hurt if you do. I've gone the psychiatric route, and the verdicts have been varied but add up to much the same thing. *Highly neurotic.* One even said, *an emotional cripple.* Whatever you have in mind about us," she went on steadily, "I doubt that I'm a suitable candidate. You deserve—" she broke off in some confusion—"well, not me."

"At my age I think I'm the best judge of what I deserve."

"But that's just it. At your age you probably want steadiness, permanence, all the qualities I can't supply."

"I want *you,* Bryarly, whatever your qualities are. We'll work the problems out together. Now shut up and say good night."

"Good night," she whispered, a single tear trailing down each cheek.

So I kissed her wet cheeks and then, for the first time, her mouth. Our lips met only fleetingly, not pressing, and parted before she could feel the faintest stirring of alarm.

I straightened up and couldn't help grinning. She was looking at me, wide-eyed as a child, with her fingers pressed against her lips.

"There. Was that so bad?" I joked.

"N-nooo. It—it wasn't so bad at all."

"A stirring testimonial. Could you possibly make it stronger?"

"I—I liked it," she confessed, crimson with confusion.

I promised quietly, "You'll like it even better next time. See you in a few hours, love."

I left her with her thoughts, reflecting with satisfaction that they were bound to be of me, as mine, two hours later prowling around her apartment, were all of her.

It was high on the fourteenth floor with most of the rooms overlooking Central Park. It was a bright, spacious apartment with two bedrooms, the smaller of which was a combination study-and-guest area with a businesslike office desk, a wall of filing cabinets, and a couch that made up into a bed.

Three steps down led to the living room with its wood-burning fireplace and acres of bookcases. Her walls were hung with paintings by Heston, powerful seascapes, New England fishermen; and over the fireplace two smaller portraits, one called simply *Caroline* of a lovely laughing woman with hair like Bryarly's and the same shape face but very different features. Her mother, I would expect. The other painting showed a happy sparkling imp of a girl, fishing pole over her shoulder, a bucket dangling from her hand as she scrambled down a rocky pile onto a stretch of sand. The little gold plaque attached to the bottom read *Bryarly on the Beach.* Bryarly with her blue-black hair dancing every which way, dark eyes bright with the sheer joy of living.

So this was my love as a little girl before she had learned to fear people and colors and life!

CHAPTER
6

Craig Burden called the day after Christmas just as I came out of the shower. A letter marked "Urgent" had arrived for me from the *Washington Star*.

"I'll pick it up in an hour," I promised.

Good old Barney, I thought, plugging in my razor. And then: How the hell did Craig find out so quickly that I was here?

I asked him the same question on arrival at his office.

"Mark told me. He visited Bryarly last night."

There was an unusual shade of reserve in his voice.

"Hey," I said, "I met her before I had any idea they knew each other." I looked at his poker face. "It wouldn't matter if I hadn't," I explained a little aggressively. "This isn't exactly a kid's game with rules of sportsmanship to follow."

"You're serious," he said incredulously. *"You,* Jake, after all these years."

"Yes, me, after all these years."

"You do realize"—he tried to phrase it delicately —"she's got problems."

"I realize."

"In that case"—he unbent all the way—"the best of luck to you both. Here's your letter."

Barney had really come through. I read the typed pages in the cab on my way to the hospital, skimming the first two which were mostly about Heston's early years in Boston, his navy service in World War II, his studies in Paris and early struggles as an artist.

When I got interested was halfway down page three, at his marriage to Caroline Allen, née Caroline Allerton, mother of a nine-year-old daughter named Bryarly. Caroline, on being divorced from Wayne William Allen, a leading citizen of Ambruster, Georgia, had returned to her home base, Boston, where she got a job in an art gallery and later met the by now famous Benjamin.

The Hestons, with stepdaughter Bryarly, occupied a duplex studio apartment in Boston and spent their summers in Heston's home in Hyannis on Cape Cod.

Three years after they were married, while the young daughter was on her annual two-week home visit to her father in Ambruster, Benjamin and Caroline Heston had drowned in a freak sailing accident on a lake in Maine.

One-third of Heston's considerable estate went to his widowed sister Lucy Raphael in trust for her son Joel; the remaining two-thirds, all his unsold paintings, and the Hyannis house went to Bryarly Allen.

Prior to the death of his ex-wife, Wayne Allen had given his consent to Benjamin Heston's adoption of his daughter. Adoption proceedings were under way at the time of the drowning but not completed.

Wayne Allen and Lucy Raphael both applied for custody of Bryarly, and it was granted to her father, despite the child's expressed wish to live with her stepfather's sister and nephew.

A cynical side note scribbled in by Barney said simply, *Father brought her to Boston for funeral on receiving news of mother's death. His application for custody came after reading of the will.*

Of course. She was quite an heiress and only—I calculated quickly—only twelve or thirteen. Her guardian would have access to her income.

I turned back to Barney's report, skimming once again over accounts of which museums had bought which paintings. The last paragraph stated, *Only known living relatives of Benjamin Heston are Lucy and Joel Raphael and Bryarly Allen. No record of a Cousin Lucretia in the family.*

Cousin Lucretia must be someone from the Allen side. I started wracking my brain for a source in Georgia . . . I'd have to look at a map and find out how near Ambruster was to Atlanta; if necessary, I'd go there myself.

Bryarly, in a short flowered robe, was practically swinging about her room on crutches.

"Don't I handle them marvelously?" She laughed aloud in delight. "Dr. Harkness says maybe I'll be able to go home earlier." She eased herself down carefully into the one big armchair. "Were you comfortable last night?" she wanted to know, and before I could answer, she said, "I forgot to give you the keys to the filing cabinets. You'll want to go through them if you write the book. All my case histories are there as well as MART records and my personal notes on the rape committees and the victims I've had to deal with."

I sat down on the edge of the bed. "How long have you been doing this?" I asked casually.

"Oh, I don't know. Ten, maybe eleven years on and off. It's not all I do. I use my degree in Library Science, you know."

"I didn't know. Do you mean you work part time?"

"Sort of. I'm a specialist in rare books. I work free-lance cataloguing special libraries, particularly for estates. It's ideal for me because in between assignments I can work for the committee. Jake"—she looked at me anxiously—"I have to ask you something. Do you really want to write the book? You mustn't if you don't have a gut reaction to it. It's too important to be done half-heartedly. I don't want you thinking it would affect our personal relationship if you—if you—you know what I mean."

"I know what you mean," I said quietly, "and I want to write the book. I have a very personal involvement in it as well as a gut reaction."

"I don't understand." She stared at me, puzzled. "Mark said you weren't so keen until you knew it was me."

"Yes," I agreed, "but that's what made the difference. I have a gut reaction to anything that changed Bryarly-on-the-beach to Bryarly-behind-the-mask."

"I—don't know what you mean."

"I mean rape," I said quietly. "You were raped, weren't you?"

The crutches dropped to the floor. She sat very straight and rigid, her face more masklike than ever. "Mark had no right to tell you without my permission."

"He didn't. You did."

Her voice was stiff with outraged pride and temper. "It seems I've been very obvious."

"Don't be a fool," I told her roughly. "I'm a trained investigator. You let me get close to you, and I put a few simple facts together. It didn't take an intellectual giant. Eleven years of your life is a long time to give to a cause without a very personal interest."

"We have many women in our organization who have never been raped."

"But not you—and not the ladies who came here to make your Christmas yesterday. Right? They were a very mixed bag—ethnically, racially, financially, and there was a forty-year age range between the youngest and the oldest, but the bond of sisterhood was very strong, very apparent."

She leaned against the chair back, closing her eyes. "They know about you and the book," she said in a curious dull monotone, "and they've given me permission to talk about them, if it will help. I've got their full case histories at home. Would you like the capsule versions right now?"

"If you want to tell me."

"Sure I do, Jake, it's all for the greater good, isn't it, so you'll never again be tempted to think of rape as a woman's question." Her eyes opened a moment to spit scorn out at

58

me, then closed, while the flat voice continued. "Let's start with Helen, who looks like the girl next door. She was only eleven when her uncle raped her while he was baby-sitting. When she tried to tell her parents, her father washed her mouth out with soap for quote 'talking dirty' unquote about his kid brother. She's been under psychiatric care for six years, and she's never had a date . . . Phyllis is a grand-mother. It was particularly kind of her to come yesterday because it happened to her four years ago Christmas. She was shopping for presents for her grandchildren, and he was hidden in the back seat of her car when she got back to the parking lot. He held a knife behind her ear while he sodomized her in the back seat of the car. Then there's—"

"Bryarly, that's enough for now. You're—"

"No, I want to." She beat her clenched fists against the arms of the chair. "I need to. You shouldn't have got me started if you haven't got the stomach to listen."

I had half risen. I sank back, and she took my bowed head as acquiescence, which I suppose it was.

"Terry Ramundo," she said. "She's the young Sophia Loren lookalike. Terry's one of our success stories. She's been married *happily* for five years, and her husband is one of our biggest supporters. She was indirectly the reason I started working for the organization."

I looked up, my senses alert again. "How come?" I asked after a while.

"We were both going to Hunter College and knew each other from a modern dance class. She was absent one day, and one of the girls brought in a small newspaper article —they always gave the victim's name in those days—about her having been raped by a man she let bring her home from a neighborhood dance. Later I heard that her father had thrown her out of the house, and when she returned to class about a week later, even though the bruises were fading, it was obvious she had been beaten pretty badly. When I started talking to her, trying to find out what her situation was, she was pretty hostile at first; she thought I was satisfying my curiosity. So I said something I had never

59

been able to say right out before—in a way, saying it helped *me*. 'Listen, I'm not prying or a gossip; I'm just trying to help because it happened to me, too.'"

She seemed to be having difficulty with her breathing, but I didn't try to stop her. This was something she seemed to have to do.

"After Terry told me about the rape, all three hours of it," she went on painfully, "she told me about the beating she got from the rapist, who was angry at her because *he* didn't perform too well. Then there was the second beating she got from her father before he threw her out because 'she must have asked for it; nice girls don't get raped.' An aunt with six children and only three bedrooms took her in, and she was sleeping on a couch in the living room. She came home with me that night and she stayed for two years."

Bryarly was far away from me, living in that distant past. "It was good for both of us," she said dreamily. "We were like sisters, and after a few months we both started training at a rape crisis center."

Her eyes opened wide again. She looked up at me almost pleadingly. "We could only make some sense out of it if we could use wh-what happened to us to help others. Does that make sense to you?"

I rose and went to her. "Very good sense, Bryarly." I put my hands underneath her arms and lifted her out of the chair. It wasn't easy; the cast made it heavy going. I held her against me, like so much dead weight, my cheek rubbing hers. She didn't object, but she didn't respond either. Only her labored breathing told me she was alive. "I want to hear everything you have to tell me, my dear love, but only when the time is right and when you feel up to it. Okay?"

"Okay," she agreed shakily, and then the tears came, and her body was shaken by great tearing sobs.

On the couch bed in Bryarly's office, which Terry Ramundo had once used, I lay sleepless that night, fitting together pieces of the jigsaw puzzle that was Bryarly. Even as I did, the nagging inner voice that travels with every reporter kept nudging me about a missing piece.

Suddenly I reached for the light, rolled out of bed, and

returned with Barney's report. I skimmed through it quickly, and the missing piece leaped triumphantly out at me.

Bryarly's mother had been Caroline Heston, formerly Caroline Allen, maiden name, Caroline Allerton. Allerton. Bryarly's last name. Not exactly Smith or Brown; you didn't come across it every day. I always question coincidence. Had she perhaps married a cousin? Or—

I turned off the light and lay in the darkness with my arms under my head. It was something else to be looked into.

Bryarly, I thought, with a kind of pain I had never known before, can I help bring you out from behind the mask?

It was probably because I was feeling her pain so keenly when I fell asleep that I experienced the rare other pain that came to me only in the night.

I woke up groaning and covered with the cold sweat that was always the aftermath of my own nightmarish dream. Grateful to be awake, I turned on the table light.

My sheets and blankets looked as though I'd been wrestling with a wildcat. Partly out of need, partly for therapy, I remade my bed.

I knew better than to try to go to sleep again. I never could. Instead, I put on slacks and a jacket and went out in the gray predawn to walk the outer edges of Central Park. It was stingingly cold, an excuse rather than a reason for the tears on my cheeks.

The taste of grief and loss and despair filled me through and through, as it did each time.

"Philadelphia," I repeated to myself, as I had God knows how many times before. "Why? Why—Philadelphia? Damn. Damn. There's got to be some meaning to it."

CHAPTER
7

The second set of keys Bryarly gave me each had a neat little tag numbered one, two, three, and four to match the numbers painted on the top left-hand corner of each cabinet. It wasn't until I started working in her office regularly that I realized there was a number-five key missing.

I tried the cabinet, and it was locked. I was certain that my not being given the key was a deliberate act of omission. I knew ways and means and people . . . and for a while I was sorely tempted. I felt positive the contents of that one cabinet meant more to my search than the overflowing files of the other four put together.

In the end I couldn't bring myself to break into the locked file. I was a guest in Bryarly's home; she trusted me. If I violated that trust and she found out, I could tip the delicate balance of our relationship in the wrong direction. Even if she didn't find out, it would still be a breach of trust.

The sooner my work was done, the sooner I could plunge into the much more vital job of uncovering Bryarly's past.

Full of good resolutions, I programmed my days, spending the hours from waking till late afternoon painstakingly sifting through the files and making copious notes. After an early dinner I would visit the hospital, where I often had to share her with other guests. The intimacy we had achieved in the first few days seemed to diminish rather than increase.

I became more impatient for her to leave the hospital than she was. At home, if we worked together during the day, even after I moved out, we were bound to be close.

Arriving on the heels of her departing dinner tray one night, happy no one else was around, I announced cheerfully, "I think I've got myself a place to stay when you break out of here. It's in the forties, two rooms, kind of pokey but clean. Anyhow, I figure I won't be in them too much, if you don't mind my camping out in your office during the day. It would be better for the work if we're together."

"No, I don't mind," she said flatly, but her face, radiantly smiling when I arrived, had taken on the closed-in look I knew so well.

"What's the matter, Bryarly?"

"Nothing's the matter."

"Cut out the crap," I said roughly. "You look as though I'd just stabbed you."

"It's just"—she looked down at her clasped hands—"I didn't know you were planning to move out of my apartment."

"But you're coming home the day after tomorrow."

She looked up at me, opening her great dark eyes and arching those winged brows. "So?" she said softly.

"B-but, B-Bryarly," I stammered. "You mean—you wouldn't mind—" With an effort I pulled myself together. I hadn't felt or behaved like this since I was in the throes of my first crush on Gloria, the golden goddess of the sixth grade. "Do you mean," I asked her calmly, "you have no objection to my staying in your apartment even after you come home?"

"I don't mind," said Bryarly nonchalantly, but her fingers

kept knotting together and a pulse in the center of her throat was throbbing wildly. "After all," she added after ten seconds, "the office is like a second bedroom."

"I'd be happy to stay, Bryarly," I told her formally, and accepting her hint in my turn, added, "in your second bedroom."

Two days later I brought her home and immediately got her tucked in bed for an afternoon nap in preparation for our delayed New Year's celebration.

I had exchanged her red satin Chinese robe for one of midnight blue and laid it over the rocking chair in her bedroom. She was wearing it when I went to her room to tell her it was time for dinner.

The dining area was five steps above the living room. I had to help her stumble up the steps on her crutches. The table was all set, blue candles lit, a centerpiece of white camellias. The food was my surprise—a take-out dinner from a Japanese restaurant.

"We're a little late," I told her as she turned to me, shiny-eyed, "but we've finally made it. This is the dinner you stood me up for."

"Oh, Jake, oh, Jake, you do the most special things of anyone I've ever known."

"Happy 1978, Bryarly."

"Happy New Year, Jake."

I pulled her chair out, helped her lower herself into it, and propped her crutches against the nearest wall. Then I sat opposite, moving the flowers slightly to the left of center so I could see her.

"Sake or plum wine?" I asked her.

"Plum wine to start, please."

I filled both our glasses. *"L'chayim,"* I toasted her.

"L'chayim," she toasted back with just the right amount of throatiness in pronouncing it.

"Your stepfather taught you well."

"My stepfather?" she said, her wineglass arrested in midair.

"Yes, don't you remember telling me about him in the hospital after they doped you up?"

"No." She set the glass down carefully and gave me a nervous smile. "Did I—tell you anything else?"

I shook my head gravely. "No state secrets, Bryarly, so don't get all tensed up. All you said was that your stepfather, Benjamin Heston, the artist, was the only *other* man you ever cared about."

Smiling in relief, she sipped her wine again.

"I was extremely pleased about that word *other*," I stated casually. "At the time I thought you meant me. Later on I realized I might be flattering myself; you might have had your husband in mind."

She choked on her wine, as good a way as any of avoiding an answer. But I have reporter's blood.

"*Did* you mean your husband?" I persisted.

After a while she stopped finger-drawing on the white lace tablecloth and looked across at me. "No!" she said defiantly.

"Me?" I asked.

"You, damn you!"

I got up, feeling like Moses on his way down from Mount Sinai. She looked a bit apprehensive, but I just said blandly, "I'll get the soup," and disappeared into the kitchen.

She exclaimed in delight when I came back bearing a tray with two covered black lacquer bowls of miso. "Did you borrow the bowls?"

"No, I bought them, so you'll have something to remember this meal by."

The radiance of the smile behind the mask broke through.

"I couldn't ever forget it, Jake—or you."

"You're not going to have to," I said gruffly. "I expect to be around for a long time. Don't let your soup get cold."

We both cupped the bowls with our hands, Oriental style, and drank the soup while our eyes exchanged messages over the rims. My eyes had challenged hers often. It was one of the few times that hers met mine, unwavering, and seemingly unafraid.

After the miso we shared a large platter of tempura, followed by oyako don and then kitsume soba.

We drank thimble-sized glasses of hot sake and cup after

cup of bancha tea. I had rice cakes and sherbet for dessert, but we were too full by then, so we decided to save dessert for a before-bed snack.

I established her on the living room couch before I cleared away the dishes, resisting all her offers to help me in the kitchen. "Not tonight," I said firmly. "Tonight"—I glanced with pleasure at the blue satin robe—"you're a Chinese princess."

"Japanese," she giggled.

"Whichever." I turned on the stereo, which I'd discovered during the week. "What shall it be?" I asked, flicking through her records. "Brahms . . . Chopin . . . Mendelssohn . . . show tunes . . . Gershwin?"

"Mendelssohn, please."

"A very good omen. I'm supposed to be descended from him."

"Truly?"

"So my mother claimed, but I admit she was prone to exaggeration. There was a gypsy horse thief on the family tree; she never liked to be reminded about him."

She giggled again. "You're funny, Jake. You make me laugh."

I grinned ruefully. "I bet no one ever said that to double-oh-seven."

"That sexual athlete!" she said scornfully. "Who cares about him?"

"Half the women in the world, I gather."

"Not me." She snuggled down against the couch cushions, easing her cast out. She lay in beauty, sated with food and sleepy with sake. The rope of her hair had worked loose from the jeweled combs mooring it and had fallen over her shoulder. It lay like a coiled cobra against her left breast, and my hand had a strong urge to follow suit.

I turned sharply and went into the kitchen. When I heard the music end, I came back to the living room to see if she wanted another record put on. I found her fast asleep, her arms around a cushion. She looked adorably young and innocent with her smudged blue-green lids and mascaraed lashes sweeping her cheeks, like a little girl who's gotten loose in her mother's makeup kit. I went to the bedroom and brought back a wool afghan to put over her. Then I closed the blinds, drew the curtains, and turned off all the lights. I closed the kitchen door when I returned to the dishes, leaving her in darkness.

Ten minutes later the screaming began, and after three heart-stopping seconds of frozen terror, I flung myself through the kitchen door and into the darkened living room, tripping over a footstool and an end table in my stumbling progress to get to her.

When I barked my skin on the couch leg, my hands sought blindly for a lamp and finally found it. I was shaking when I turned on the lamp, but not as much as she, sitting in the center of the couch with her eyes wide open and staring, and her mouth wide open, still screaming.

"Bryarly! Bryarly!" I shook her hard. "Wake up, damn it, wake up."

Shudder after shudder shook her; then the blank staring look faded away and she began to sob. "The cat, dear God, the cat. It's red all over."

I sat down on the couch and swept her hard against me, my arms holding her for dear life. I could feel her heart pumping against my chest like an overworked car engine. I still hadn't recovered from my fright; mine probably sounded the same.

"Tell me about it, dear," I murmured; but all she could say was, "The cat, it was so heavy sitting on my chest. Its face was red with blood." After a while she whimpered, "Red, red, just like their coats."

I comforted her silently with my hands and arms, rather than with words, all the while making mental notes. *Red cat, red coats.*

Suddenly Bryarly pushed away from me. "It's all right, Jake, I'm awake," she said quietly. "Did I have a nightmare?" Before I could answer, deep reproach sounded in her voice. "You turned off all the lights."

"Do you never sleep without a light?" I asked.

She tried to answer lightly. "Not if I don't want to wake up screaming. Did I frighten you? Sorry."

She pulled away from me and struggled to her feet, avoiding the helping hand I held out to her.

"If you'll excuse me, I think it's time I went to bed. Good night, Jake. Thank you for everything."

But she didn't look at me when she said it; all the spontaneity had gone from her voice. She swung along alone on her crutches, never once looking back. I had come too close, so she had gone away from me again, in spirit as well as in fact.

CHAPTER
8

Around the middle of January I took a week off to go to Washington. Our research work was going well, but the distance between Bryarly and me had never been bridged since the night she woke from her nightmare, screaming.

I thought perhaps a few days apart would be good for both of us.

I didn't say so to Bryarly, merely offering the excuse of several business appointments scheduled for me in Washington. I also mentioned that I had not seen my younger daughter since before I went to England. When I phoned Nancy to tell her I was coming home, she agreed to drive up from college and stay with me at the farm over the weekend.

The morning I was to leave, Bryarly seemed to be oversleeping. I had to tap on her bedroom door to say good-by.

"Come in," she called.

I opened the door and found her sitting up in bed in a white quilted bed jacket reading a paperback.

I said awkwardly, "I thought you overslept. I'm leaving now. I wanted to say good-by."

"Good-by, Jake. Have a good trip," she said chillingly.

"Take care of yourself."

She nodded distantly and looked down at her book, but still I lingered. "Are you sure you'll be all right?"

"Quite sure. I have friends to call on if I need anything."

Now, why did I think that message was directed rather pointedly at me?

I shifted from one leg to the other. I suddenly wanted in the worst way to stay.

"You know, I don't really have to go," I said, coming around to the side of the bed she was facing. "I could delay my appointments. I have the feeling you—"

She was looking at me a little more kindly. "The feeling I what, Jake?"

"You might need me." After a few seconds of silence, I added doggedly, "I don't ever want to be away when you need me, Bryarly."

Her expression softened even more. "I'll be fine, Jake, truly. Several of my friends have offered to come by during the day or sleep over if I need them, but you know yourself I'm perfectly capable of being by myself now. Anyhow, you—you won't be gone that long, will you?"

"Not more than four or five days," I said, ruthlessly shortening the allotted time and planning to shorten it more if possible.

As it happened, I doubled the time because Nancy came down with the flu on our second day at the farm and I didn't want to leave her until she was well enough for me to drive her back to school.

As soon as I got back to Washington, I packed a bag and caught the first shuttle flight to New York.

By the time I got off the cab on Central Park South, my heart was thumping like a teenager's getting ready for his first date. I had my keys, but I rang the bell of the apartment so as not to give her a fright.

I gave it a good peal, once, twice. Maybe she was out

shopping, I thought, disappointed, turning first the top and then the bottom key in their locks.

I walked through the living room with its blinds drawn, and into the empty office, laughing aloud a bit ruefully at the monstrous ego which could believe that after ten days she would be sitting there waiting for me whenever I chose to appear.

I dumped my suitcase on the office couch and then returned to the living room, frowning a bit. Why would the blinds still be drawn in the middle of the afternoon?

I had a vague premonition even before I saw the big envelope propped against the pewter vase on top of the fireplace. It had my name scrawled large across it in Bryarly's now familiar handwriting. She hadn't been angry when she scribbled it, at least not too angry to tease, because the name written on the envelope wasn't Jake but GERARD in great capital letters.

I drew out a single sheet of typing paper with a simple four-line message.

Dear Jake:
I've decided to go up to my house on the Cape for a bit. Make yourself at home as long as you want. Lots of basics in the refrigerator and freezer. See you soon.
B.

I swore long and loudly before I snatched the desk phone off its cradle and dialed Mark Lorrimer.

"Mark," I barked into the receiver when the Lorrimer network of secretaries finally put me through to him, "have you an address for Bryarly's house in Hyannis?"

"Yes. Why?"

"I just got back from Washington and found a note saying that's where she is."

"This time of year with a broken ankle in that isolated place? She must be nuts."

"Exactly. The address, please."

"Are you renting a car? I'm not sure Air New England runs its regular flights now."

"If it doesn't, I'll hire a charter. Have you got that address?"

Eventually his secretary provided one, and I wrote it down on a slip of paper which I tucked in my wallet while I dialed Air New England. Round about the third digit, my eye fell on her filing cabinets, and I crashed the phone down without finishing my number. I walked across to cabinet number five, which had attracted my attention by a most unusual sight—its top drawer was not quite closed. For the first time ever since I'd moved in—unlocked. I pulled the drawer out all the way and then in swift succession the other three. Not only unlocked but empty. She must have taken with her whatever files they had contained.

Why? I wondered, dialing again. My mind nibbled savagely at that same simple question all the while I dealt with arrangements for my flight. Had she taken her files *out* of or *into* protective custody? If so, why had she and what were they? Someday soon I would have to press her harder for some answers. I was, after all, an investigator, not a psychiatrist; a writer as well as a would-be lover.

After twice losing my way, it was fairly late in the afternoon when I made the sharp right arrowed on the map by the car agency man and went barreling up and down the narrow strip of stony road bordered with towering pine trees and idiotically labeled Melody Lane.

He had said I couldn't miss the house once I found Melody Lane, and that, at least, turned out to be true. After playing hide-and-seek among the evergreens for two spine-crunching miles, I came to a small snow-covered beach, dotted here and there with scrawny scrub bushes and rock piles and ending in a gravel driveway that led to Benjamin Heston's house.

An old painted wooden signpost hanging from a tree read HESTON HOUSE. Underneath, in much smaller letters, the name B. ALLERTON had been added.

The house was big, sprawling, and very well kept, a typical weathered-shingle Cape Cod. Suitcase in hand, I marched up to the front door and rapped loudly. After a while, when no one answered, I tried the side.

Bryarly's voice cried out, "The door's open, Pete," and I pulled out the storm door, pushed in the inside door, and found myself in a huge New England kitchen, gulping in the marvelous smell of baking bread.

I couldn't see Bryarly. Then a muffled voice said, "Put the stuff on the table, will you, Pete, and give me a hand up."

I followed the sound of the voice and discovered her flat on the floor in front of the stove checking inside the oven.

I dumped the suitcase, and said fairly mildly, considering the state of fury I was suddenly in, "You are some kind of damned fool!" and went to help her up.

She looked rather dazed when I got her onto her feet. "Wh-what—h-how did you get here?"

"By cab, plane, and car. Who's Pete?"

"A painter who acts as my caretaker here for room and board. He and his wife live in the garage cottage, and he uses Benjy's studio when I'm not here. He went to get me some things from the store." She looked over at my suitcase. "Are you—staying?" she asked a bit nervously.

"Probably. Certainly for now. We'll discuss it," I said with a fair amount of *chutzpah* for an uninvited guest, "after I stretch out on the nearest bed for an hour or two, if you'll be so kind as to tell me where I can find it."

She led me out to the hallway, still looking slightly dazed. "Up the stairs," she said. "First door on the left. I think the bed may be made up, but I haven't been up to the second floor. I stayed in the den this trip to avoid steps."

I snorted. "So you had that much sense."

"Are you annoyed with me, Jake?" she asked forthrightly.

"Annoyed?" I repeated. Then I said it again, sort of tasting the sound of it. "An-noyed. My dear girl, from Washington to New York to here, I've managed to be in transit this whole dismal day. Luckily for you, I'm too damn tired to wrap those crutches around your neck, which is what I very much yearn to do and possibly may a few hours from now."

Those few hours later, showered, shaved, and rested, wearing corduroy slacks and a fisherman's sweater, I came downstairs and followed the trail of lights to a comfortable shabby living room hung with Heston seascapes. A wood and pine cone fire snapped, crackled, and popped in the open fireplace; and Bryarly, in jeans and an Icelandic sweater, sat sprawled in an oversized wing chair with her cast propped casually on a needlepoint hassock.

Her crutches lay on the floor. She glanced down at them with a spark of mischief in her eyes. "Would I be safer hiding these or have you lost the ambition to wrap them around my neck?"

"I haven't lost it," I said amiably, sliding my tail down in a smaller sister of her chair on the opposite side of the fireplace. "But fatigue has given way to hunger. Is that dinner I smell?"

"Supper," she corrected. "You're no longer in the elegant East."

"So long as it's food."

A small gateleg table drawn up to the curtained window was set for two with gay blue-and-white-checked place mats and two big pewter bowls.

"I was just waiting for you," Bryarly said, pushing herself up from the chair. "Can you carry for me, please."

"Gladly." I handed her the crutches, and then followed her brisk progress to the kitchen.

"You use those crutches like a pro now," I told her, pouring out two huge glass tankards of cider from the ceramic jug she indicated.

When I came back from carrying the mugs inside, she pointed to an old-fashioned china tureen. "If you'll take the stew in and sit down, I'll be right there with the bread. Watch it, it's heavy."

I dumped the tureen onto the center of the table, eyeing Bryarly expectantly as she followed with a basket of bread —several different hot breads, I discovered, when we were seated and she passed the basket across to me.

Using a silver ladle with an ornate handle, she filled both our bowls to the brim with stew. I took a quick taste, burnt my tongue, cooled my mouth with cider, took another more cautious taste, and then bit deep into a whole-wheat roll.

"My God!" I said reverently, and Bryarly, who had been watching me with smiling eyes, laughed out loud.

"You've been hiding your best attribute," I told her. "I never dreamt you could cook and bake. Please, you've got to marry me. I can't lose out on a good thing like this."

"You already have," she said with her mouth full. "The cook-baker is Ruth, and she's already married to Pete. If you like her stew, just wait till you try her fish-kebab."

"Anytime."

For the next ten minutes, while we silently demolished the contents of both basket and tureen and downed our tankards of gently kicking cider, there were no sounds except the snap and hiss of the fire and the outside wails of trees pummeled by the wind and water crashing onto the rocks and beach.

When I had room for not a drop more, I said, "I've died and gone to heaven." I pushed my chair back from the table and watched Bryarly scoop up the last bits of gravy in her bowl with a small crust. "Is Pete's wife often this good to you?"

"She always cooks for me when I'm here and in summer for my guests."

I cleared my throat. "In spite of my disappointment," I said with pretended pomposity and a heart turning cartwheels, "my offer still holds."

"Of-fer? I don't understand." But her frightened eyes said she did.

"I'll still marry you," I said gruffly.

"Oh, Jake." She shook her head and bit down hard on her lower lip, then said again, "Oh, Jake." After a bit she shrugged. "You know I can't. I—I don't suppose it's any comfort to a man being turned down, but I wish I could." The faintest glimmer of a smile flickered across her face. "I've had a number of proposals in the last thirteen years. Every time I said no, I thanked God for Benjy, who made me free and independent so I could please myself. This is the first time I wish I was able to say yes instead of no. But I can't."

"Are you afraid to go to bed with me?"

Her face turned scarlet, her mouth shaped a round *No*, and then, with that occasional flash of honesty I loved, she answered simply, "Yes."

"But you married after it happened," I persisted, hoping she would tell me the truth. "How about the physical side with your husband?"

She turned away from me abruptly, saying in a muffled, anguished voice, "We—we worked it out."

"Then why couldn't you and I do the same?"

She said wearily, "Marriage is out. An affair is out. I didn't cheat, Jake; I told you that from the beginning."

"You told me," I acknowledged. "I just don't accept it. However"—I shrugged—"I'm too beat to go into it now. Let's do the dishes." I got up and lifted the empty tureen. "To be continued in the morning. If the weather report turns out right, we'll probably be snowed in. It will be a good day for fighting."

"There's apple pie," she offered timidly. "Ruth's apple pie has to be tasted to be believed."

"I'll have it for breakfast."

CHAPTER
9

Getting turned down by the woman I wanted to marry —even though I was expecting to be and the offer itself was just a trial balloon—is still not the stuff of which sweet dreams are made. Unexpectedly, I had a nightmare of my own that night.

I woke to the shadowy candlelight and Bryarly bending over me, awkwardly trying to hold onto one crutch and coax me awake at the same time.

I muttered in a thick voice, "Huh, whatsa matter?" and her slender fingers traced lines of concern across my cheeks.

"I think you had a nightmare."

I sat upright, disclosing my bare chest and pulling the blankets a bit higher so I wouldn't disclose the bare rest of me. "So I did," I said wearily, rubbing my head. "Damn." I reached across the Delft candlestick she must have brought upstairs with her and switched on the bedside lamp. "I thought I'd done with that one, it's been such a long time."

I smiled up at her troubled face. "Sorry I brought you all

the way up the stairs. Sit down. You look as though you're going to fall over on that crutch."

She eased herself gingerly down onto the side of my bed, holding the one crutch over her lap.

"You see," I told her, grinning wryly, "you don't have a corner on neurosis. I'm nightmare-ridden, too. What time is it?"

"Just past two in the morning."

I eyed her jeans and sweater. "Haven't you gone to bed?"

"No, I—I couldn't sleep. I was reading by the fire. When I went out to the hallway to get another log, I heard you moaning and groaning."

I made a face and said again, more briefly, "Sorry."

"I don't mind," she said softly. "It makes you more human, somehow, more approachable."

I took her nearest hand, playing with her fingers. "Bryarly, if you only knew how human I am."

She stiffened a little, taking fright, and I let go of her hand, yawned, and then asked, "Are you sleepy now?"

"No, unfortunately, wide awake."

"Me, too. Why don't you scram out of here and I'll throw on my clothes and come down and share your fire?"

She nodded and stood up, and I shouted after her, as she hobbled along on one crutch, "Can you manage the stairs going down?"

"Yes," she shouted back. "I'll hold onto the bannister."

In fifteen minutes when I came downstairs, the gateleg table was again set with place mats on which sat two steaming mugs of tea and two tremendous slabs of pie.

I took one taste of the pie and uttered a single awed, "Wow! That," I said when I had finished, "was a religious experience. Excuse me."

I went out into the hallway and came staggering back under the weight of a baby tree trunk, which I unloaded onto the fire. It blazed up fierce and hot, and I brushed off my hands and started tossing the couch cushions onto the floor.

Bryarly came back from the kitchen carrying something

that looked like a bed warmer. "What on earth are you doing?" she asked me.

"Creating twin love seats to set us up near the fire. By the same token, what on earth is that object you're carrying?"

"A popcorn popper. Do you like popcorn?"

"Yes, I do, my poppet."

"I should think," she told me, her nose pointed disdainfully upward while she shook the popper vigorously over the fire, "that a writer would know a pun is the lowest form of humor."

"Not to us Coney Island kids," I retorted.

In a surprisingly short time she produced a huge bowl of popcorn. We bundled down on our love seats with two cushions each propping up our heads and the popcorn bowl stuck between us marking an unspoken border.

"Tell me more about Coney Island," she wheedled.

"Someday I'll take you there," I said lazily. "Preferably when it's still winter and you're not on crutches. We'll walk along the boardwalk, inhale the perfume of the Atlantic, and I'll tell you tales of my misspent youth, particularly my daughters' favorite, the story of Slumschick."

She hoisted herself up and leaned over me. "The story of *what?*"

"Slumschick. And it's *who,* not *what.* They're people."

"You have got to be kidding."

"Word of honor."

"Tell me about them now. Pretty please," she added, coaxing.

I lay on my back, staring reflectively at the ceiling. "What will you tell me in return?"

"Anything you want," she promised rashly. Then she took a quick look at my face as I turned on my side again, with my eyes questioning her, gulped, and added, "Almost."

"The Slumschicks," I said, grabbing a handful of popcorn and lying back again, "lived one floor below my family and next door to my friend Jerry Crook. Mr. Slumschick was a cutter in the garment district, a gentle, mild-mannered guy, not more than five foot four, with a Yul Brynner head. His wife Annie topped him by three inches and was twice as wide, and she had the voice of a Fulton Market fishmonger. There were three Slumschick daughters, Fanny, Rose, and Tillie; the middle one, Rose, was in my class at school."

I paused to nibble my popcorn and lick the salt off my fingers. Then I went on. "Now, Max, the superintendent of our apartment house, used to sell tickets for the Irish Sweepstakes—strictly illegally, of course—and one year we had a winner in the neighborhood. You can imagine the big excitement that swept Coney Island and our building in particular, because this meant at least one book of our tickets had gotten across the Atlantic, so we all had a chance.

"My gang, which consisted of Jerry, Joey Mandelbaum, Pete Kelly, Tony Pisatti, and me, hatched a really fiendish plot. There was a phone booth in the drugstore—which in those days was a combination pharmacy and ice cream parlor—on the ground floor of our building. We went into it and dialed the Slumschick number. When the lady of the house answered, I said in my best supposed-to-be-Oxford English accent, "Is this the residence of Slumschick?"

"Oh, you little beast!" Bryarly breathed.

"Kindly don't interrupt the speaker," I said severely. "To continue: when I got the madame to admit that she was who she was, I informed her that I represented Lloyds of London." I smiled reminiscently. "Mrs. Slumschick screamed, 'Vat? Vat?' and I repeated that it was Lloyds of London and her ticket had been picked and she was in line for the grand prize.

"First I heard her screaming over the phone, then she hung up, and we could hear her screaming all the way up on the third floor. 'Ve von! Ve von!' The voice kept getting nearer and nearer to us, and the next minute she was in the store. We were all still grouped near the phone booth, where we had collapsed laughing, only now we were beginning to get a bit nervous. The store owner—his name was Max, too—was eyeing us a bit suspiciously, especially when Mrs.

Slumschick shrieked again, 'Ve von, ve von! Mexxie, serve multed milks for evvyone.'"

I stopped for breath, and Bryarly demanded indignantly, "For heaven's sake, finish it. What happened?"

"What happened, Jerry listened through the wall and told us later, was a rip-roaring fight between Mr. and Mrs. Slumschick. When realization dawned, she assumed he was the guilty party. As soon as he entered his castle that night, the dishes began to fly along with her tongue. "Precktickal jokes, is it? I'll give you Lloyds of London.'"

"And that was all?"

"That was all." I rolled over and grinned down at her. "Except that a few days later, when I walked into class, Rosie Slumschick marched over to me, and without saying a word hauled off and whacked me so hard across the face, I thought she'd broken my jaw. Then she marched off."

"What did you do?"

"Nothing. I figured I deserved it."

"Yes, you did, you monster," said Bryarly in a schoolmarmish voice. Then she broke down and giggled. "It's a great story."

I asked quietly, after a short silence broken only by the munching and crunching of popcorn, "Haven't you a great story to tell me in return?"

She used the edge of the couch to lever herself up on her feet. "No," she said, "just a very ugly, sordid story, but you're not going to give me any rest till you hear it, are you? Wait here."

She pulled her crutches under her arms and swung out of the room. When she came back, she was holding a slim file, which she flung over onto my lap.

The filing tab read: *A case of rape in Georgia, 1963.*

I looked up quickly. Bryarly was seating herself in one of the wing chairs. I patted the cushions beside me. "Why don't you come back here?"

"No. Not now. Read it, please," she said, her face turned away from me.

I started on the first page. *A naked Venus knelt at the*

center of the fountain . . . I directed my eyes across to a profile that might have been chisled in marble. *She reached up suddenly and yanked off the silver crown* . . .

I continued to read slowly, deliberately, not wanting to miss a single word or nuance or shade of meaning. Not till the final page did I realize that my palms were hot and damp with sweat, my throat ached from the rasp of short, shallow breaths, and I sat staring sightlessly down at the one last paragraph I had read six times and committed to memory for all time to come . . . *Hattie, she sobbed out wildly as they both stumbled into the house. I want a bath. I want a bath. I want a bath.*

CHAPTER
10

When I thought I had control of myself, I went and sat down on the arm of her chair, put my hands on either side of her face, and lifted it to my searching eyes.

She gave me a twisted travesty of a smile. "Jake, for heaven's sake, don't look so tragic," she said lightly. "It was more than thirteen years ago."

"And have you forgotten a day of your life since?"

She jerked her face free. "No."

"Bryarly, I'd give my soul right now to be able to take you in my arms and comfort you, only a man's arms aren't a comfort to you, are they? They're either an insult or a punishment."

"Up till now," she whispered, struggling to her feet.

Very slowly, hardly daring to believe she meant it, I put my arms around her, holding her loose and easily at first. When she made no movement of withdrawal but instead put her head down on my shoulder with a tired, contented little sigh, I tightened my grip till she gasped.

I slackened my hold at once. "Did I hurt you?"

"No, no, it feels so good. I had forgotten . . . it's been so long . . . a man's arms *are* comforting. Hold me, Jake, please hold me tighter."

I held her tighter, my sweater soaking up her tears, but let go the moment she strained away.

"Let's lie down again, dear," I said, and she let me take her hand and help her hobble to our bed of cushions.

When I had built up the fire again and, at her direction, fetched some afghans from the antique Dutch cupboard in the hallway, I lay down beside her, this time firmly removing the half-empty popcorn bowl from between us.

We lay very close but under separate afghans, the interlocked fingers of our hands the only point of contact.

"What made you write it up the way you did?"

"You mean third-person?"

"Yes."

"It was the only way I could do it. Things—they got so goddamn messy, not just the rape, but afterwards. I—I just couldn't talk about it then, and Cousin Lucretia . . . well, someone suggested writing it; she said it didn't matter how I did it as long as I got all the poison out of me."

She stopped to draw some long, deliberate breaths and then continued less incoherently, "I tried a couple of times without getting anywhere. Then I found that writing it as though it had happened to someone else, it came out easier. At the crisis center, with the girls who have trouble talking, I always suggest writing it down. You'd be surprised how often it helps."

She began to laugh then, sounding genuinely amused. "That was pretty silly of me, and you a writer. Of course, you understand."

"Bryarly, darling, I understand a lot more than you think."

She sat up and bent near to me. Then her hand let go of mine and moved across my eyes and cheeks.

"You've been crying," she said in wonder. "I can't believe it, you've been crying."

"Why is it so hard to believe?" I asked huskily, kissing the fingers that had wandered down to my mouth. "I love you, Bryarly."

"I may love you, too, Jake. I'm not sure because neither am I sure I know what love is anymore. Either way, no good can come of it."

"Don't say that, loving is a good in itself."

We lay quiet for quite a while till presently, hearing her stir, I asked, "Is the one you showed me the only file from your number-five cabinet?"

She gave a rueful chuckle. "You don't miss much, do you, Jake? No, it isn't the only one. I have my notes on a girl who was raped in 1777. I got the idea for the book from her. This country's bicentennial was also the two-hundredth birthday of practically no change in attitudes about rape. The victim is still crucified afterwards, and the law is less concerned with protecting women from rape than guarding the occasional man against false accusations of rape. The women's movement is just beginning to get some of those laws changed."

She let go of my hand and moved a few inches away from me. "I also have a file on my life before the rape and after," she told me in a flat, precise voice. "I'm sure you noticed that I wrote up one for all my other case histories. I saw no reason to except myself. I suppose you'd like to see that file, too?"

"Or have you tell me about it, I don't really care which," I said, ignoring her bitter emphasis. "After all, *I* gave you my capsule confession."

"So you did, those poor but not poverty-stricken parents in Coney Island," she jeered gently. "Well, mine were fairly well-to-do, but a most unlikely combo. My mother was descended from the New England Allertons, not the Mayflower ones but relations of theirs who came to the New World about ten years or so later. Their branch became a well-known Cape Cod whaling family. In the middle eighteen-hundreds one of the Allerton captains married the beautiful half-Chinese girl that all his contemporaries politely pretended was under the guardianship of another older captain . . . on the theory, no doubt, that gentlemen in glass ships shouldn't throw accusations. The youngest daughter of the marriage was the first Bryarly Allerton; I'm afraid I'll be the last."

She clasped her hands behind her neck and stared off into space. "My father's oldest known ancestor, Tobias Allen, came to Virginia as an indentured servant. Just after the Revolution, with his indenture worked out and a little money in his pocket, he settled in Ambruster, Georgia. In a few generations the Allens were the biggest frogs in town after the Ambrusters, who founded it. My mother and father could never even have met if it weren't for World War Two. He was stationed near Boston, and she lived there. I don't know what got to her about him, the uniform or the Southern charm. Or maybe she was in love with love."

She drifted off into private thoughts for a minute and then went on briskly. "After the war he got a job in a stock brokerage firm in Boston, and all went well till I was about three years old. Then his father died quite suddenly, and when they went home for the funeral, my grandmother Allen insisted that he must stay.

"I suppose," she said, chewing her thumb reflectively, "there was some justice on her side. His sisters were married and scattered; he was the only son, and there were a lot of businesses to be run. His father owned a real estate firm, a—don't laugh—peanut farm and factory. He had an interest in a local bank and a couple of other pies. But my mother was used to Boston and living in Ambruster must have been sheer hell for her. Her whole life was dominated by a mother-in-law who detested 'that Yankee girl' her son had married. And, though I can't remember it, from what I pieced together years later, my father reverted to being his mama's boy rather than my mother's husband."

She shrugged. "The end was inevitable. In December of the second year she took me home to Boston for the holidays and we didn't go back. Their divorce came through in about two years, and after that I only saw my father for two weeks every summer, which was two weeks too much. To my grandmother Allen I was always that Yankee girl's daughter, my father's new wife was jealous of any interest he showed in me, and my stepsister Maggie Louise and I had a mutual hate pact.

"My life in Boston the rest of the time was marvelous. Mother worked in an art gallery right near our apartment. I used to drop by there after school every day. Every summer we went to the Cape, first visiting my Allerton grandparents. After they died Mother rented rooms for us in a sort of artists' boarding house. Then we started coming here to Hyannis to Benjy's house."

"After your mother married him, you mean?"

"Before, too. Mother was very wary about getting married again."

"It runs in the family, I see," I said dryly.

She grinned at me, unconcerned. "I expect so. Whatever. Mother kept him dangling for years. Of course, they lived together, which I didn't realize till a long time afterwards. But one day Benjy put his foot down, and they had a bang-up quarrel on which I shamelessly eavesdropped, though I didn't understand more than half of it. He said he was tired of this hole-and-corner living; either she wanted him or she didn't; she was going to marry him or else he was walking out. God, I was terrified."

"Of the quarreling?"

"No, of his walking out. I adored him. Anyhow, I didn't have to worry. Mother cried and carried on, but she wasn't about to lose him. The next day she took me shopping for wedding dresses for the two of us, and they were married within the month. They had a marvelous honeymoon in the Greek isles, and I"—she laughed with remembered delight—"I had a marvelous time here in Hyannis with Aunt Lucy and Joel. Lucy Raphael was his widowed sister; her son Joel was, and still is, my best friend."

I asked lightly, "Do I have to worry about him?"

"He's a solidly established doctor in Boston, married, with three kids. I'm godmother to the oldest two."

"But," I said, watching her giveaway face, "he was in love with you at one time?"

"Long, long ago, and it was never any good. He knew it without even asking. But he and his mother were good to me when I needed friends and kindness . . . good above and beyond anything our relationship called for. It's not something one would ever forget. Or should."

"When your mother and Benjy died, you mean?" I asked gently.

"They were drowned," she corrected fiercely, "only three years after the marriage. The day of the funeral I overheard something I wasn't supposed to. The lake they went into had a tremendous undertow. It sucked them down so fast and furiously they never even came up once. When the divers went down for their bodies, they were both standing upright at the bottom of the lake. For years and years I had a nightmare vision of the two of them standing there facing one another while they drowned, with bodies arched upward like ballet dancers, arms reaching out, their faces contorted in the final agony. I kept picturing little fishes playing in Mother's long hair as it streamed out behind her."

I moved swiftly to pull her up against me. The voice muffled against my sweater said, "It still haunts me."

"I know, darling, I know."

I continued to comfort her while she wept softly. When she was calm again, I told her, "I did learn about the custody appeal."

"Then you know who got me and why." She lay back against the cushions, smiling disagreeably. "I had no idea of it at the time, but I was a considerable heiress. At the judge's hearing, Aunt Lucy offered to take me at her own expense, not using any of the income from my inheritance, but my father had the law on his side. I went back to Ambruster with him."

She gave an involuntary shudder. "I was twelve, and from then until I was fifteen I was a miserable square-peg, tomboy Yankee. At my sweet-sixteen birthday party, considered as obligatory as the wedding ceremony in Ambruster, I decorated the wall for the first half of the evening, pretending not to care but dying a thousand deaths while Maggie Louise and her friends snickered and sneered. Miss Annabel—which is what the whole town called my grandmother; her name was Anna Belinda—didn't help any, shaking her head every time she caught my eye and commiserating quite audibly, 'No Allen woman was evah a wallflowah!' "

She caught my eye and gave me a bittersweet smile. "It's funny now, but at sixteen . . ."

"I feel quite sure," I cut in smoothly, "that you weren't a wallflower long."

She grinned. "Right on. Never after the first half of that night. Miss Annabel said, 'Poor thing,' just once too often, and I told myself, 'Okay, that's it.' The first boy who came by after that was sweet on Maggie Louise, which suited me just fine. I harpooned him with my biggest, sugariest smile and then wove him further into my net with a barrage of compliments. 'If you aren't the handsomest thing in that sincere blue suit. I do declare, no matter what Maggie Louise says, it's the exact color of your eyes.' Of course, he demanded to know what Maggie Louise had said, but I just hung my head, the picture of maidenly confusion and reassured him tenderly, 'You mustn't mind her funning; Maggie's always so full of jokes. I just love eyes like yours myself.' "

"Bitchy," I said, "but bright."

"I thought so," she returned complacently. "I had him eating out of my hand by the end of the evening, and two other boys as well. I danced all the second half of the night. Maggie Louise looked fit to bust, and Miss Annabel actually gave me an approving smile. For the next three years I became a typical and popular Georgia peach. Sugar and flattery were my daily diet. I shoveled it out, and I gathered it in. If Maggie Louise had two dates in a week, I tried for three. If she went to one party, I made sure to go to two. I turned myself into a puppet, just as damned silly and empty-headed as she was. In my freshman year I crowned my idiocy by getting engaged to Randy Ambruster, probably, looking back, for no better reason than that she would have given her eyeteeth with a few molars thrown in to get him. He was the biggest fish in the local pond, and the Ambrusters were filthy rich."

"Why were you ready to return his ring before the . . . the . . ."

"Rape, Jake, the word is rape."

"Before the rape."

"I went to bed with him," she said, trying for a light, airy note but clutching at the top of the afghan with both hands. "Listening to his ardent entreaties and deluding myself that this was true love, I let myself be carried away on the wings of passion. Except"—her voice grew hard and remote—"that the passion seemed ridiculous and I wasn't so much a shrinking virgin as a bored one. I remember being horribly embarrassed by his puffing and panting, and after it was over, all I could think was, 'So that's sex. What in the world is all the fuss about?'"

"So you decided to break up with him?"

She gave me the slanting smile, which meant she was really not amused. "No, *he* decided. It seems that for him, too, there were a couple of highly important missing ingredients in our coming together; one, a lack of pain, and two, a lack of blood. It never dawned on him that I was a highly active if not athletic young lady. His immediate inexperienced conclusion was that I couldn't possibly be a virgin. He complained to his frat brothers that same night about how he'd been had, and I was instantly labeled fair game. Since I was second-hand goods already, why should I object to a spot of rape?"

A little roughly I pulled her across her set of cushions onto mine. I kissed the sides of her head and the corners of her mouth and her restless hands. She didn't speak, just sighed a little; then much to my surprise, she fell fast asleep in my arms. When I was sure she wouldn't awaken, I laid her gently back on the cushions and pulled the afghan up to her chin. After a while I slept, too.

CHAPTER
11

I stayed in Hyannis for three days, gaining a pound each day under the care and feeding of an unobtrusive Ruth, who was seldom in evidence but whose superb meals appeared on the table with clockwork precision. Dishes, ashes in the fire-place, and any other mess and clutter we created vanished the moment we turned our heads.

Bryarly and I did no more true-confessing or open-heart dissection of our feelings in that time, but we did achieve an easy camaraderie that I considered more than hopeful. Friendship in love is not to be despised.

The work was waiting, however, and when Bryarly told me she had promised to fly down to Boston the next day for her goddaughter's eighth birthday party and I could go back to New York or stay on in Hyannis as I pleased, I pleased to go.

"You don't have to fly," I said promptly. "The roads aren't too icy anymore; let me drive you."

"Well . . ." She tapped her laced fingers against her mouth.

"Don't worry," I said sardonically. "I'll drop you off at the door and drive away immediately. You don't have to introduce me."

"That's not what I was worried about!" she said indignantly, lowering her hands and casting me a look of dislike.

"No?"

"Noooo. Okay, damn it, yes. You are so doggone persistent. You're like a woodpecker, you bore from within."

"I believe you mean a termite. Are we driving or not?"

"I guess so."

"You're welcome."

To my surprise she blushed vividly at this mild rebuke, lowering her eyes and speaking in the rapid tones of a rehearsed speech. "I'm sorry, Jake. Yes, thank you, I'd appreciate the drive."

The next morning she came to Ruth's farewell French toast breakfast in full war paint and one of the side-slit dresses she affected. The mask was on, and her guard was up. I wasn't surprised that the ride to Boston fairly sizzled with silent hostility. I *was* surprised when, halfway there, she broke the long silence to tell me, "I called Joel and Cathy last night to tell them we were coming."

"We?"

"Well, I said you were driving me from Hyannis, and they said I should invite you to dinner after the party," she reported with doubtful enthusiasm.

"Would you prefer me to accept or decline?" I asked carefully, and received an elaborate shrug and monosyllabic grunt for reply.

"Would you translate that into understandable English, please?"

She sighed exaggeratedly. "It's up to you, Jake, but it would be a bore for you hanging around through a kid's birthday party."

"Not at all. I always enjoyed my daughters' parties," I assured her cheerfully. "I'll be happy to accept."

A look of dismay flashed across her face, and I stifled a grin as she stared suspiciously at my profile.

"Tell me about Joel," I suggested. "Benjy's nephew, your best friend and father of three. What kind of doctor is he?"

"A psychiatrist."

I groaned.

"Don't be a bigot! He happens to be nice, extremely nice, and quite normal."

"Then why is he a psychiatrist?"

"Because of me, I think," she said quietly.

When we arrived at the Raphael house, the party was in full swing. I was introduced to Cathy and Joel Raphael in the midst of the hullabaloo while Bryarly fended off the rapturous attacks of their offspring. Then I was elected to go down to the playroom to supervise a Ping-Pong tournament.

An hour and a half later the doctor and I, having been offered the mind-saving bonus of coffee and a slice of birthday cake alone in his den, were seated on opposite sides of his oversized desk. It didn't require my investigative techniques to get him to talk. He wanted to.

"I definitely became a psychiatrist because of Bryarly," he confirmed as soon as the subject came up. "She's been part of my life since I was eleven years old and Uncle Benjy fell in love with Caroline." He smiled ruefully. "Of course, I used to think she was a real pain in the neck then, tagging after me in Hyannis and everywhere I went. Still, a lovable pain in the neck. In Boston I used to play big brother when she had a problem. I felt really rotten when her father took her home to Georgia. Coming on top of Caroline and Uncle Benjy, it was like another bereavement, losing my little sister."

He slapped the desk hard with the flat of his hand. "Seeing her now, that beautiful, calm—seemingly calm —poised woman, you would never believe what a *sparkling* child she was. She danced, not walked; she sang, not talked. God, she was alive!"

"Bryarly on the Beach," I murmured.

"Exactly. He caught the very essence of what she was then. We didn't see her again for nearly seven years, and the early weekly letters had dwindled down to practically nothing. Then one day my mother got a collect call from Bryarly in a hospital in Atlanta. It didn't make sense at first. She kept saying Cousin Lucretia had told her to call; would it be all right for her to come and visit. Mother said yes, of course, and Bryarly broke down and cried so hard she couldn't talk. At which point a man took over the phone and introduced himself as a doctor at the hospital. When I came home in the late afternoon—I was in my second year of medical school and it was exam week—Mother was all packed and ready to go. I listened to her explanations while I drove her to the airport. Two days later she was back with the lovely-looking automaton that was Bryarly. She moved, she spoke, she dressed, she ate, but she wasn't alive."

He looked at me broodingly. "She leads a very full, very busy, very interesting life. She does good works. She travels. She dates. Has friends. But, in spite of it all, I don't think she's really been alive since. Ailurophobia. Erythrophobia. Fears she's never begun to explore. It's obvious you're in love with her. Do you have any idea what you're up against?"

"I think so."

"I've been that road myself, but the timing was all wrong. It was too soon; she was too tormented. For her sake, I gave up without a fight."

"For both our sakes, *I* won't."

He tilted his coffee cup in salute. "The best of luck to you, Jake. I'd give a lot to see that girl happy."

"Thanks," I said. "I may need your help as well as your wishes. To start, I'd like your mother's address."

"My mother lives in Sarasota. She married again and went to Florida after Bryarly moved to New York." He scribbled on a piece of paper. "Here you are. I'll write to her tonight myself and give you a character reference."

"Thanks," I said again, carefully folding the paper into my wallet. "You've been quite frank, I appreciate it."

His eyebrows lifted. "But you wonder, how come?"

"I do."

"Bryarly confides in me as much as she does in anyone,

which isn't overmuch. I do know you're aware of her past, and I sense the feeling between you isn't a one-way street. It's Bryarly I'm trying to do something for. If you get helped along the way, that's incidental."

We smiled in mutual understanding and sipped our coffee silently for a moment. Then I had another thought.

"Who," I asked, "was the Cousin Lucretia who advised Bryarly to call your mother?"

"Now that," he said softly, "is something I've puzzled about for thirteen years. We never found out. There isn't a Cousin Lucretia in her family or in ours. But she said it several times, not just over the phone but when my mother first got to Atlanta. Later she denied it flatly. 'I never heard of a Cousin Lucretia in my life,' she told me, looking me straight in the eye that challenging way she has when she's lying in her teeth. Have you ever seen it?"

"Have I not!" I said wryly as I took out my notebook and ruffled its pages backwards. "Here it is," I said and read aloud to him, "'Cousin Lucretia, I'm so glad you're back.'

"That," I said in answer to his puzzled stare, "is a direct quote from Bryarly when she was dazed and drugged. The other evening, when she was in full possession of her senses, if a little emotional, she spoke of Cousin Lucretia quite lucidly."

"She did!" he exclaimed jubilantly. "In what way? What did she say?"

I cast my mind back. "I had just read the case history of her rape," I recited precisely. "We were discussing her reason for writing about it in the third-person. She said that Cousin Lucretia came, and then that *someone* had suggested she try writing it out."

"This is quite a breakthrough, Jake."

I said ruefully, "I'm afraid I'll have to take your word for it. Sometimes I feel as though I take two or three steps backward for every one that goes forward."

"It may seem like that, but it isn't so. She's changed already. Cathy and I can see it even if you can't. She's —she's—"

"Yes?"

"Less wary, I think," he said thoughtfully. "It's not something that can be seen, but it very definitely can be felt. And there's something else, Jake."

"Yeah?"

"She's never brought a man to our home before."

"She wasn't too thrilled about bringing me. I had to push quite a bit."

He grinned. "Think again."

I thought for a while, and then a slow grin spread over my face, too. "You mean if she hadn't really wanted me to come, she didn't have to tell me about the invitation."

"Bingo!" cheered Bryarly's best friend.

CHAPTER
12

An answer from Lucy Raphael to the letter I had written her arrived at Craig Burden's office within a week. Craig lent me a small office to read it in peace; it looked like a small book.

I unfolded the typewritten pages, headed *Mrs. Steven Rose*.

> *My dear Jake,*
>
> *Your very welcome letter did not come as a surprise because Joel had already written me to expect it. Bryarly is as dear to me as a daughter, and if answering questions can in any way help her to happiness—she has, I think, everything but that—then I will gladly tell you what I can about the painful subject of her rape.*
>
> *The first thing I knew about it was a phone call from Bryarly asking if she might visit me, only the words she used were "come home." After all the years that had passed, with our correspondence reduced to an exchange of birthday gifts and greeting cards, you can imagine it was a shock, especially when she sounded quite hysteri-*

cal and broke into uncontrollable sobbing when I said yes.

While I tried to calm her, a strange young man took over the phone, introduced himself as Dr. Winger or Wingard and explained rather tersely—I suppose he couldn't talk quite freely with her right there—that Bryarly had been raped the week before, treated at the local hospital, then later brought to the Atlanta hospital for some minor surgery. I can't begin to explain the tone in which he said she was experiencing some family difficulties and was in great need of a sympathetic friend or relative, but it had me packing my suitcase the minute I got off the phone. I arrived in Atlanta that night, checked into a hotel and was off to the hospital in the morning.

I was lucky enough to get to the doctor first (I do wish I could remember his name; I shall always feel eternally grateful to him). It seems that after the rape, Bryarly was cared for at a local hospital and then dismissed. The treatment she received there was so traumatic that later, when there was hemorrhaging and her doctor decided that the damage to the genital tissue required minor surgical repair, she refused to go back.

I firmly believe that the unbelievable callousness, of those whose duty it was to protect her, harmed her almost as much as the four bestial young men who held her down and savaged and humiliated her. I remember her saying once long afterwards, "Until I got to the hospital and spoke to the police, I thought the rape was bad!"

I was prepared to be shocked when I got to Bryarly's hospital room, but shock is hardly the word. I remembered a beautiful happy child. What I found was a white-faced ghost-ridden girl with great frightened eyes, sunken cheeks, constantly twitching hands and feet and body. She jumped at the sound of a voice, burst into tears when she was spoken to.

I was ready to take her right home, and she was ready to leave the hospital. The only thing that worried me was whether she would need to return soon for the police case.

"There is no police case," she told me in a dull, dead voice that made my stomach turn over. "Webb Carlin's cousin is a police lieutenant in Ambruster. Hank's uncle is head of pediatrics at the local hospital . . . the records disappeared. The boys' testimony is that it never happened. I took them all on, but it wasn't rape. I begged my father to bring the case, but he and his lawyer said there was no chance I would be believed in court, and it was best forgotten. He didn't mention that he and Randy Ambruster's father were heavily involved in business with the Hunnicutts' bank."

I was too appalled to say anything, and Bryarly began to laugh, a dreadful sound. "Besides," she said, "I committed the greatest crime of all. I took a bath and destroyed the evidence. I couldn't get anyone but Hattie to understand why I wanted a bath. Why I want one right now. Oh, God, God, I don't think I'll ever be clean again."

She and I left for Boston the next day. I notified her father—she refused to—and I must do him this much justice. Far from objecting, he seemed to think a change of scene would be beneficial, and he expressed gratitude to me for my trouble.

What did amaze me, weeks later, was to learn from Bryarly that she had never been told of her inheritance. She had begun to speak about looking for a job, saying she couldn't sponge off me. When I told her she was Benjy's heir, she was dumbfounded. Her father had always been generous about clothing, allowance, a car, but he had never mentioned it was her own money he was lavishing on her or using for medical and college bills.

She went to the Boston lawyers at once to ask if it were possible to receive the money directly. It wasn't. She was nineteen, and her father was her guardian for another two years. He agreed, however, to pay her college expenses—she transferred to Boston U.—and all her *other bills, including room and board to me, which she insisted on and I accepted for her pride's sake.*

He wrote a letter to her expressing his hurt that she should deal with him through lawyers; she never answered it. She could not forgive him for what she regarded as his weakness and betrayal.

She took speech lessons, determined to erase every trace of accent that identified her with him; dropped the nickname Lee that she had been using. When she was twenty-one and came into her inheritance, she legally dropped her father's name in favor of her mother's. She never had anything to do with her father's family again until years later when he came to New York for a cancer operation, I think in hopes that they could be reconciled. They were, but I doubt that the bitterness could ever be erased.

Bryarly led a very limited existence the two years she lived with us. She went to school during the day and spent every evening at home. Her recreation was an occasional movie or concert with Joel, or an art exhibit with me.

She made no other friends. She wanted none. She was utterly dependent on us, and it was a horrible complication when I realized that my son had fallen in love with her. It was all quite hopeless, and I was torn between my love and duty to both of them. Then there was Steven, my present husband. He had sold his art supply business in Boston and moved to Florida, where he opened a small gallery. He wanted me to marry him and, of course, move there. I felt Bryarly needed me. I thought Joel should move out, as he wanted to; it was torture for him sharing the same house with her.

Bryarly, however, was nobody's fool, even if her fears and needs had caused her to cling to us rather longer than was good for her. I've always suspected she may have overheard something, or perhaps she just observed the obvious and called on the strength she always had, even if it lay dormant for a long while.

The year she was twenty-one she went to spend the

summer in the house in Hyannis, which she had given strict orders the year before should not be rented out again. That house meant more to her than all the money in the world, and I suspect it was the beginning of her healing.

A few days after she drove up there alone—I was planning to follow in a few weeks—I received a long letter from her (though not so long as this one) full of love and gratitude for what we had given her but expressing her determination to go on without using us as crutches any longer. She had transferred to Hunter in New York for her senior year and registered with a real estate agent for an apartment.

I spent most of the summer with her at Hyannis; Joel came up in August. Steven and I were married there over the Labor Day weekend, and I moved to Florida, leaving my apartment for Joel.

In the fall Bryarly moved to her own apartment on Central Park South in New York, and got all kinds of safety locks installed. When I fretted about her loneliness, she got herself a German shepherd and a psychiatrist. The psychiatrist she gave up after six months; the dog, Caleb, and she were inseparable till he died last year.

After Hunter she went to Columbia for her master's in Library Science. Then she did a short stint at the Mercantile Library in New York but gave it up for free-lance cataloguing, so she could have plenty of time to carry on with her volunteer work for various rape committees and be free to spend her summers at Hyannis. Steven and I usually spend Augusts with her, and she comes to us in Sarasota in December to escape what she calls the "red Christmas celebrating." Joel and Cathy bought a place near hers in Hyannis after the babies started coming.

I think that covers almost everything I have to tell you. You can see for yourself that Bryarly is bright and beautiful. As a trained observer as well as a man in love, you must sense that her security is nonexistent, her *stability sadly brittle. More than just her innocence was lost in that terrible episode. It shattered her trust and her faith along with her ability to love.*

My son seems to think that you may be the one to restore her, my dear Jake, and I pray with all my heart that he may be right.

I would be most grateful to have you keep in touch with me from time to time.

*With all good wishes
and warmest
regards,
Lucy Raphael Rose*

CHAPTER
13

Maybe it was the letter—God knows it was enough to give anyone who loved her nightmares—but I dreamed again that night and woke once more to find Bryarly bending over me, vigorously shaking one of my shoulders while she urged in a voice of loving concern, "Jake, wake up, wake up, you're having another nightmare."

I shook my head against the grogginess. My eyes blinked away the glare of the bed light.

"Sorry," I said thickly, after a bit. "It doesn't usually come back so soon. Maybe I had better get my own place. I can't keep disturbing your sleep."

"You didn't," she said and slid the crutch from under her arm and sat down trustingly on the bed beside me. "I was reading. Don't you know by now I'm a night owl?"

Tentatively, she took my hand, pressing it between both of hers.

"Have you ever told anyone about your nightmare?"

"No."

"Why not?"

"Because it doesn't make sense."

"Maybe it will to me."

"If it doesn't to me," I muttered, "how can it to you?"

"Try me."

"Okay, Doctor, you're on," I decided cheerfully. "But on my conditions. Lie down beside me."

Her pale cheeks went to scarlet and then back again to dead white in five seconds flat.

"But you're—you're—you're—" I lay looking up at her with a wicked smile, refusing to help her out, and she finally stammered her protest in full. "You kn-know I c-couldn't."

I twitched at my blankets. "See, three layers. You just get under the top one. We'll have the comfort of being close—" my smile again provoked her to deny it would be comfort —"without any danger of your making contact with my nudity."

She blushed violently, and I gripped her fingers hard. "Your hands are chilled," I said persuasively, "and I'm still shaking. Besides which, bundling is a good old New England custom; nothing could be more suitable."

"Come lie with me and be my love," she misquoted unexpectedly.

"No, not just yet; someday maybe if we're both very lucky. Right now you're too fearful, and I, dear girl, am too fatigued. So"—I reached up and drew her gently down —"just lie with me and be my friend, and I'll tell you *my* neuroses."

She giggled at that, a nervous un-Bryarly giggle, but made no further resistance, just lay on her back, her body as straight and rigid as a tree trunk, while I turned on my side, drawing closer to her. For several moments I did not speak, savoring the delicious warmth of her and the proximity, despite the separating layers of wool, of one or two exquisite curves.

After a bit she said impatiently, "Well?"

I closed my eyes, seeing it clearly in my mind, trying to describe it so that she would see it, too.

"It begins like the picture on a three-dimensional movie

screen, colors and figures whirling toward the audience and finally settling into just one piece of wide-screen action, in this case of six little Indian boys playing on a spit of land jutting out into the water. Two are fishing, two are wrestling, and two are seesawing on a half-submerged log. Their faces are blurred so I can't make out the features. They are all different sizes, but they all six wear the same exact outfits of deerskin breeches and fringed jackets and moccasins, and three of them have on beaver-skin caps. The smallest of the boys has more ornamentation on his jacket; that's the only difference. That, and the color of their hair. Four are fair and two are dark. Did you say something?"

"I said, 'fair-haired Indians,'" she murmured.

"It's my dream," I pointed out with dignity.

"*Scusi.* So it is." The words were light, but her voice sounded strained. I couldn't think of any reason why it suddenly should except—I moved a little away from her.

To my astonishment she moved right after me. "Go on, please," she said, unaware.

Trying to keep her that way, I continued slowly, "The hair is important, not so much because of color as of style. The ones without caps are wearing it clubbed at the back of the neck and tied with ribbon à la the Father of our Country. That sets the period of the dream for me."

"Colonial." It was the barest whisper.

"Colonial," I agreed.

"Is that all?" came the same husky whisper, and again, unaware, her hand moved up to where the blanket had moved down and roamed restlessly over my bare arm.

Carefully controlling my pleasure, I said, "No, it's just the first frame. Then that picture dissolves, and two maps appear on the screen. To the left I see a long, winding river marked the *Hudson* and a big land area marked *West Chester.* In the center is the single word *Tarro.* I looked it up long ago and discovered it was the Indian word for wheat. That's where Tarrytown, on the Hudson, gets its name. Then the six little Indians suddenly appear again, faces still blurred, standing single file, balancing themselves on the borderline of the land and the river. They are all looking to the left, where another much smaller map slowly takes shape. When the form of the second map is complete, it changes in color from white to pale pink and then to a deep red"—I felt her involuntary shudder and hurried on —"then a single word appears underneath it: *Philadelphia*. But the strange thing is that somehow, in my dream, even before I see the word, even though the map bears no resemblance at all to the shape of the present-day city, I know deep down that it *is* Philadelphia. Does that sound weird to you?"

"Of course it's not weird," she said with a forced laugh. I was too busy sorting out my own feelings to remark how pale she'd gotten. "It's just a—just a dream."

"I'm awake in the dream. Somehow or other I've gotten myself from the Hudson Valley and over to Philadelphia, but when I reach out to touch it, it just crumbles into jagged bits like the pieces of a jigsaw puzzle. The colors blur and fade, the pieces fly up in the air, and suddenly where Philadelphia was, there is nothing."

I had never spoken about it before to a living soul. Talking about it was like living the dream over. My throat was dry and my cheeks were wet, and the pain was there, that unutterable, unbearable pain. "That's when I feel a grief so great, I think I'm dying myself. Philadelphia is gone, and this, for some reason that the dream never discloses, leaves me cold and alone and bereft."

A soft hand crept up to my cheeks; slender, sharp-nailed fingers sopped up the teardrops. "Don't cry, Jake dear," begged a voice of silk and honey.

I seized the fingers and kissed them, pointed nails and all. "I'm not," I said huskily. "The tears seem just to be there after the dream."

"Is that the end of it?"

"Not quite. After Philadelphia goes, I try to hold on to the dream. There's this feeling I have that the Indians can help me out; they can tell me about Philadelphia. I beg them to tell me, but they act as though I'm not even there. Still lined up in single file, they march right past me, right through me, right on down the Hudson Valley and out of my life. They're reciting some kind of song or chant as they go, always the same one. The song haunts me, but it's gone. I never can remember it when I wake up. I come to moaning and groaning and wet-eyed, and for hours after, there's none of the usual relief in finding out a dream is just a dream. I'm drained, empty, it's as though I've lost someone I dearly loved."

"Is—is that how you feel right now?"

"Not holding you in my arms, love. In case it's escaped your notice, that's what I'm doing. With you in my arms, Bryarly, I find myself dreaming wild, crazy, improbable dreams of happiness for both of us."

"Don't, Jake. It isn't any good. We're never going to—it couldn't ever—Even if I had wild, crazy hopes myself, you've just proved to me it's never going to be."

"What the hell are you talking about?" I asked in genuine bewilderment.

She dropped her head on my shoulder and sobbed, "Don't you see, you lost Philadelphia, too? It wasn't ever meant to be. *We* weren't meant to be."

"Jesus Christ!" I howled. "You bloody nutty little neurotic! And I'm just as bad. I should have my head examined for telling you. You mean to say you're going to read some deep symbolic meaning into this? Because the city of Philadelphia went up in smoke in my nightmare, so will we?"

"Wh-what makes you th-think it's a c-city?" she hiccuped weepily.

"It's the only Philadelphia I know."

She mopped her cheeks with her pajama sleeve. "Your reporting instincts have failed you for once," she told me, sliding out from under her blanket and swinging herself awkwardly up into sitting position. Withdrawal made her arrogant and assured again. "In colonial times, Philadelphia was a popular name. If you were bereft in your dream, it's because you lost a girl named Philadelphia, not a city."

I sat up myself, swearing softly. "I never thought of it. Do you know—?" I looked at her rather shamefacedly. "Once —in the beginning—it was driving me so crazy, I—I went to Philadelphia. Believe it or not, I walked the streets there for two, three days, expecting something to happen. When it didn't, I gave up in disgust, resolving to put it out of my mind."

"You have enough information to trace her now."

"What do you mean?"

"Her name was Philadelphia, and she lived in the Hudson Valley just before the Revolution broke out. She was connected somehow to six little Indians. I know it's not much to go on, but there are historical societies . . ."

It was bending the truth a bit, but I thought it best for Bryarly to get her off this kick. "I tell you, I don't care anymore!" I cried impatiently.

"I care, Jake."

The words were like a gauntlet flung between us.

"You really mean it? You think there's some symbolic connection between this Philadelphia and us?"

"I don't just think it. I'm certain."

"And you won't rest until I've investigated it?"

She bit her lip, not answering. Her eyes gave me a look of glowing entreaty.

"And if I don't choose to investigate?"

Again no verbal answer, just her hands thrown out in a gesture that said it all.

"Blackmail, Bryarly?" I asked gently.

"Jake, please, Jake." Her lips began to tremble again. "It's important. I wish I could tell you . . ."

I said gruffly, "Don't start crying again. I've had all the emotion I can stand for one night, and so have you."

"Jake," she asked me carefully, "can't you think of this as an investigation you've been assigned to? I've told you how it is—how I *know* it is. What you'll be doing is going out to find the proof for both of us. I don't know exactly where, but it's there to be found."

"How do you know?"

She turned away from me for a moment and then turned back. Her eyes met mine unflinchingly. "When you bring the proof back to me, I promise you, I will answer that question."

"What about the rape research?"

"It can wait a few days."

"That's all I'll give to it, I promise you that, no more than a few days."

She flung herself at me with a cry of joy that changed to a yelp of pain as she banged her cast against the side of the bed. As soon as I made sure she had done no real damage to herself, she began hugging me with enthusiasm. Deciding I deserved something for the wringer I had been put through, I responded so warmly she took instant flight.

Crutch retrieved, standing in the doorway, she said a bit pathetically, "Is there anything you need?"

"Bryarly," I said wearily, "will you please get the hell out of here."

She stared back at me, puzzled and affronted.

"I wrote an entire book on the evil of men who mistreat women," I told her pleasantly. "If you don't *amscray* this minute, I might wind up one of my own statistics."

She whisked out of sight, I turned off the light and was asleep before the clop of her crutches died away down the hallway. As so often happens when I'm wrestling with a story, my brain and my subconscious got together during the night to bring up a number of important points.

I awoke in the morning fully alert and held a brief dialogue with myself.

Wouldn't you say she came up extraordinarily quickly with the notion of Philadelphia's being a girl rather than a city?

Not necessarily. You just didn't see the trees for the forest. Reporters are supposed to see both the trees and the forest. Cool it, Jake, your professional pride isn't at stake. You were just too emotionally involved.

Well, for someone not involved at all, didn't that spate of information on the name Philadelphia come tripping off her tongue rather smoothly?

She's a librarian, Jake. Their heads are stuffed with odd bits of information.

Mmm. Try this one on for size. The period of the dream is colonial, which covers a long stretch of history. How come she said Philadelphia lived "just before the Revolution broke out?"

You're really straining, boy. Many people use the terms colonial and Revolutionary interchangeably.

But she's a librarian.

Cut the sarcasm and use your common sense. Do you have any idea what you're trying to say—or prove?

That's the damnedest part of it. I don't. But I keep remembering she said she knew of a connection between Philadelphia and us. I took that to mean she just felt certain . . . Now I'm not so sure . . .

Come on now, climb down out of Cuckoo-land; what else could she have meant?

That she had positive knowledge.

Positive knowledge of a girl who may or may not have lived two hundred years ago. Boy, you've been living in her home too long. That's really from outer space.

Don't you think I know it? Christ! I'm getting more whacked out than she is.

CHAPTER
14

I had followed thin leads before, but this one was ridiculous to the point of embarrassment. The New York Public Library and the New York Historical Society bend over backward to be helpful to researchers, but they need a little something solid to go on. A name and a notion are not exactly the material of which evidence is fashioned.

Doggedly, having a promise to keep and a couple of ghosts to lay to rest, I dug on into the past. After a couple of days, when I had exhausted the resources of the city, I hired a car and drove up to Westchester County with a long list of historical groups and a longer list of scholars and history buffs who might be helpful.

I made my home base a motel near Tarrytown in the heart of the region that was once the breadbasket of the thirteen colonies, researching during the day and interviewing at night, zigzagging east and west across the county, north and south along the Hudson.

For my week's work—I had promised Bryarly a couple of days—I came up with zilch. It was a toss-up on the seventh morning, while I dipped toast into the eggs with home fries that I had been eating with monotonous regularity, whether I headed straight back to the city or . . .

One day more, said the nagging voice in my head that so frequently prods me into unwished-for action. Okay, damn it, so one day more it was, and then definitely home-bound.

Or rather, Bryarly-bound. My annoyance melted as the eggs petrified on my plate; my mood softened as my toast got hard. Home-bound or Bryarly-bound, they were one and the same now.

The irritating thing about the nagging little voice is that it so often has a more intuitive grasp of what's going to happen than I do.

It started off as just a casual chat with a librarian in Croton-on-Hudson. I produced my list and she studied it as many librarians had done before her.

"Dear me," she murmured. "This is really quite comprehensive. I don't know that we have anything to add to it. Of course"—she nibbled a finger thoughtfully—"there's the Hudson Valley Art Historic Society. One of our local artists was mentioning it just the other day. It's very small, of course, and not open to the public yet . . ."

I got ready to dismiss the Hudson Valley Art Historic Society and offer my thanks and take my leave, but she hadn't wound down yet.

"Mrs. Reuter has written for permission to view," she told me beamingly. "There are supposed to be at least eight or nine De Kuypers. Not another folk art collection in the country has that many primitives by Lucretia De Kuyper."

My heart was battering against my ribs. I was all over sweat. They were both part of the wild, wonderful elation that sweeps over me when I'm going after a big story and it suddenly begins to break for me.

"Lucretia De Kuyper," I croaked. "Who is—was—she?"

"I really don't know," she said regretfully. "Perhaps Mrs. Reuter . . ."

"Lucretia De Kuyper," said Mrs. Reuter briskly, slapping a cup of coffee and a prune Danish down before me, "is

probably one of our oldest-known and best primitive paint-
ers. Maddeningly little is known about her personal life,
considering."

"Considering what?"

"That she was related to the Van Durens and that some of
the original Van Duren property in Tarrytown still stands;
that there's still one family descendant, Philippa Jansen,
alive and living there. There are bound to be family records,
but they have always been guarded the way the government
guards the records on Lincoln's assassination. And it's been
the same with the paintings. But now that Philippa's
incorporated this Art Historic Society, we've all been
hoping—After all, she's an artist herself, a very successful
sculptor, though she hasn't produced much these last few
years."

Philippa. Philadelphia. And Lucretia. The mysterious
never-to-be-mentioned Cousin Lucretia.

I called Bryarly from the motel that night after a half
dozen calls to Washington.

"Seventh day lucky," I reported to her.

"You found out something?"

"Not yet. Not really. But I've a feeling I'm closing in. I'll
let you know more about it tomorrow. That's not why I
called. How are you?"

"I'm fine," she said. "I saw the doctor today. I'll graduate
to a half cast soon."

"Are you missing me?"

"I've been extremely busy the entire week," she evaded
the question. "I went to see *A Chorus Line* with Terry and
her husband. Mark took me to lunch one day and to dinner
one night. I attended a MART meeting, a Metropolitan art
exhibit, and filled in at the Rape Crisis Center two afternoons. In my spare time I started *The Thorn Birds* and read
two Barbara Cartlands."

"Sooner or later you're going to have to break the news to
Mark, and what the hell is a Barbara Cartland?"

"Break what news to Mark? Barbara Cartland writes
perfectly dreadful but somehow fascinating Cinderella peri-

od romances with Heathcliff heroes and heroines who have tip-tilted noses and tip-tilted breasts."

"The news to Mark is that you're out of circulation. Then why do you read them?"

"You're being premature, and I have no idea. It's my secret vice, like drug addiction or alcoholism. My friend Sylvia says they fulfill our childhood sexual fantasies."

"You can give them up, then," I said calmly. "That's what I'm here for now. Have you any particular fantasies that need fulfilling?"

I heard a gasp at the other end of the line, grinned, and continued amiably, "You haven't answered the original question. Do you miss me?"

"You unutterable bastard," Bryarly said with great dignity. "I miss you horribly, continually, and unbearably. *Now* are you satisfied?" The crash of the receiver momentarily deafened me.

My grin more Cheshire than ever, I dialed again. She had stayed right where she was and picked it up on the first ring. I didn't even wait for her "Hello." "Bryarly, I love you," I said. "I miss you, too. Horribly, continually, and unbearably. Are *you* satisfied?"

"Yes," said a small voice at the other end.

I judged she wasn't far from tears. With my shoulder so far away, it was time to lighten the atmosphere.

"Have you ever heard of Philippa Jansen?" I asked in an abrupt change of subject.

"The California sculptor?" she asked doubtfully.

"She's a sculptor, but she lives in Westchester County."

"Must be the same one. She had to give it up. I heard that her hands are crippled with arthritis. What about her?"

"With any luck I may see her tomorrow. It seems she's from an old Hudson Valley Dutch family. She had an ancestor named Lucretia."

"Lucretia?"

"As in Cousin Lucretia."

There was a short silence with a lot of deep breathing.

"Are you still there?" I asked presently.

"I'm here. Will you call me tomorrow if there's anything —anything—"

"If there's anything to report, I will. Or even if there isn't. Good night, my love."

"Good night, my—friend."

I was laughing softly when she hung up, quite gentle about it this time.

CHAPTER
15

Just before eleven the next morning I telephoned Philippa Jansen.

"Mrs. Jansen? My name is Jake Ormont. You don't know me, but—"

A cool incisive voice broke in on my introduction. "The polite preliminaries are quite unnecessary in your case, Mr. Ormont." A glimmer of amusement crept in. "It's not every day that the directors of five top art museums and national galleries call me to attest to someone's credentials. When would you like to see me?"

"As soon as possible."

"One-thirty this afternoon. Do you know the way?"

"I have the address, but I could use some directions."

She supplied them crisply, and much to my chauvinistic surprise, they led me to her without any difficulty. Fifteen minutes early I turned in at the dirt lane she had indicated, followed the snake fence on the left whichever way the road wound, and arrived at a small circular drive.

In front of me, through a grove of shivering, bare-leaved

birches, I glimpsed icy gray patches and sun-dappled reflections on the river. When I turned to view the house, I felt a kind of impatient sadness. It must have started out as a typical Hudson Valley Dutch farm house built into the side of the sheltering Westchester hillside. Evidently, each succeeding generation had added an architectural atrocity from its age, including the final monstrosity of a Victorian porch and gallery.

The top half of a Dutch door swung open suddenly, revealing the top half of a woman.

"An abortion," said the cool amused voice from the evening before, "but I call it home."

She had a young-old face scrubbed clean of makeup, short curly gray hair and deep blue eyes. She was lean and small and straight. Somehow, a sculptor, and that decisive voice —I had expected a much bigger woman.

I slammed the car door shut and went toward it. "It must have been a lovely and simple building at one time."

"Yes, it was. And it will be again if I can convince some foundation or other that it's a worthwhile project." She opened the bottom half of the door. "Come in. It's freezing out there. I take it you're Mr. Ormont?"

"Yes, Miss—or is it Mrs. Jansen?"

A smile of great beauty illuminated the fine plain features. "Miss, Mrs., Ms. I have no emotional preference."

"I want to thank you, then, *Mrs.* Jansen, for giving me your time."

"Not at all. I've a very inquisitive nature. The build-up piqued my curiosity. Did you count on that? Let me take your coat."

Having taken it, she tossed it carelessly over a wooden hutch chair along with my scarf and gloves, then crooked one finger to indicate that I should follow her. She led me into a very small and delightful room that could only be termed a parlor. It contained a great dark cupboard and sideboard with a quantity of pewter plates and tankards and several armchairs covered in the same gay flowered chintz in which it was curtained. A welcome fire blazed in the fireplace, and I went toward it gratefully, taking the chair she pointed to while she sank down on a hassock, tucking blue-jeaned legs beneath her.

"Say your piece, Mr. Ormont," she told me blandly. "I'm all ears."

The ears, when I looked over at them, were hidden behind the crop of curly hair. It was the eyes that studied me intently, their blue depths kind but keen. They seduced me into a much more total honesty than I had intended.

"I've been all over New York City and Westchester, and you're about my last hope. I'm hunting for something I'm not even sure exists. Someone."

"And that someone?"

"Philadelphia."

"Philadelphia." She drew out each syllable separately. "Her last name?"

"I have no idea."

"And why have you come to me?"

"Because I heard about your collection of paintings by Lucretia De Kuyper, and I believe there might be a connection between Philadelphia and Lucretia."

"Anything else?"

Under her glacial stare, I was feeling more and more like a schoolboy called to order. "There were—may have been —six little Indians," I blurted out.

She unfolded herself gracefully from the hassock. "Mr. Ormont, I don't know why you've come here, but I don't like being used or treated like a fool."

I knew I was expected to get up, too, but I didn't.

"I wasn't trying to do either. *I'm* curious now about why my—my simple-minded, if you will—request should have made you assume I was."

If simple scorn could have scorched and frozen me at the same time, her voice would have done the job. "Anyone who has seen the paintings—and there have been many over the years—would know about Philadelphia, Lucretia, and the six Indians. But to use them in this ridiculous mumbo-jumbo—really, Mr. Ormont, of all the gambits for getting at my family records, none has been quite so blatant."

"Mrs. Jansen," I said quite courteously, "what makes you think I'm after your family records?"

"You're a writer, a reporter," she said furiously. "I'm quite aware the records will furnish the worth of several books. But I'm the one to determine when and what, Mr. Ormont, and above all, *who* does the writing."

I regarded her steadily. "If you recall, in the first minutes of our meeting, you mentioned my credentials. I'm afraid you've made it necessary to repeat them. I'm already a best-selling writer, not only of books but of movies and articles. I appear on national TV, hobnob with senators, and have dinner at the White House. I make a great deal of money, some of which I even manage to liberate from the hungry jaws of the IRS. Now think, please, Mrs. Jansen. Is there really anything here so earth-shattering that I would lie, cheat, and God knows what else you suspect, to get my ambitious hands on it?"

She sank down on the hassock again, with her elbows on her knees and her fists against her mouth. After about two minutes, her fists came down and away, and a disarmingly apologetic smile replaced the anger.

"Oh, dear. I'm getting much too cynical. But you must admit—How did you hear about Philadelphia?"

I told her. All about my dream. All about the Indians. About the anguish that came with the loss of Philadelphia. I told her of its recently having been pointed out to me that Philadelphia might be a girl, not a city.

"And Lucretia De Kuyper?"

I shook my head. "I never heard of her until yesterday. I only learned—quite recently—of a Cousin Lucretia who —who—well, seems to be involved somehow in the life of my—a friend of mine."

"May I know your friend's name?"

"Bryarly Allerton."

"You're doing this because of her?"

I nodded. "She—she has deep emotional problems." I looked at her squarely. "With reason. Now, somehow she's gotten it into her head that our fate, hers and mine, is tied up with Philadelphia's."

"And Cousin Lucretia?"

"She won't talk about her. She usually mentions her only when she's unaware, under drugs, after surgery."

She came and patted my shoulder like an old friend.

"Come with me, Jake. I have something to show you."

I followed her across the hallway and into the room opposite. It was a large bare room with white painted walls and long, uncurtained windows. It was all hung with paintings—an improvised art gallery.

She pressed the switch, turning on a brilliant overhead light, then started flipping up the bamboo blinds.

I looked at *Skating on the River, Return of the Pigeons to Tarrytown, Spearing Sturgeon in the Hudson.*

Rough, vibrant paintings. Vivid and alive. Making up in power what they lacked in professionalism.

"Look there between the windows, Jake."

I looked, and a great lump rose in my throat. I bent forward, knowing even before I read the little plaque underneath. *Our Philadelphia.* Painted by Lucretia De Kuyper, *circa* 1770.

She was young and lovely and happily alive from the top of her sun-gold head to the tips of her square Dutch shoes. She had a wide, laughing mouth; flyaway buttercup-blond hair; a slim, straight figure; and the deep blue eyes of the woman who stood at my side. She looked out at life with an eagerness and innocence that spoke for themselves. Either life or the painter had not yet dealt harshly with her.

Philadelphia, I thought, my Philadelphia . . . It was a moment of discovery, like the one in which I first saw Bryarly. I was stunned by the shock of possession I felt toward the girl, that darling lifelike girl laughing out at me from the prison of the wood frame.

"Jake," said a soft voice at my side. She must have said it several times before I groped my way back to earth.

I turned, uncaring that she would see the glitter of tears in my eyes.

"I was going to show you the other rooms of paintings," Philippa Jansen told me, "but I think perhaps they had better wait. If you'll come upstairs with me . . ."

We reached upstairs by way of a detached series of staircases, our heads bent to keep from hitting the low ceilings. I caught a glimpse of an old-fashioned four-poster bed with dark red hangings as she took me past a small bedroom and into a dark bare room with a long wooden work table and rows of shelves for boxes and what looked like ages-old account ledgers and record books.

There was one filing cabinet. She unlocked it with a key hidden under one of the ledgers.

"Take out the top box, please. It's a bit heavy for me." She held out her hands, both a little veined and twisted. "There's not much power left in them," she said matter-of-factly. "Arthritis."

"I know. I heard. I'm very sorry."

"No need to be. I had early success and a good run for my money. After my husband died and the career was over"—her voice was entirely without self-pity—"I had this place to come home to. I'm past sixty. There's enough here to occupy me for the rest of my life. I've been doing the research for the last two years . . . perhaps I've found the writer."

I had lifted the top box out of the file drawer. I turned to her sharply. "I hope you don't mean me."

"Why not?"

"It's the contemporary scene I'm interested in, not the past."

The blue eyes twinkled across at me. "That's why you're here on the trail of a girl who lived two hundred years ago."

"That's different," I mumbled defensively. "Bryarly . . ."

"Ah, yes, your Bryarly. You're deeply troubled about all this, aren't you?"

"I suppose so." I followed her down the stairs, carrying the box and forgetting to bend low.

She heard the smart rap of my head as it hit the ceiling. "I warned you," she said without turning around even when I swore.

Back in the little parlor, I continued answering her as though there had been no interruption.

"I've always thought of myself as an entirely rational

being. I believe in solid evidence, things I can see, touch, taste. This damn dream nonsense . . . and Philadelphia. I'm beginning to be terrified that Bryarly may be right. Because of the past, because of things that have nothing to do with either of us, we may lose our chance for happiness."

"Sit down, Jake. You don't mind my calling you Jake, do you? I'd like you to call me Philippa. Sit down near the fire, and open the box. Have you got an hour or two to read? Good. Put your feet up on the hassock. Take off your shoes if you'd be more comfortable. Read it, Jake, then we'll talk. I'll get you a cup of herbal tea and some sourdough bread."

I slipped off my shoes and my jacket, propped my feet on the hassock, and slouched down on my tail as I lifted the sheaf of pages out of the box.

The file cover on the manuscript read:

A Secret History of the Van Duren Family of Van Duren Manor on the Hudson, including Private Papers, Unpublished Records and Documents and Selected Correspondence.

I turned to the second page.
My weariness fell away. My depression vanished.

Part I
Lucretia De Kuyper. Inn Keeper.

The lover was lost in the newshound as *A Secret History* unfolded.

Journal of Lucretia De Kuyper
The first day of January
in the year 1759

My brother Hendryk, as has been his Habbit these last years since I took over the House Hold Business Accownts, furnished me with the Variety of Legers I told him would be necessary to Complete the twelve Months. He Grumbeled without ceasing, I might add, over the Sum of Monies expended. What a Miser the man has become! God's Mercy, how can that Gentil boy in the picture over the Mantel holding onto one of my long Braids of Hair and casting such a look of Brotherly Affection upon me have so Changed? How well I remember the Day that I fell from my Pony and it was he who lifted me up and Tended to my Hurts. Could Marriage alone, even to such a one as Catherine, have Soured him Thus?

I digress, and what use? Such speculation is Fruitless. He is what he is . . . and I? Well, to such Petty straits am I redused that this brand new Leger which serves as my Journal I filched from among those he Bought for his Business Accownts.

Moments ago I Ruffled through the hundreds of blank Pages. Pray God that at this year's end the days and weeks and Months that strech ahead will not turn out as Empty. If it please the Almighty, may I have more to write about than how many Alphabet Letters or Mathmatickal Tables I have managed to stuff into the heads of Catherine's Dull-Witted daughters or how much wool I have carded or Spun. Mornings to teach, Afternoons to Spin. Spinning in the Parlor, Spinning while at Tea. A Perfect Paragon of a Spinster, that is I.

The Jagged peace of framed Mirror in the childrens' Chamber, which I use to Neaten my Hair, is kinder than Nature. Just yesterday I caugt a Fuller Glimpse of my face in the great mirror in Catherine's Bedchamber, which was once my Mother's. I could hardly believe what I saw. Tight lips, tight Braided hair, taut cheekbones with their Pox marks—in Truth, the Tipical prune-faced Spinster.

How cruel the years are. How cruel is Time. Ah God, what became of the Healthfull laughing girl Betrothed to Johann? He died, then Mama and Papa. And I recovered to endure the doubtfull Benefits of my brother's Tender Care. Tender Care! So Papa wrote in his Will, entrusting me to Hendryk, not trusting me—since I am Female—with Monies of my own.

Full well he knew Hendryk to be Weak, and I, his dear loved Daughter, to be Strong. He knew that Hendryk would be ruled by Someone but did not think to Protect his own Flesh and Blood from Hendryk's wife. So the irony is that a Woman calls the Tune, and I am today the same Unpaid Servant that I have been these last eight years since my Father's Home became my Brother's House.

I Estimate that in these eight years of Spinning, as I Tread Back and Fourth about the Great Wheel, I have walked five and twenty thowsands of Miles. Would God my Feet had carried me instead that Many Miles from where I am:

10th Jan., 1759
New York City

My Very Dear Lucretia,
And very dear you are to both Cornelius and me even though I Purpose to start this letter by scolding you amazingly. How could you fail to come to us when you knew how Vastly we wanted you to join in the Merryment of our Holiday Festivities? You cannot put the Blame on Catherine this time, for though I know it is the Delight of her Warped Nature to deny you any rational Plezure, in this case I feel sure your brother could have prevailed. Hendryk's business Dealings with Cornelius are of too much value for even Catherine's Mean interference. Just a few words, a few lines from Cornelius, had he your Leave to send them, would have Turned the Trick. But you would not give him leave. No, no, my dear Couzin, in this case I must Confess I believe it was not Catherine but your own fierce and stubborn Pride that kept you from us.

I say again what I have said before, though I begin to Despaire that you will ever believe me. Your Presence would not be a Burden. How could it be when you are so much wanted by all of us? Rachel and Pieter both fretted that dear Couzin Lucretia was not there to see what St. Nicholas browt to them. And I know little Jacob and baby Carl would have been less Fretfull had you been by, as they always are. You have been told numerous Times that Cornelius and I would Joyfully recieve you as a permanent Member of our Household, so why do you consider a month's visit as an act of Charity?

Of a truth, dear Couzin, such Stiff-Necked pride smacks more of a Haughty Spirit than Independency. But enough of this for now. I will address you with more of the same when next we meet, which brings me to the second Object of this Missive.

Dear Lucretia, I Beg you most Ernestly to come to us in Pearl St. as soon as may be but not later than the last week in March. I am antisipating my Lying-In early in May, and allthough Cornelius has already secured the services of Mrs. Schooner, the Mid-wife who attended me for my last two birthings, you know I cannot be Comfortable if you are not by to assist. Indeed, your Presence has ever been of the greatest Comfort and Reasurance to me, so that my mind will not be at ease untill I am certain you will be with me.

Therefore, even you must Acknowlege that your agreement would Confer a Favour. You see, dear Couzin, I am less proud than you. I do not hesitate to plead with you most Fervently for a gift that it is in your power to bestowe, namely Yourself.

If you wonder why I appoint such an early day, pray recall that my little Carl entered this Vale of Tears some weeks earlier than expected, and the enormuss Activity within me of this unborn babe of mine leads me to believe that she may well do the same.

You Observe, I trust, that I call the baby "she." I do so because I do indeed pray for another daughter. How Turnabout life is. I almost wept at Rachel's birthing because I was so sure Cornelius would be greeved that his First-Born was not a son, and now I have three sturdy sons, God bless them, and I long for another sweet daughter.

As for Cornelius, what a Satisfactory Husband is mine. He says he cares not a whit weather it be male or female. That the child and I be helthy is all that concerns him, and he is as pleased as though this fifth Lying-In was my first.

He has even consented, albeit reluctantly, that if a girl-child, her name shall be Philadelphia. He grumbeled for some time that it is a Heathenish-sounding name, but I reminded him not so. It was the name of a city first mentioned in the Holy Book, and it denotes Brotherly Love, which any daughter of ours will receive a-plenty. The Truth is I believe my dear Cornelius is still inclined to Jelousy of the city of my birth and my family and where he believes my Heart's first allegance still lies. Though I deny it for his Comfort, to you I may Confide that there is some truth in what he says. To him, however, I point out oftimes that Pieter, Jacob and Carl are proper Dutch names and proper little Dutch Men. This pleases him beyond all else, this despite that he proudly regards himself as English. Indeed, no British Lord could be more unswerving in his Devotion to the German King on England's Throne than my dear husband. So strange men are, my beloved Cornelius no less than others!

In Conclusion, this time without your leave, Cornelius is penning several lines to both your brother Hendryk and his wife Catherine Detailing our great Need of you. His letter to them should arrive by the same Post as this one of Mine to You. Pray let me Hear soon by your own Hand that I may expect you.

> *Your Couzin by Affection and*
> *Marriage Both,*
> *Annette Du Bois Van Duren*

> *2nd Feb. 1759*

My dearest Lucretia,

How Happy, how very Happy I was to learn that you will surely come to us in March. Pray bring all your most Cherished Possessions, for if I have my way you will never Leave us again except it be to a Husband and Home of your own.

I am monstrously heavy and awkward but otherwise well, though untill your letter arrived to cheer me, my Spirits were somewhat Depressed for Cornelius has had to Depart the city for a short period.

It went sorely against his Inclination at such a time,

*but our Manager of the Mill and holdings in our Manor
at the Tarrytowns wrote in haste that the Tavern and
Ferry Crossings were being so ill-managed by the
wretched drunken Simpson, over whom he had no
awthority, that it was a necessity for Cornelius to
journey to Westchester County despite the Unseemly
Wether.*

*I will write no more now. Rather we will soon be
talking.*

*Your loving Couzin,
Annette Van Duren*

Journal of Lucretia De Kupyer
12th Feb. 1759

I am in Receept of another Letter from Annette expressing her
joy that I consent to journey to New York City as soon as may be.
She may well be Surprized for I antissipate that I will arrive sooner
even than her Desire.

The truth of it is that I have taken a most Desperate Rezolution. I
had hid Annette's letter, after my first Reading, in the box on my
wardrobe floor where I keep my other Correspondense and my
Journal. In the evening after the three girls were safe asleep, I re-lit
my Candle and read it again. Then I read her Former Letter, asking
that I become a permanent Member of my Cousin's House Hold. I
thought Wistfully but Hopelessly of exchanging Catherine's dullness for Annette's Spritely Society and my brother Hendryk for our
Cousin Cornelius, of living among their Lively and Spirited Children instead of with my neaces. (How much I would like to love
them and how sad it is that I cannot, but they are too much their
mother's daughters, Shallow and Spitefull; their Natures make a
mockery of their Beauty.) Only the thought of little Bram deters
me. How I love that child . . . but he is not mine. He is the son of
my brother and his wife, the Apple of their Eye, and perhaps it were
Also better that I leave before my Heart is too much Bownd up in
him.

I lay the letters aside and turned over the pages of January during
this year of our Lord 1759. Six hours of spinning today . . . Kitty

has at least mastered the 7 and 8 times Table . . . Seven hours of Spinning . . . Hendryk and I worked over the House Hold Accownts . . . Catherine had one of her Histerickal Fits today . . . Bram in disgrace for Gobbeling down the fruit tarts Destined for lunch. And I am to Blame for his Offense, according to the Gospiel by Catherine, for not Supervizing him better . . . Six hours of Spinning . . . Bedelia learned to spell her Name . . . Five hours of Spinning . . . Little Margaret had the toothache . . .

Dear God in Heaven, I beseeched Him, reading, is it meant that I shall spin my Life away?

The days of the Month read as empty and Awful as I had feared when this year's Journal Commensed, and all on a sudden I found myself Unwilling any longer to Resine myself to such an existence. Ashamed, too, that I have been content so long merely to Pity myself and Endure it. I seized a sheet of paper in an Impetuous move to tell Annette that my Cherished Possessions would Accompany me for permanent Residency, and then the thought darted through me with the speed of an Arrow that there existed another more exsiting Possibility.

I made up for these eight years of drifting along, Unhappy and Irrezolute in a Life I detest. I wrote immediately, addressing myself not to Annette but to Cornelius, and I made a fair copy of my letter, directing one to him at Home and the other to his Manor in the Tarrytowns, since I know not wether he will still be in Westchester County or have already left for his home in New York City.

My Proposition to Cornelius was simply this—that he employ *me* to manage his Tavern and Ferry Crossing in the Tarrytowns! I dare not flatter myself, I can only pray that I used Perswasive Argument. It is not Unknown for Women to be so employed in Assisting fathers, Brothers, or Husbands. Why then should an Able Woman not be in charge with hired men to Assist *her*?

I am not Unskilled in House Hold Maintenance. A Tavern merely encompasses a larger House Hold, and that for only part of the year. Not many take to the roads in the uncertain Wether of the Winter months.

I can keep accownts, do I not for Hendryk? I can supervize servants, have I not for Catherine? I am accustomed to hard work, long hours of Labour and but littel pay for Same. Has this not been my life for eight long years?

I Concluded my letter by reminding Cornelius of how often I have heard him Describe the "Wretched Men" who do duty by him at his Tavern property. Could a Woman do much Worse? And might she not do far better? Do but let me try for a Six-month, I urged him, after Annette has fully recovered from her Lying-in. If you are not Satisfied at the end of this Period, then I will abide by your Jugement.

In a hasty Post Scriptum, I bade him not take the Trouble to Reply to me by Mail as I proposed to follow my letter so swiftly, the Likelyhood is that I would have Departed for New York before any answer could arrive here in Poughkeepsie.

After eight years I am in such haste to be Gone, I intend to leave as soon as my Preparations and Packing can be done.

Oh my little Bram, how I grieve to leave you Behind, but Otherwise my Life cannot but be better.

Estate Book
Van Duren Manor
20th February, 1759

Agreement reached with Mr. Thruftwood today over the purchase of sheep in the Spring. Am greatly please at the Prospect of improving our Stock . . . It has been of much Concern to me to be absent from home and my Dear Wife at such a time, but now that I know Lucretia to be with her, I am more easy in my Mind. Lucretia is always an Aid and Comfort to Annette, most particularly during Pregnancy.

This being the Case, I have had to give Serious Consideration to Lucretia's astonishing Proposal. My first thought, I admit, was to reject it out of hand . . . a Woman in charge of a Tavern, no, it could not be. But then I recalled, as she reminded me, the "wretched men" that over the years I have had to Endure in charge. These Pages, if I read Bakwards, are filled with a Catalog of their Iniqwities. It is true that Lucretia would bring to the job higher Qwalifications of Integrity, Qwickness of Mind and Willingness to Work than any man who has ever been my Inn Keeper at River Cross Tavern.

I am Resolved. She shall have her Six Months. Tom Nease and his wife have said they can manage both Tavern and Farm till I hire another man. They expected it to be a Matter of Weeks. I am sure they will not Object to the extra monies for Several Months. Lucretia must stay with us until my Annette is Full Recovered from her Lying-In.

Journal of Lucretia De Kuyper
Pearl St., New York City
26th Feb. 1759

The days since I arrived here have sped by on Wings of Happiness. I play Noisey games with the children of the kind Catherine would never Allow but Annette sits by beaming with Plesure at our Joy. Today we were Indians hunting in the Forest, and my dear Cousin's Sunday Bonnett provided the Fethers for our hair. In the Evenings, when the children are a-bed, are the Coziest Times of all, for Annette and I sit in our night Shifts, blanket-Wrapt, with our chairs drawn up to the fire, our feet on brass warmers while we sip hot chockalate and talk, such Wonderful Talk as I have not Indulged in since God knows when, of Life and Love and the Past and the Future.

It is true Annette knows much more of such things than I, having known a man's Love, faced Birth and Death . . . and what have I but some eight-year Memories of Johann's tenderly Smiling eyes and a Handfull of Kisses? Yet this noon when Cornelius' message came, I would not have traded Places with Annette despite the Hunger I have sometimes felt for more of those Kisses and Strong Arms about me. 'Fore God, I would not now trade Place with the Queen of England.

Come next month I will be full eight and twenty, and for the first time in my life I am to have the Dignity of Choosing my own Path and Making my own Way. I am to be Inn Keeper at the River Cross Tavern.

I will have all provisions as well as Income. Imagine, the best of food Van Duren Manor provides, and none of it Gruged me, and cloth for my skirts and petticoats that *I* need not spin. The Per cent of the Tavern's per Annum earnings that Cornelius agrees to pay me can all be put by. I will have no need to spend. Because of these savings, if I grow Old alone—and I have long since faced that I shall—I need not be Dependent.

Not to be Dependent. For that I thank You Fervently, dear Lord.

There is something else, and it seems almost most Marvelous to me of all. I am to have a room of my Own, the one behind the Bar Room, with the windows overlooking onto the Hudson River and the stove of the type Desined by Mr. Franklin, so that the room is cool in summer and warm in Winter, Cornelius says. And there are two Shelfs for Books, empty now, but I may fill them as I wish from the Manor House for the long Winter evenings when the Tavern is Desolate of guests and I am alone save for the Servants.

He warns me of the Lonelyness and the Desolateness as things I must face up to, never knowing what it is like to live as an outsider in the Home of others.

I Embrace the Lonelyness, I thank God for the Freedom. A room of my own where none can Intrude against my Wishes. It is almost too Wonderfull to Believe.

Journal of Lucretia De Kuyper
3rd of April 1759

So Weary I am, so very Weary, yet far to Exsited to Sleep. I shall Remember this day all my Life long.

Annette and Cornelius and I took Breakfast together with only Pieter by; the other children were with their Nurse. Barely had Cornelius left for his Work Day and Pieter run off to his Lessons, while Annette and I stayed at Table for a second cup of Tea, than her Pains began.

I tried not to let her see my Worry, for her Labour was full five Weeks early, and so many eight-Month Infants Perish. But I read the Fear in her eyes that was in my own Mind.

I sent messages at once to Cornelius and to the Mid Wife. I helped Nurse bundle all the children into their clothing and off to Annette's good friend Annie Vroom.

Then I went to the Bed chamber where a young Maid was helping Annette into her night Shift. She was Trembling more than Annette, and I bid her get back to the Kitchen to see to the hot water and send me one of the older maids. Thank God the one who came to us was older and had Sense for by this time Annette was in Dire Straits, and it was Plain to me she would not wait on the Mid Wife.

I have helped at many births but never been fully Responsible at a Lying-In. Thank God for my past Learning. The Child came Fast, and there was Trouble for the Cord was tight-Wrapt about its neck and it was turning Blue. I tried to pull the cord free, but all was so Slipery I failed. I dared not use the knife and risk cutting the Throat. In desperation, seeing its breathing stop, I Held the Child High, still attached to Annette and used my Teeth.

In Seconds the throat was Freed and Air flowed into the Lungs, the Blue turned to the helthy glow of pink flesh and the little Mouth opened up to let out no Feebel Wail but rather an Hearty Yell. Never was there a Sweeter Sound to my Ears.

Now I could use the knife to cut the Cord and I thrust the Baby into the Maid's arms while I tended to Annette.

"Boy or girl?" she Whispered to me some Moments later and I turned, Bewildered, to the Maid, who now sat close to the fire, Crooning to the Infant in her arms, for I had been too taken up in the Work at Hand to notise.

I drew the blankets from around the Babe and smiled in Satisfaction. Then I re-wrapt the Child and brought it to lie in Annette's arms.

"You have your daughter, dear Annette," I told her. "Here is your Philadelphia."

Annette smiled Tenderly down at the Infant and then just as Tenderly up at me. Her words are Imbedded in my Brain for all Time to Come. "Let us say rather *Our Philadelphia,* for you gave her life, too, Lucretia, so I think it only fair to say that *we* have a daughter."

I am not much given to Weeping for ither Joy or Woe, but at this, Tears Stung my Eyes. I put out my Hand to the Child, and those tiny little Fingers gript one of Mine in a Veritabal Strangel Hold. A tiny corner of my Heart, which I had not Known till now had been long Frozen, began slowly to Unthaw at this Firm Touch.

"Our Philadelphia," I said aloud, and now the tears threatened my Voice, too.

Just then in the Comick manner of Every Day Life, just when High Drama seems to be in the Air, Cornelius burst into the Chamber and rushed towards the Bed.

"Annetje, my God, Annetje, dear one," he bawled, "has your Labour begun so soon?"

His "dear one" and I both burst out into high-pitched indeed Histerickal Laughter.

Feebley she indicated the Bundle in her arms, while I clung to the Bed Post and laughed on.

"Meet Philadelphia Lucretia Van Duren," said Annette, and as he bent to the Babe, her eyes met mine across his bowed head. I saw again her mouth shape the words "Our Philadelphia," and I went away and left them.

But this night, though I am weary to the Bone, I cannot sleep. For I, who have never Wedded or Lain with a man, am not utterly without Life's Fullness. What Mistery of the Body is this that I should feel this Tumult inside me, almost a Swelling of the Breasts as though they held Milk for her, just as I felt that Tug at my heart when those perfect little fingers curled so tightly around mine.

Our Philadelphia. Annette spoke Truly. Not just she, but I, too, have a daughter.

Journal of Lucretia De Kuyper
9th April 1759

Philadelphia throve well until yesterday, sqwalling lustily to make her Hunger known, sleepy and Content at other times. Then she became constantly Awake and Fractius.

It was not until this morning we discovered the reason for her Fretfulness; Annette has not a sufficiency of Milk.

The baby howled, Annette wept. In Vain I tried a sugared glove tit for the child and Words of Comfort for the Mother. They both continued to Howl. I must say I was at my witts' end when Cornelius took Charge, hunting through the Advertisement pages in back copies of *The Gazette,* which had been stocked in the kitchen for the fire.

He remembered to have read in one of them not too many days back About a Wet Nurse to hire out.

The papers were sent for and gone through, and Cornelius found the Advertisement, which he read aloud to us. *A woman with a Choice Breast of Milk to take a child at home or go into a family to Suckle. Inquire of the Printers.*

Annette wept afresh. "A Stranger, a hired Servant to nourish my child."

"If necessary, and it is necessary, yes," said Cornelius more sternly than he was Wont to speak to her.

Annette sobbed out something about her lack as a Woman, then moaned, "I'm so ashamed."

"So you should be," my Cousin said to her, still severe, "making so Big a Fuss about such a small Matter. As for wether you are enough Woman for me, my Annetje, we will discuss it when you are fully restored to Helth."

"Cornelius! Lucretia is in the room."

But I was already on my way out thinking of those words in the Bible, the Way of a Man with a Maid . . . Truly it can be most marvelous.

Cornelius joined me in the Parlor soon. He had torn the Advertisement from the Newspaper, and we drove at once to the Printing Office, where he secured the necessary information. From there it was but a short carriage ride to the modest Residence with a Cooper's shop in the rear, where we had been Directed.

The Cooper, Mr. Sayer, was a surly man, and I misliked the Servile Manner that replaced his Curtness when he learned our Errand. I could see from Cornelius's expression he was of the same Mind. But Mr. Sayer hurried away to Fetch the Wet Nurse before we could Assent or Refuse. I walked over to the rear doorway through which he had disappeared and heard a Murmur of voices, the woman's low, the man's harsh. There were Several Exchanges between them and then the man snarling, suddenly loud, "You'll do as I say. Now put a plezent Expression on your face, you Black Bitch or you'll feel my fist again."

Cornelius, standing at the far end of the room, heard Nothing. Before I could prepare him, the Cooper was back and the Woman with him.

She was not black but a pale golden brown color like the dye I got for my spinning wools when I mixed black walnuts with onion skins. Allthough marred by a dark bruise on one high cheekbone, she was exceeding Comely, one of the Comeliest women I have ever Beheld, with her hair pulled straight back and piled in a knot atop a head held high as any Queen's.

Cornelius and I both stared, all Amazed. He found his tongue first.

"You had a child?" he asked gently.

She turned her head away, and the Cooper admonished her warningly, "Answer the gentleman."

She said, as though the words were wrung from her, "My baby, he died a-birthing."

"I'm sorry," he told her gently. "My little girl is fine, but my Wife has no milk. Have you—"

"These black wenches are like cows," the Cooper interrupted, making me blush for his Corseness and her Humiliation.

"And would you be willing to—"

Mr. Sayer interrupted again, "It's for me to say if she's willing. I own her."

Cornelius cumpressed his Lips, trying to hold back his Distaste as he moved aside with the man, no Doubt to Discuss Terms.

The Woman, standing alone looked so Forlorn, I could not help reaching out to touch her. "Don't be afraid," I said. "My Cousin's Wife is a Kind Woman. She will be gratefull and very good to you."

"And he?" She jerked her thumb towards Cornelius. "He be kind man and good to me, too?"

"Yes, I promise you, he will be good to you, too. You have Nothing to fear."

She looked at me almost with scorn. "When men are good to me, then I have plenty fear."

It took me a full minute for her Meaning to Penetrate my Mind. Between shock and pity and embarrassment, I found myself again Blushing like a school girl. "No, no, I assure you, he will not be good to you like—not in the way you mean."

I misdoubt that she was Convinced, though she said nothing, just standing there, passive, head bent. My heart was Renched with pity and with shame, too.

I had dared to pity myself in the past and thought my lot was Hard. If ever I think so again, I must read this page over and remember the emotions I felt standing in the Cooper's shop trying to Comprehend what it must mean to be a Woman and a Slave.

In ten minutes it was Settled. A paper was signed and monies passed. The Woman went to the Attic to fetch her things and came back with what must be her pitiful possessions tied up in a shawl.

The Cooper took a visious hold on her upper arm. "Thomasina," he said to her with a sly smile on his face, "this gentleman is Mr.

Van Duren, and you do what he says for the next months till I come to Fetch you away. You behave yourself, hear, Girl?"

She answered him, "Yes, Sir," in a submissive Way I instinctively knew was forenn to her Nature.

"That means none of your uppity ways. I don't want no bad Reports. You know what will happen to you if Mr. Van Duren isn't pleased, don't you?"

"Yes, Sir."

The man turned to Cornelius. "Whale the tar out of her if she gives you any sass; it's the only langwage she understands."

"I hardly think," I said icily, unable to control myself any longer, "that it would help the flow of milk. Come, Thomasina. The carriage is outside."

I swept out, head held high, and Thomasina Swept out with me, her head even Higher.

When Cornelius took her arm to steady her up the carriage steps, she shrank from his touch, but once inside she drew a deep breath and exchanged a small Secret Smile with me. Then she looked straight ahead, Solemn and Silent again.

We could hear Philadelphia wailing the moment we entered the House, and Cornelius was so eager he would have rushed Thomasina to her at once if she had not told him with Extreme Positiveness that it would be better for the baby if she first Cleansed herself.

So she and I desended to the Kitchen, where ignoring the Cook and her helper, she calmly set about cleaning herself with hot water and soft cloths, face and neck, hands and arms, and then quite calmly, Slipping off her Blouse and lowering her Shift, her full ripe Breasts.

I Eskorted her into the little family dining parlor leading out from the kitchen. There was a rocking chair drawn up to the fire, and I bade her be Seated while I fetched Philadelphia.

She was sitting very Uprite on the edge of the seat when I came back with the baby and a Shawl of my own which I flung about her shoulders. She was marveling at its softness as I put the baby into her arms and bade her again to be Comfortable.

She sank against the cushioned chair back, shifted Philadelphia up, and at once the child turned her face towards the Welcoming

Softness. The greedy little mouth reached for the full Breast, clamping onto the Nipple in a way that made Thomasina Wince.

Then there was no sound except the Crackle of the Fire and the Smacking Noise of the Baby's lips as she Sucked.

I sat on a stool and Watched until Prezently Thomasina removed the Baby whose angry howl was cut in two as she was Transferred to the other Breast.

"Ah, that be good," I heard Thomasina sigh and realized she must have been in Sore Pain for her Breasts were full to Bursting.

Slave or no, I thought, it is she who Nourishes *our* Philadelphia. And with that passing thought such a pang of Jelossy as I had never Known I was Capable of shot through me.

As it did, my eyes met Thomasina's. Seconds later, with cheeks Burning Hot and fast-beating Heart, I fled the room, for her eyes were the Mirror of my own, or what had been in them an hour Before, only it was *she* now, the Slave Woman, who pitied Lucretia De Kuyper!

Journal of Lucretia De Kuyper
18th April 1759

Philadelphia grows Visibley fatter day by day. She Thrives, Annette is Rekonsiled, and so, I think is Thomasina. She no longer Shrinks Away when Cornelius Approaches her, and Indeed in more ways than Nourishing the Baby, she has been God-sent for this House Hold. When Cook slashed her hand to the bone, cutting a side of beef, Thomasina not only stawnched the Bleeding but Treated the Wound with Herbs and Remedys of which neether Annette nor I have the Receipts, so that the Swelling and Festering soon Subsided. Then she did the cooking for this last week, and even Cornelius, who is most Partickular in matters of the Table, Complimented the Superiority of the Meals.

It is setteled that I am to leave Pearl Street on the first of the coming month to take up my Duties as Inn Keeper. This morning when Annette sighed as she several times has that she knows not how she will go on without me, I Voiced the Notion which has taken fast hold of me during these last Days.

"You will go on fine, as you always have Before this, Annette, in especial if you have Thomasina."

"But I will not have her for long."

"You will if you want. And you should want. Think, Annette —Philadelphia will need her till she is weened. She is a Healer, Cook, Housekeeper. I doubt not she has Other Abilities we have not Tried yet."

"But she is a Slave, and you know Cornelius is opposed to Slavery."

"Then let him pay her a Wage!" cried I impatiently. "Good God, Annette, he would be buying her *out* of Bondage, not into it . . . If you had but seen the man who Owns her!"

Later I sat with Thomasina as I Generilly do when she Suckles Philadelphia. A Strange Bond has grown Between us since the Moment when I saw my Soul in her eyes and she, I think, hers in Mine. My Wicked Jelossy is Gone. She gives Life to Philadelphia, which is all that should Matter.

One pressious little infant torn between three who would be her Mother.

Journal of Lucretia De Kuyper
20th April 1759

I taxed Thomasina today with Mother feelings to Philadelphia, and she denied them.

"I be cow to this calf, nothin' more," she said in that Husked Sing-Song voice of hers that I cannot help thinking Men must find Allurring. "I cannot give my heart to what Mite be taken Away like I be taken from my Mama, like my baby be taken from me a-dyin'."

"I am sorry about your baby," I murmured Helplessly and was shocked when she shook her head.

"Not I," she said Feercely. "I no wanted Mr. Sayer in my bed, I no wanted his baby in my belly. I laugh when he tells me baby is dead. That's why I have Mark on my face. I saw you study on it."

"He hit you in Childbed!"

"I say to him, 'that's one of us got away from you, Mr. Sayer, sir,' so he hit me. Nothin' new in that, he allways Hittin' out at me. I run away one time, he allmos' kill me when he get me back." She shrugged. "Next time he kill me sure."

"Next time?"

"When Mr. Van Duren try to send me back, I run again. He cotch me, I be killed sure. Not so bad. Better dead than makin' more babies for Mr. Sayer."

I stormed into Cornelius' private Study, where he was working at his Business Accownts.

"Cornelius, you must buy Thomasina from Mr. Sayer. You must not Permit that she go back to him."

I Repeeted my Conversations with Annette and Thomasina. If I had my Way, I would have sent him out of the House to Negotiate her Purrchase at Once. I had to be Satisfied with his Promise to give Serious Thought to the Idea.

Household Account Book
Pearl St., New York City

This 23rd day of April, 1759, I purchased the Slave Woman called Thomasina from Mr. Sayer, the Cooper, for the Exorbitant Sum of one hundred pounds. It goes against my deepest Convictions to buy a Human Being like a Piece of Livestock, but neither my Wife nor Cousin would give me any Peace until the Deed was Done. After meeting with the Cooper and having to endure his Coarse Manners and Sly Innuendoes, I can see why they were both Loth to Return Thomasina under such a man's Protection. Duly entered, 23rd April, 1759. C. Van Duren.

Household Account Book
Pearl St., New York City

I summoned Thomasina to my Study last evening to apprise her that I had bought her from Mr. Sayer but, since I am Unalterably Opposed to Slavery, I would pay her a small Wage, though not as large a one as would be usual if I had not had to lay out a Huge Sum for her Purchase. Eventually, I promised, she would have her Freedom.

There was no change of expression on her face. She only closed her eyes for a Moment, then opened them to say, "This be True? I live here now?"

I assured her I would hardly jest on such a Matter. Then to my astonishment she went down on one Knee to seize my hand and Kiss it. On rising she demanded to know what Sum I had Expended for her.

So bemused I was by such Impudence, I told her, only to have her demand further how much Wage I proposed to give her.

"Five pounds per year," I answered, amuzed now rather than angry to be Inquisited in this Court-Room Manner by one who had just become my Property.

"No," she said. "I work for you free, you give me no money. Then *I* am Free, and you pay me usual Money."

My slave, and she issued her orders as grandly as a Dutchess. Lucretia was right, as allways. This may be the best day's Work I have ever done. Duly entered, 24th April, 1759. C. Van Duren.

Household Account Book
Pearl St., New York

This morning at the Tide I escorted my Cousin, Lucretia De Kuyper to my trading sloop, The Old Amsterdam, lying at Harbour in the Hudson. Capt. der Horst will bring Lucretia up-River to the Tarrytowns to take up her Duties as Inn Keeper at my Tavern. I pray God this Decision be a wise one. My friends who are apprized of it tell me I belong in Bedlam. Duly entered, 1st May, 1759. Cornelius Van Duren.

Journal of Lucretia De Kuyper
River Cross Tavern
3rd May 1759

I am here at last, and it is more Wonderfull even than I contemplated. My room is not a great Size but Snugg as I could wish and large enough for a Sturdy four-poster Bed, which by Cornelius' orders, had fresh new Hangings and Coverlet in a Bold blue-and-white Checquered Gingham. There is a Rocking Chair and a Corner Chair covered in the same cheerful Cloth and the lovelyest dressing table of Mahoggony with ornamental Shell carvings. My Mother's Travel Desk folds up to make a handsome Fire Screen when not in use for my letter-writing.

A Friezeland clock hangs on the wall, and my Chamber pot is of pewter as in the Great House. Indeed I think both were Transported from there as was my Fether bed Mattress, which goes on top of the one made of corn husks.

So much for my Creeture Comforts.

Journal of Lucretia De Kuyper
River Cross Tavern
20th May 1759

I have been Keeper of this Tavern near on three weeks. Never
have I been busier and it is near ten years since I have been so
happy. Allredy I have Dismissed Several from my Servise and
Employed Others, Thankfull that Cornelius gave me full Authority.

I have now for my Cook Mrs. Wallace, mother to one of the Van
Duren Farm Tenants. She is a small spry woman who was living a
most Miserable Existence in the home of her Son. When she heard I
had rid myself in just two days of the Slovenly slut who took place
of Mrs. Nease, she came to Seek me out to ask for the Position.

The first thing I noted about her was the Cleanliness of her Garb.
Her rough Hands Proclaimed her a Worker but were Likewise
Spotless. Despite her years she seems a woman of Dignity and I
misliked the Humble Way she Approched me.

"You live with your son?" I asked by way of testing her. "Why
should you wish to trade a comfortable Home for a Kitchen Bed?"

The Humility fell away from her. "Better a Kitchen Bed than a
child's cot in the home of my Son's Wife." Then, as though Fearfull
she might have said too much and never Dreaming that *I* understood her Feelings all too well, she tried once more for Humility.

"If I say so myself, I could cook for Mr. Van Duren's own table
and not be shamed, not just in his Tavern. He's stopped by my son's
many a time only to taste my Pies. I have cake Receipts handed
down in my family for one-hundred Years. I can sew and spin and
Scrub." She looked up at me, and the look I saw in her eyes was
Despirate. Good God, I thought to myself, is that How I looked all
those years with Catherine?

"Please, Miz De Kuyper, ma'am, you won't be sorry, a Kitchen
bed will suit me fine, it's warm in the Cook House, and it's a big fine
bed. Mrs. Nease, she told me she and Tom used to sleep comfortable in it with their Grandson. I'm not a big eater and if I could just
have a few pence a week for my Stocking . . ."

I spoke more Bruskly than I meant to because it was Painfull to
me to see a Woman so redused to Begging, saying we would give it a
month's Trial. But by the end of the first day I knew that I had
found myself a Treasure, for she made the most Savoury Stew for

the evening meal that ever I have eaten. There were nine or ten guests in the Tavern that night and most of them ordered a Second Dish.

The kitchen is scrubbed and clean enough to please the most Partikular Dutch House Wife. Mrs. Wallace is a woman who cannot sit by Idel. When she is not Cooking or Baking, she spins, she sews, she searches out Work the way a Preecher searches out Sin. She is Touchingly Gratefull to me and shows it in many ways, including the care of my Wardrobe. She is making me fresh Aprons and Caps and some Summer Dresses. She took charge, too, of my Friezeland Clock, marching in every six hours to wind it until I ernestly Besought her to Hang it in the Tap Room and trouble me no more.

Besides Mrs. Wallace, I have Sally, a girl of some 16 summers, who I hired away from Dusenberg's Tavern in Cortlandtville, when one of the cattle drovers stopping by informed me she was wishful to make a change. It was my intent to Train her to help me in the Bar Room, but as Sally is more Experiensed than I, the training seems to have Worked in Reverse. But she does not Presume on this, so we go on very well Together, and she has a Saucy Flounse to her Walk and a Merry Smile and Manner that make her Popular in the Tap Room of an Evening. As Inn Keeper, *I* am more sedate and Aloof and alas! not so Young or Pretty. The men laugh and qwip with Sally, they are more Respecktfull of me.

Young Ben Harmer, a boy of about twelve years, and his younger brother by one year Obidiah, both orphaned, are my other two workers. They assist me wherever they may be needed, to run errands, to answer the Ferry Bell if I am otherwise occupied, in the Bar, serving meals, cleaning up. When the work day is over, they go next door to the Cook House with Mrs. Wallace and spread their mattresses out near to the warmth of the Bee Hive Oven.

There is a vast amount of work to be done, and I do my share, but not so much as the others. The difference is in being the one they work for rather than a worker. The difference is in being free of Servitude if not of Service. May God bless Cornelius, I will never forget so long as I live what he has done for me.

Journal of Lucretia De Kuyper
3rd June 1759

My day begins early and ends Late for the Traveling Season is upon us, and we are Crowded almost every night. We have had as many as twenty-six persons staying over for the Night, with Pallets spread all over the floors. Last night there were nineteen.

Mrs. Wallace has the fires started and the Ovens going before I rise, and I help to prepare the Breakfasts, which Sally carries in to the Common Room. By the time the cleaning-up is done, we must prepare for the mid-day meal.

It grows Qwiet in the early noon when some guests leave, but by late afternoon others come and the Common Room is all a-hum.

The gentlemen eat Mrs. Wallace's ampel Servings with Gusto, then settle back in their chairs, opening waistcoat buttons to accomodate their Expanding Stomacks, belching Freely and telling stories, some of them rather Warm, I suspect, for their Voices lower discreetly when I come near—but not Sally. With her they laugh and flirt Prodigiously. The room is wreathed in the smoke of the Clay Pipes, a rack of which stands at the fireplace to be Rented Out. As the night goes on I light the candles and we convert the Hutch tables to Chairs, pushing them near the fire. The gentlemen play at Backgammon and chess, while the women—if women there are, which is but seldom—retire to their bed chambers, which may be more Genteel but not near so much Fun.

The gentlemen more intent on drinking than Games shift gradually over to the Tap Room, and the night rings constantly with the shots of their Firing Glasses as they bang them down to make a Point in Argument or Acknowlege a Toast. I am grown Accustomed and no longer Jump at the sound as I did in the Beginning.

News of the day is passed up and down the River in Taverns such as mine. It is surprizing, living what might be considered Retired here, how much in the know I am of what goes on in Boston, Albany, and New York.

Journal of Lucretia De Kuyper
9th June 1759

To my surprize a letter today from my brother Hendryk, which made me laugh and Cry both, so Hendryk-like it was, so full of Hurt Dignity and Reproche. He informs me that it was not by any wish of his that I had left his Board. He cannot approve of my present Unwomanly Occupation, but I am his dear Sister and his Home is Mine to Command at any Time. When I grow Weary of this Foolishness, I have only to inform him and he will Fetch me back to the safety of his Roof.

I can only suspect that it is Catherine who grows Weary—of Managing her own House.

But then he spoke of young Bram and how much he missed his dear Aunt Lucretia, at which I could have wept. For I miss Bram, too, and I miss Philadelphia, the child and the babe who have both wound themselves around my Heart. Thank God I am so occupied here, there is no time for Pining.

Journal of Lucretia De Kuyper
14th June 1759

Cornelius' Farm Manager came by to inform me that Capt. der Horst is on his way to New York with the Van Duren sloop, the Old Amsterdam. In a few days he will return with Annette and Cornelius and the children to spend their summer months at the Manor House here in the Tarrytowns as they usually do to avoid the Heat and Sickness of the city.

I am so eager to see them, to snuggle our Philadelphia in my arms again. And though many would think it strange, I must admit that I am eager to see Thomasina, for I learned to enjoy her company greatly.

Journal of Lucretia De Kuyper
4th July 1759

I did not know I could be happier until Cornelius returned from his business trip to Poughkeepsie bringing Bram on the Saddle before him. Since Bram and Pieter are of an age, he perswaded Hendryk and Catherine without too much difficulty to spare him for a month's visit.

So now I have my two dear little ones with me. In fact, I have with me the family of my own creating. For Annette is the sister I never had and Cornelius is far more my Brother than ever poor Hendryk can be. Mrs. Wallace has taken on the Role of my mother, looking after my Wellfare, Skolding me if I do not care for myself in a way I find very Pleasing. And then there are the children. I love them all, Rachel, Jacob, Pieter, and Carl, too . . . but Bram is of my Flesh and Blood and Philadelphia the child of my heart. Lastly, there is Thomasina, and she, I think can Truly be called my Friend, if there be such a thing, my Friend of the Soul. There is a Bond grown up between us that I think will never be broken. We talk much, but we also understand One Another without Speaking. She knows my Simple History. Someday when she is ready, I will know Hers.

Journal of Lucretia De Kuyper
3rd September 1759

It rained this morning, we are less full of guests than might be expected, and I was Restless. So I took myself some hours of Holliday and walked the quarter-mile to the Manor House. Cornelius was at the Mill and Annette had retired to her Bed chamber, feeling poorly. I pray to God she is not with child again. It is too soon!

I found my way to the Family Eating Room adjoining the Kitchen where Thomasina nurses Philadelphia, and she was there, suckling the child.

In the instant before she saw me, the look she cast upon the child, the very way she held her in her arms, Betrayed her Inner feelings. She could no longer Deny to me that she loved the Baby with all her Heart, and she did not even make the Attempt.

"I never meant to love another soul," she told me, and then her sad savage History poured out.

She came Originally from the Dutch Indies, having been born on the Island of Arubba. Her mother was a slave on a great Plantation, working inside the House as maid to the Mistress. Of her father she was not sure, but she suspects he was the white overseer, Thomas Leuven, who would often bring her candy and treat her with Careless Kindness. Her mother was teaching her to be a lady's maid when money troubels caused the Break Up of the Plantation, and Mother and Daughter were sold separately, Thomasina to a Master who took her immediately to his bed.

"How old were you?" was my first Horrified Interruption.

Thomasina shrugged. "Twelve. Maybe thirteen."

She resumed her story. The new Master tired of his reluctant bed partner. She was sold. And sold again. There were many masters. Many beds. Eventually she went to a ship's Captain, who, Misliking her Haughty Ways, sold her in New York to the Cooper.

Always she had avoided pregnancy, in ways, we soon discovered, not too different from those the Mid-Wife Mrs. Schooner had shown me and I had urged her to show Annette. But Mr. Sayer had wanted her to breed for Profitt and beat her when he found out she avoided Conseption and Watched and made sure she could not repeat the Offense.

He did not foresee the death of their infant, but when it was Still Born, his Mind Immediately dwelled on another Avenue of Profitt and he advertised her like a Milk Animal.

Knowing better than to offer pity to this proud Woman, I put my Hand out impulsively to her, saying, "And a lucky thing for our family that he did, Thomasina. Philadelphia needs you more than anyone, and you belong with us."

She smiled, which was rare for her. "Belong *with* . . . I like that. Better than belonging *to* . . ."

Who can believe the life of misery and outrage concealed behind her Serene Air as she sits giving Nourishment to the child?

Journal of Lucretia De Kuyper
8th Sept. 1759

Hendryk came for Bram today. I cannot complain. What was to be a month's visit has extended into more than two, but oh it is hard to relinqwish him again. All ready he is promised to us for the summer next, but that is so long away.

To my surprize I was not Displeazed to see my Brother. Now that I am not Dependent on him, my feelings have changed. I would never live with him again, but I need no longer Despize him.

Journal of Lucretia De Kuyper
15th Sept. 1759

The Manor House is empty. They have all taken ship for New York City. The last morning before he left Cornelius and I went over the books together. It was a proud moment in my Life. The Tavern has prospered under my Governence. It is gaining Reputation; those who work for me are happy and well-fed. What must be most Important to a hard-working Dutchman such as Cornelius, the Profitts speak for themselves.

If he raised an Eye Brow at the Wages I pay Mrs. Wallace and Sally and the money I am putting by for Ben and Obidiah, he did not do so Notiseably . . . and I only said when we came to those itims, "The Labouror is worthy of his hire," pointing again to the profitt Line.

"You have done ably, Lucretia. I am more than satisfied with my Inn Keeper. And are you satisfied to stay on?"

"More than anything," I whispered, as close to tears as ever I have been.

Not I, his Cousin; not I, a woman; but I, the Inn Keeper have done ably. I Repeet myself, but oh indeed it *was* a Proud Moment in life.

Journal of Lucretia De Kuyper
4th Nov. 1759

The winds of Winter threten and for some days now, seldom are there more than a half dozen of guests. As winter settels in, even those numbers will Dwindle.

Sally has left on a visit to her Family in Albany but Promised cheerfully to return in the Spring if she doesn't catch herself a Husband before then.

Mrs. Wallace has far less cooking to do, so we had the big Drive Wheel set up for her in the kitchen, and she spends half her daylight hours spinning. I urged her not to feel Oblidged to, but unlike me, it is her pleazure.

The boys do all the outside chores, bring in the wood and help to wait on our few Guests. I spend two hours of every morning teaching them their Letters and Numbers and make them Study another hour. To think they were never taught to read or write!

I am approching the Season of Lonelyness Cornelius spoke of when he hired me, and I love it. I love it. Picture me snugg in my Chamber with the Curtains drawn and the Sperma-Cetti Candles giving a bright glow to the room. My chair is drawn up to the bed so that I can sit with my legs stretched out upon the Mattress, most Un-Ladylike but so comfortable. Propped up on my lap is a Book. The one I am prezently reading is *Tom Jones,* which makes me laugh till the tears run down my cheeks. Annette sent three boxes full of books from the Manor House before she left, Tomes of History and Travel but mostly the Novels she and I so enjoy. The Van Duren Library, I confess, is too sober for me, mostly Books of Sermons and Essays on Behaviour. When it comes to reading, I am all English. Most of those old Dutchmen thought a Library incompassed a big Dutch Bible with silver clasps.

In a little while there may come a light tapping at my door, and when I answer, there will be Mrs. Wallace holding a small serving Tray on which stands a pewter mugg of tea and a large slab of cake or mayhap a small dish of Bisquits. She thinks of me as a Child in Constant Need of Sustenance, and though I protest this aloud to her, I admit I relish the role. Certainly I relish the tea and cake. There is something sinfully Wicked and Delightful to be warm and cozy and idel, reading and eating at one and the same time.

Journal of Lucretia De Kuyper
Pearl Street
10th December 1759

Oh dear, oh dear, my worst fears are Realized. I had only to look at Annette to know that she was Pregnant again. As soon as we were alone, she Confessed it. Of course, she did not utter such a word as *Pregnancy . . . With child* is as daring an expression of her Condition as she will ever use. (In the unlikely Event that I Someday have a Man of my Own, I must ask him why it is Permissible to do what they have done but Highly Improper to call the Result by its Proper Name.)

She expects her Lying-In to be mid-May if the child be Punktual, but antisipating otherwise wishes me to return here early in April. Indeed if it were up to her, I would not return to the Tavern at all this Winter, but I can be Stubborn, as she knows, and I told her it would be wrong to accept Monies from Cornelius and not to Perform my Duties.

Truly I am not Completely Reluctant to go back. It is good to be here, and I will enjoy all the Dinners and Parties and Feasting for St. Nicholas Day and Twelfth Night. I will enjoy the childrens' faces all lit up when they receive their Gifts. Annette is here and Thomasina and our Philadelphia.

But I find in me a growing Need for the Winter Solitude of the Tavern. I have Mrs. Wallace there for company when and if I want it, and the boys, too, so there is Young Life about the Place; but I have an almost Greedy Need now to be Often Alone. I read in my room and I walk along the River in all but the wildest Winter wether, and I am Strangely Happy. I, who once Railed against my lot in having to live out my Life Alone. Perhaps for all that happens in Life, God sends Compensations. This then must be Mine.

Journal of Lucretia De Kuyper
Pearl St., NYC
3rd April 1760

I arrived in New York last night by deliberate Intent because it is a year Today since the birth of Philadelphia, and I knew that with Annette's love of Partying for all occasions, there would be a Festivity of some Sort, and I was Wishfull to be part of it.

My Surmize was Correct. There was a small Childrens' Party in the afternoon, which her Elder Sister and Brothers enjoyed far more than the Honoured Guest, and Tonight there will be a small dinner for the Van Duren Connections in New York.

Annette was here just a few moments Since, exclaiming in Horror at the Condition of my Wardrobe, but I fear me the Elegant Gown she sent in by her Maid will do me no Service. The Colours that become her dark Beauty do not become me, and she, as she Pouts Prettily to hear Cornelius say in the French fashion, is *Petite*, unlike my Taller, more Angulor Frame. Yet she Persists in trying to Robe me like a Tipical Round Rosey-Cheeked Dutch Doll!

Ah well, I shall Alter the Dress for Tonite. I would not Injure her Feelings, and when all is said and done, it is no Worse than any Other. I have Grown Accustomed to my Linsey-Wool petticoats and plain dresses with their crisp white Aprons. They suit me Well. And what suits me Best, though Heaven Forbid that Annette ever learn of it, is the Breeches and Man's Shirt that Mrs. Wallace sewed for me. They are less Cumbersome to me when I Tend the Ferry, and they give me a feeling of great Freedom when I walk.

Journal of Lucretia De Kuyper
4th April 1760

Today I had an hour in the Garden alone with my dear little Name Sake, Philadelphia Lucretia. What a Froward Child she is, Prattling all ready like one much Older and staggering about on sturdy Leggs. No Dutch Doll she ither, nor yet a Beauty in the French style like Annette. I would not wish my Life away and yet sometimes I feel Impatient for the Years to Unfold that I may see what becomes of her. Whatever, I am Convinced it will not be Ordinary she is no Ordinary Child. Or is that just my fond Imaginings?

Journal of Lucretia De Kuyper
9th April 1760

Today is another Anniversary in the Family, all though it occurred to none but me. It is a year Today since Thomasina came to this House. Now none can Imagine not having her here.

I had prepared my Gift well in advanse, and I brought it to Her in the Kitchen. It was just a small picture done from my Memory, but when I looked at her, I saw that my Memory had served me Well.

"I have a Prezent for you, Thomasina," I said and brought it from behind my Back.

I untied the Ribbons and unfolded the Parchment, and she looked in Astonishment at the Sketch I had done in Charcoals of herself. It showed her seated in the Rocking Chair, her back very Strait, her Head bent to the Infant at her Breast.

She was Surprized beyond Mezure when I assured her that I was the one who had sketched the Picture. Indeed, her Wonder and Admiration have given me a great Conceit of myself. I explained that I was used to draw and paint a good deal when I was young. Encouraged by my Mother, but had Stopt for almost Ten years.

In the long winter nights of Idleness at the Tavern, somehow I had Resumed, starting with such charcoal sketches as these to amuse Ben and Obidiah and going on to Colured Paintings. The boys and Mrs. Wallace, too, had Encouragged me to believe I was as good an Artist as any, but I did it for my own pleazure.

Reverently, Thomasina rolled up the Sketch and tied the Ribbons round it with extra care. Then her hand reached out slowly, and for just Several Seconds her fingers trembled against mine, Uttering the thanks she was Unable to Speak.

BRYARLY

Journal of Lucretia De Kuyper
17th May 1760

Early this morning, punktual as may be, Annette's Labour began, lasting all the day Long. It was a Difficult Labour and Difficult Birth, and there were times when Mrs. Schooner and I both doubted that she or we had the Strength to bring her through it.

The child is a boy, a Puny Sickly one, I fear, but mostly I fear for Annette.

"Mrs. Schooner," I whispered fiercely to her, sinking Tiredly onto a stool and watching as she gently Cleansed the Infant, "either you or I must tell him, she should not have any more Children. I think another Birthing would kill her."

She nodded Agreement, but when I cast her in the role of the one who should Address Cornelius, she reeled back in shock, reminding me, "I'm not a Member of the Family."

"But you are a Mid Wife . . . he would accept it. I'm his Cousin and a Spinster. If I spoke on such a Subjeckt, he would be Embarrassed."

Reluctantly she gave in to my Pleadings.

Journal of Lucretia De Kuyper
20th May 1760

Mrs. Schooner spoke to Cornelius. She Reported to me that he listened Courteously to what she had to say and thanked her. One can only Hope he takes it to Heart.

It is Annette's Fancy to call the boy Philip, which is the name of a Van Duren Great-Uncle. But I think probably it is the Pairing of the Names Philadelphia and Philip which Appeels to her.

Annette is Recovering and I think the child will live, though I fear he will Allways be Deliket, but Thomasina has the care of him, and if anyone can Raize him, it will be Her.

Journal of Lucretia De Kuyper
1st June 1760

I am Home again, and the Tavern business thrives so, I have Scarce a moment free. Sally never returned, so it is to be Hoped she

151

caught her Husband! Acting on Instructions from me before I Journeyed to New York, Mrs. Wallace hired Tom Nease's youngest girl Mary, and I agree with her Report that Mary has worked out well. She is a strong Buxum girl full of helth and good Humour. I am full of admiration for how she Handels the men in the Tap Room, Encouragging and Fending them off at one and the same Time. I wish I had the nack of it.

My littel family here, Ben and Obidiah and Mrs. Wallace were Rejoyced to see me, but there is no time for Lessons nor will there be Probebly untill the last qwarter of the year when the Travel falls off.

Annette does not feel Eqwal to the Trip, so the Van Durens will not be staying at the Manor till later in the summer than is usual, but Bram is Promised to me for the first week in July. I have not said so to Hendryk, but I Purpose to Keep him Occupied by letting him work with Ben and Obidiah in the Tavern untill Pieter arrives. Mayhap I will have him do so even a little Afterwards. It will do him no Harm, I think, to learn that there are others whose Lives are not so Fortunate as his, and that Reading and Mathematickal Lessons may be a pressious Gift rather than a Chore!

Journal of Lucretia De Kuyper
30th October 1760

The Days are shorter, Dark falls sooner, and the Guests are far Fewer. We are on our Winter Skeduel, with the Cook House closed and what meals we need all made here in the small Kitchen.

I have Resoomed my School, which is what Ben and Obidiah call their Lessons, also my Sketching and Drawing as well. Mrs. Wallace smiles and nods at us over her Knitting, jumping up every so often to Press us to swallow a bowl of Soup or some bread and cold Meat.

The Large Family Guest Room back of mine is Scarcely ever in Demand now, so I have set up my Mateeriels there for my more Serious Painting, which I do not wish to do in the Kitchen under the Eyes of Others, Despite of how Unvariably Kind my Criticks are.

Journal of Lucretia De Kuyper
11th November 1760

I made a Wonderfull Discovery today. Would that I had found it Sooner. In the afternoon I Bundelled up Warmly, with my Breeches under my petticoats, and went for a long walk. I was lost in medditations and Wandered Far. Somewhere near the Northmost Boundaries of the Van Duren Land, at the bottom of the narrow Track that leads to the River, I came to what must be a Peckuliar Fenomenem of Nature. The mighty Hudson had so eaten away at two points of the Land that it looked as though it had been Skooped away by a Giant Shovel. Between these two Points, the Land is intact, and it Projects itself right into the River, firstly a Narrow little Neck and then a Large Patch, almost Triangulor in Shape. The appearance it gives is that of a small Island into the Hudson. It is Enchanting!

I sat down on a Bowlder to rest untill I was forced to Rize by the Chill on my bottom. Next time I shall bring a Blanket to fold over the Rock. I hope the Snows are İate so I will not have to wait till the Spring. If I could have my dearest wish, it would be to have a little Cabin bilt there, surrownded by the tall sweet Pines that abownd here.

I must ask Cornelius if this is part of his land . . . If only I could buy just the Smallest Piece that incompasses this Island. I know the Van Durens never Sell, but surely this one Patch the Lord of the Manor would not miss amongst his Thousands of Acres!

Journal of Lucretia De Kuyper
20th November 1760

A letter from Annette this day detailing the Alternative Means by which I may come to New York for the December and January Festivities forsed me to admit to myself that Truly I would be better pleased to stay at home. Home to me has come to mean this Tavern, where I am Treated with the Respect due Miss De Kuyper, Inn Keeper. In New York I am Miss De Kuyper, Spinster, the pox-marked badly Dressed old Maid Cousin the Van Durens are so Unakountably kind to!

Poughkeepsie, New York
19th of Dec. 1760

My derest Sister Lucretia,

*I take my pen in hand to Ackwaint you with the
saddest news it has ever been mine to tell. My Beloved
Wife Catherine is no more. She died most Horribly, but
of that I cannot Speak. Suffice it to say that the House
and the Children are in the Utmost State of Confuzion
and I know not which way to turn. It would be of the
most Inestimable Value if you could come to us for a
while and Set things Strait, as I feel you alone could do.
My Daughters are Distracted with Greef and I amost
fear for Bram's Reeson.*

Your loving brother Hendryk

*Journal of Lucretia De Kuyper
24th January 1761*

I am wildly Distrawt and know not what to do. A long-Delaid
letter from my brother reached me today, and in it he informs me
that Catherine is dead and his Family all need me. He sent the letter
to me in New York, but I had left for Home before its Arrival so
Cornelius posted it in one of his, not according it any partickular
Hurry. As indeed why should he, having not heard the Dredful
Tidings. No doubt Hendryk meant me to Impart them, which I did
at once. And I wrote to Hendryk, too, explaining the Terrible Gap
in Time since his Plea to me and the Gap there still must be till I
can go to him, which is caused by the Wether. The Snows are Deep
on the Ground, and Travel is Impossible. Why oh why did he give
such Meagger detales? I know Catherine was not with child, and
she was in the best of Helth when last I heard from Hendryk not
long before St. Nicholas Day. What is this about Bram's Mind
being Effected? I shall go wild with angziety if I do not hear soon.

*Journal of Lucretia De Kuyper
15th February 1761*

I am here at Hendryk's Finally and through Great Good Fortune
a full month earlier than my Best Expectations. There was a Brake
in the Wether, during which friends of Cornelius traveling from
New York to Poughkeepsie, having heard through his Kind Offices

of my Need, stopt by for me. I Housed and fed them for the Night in Royal Stile and would not, of course, accept of Compensation, which seemed only Faire, though in Justice, it comes out of Cornelius' profitts. My dear kind Cousin.

The children were all redy a-Bed when I arrived and Hendryk was from Home. So I Secured a Candle from the maid and found my own way to a guest chamber. She is new since this was my home and seemed dowtfull, so I assured her I would not steel the Silver Spoons and bade her tell my brother I would see him in the Morning.

Journal of Lucretia De Kuyper
16th February 1761

Hendryk and I breakfasted alone early this morning, and he related the entire wretched Story. Though I had no love for her, and Death cannot change that, I could not but feel Pity for the Traggedy of Catherine's Passing. She was Supervizing the Week's Baking and her cotton petticoats caught Fire. I shudder, remembering how often I used to warn her, as she swept Carelessly about the open Coals, that linsey-wools were safer for under-Skirting, but she ever preferred the Softness of Cotton near to her Skin.

To my mind one of the Worst Feetures of the Affaire is that Hendryk and Bram were near by and, hearing her Skreams, rushed to the Kitchen. It seems she cried out . . . Indeed they were her last Desperit words . . . "Hendryk, help me!" and Hendryk, he admits, stood Froze in his Horror for Several Seckonds while Bram rushed right to his Mother.

But then Hendryk made a Recover and Ran and threw her to the Ground, pushing Bram aside and out of Danger and smothering her with a Blanket brought by one of the Maids. Still nothing they did Availed them.

The Affect on Bram of seeing his Mother Blaze up like a Torch and then Die before his eyes was such he did not move or speak for Several Days. Ever since he has avoided Hendryk.

Myself, I think he is like a Wounded Animal that will steal Away to lick its Wounds in Privasy, but Hendryk is Convinsed the boy blames him for those few Seckonds of Delay before he came to Catherine's Aid.

I tried in Vane to bring Hendryk to my Point of View. He persists in this Notion that his Son blames him for his Mother's Death. Truly it is his own Guilt praying on his Mind; I think he blames himself. God knows as many or more Women die by Kitchen fire as in Child bed, but he is Unconsoleable. It appears to me that it is he who avoids Bram, who was formerly his Darling.

My Task here, I think, is to reach them both.

The girls, I thank God, are in good Hands with Catherine's Cousin Gretchen, now widowed and living in a Cottage near to us. She keeps them by her most Days.

Journal of Lucretia De Kuyper
1st March 1761

I have just left a Meeting with Hendryk in his Private Parlour and I am Dazed by the News he imparted. Catherine is less than three months dead, and All ready he and Gretchen are planning to be Wed!

So much for a man's Greef.

Of course, Hendryk insisted in his old Pompouss way that he was doing this for his "dear childrens' sake." But I notised that he avoided my eyes when he said so. I could not help remembering that Gretchen's Husband left her in very good Circumstanses and there are no Inconveenient children of the Marriage. Also, she is very pleasing to the Eye.

He was kind enough to Hint that this Step would not have been Necessary had I been willing to do my Sisterly Duty and give up the Tavern to take Catherine's place here. What he really means is my former place as her Unpaid Worker. I made it qwite Clear to him when the Subjeckt first came up that I am not so Sisterly. Hence, this Marriage.

Journal of Lucretia De Kuyper
5th March 1761

Hendryk and Gretchen plan to be Wed within the week, and the Children have been Informed. The girls were Prepaired, almost, I think, they were Antisipating, but for Bram it came as a compleat Shock and his Condition is Indeed Piteous.

156

It is to be a small and qwiet Wedding, and Gretchen will move into the House at Once, so there is no longer need for me here. Hendryk is looking into the Skedules of the Stage Coach on the Boston Post Road, as eagger to hurry me away home as formerly he was to bring me here.

Later in the same day

Early this Even Hendryk called me into his Private Parlour and made me an Amazing Propozal, in short, that I take Bram home with me untill such time as he had adjusted to the Situation of his Father's having a new Wife. He began by speaking of a stay of Several Months, and before we were finished, he had enlarged the Proposed Visit to Include the Summer.

How well I know my brother and how often I Wish that I did not. He Lies. To Himself as well as to me. He is not Propozing a Visit, he means for Bram to live with me!

It has Allways been Hendryk's Weakness, one of them, to hide away from Unplezant Truths. This Truth is that ever since Catherine's Death, he has seen his son's eyes as the Mirror of his own Soul. Into that Dark Mirror, with its ugly Truths, Hendryk cannot Bare to Look. Hence, better to take away the Mirror even if it be his once Beloved Son.

I am so full of Pity and Disdain for him, I know not which is Stronger. And my heart goes out to the child, who has shortly lost his Mother and is now to lose Home, Sisters, and Father, too.

I was more than ever Convinsed of the Riteness of my Deducktions when Hendryk, the King of Mizers, offered me a Monthly sum for Bram's Keep and Expenses. It was on the tip of my Foolish Tonge to Decline, but I held myself back in time. Why should he not pay? My own money can be Husbanded to Provide for Bram in the Future if there is need.

I am Ashamed, so ashamed. Even as I sit here, sorrowing for Bram's loss, my heart Overflows with Joy, Sellfish Joy. Bram is to live with me, to be Mine. Mine to look after, Mine to love, Mine to be the Son I never had, the one I have always Wanted.

Evening, still the 5th of March

Bram came to my Bed chamber wilst I was Neatening my hair, just before Supper. Hendryk had told him that he was to go home to the Tavern with me for a Visit.

"Shall you like that?" I asked, smiling Falsely, for the Pain I saw on his Face was like to make my Heart brake. He was so Sobber and Seerious for such a small boy, so much Older-Seeming than his Seven Years.

"Shall *you?"* he asked like a little old Man, and there, I saw, was the Crux of the Matter.

He knew. He understood. This child who was wiser now than Hendryk would ever be clearly saw his father in all his Weakness and lack of Charackter. Mayhap the one he did not Fully understand was me.

I laid down my hair brush and turned to Face him.

"Bram, *mijn kleine liefde,"* I told him with all the Tenderness of a heart Overflowing with love for him, "if this very minute I could have come true the one Wish I want in all this World, it would be to have you come Home with me and never go away again. So Sellfish I am, so Much I want you to be with me."

If I live the Full A-lotted three score and ten the Bible speaks of, never shall I forget the Joy that came onto his face at my words. His eyes had seemed cold and bleak and grey before, like the Hudson before it ices over in Winter. Now they were clear and blue and sparkling like the River running its merry Corse in spring.

As I have tried many Times to paint the look of a flower unfurling its pettals to the Sun, so some day I may try to paint Bram as he looked in that Moment, when the Shut-Away look left his face, and his Life seemed to open up to Happyness once more.

Journal of Lucretia De Kuyper
3rd April 1761

I think no matter where I am, close to her or A-part, I will allways Celebrate this date when Philadelphia Lucretia Van Duren made her Entranse into the World. It is two years today since her Arriving. She is at home in New York, but Even So, we had a Grand Speshal Supper here, and Mrs. Wallace made a great St. Nicholas cooky, which Captivated Bram and Ben and Obidiah. They thowt it Exqwisitely Humorous that we should have a St. Nicholas Cooky in April and a party for an Honoured Guest who will not arrive in the Tarrytowns for another Seven or Eight Weeks.

Bram remarked to me as I was tucking him into his littel Trundel Bed some hours later that I did Peckulyer things. I asked cazually if he minded. He shook his littel straw head with Vigour and Bounced out from Beneath the Coverlett to hugg me. "They're fun-peckulyer things," he said, snuggeling down again. "You're a fun-peckulyer Lady, Aunt Lucretia."

A great Lump rose in my throat.

"Are you happy living here with me, mijn Bram?" I could not keep myself from asking, despising my Weak Need even as I did so.

Bram's eyes, which had just closed sleepily, opened once more and slanted wizely up at me.

"I like living with you, Aunt Lucretia, forever and ever." The blue eyes closed again. "And with Ben and Obidiah and Mrs. Wallace, too," he murmured sleepily.

It is true that Ben and Obidiah have been gentil and good with him, showing Cumpassion beyond their years, and he has become Mrs. Wallace's darling. But that is not why, when I left his chamber, I stopt in the hallway and leaned my face against the wall and Wept. My tears were for myself, tears of Joy at being Bram's "Fun-Peckulyer Lady" whom, in all his young innocence, he wants now to live with forever and ever.

Journal of Lucretia De Kuyper
19th August 1761

Of the three Summers I have spent at the Tavern, this one has been the Busiest of all and the Happiest. I think, perhaps, the Happyest Summer of my Life. I do not Count the one I had with Johann when we walked and Talked, Hands Entwined together, and dreamed Lovely Dreams destined never to be. The Lucretia who did That was a different Lucretia, young, oh so Young and un-Tried by Fate. I am older now, Wizer, I hope, and I have learned that Dreams may die and life go on, One's Purpose can be Bent or Shaped Differently. When I was twenty, I wanted the World to my Order, but now, more than ten years later, I find myself well Content with the Corner of the World that has been given me.

There is my Work and the Pride I take in being what Cornelius calls, despite Annette's Shocked Protests, "the best damn Inn Keeper in the County of West Chester."

I have my dear small family here, my books and painting, my Island. In December there will be the Joy of Holidaying in New York, and this Year I look Forward to it as the Young Ones, for Bram and Ben and Obidiah are to go with me, and their Joy will be my Joy.

Truly I can say my Lot is a good one, my Way has fallen in a most Plezant Place, I have Helth, Pride, Independency, Occupation, and Loved Ones. What more could I ask? Annette would say a Husband, but if I had one, might I not lose two of the things I most Value, my Pride and Independency?

What has made me all on a Sudden so Wretchedly Phillosofficall? And why should I worry about a Choise that will not be Offer'd me? Men wanting Wives are not roaming the Highways and By-Ways of West Chester in search of Gawnt and Over-Grown Spinsters well past thirty.

I will be Honest, Confiding in these pages what I could not say to Annette or even Thomasina, who knows my Heart more than any other. Yes, there are times when I am Lonely on the Night, and I lie in my bed and think how it would be to reach out to Someone Close . . . but when Daylight comes, Safety and Sanity come with it, and I am Restored to Contentment.

Journal of Lucretia De Kuyper
17th October 1761

As of this day I am one and thirty. We had only three guests in the Tavern, and it was a day of Prezent-giving and Festivity. Mrs. Wallace made a Pork and Cheshire Pie for our Supper and Waffers filled with Cream and Marmalaid, on which I stuffed myself as greedily as the boys. Ben had fashioned me four Frames in Sturdy Oak and Birch for my favourite Paintings. Bram, helped I am sure by Mrs. Wallace, had made me a Pillow of Hops to Indoose Sweet Sleep and an Oranj Pomander stuffed with Cloves. She herself had knit me a small-sized wool blanket of a blue plad Pattern to carry on my walks.

The biggest surprize, I must confess, was my Gift from Obidiah.

It was a Replicka, very small, very Exact, of the big Dutch Cupboard in the Best Guest Parlour. I could hardly believe it when he told me it was work of his own Carving. I know he is allways wittling away at Peeces of Wood, but never had I been Aware he had such Skill at this. Truly, he, not I, is the Artist, and now I know how I must Gide his Future. It had allways troubled me a littel that he and even more Ben, with his qwick sharp intelligense, are ment to be better than Tavern boys.

I must write to Cornelius.

> Pearl St.
> 9th November 1761

My dear Lucretia,

I have set enquiries in train and have good hopes of Eventually interesting the proper persons in Ben and Obidiah. Nothing is certain, but my friend Joris Van Derbeck has personal knowledge of a Cabinet-maker in Philadelphia, a fine artisan and a man of sterling Worth, a Quaker like my Annette's people on her mother's Side. He has been blest with five daughters and no sons, and now in his middle years, he feels the lack. This might be a fine Opportunity for the boy.

If you will have posted to me the Carvings that you spoke about, I will take Measures to have them sent to this Quaker man in Philadelphia with covering letters from Van Derbeck and myself.

Now as to Ben, who should have been Apprenticed some years ago. You must be Aware that his Fourteen years are not in his Favor. However it happens to have come to my ears that Capt. Arend Bogardus, the Ship-owner and Importing Merchant with whom I do much business, has been on the Watch for a likely lad, he having no son nither, nor any child at all for that matter, being a Widowed man of long standing.

I approached him on the boy's Behalf, and when you all come to New York, a meeting with Capt. Bogardus will be arranged.

You do not mention Bram in your letter, so I feel it my Duty to do it for you. For the rest of this winter and through the summer it will do him no harm and perhaps much good to keep him by you and Provide his Lessons. After that, it will not do. My dear Lucretia, I know how much the Boy means to you and that you want the Best for him. If you are Correct and Hendryk does not mean to have him back, and I accept your reading that he means not to, then I think you must plan for his Future as well as for the little Orphans.

Let him be included in my Household so that he can have proper Schooling in New York. You will still have him for the long summers and in December and January when you come here.

Think about it, Cousin, and remember that it is in the light of Bram's well being you must Consider my Proposal. Annette bids me say, as I am sure you do not need telling, that she will care for him as her own. He is, after all, of my blood, too. Hendryk I do not understand!

Your Affectionate Cousin,
Cornelius Van Duren

River Cross Tavern
18th November 1761

My dear Cornelius,

One of the Cattle Drovers who stopt by Unexpecktedly at this Season will carry Obidiah's Carvings to New York, where he has personnal conserns, and will Deliver same to your business Residence. He will arrive shortly. As you know, the Drovers Drink without Pay as a Return for all the News of the Day, which they Garner and Give Out. However, for this added Servise, I proferred him Free loging as well, besides some small coin, so you need not pay him agen.

As to Bram, however Relucktantly, I must Abide by your Jugement. It Matches my own. Pray tell Annette I have no Fears for Bram in her Hands. I trust them as my own. Ever you have both been True Friends to me and mine.

Your Gratefull Cousin,
Lucretia De Kuyper

Pray kiss my Littel Philadelphia for me.

Journal of Lucretia De Kuyper
3rd December 1761

An Unexpected Brake in the Qwiet of our days.

It was Clear and Sunny, so after Lessons, I Wrapt myself warmly, hung my plaid blanket over one arm and my Basket over the other, then took the long walk to my Island.

I spred the blanket over a Rock to keep out the Chill when I sat. I had just Uncovered my Basket, taking out cheese and bread and a good New York apple for my Dinner, also the book *Tom Jones*, which I am reading for the third time, so Entertaining it is, when I heard Sounds behind me.

I turned, Surprized, for never in the two years that I have been coming here, has any other Living Soul disturbed my Paradise.

There was a gentleman making his way through the Woods. He had left the road and come onto the Rugged path, walking and leading his Horse. I turned back Rezolutely to my Book and my Meal. If he had Dismownted and left the Road for the Uzual Reason, not notising me, it would save him Embarrassment to think me Unaware.

I was Mistaken, however, in thinking he had not Notised me. A Voice behind me said, "Good morning, Young Lady. What in the World are you doing here?"

His voice was clear and plesant and Carried an Unmistakeable Ring of Awthority. It was the Awthority I found myself Resenting as I turned about to show him that I was Nither Young, nor perhaps by his Notions a Lady. I was an Inn Keeper, littel thow he knew it, with Awthority of my own.

I said calmly, "I should think it was Self-Evident, Sir. I am Reading and Eating my Dinner."

"So you are," he said just as calmly as he threw his Reins over a Tree Branch and sat down Beside me. Regardless of his fine Breeches. He took off his Tricorn Hat and threw it down just as Carelessly. "You remind me I am qwite Hungry," he said. "Will you share your Food with me?"

I was Taken Aback by these Free and Easy Manners. In the

Tavern, where the men are not allways Gentlemen, they still keep more Distants and Respeckt between us. But even as I thowt of Ways to crush such Arrogance, he broke off a peace of my Cheese and a good-Sized Crust of bread from my Loaf.

He started to eat with good Appetite and gaze out at the River, as though he were entirely Free of Care. I could not help satisfying *my* Curiosity by demanding to know what he was doing in this place.

"Looking over the land," he said eazily. "I hope to Purchase a Farm."

"From whom?" I demanded, with a Feerceness born of Fear. "Cornelius Van Duren?"

He nodded, his Delft-blue eyes krinkeling up at the Corners.

I was in such Distress I could not Keep myself from crying out like a foolish child, "Not this Land? Not my Island?"

"Island?"

I indickated it with a Wave of my hand, and the Eyes krinkeled up again. A broad Indulgent Unbearably Patronizing smile came over the Wether-Beaten Face so surprizingly Tann'd for the Time of Year.

"My dear girl," he said to me with Tottally Exaggerated Curtesey, "in the first place this Grubby Patch of land is a Peninsoola, not an Island. As for the second—"

I jumped up. "It's not Grubby. It's not—" And then I stopt. Suddenly aware what a Silly Specktakel I was making of myself, I blushed and blushed with mortifikation. My hands were shaking as I bundeled my Belongings back into the Basket.

"I must go. The Sun will be down soon. Good afternoon to you, Sir."

"Why not ride?" he suggested. "It will be faster than walking. I can take you as far as the Van Duren place." He reached for his Tricorn and stood up Beside me. "My horse can carry Double."

I notised then that, since I was tall for a woman, then he must be short, for standing there on Levell Grownd, we were of an exact Hight.

Our eyes Locked, and when the Delft blue of his darkened suddenly, I saw something in their Deppths that I prayed he did not see in mine. It would have too Much Betray'd first the fluttering Pulses of my Body and next the Starteling Leap of my Heart from below my Bodice clear up to my Throat.

I do not remember saying Aye or nay, but I was on his Horse before him and we were back on the Road again.

It was a Silent Ride. My thowts kept me Busy, and I Prezume that his did the same, for he spoke not ither.

Where the Road grew wide, he put the Horse to a Trot, and one of his arms reached arownd me to hold me Steddy in the Saddle. Even thru layers of cloathing, wherever his Flesh Encowntered Mine, I Flamed to his Touch.

A few yards from the Tavern, I spoke for the first time, telling him he could let me down at the Tavern door.

"Here?" he asked, wrinkeling his brow in Puzzlement. "You are staying at the Tavern?"

"Yes." He had stopt now, and I slid out of his arm's embrace and down from the Horse. "I allways stay at the Tavern." Standing there in the road, I sketched him a curtsey, like any grand Lady. "I am the Inn Keeper."

"The Inn Keeper!" he repeeted, as one Stunned. "Mrs. . . ." He looked down at my hand, and I splayed the Fingers out, correckting him. "*Miss* De Kuyper."

"Miss De Kuyper. Yes. Of corse." He said it more to himself than to me, and as thow it was Some Thing he ought to know. I waited for more, then shrugged and turned to mownt the Kitchen steps.

As I was Opening the Door, he called up to me, "Have you a Stable lad to tend my Horse?"

I whirled arownd, gaping at him Stoopidly.

"My horse," he repeeted, "and lodging? You do have lodgings in your Tavern?"

I swung open both halves of the Dutch Door, and he followed me into the Kitchen, describing to me the type of Lodgings he desired. No shared beds. No shared rooms. Apparently only the Parlour Room next to mine would do for such a partickular gentleman, despite it was large enuff to Sleep an Entire Family and uzually did in Season.

While Ben went outside, Bram trailing after him, to take the Horse to the Stables, I showed my new guest through the Parlour Room for the welthy. To discourage him, instead of taking him instantly through the private hall entranse, I led him to it by way of the Common and Tap Rooms and my own Chamber.

Undaunted, he was pleased to approve it and did not even Flinch when I told him the charges, slitely redused after summer but still no small Sum.

In the winter, when the Parlour Room is freqwently Uninhabited for months, I paint there. I had forgot that a half dozen of my paintings were skattered about the room, stakked up agenst the walls, and one, in Unfinished State, still on the Wooden Prop Ben had Carpentered for me. My Strange Guest walked around the Room, lifting and inspeckting each in Turn.

When I would have Removed them, he put up his Hand to stop me, saying he wished to Study them at his Leezure. Silently, Rezenting his peremptory Manner, I went to put a Match to the fire allredy laid in the big Fireplace and found myself Bundeled aside while he Performed this Act.

As the Fire Blazed merriley, he Studied the Double Row of Happy Children tiles around the Fireplace.

"Charming," he said, "but a bit of a Waste for an old Batchelor."

I am not verry Knowledgable about Men in Personnal Dealings, only in Business, yet it seemed to me that my Guest was going out of his Way to Inform me he was Unmarried and Childless.

Did he perhaps think that because I was an Inn Keeper and not qwite a Lady, I was also—I coloured up at my thowts, then shrugged Inwardly. If so, he would not be the First. I had sqwelched many Another with Similar Ideas in Mind.

So I ignored his Alluzion and asked qwietly if there was any-thing else I could get for him. "You may have your Supper in the Tap Room or, if you prefer, here in your Room. We have no other Guests at Prezent, so I am afraid it will be Simpel Fare."

"Where do *you* eat?" he enqwired.

"In the Kitchen," I told him coldly, "with the rest of the Staff," and he answered that he would do the same. Dismayd, I tried to perswade him Otherwise, but he did not have those Dutch-Delft eyes and that sqware Dutch chin for Nothing. He was as Stubborn a Dutchman as ever I have met. In the Kitchen he would eat or Nowhere, and his smile mocked me, for he knew as well as if I had said it, that I longed to answer him, "Nowhere," but my long Training would not Permit of it. I was Inn Keeper, and he was a Guest.

I submitted and stalked from the Room.

After Supper of the Same Day

I must have been more Weary than I knew. I laid down on my Bed, meaning to rest for just ten minutes, and when I Awoke, I fownd to my Consternation that two hours had Gone By.

I heard no Sound in the next room and hurried to the Kitchen. He sat there in Mrs. Wallace's favorite Big Rocker, mightily at Home, with the three boys at his feet, their Faces Worshipping him.

"But how did you get away from the Piretes, Capt. Bogardus?" Bram had just asked him when they spyed me.

Capt. Bogardus. I Frowned to myself. It seemed to me I had heard that name Some Where Recently.

The Captain notised me at the same moment as the boys. He got up, bowing, while Bram hurled himself at me, showting, "He's fought with real-life Piretes, Aunt Lucretia."

At the same moment Mrs. Wallace turned from the table to tell us, "Supper is reddy. Sit you down."

I must admit that Capt. Bogardus made a plezant sixth to our Table. The Atmosphere a man creates is indeed Different Some How. The boys were enthrawlled, even Mrs. Wallace was Captivated . . . and I, I must be honest, I, too, was Charmed a littel, thow still warry.

When we were cleaning up after the Meal, he did not leave but took some Coins and offered them to the Boys. "Can you three go up to the Manor House and bring my Luggedge here?"

I looked up from the Tub of hot water, where I was Rinsing the Dishes. No dowbt there was a qwestion in my Eyes, for he answered without my Asking, "I thowt at first to stay there, but I prefer it here."

"Are you a guest of Mr. Van Duren's?" I asked.

The corners of his eyes krinkeled up in that way he had. He did not Troubell to keep the Amuzement from his Voice. "I would hardly stay in his house otherwise."

I bit my lips and returned to the dishes. The boys pocketed their coins and rushed out, banging the door. He took advantage of Mrs. Wallace's Removing herself to the Common Room to put back the good Pewter Tankards to Approche me.

He said Gently, "Why are you distressed, my dear?"

I Stared up at him, all Amazed at the Intimacy of this Address. I said coldly, trying to put him at the Proper Distants, "I cannot understand, Sir, why a guest of Mr. Cornelius Van Duren should choose rather to stay in the Tavern."

His mouth Twitched. "Can you not?"

I looked up agen, Startled, and he said Easily, "I wished to meet Young Ben. Your Cousin had Promised to arrange it in New York, but I was traveling this way after my visit to Rhode Island, so I . . ."

I was mortified beyond Measure. Now I reckolleckted his Name. He was the man, the Widower, who Cornelius had said might find a place in his business for Ben. The Personnal Alluzions I had taken to myself had Reference to his Childless State.

Lord Allmighty, was I becoming the Sorry kind of Spinster who reads meaning that is not there into every man's words?

Mrs. Wallace Returned, and I wiped my hands dry and gave the Captain a Candle to light him to his Room. The boys returned with his Portmantow and Saddle-Bags, and I bade them Fetch everything to the Parlour Room. I stayed with Mrs. Wallace till the boys were a-bed and my guest might have settled for the Night. Then I went to my own room to be Soliterry. I had much to think about and much of it unplezant. I did my thinking, as I so often do, by writing in this, my Journal, but I am done with writing now, and still . . . and still . . .

Journal of Lucretia De Kuyper
Early morning
4th December 1761

Last night there was a tap on my door, not on the Outside door leading to the Tap Room but the one opening up to the Guest Parlour. I was sitting close to the stove, my feet planted on the Foot Warmer, wrapt in a Shawl over my Flannell Night Dress, and I hesitated a moment; and then long Custom prevailed. I was the Inn Keeper.

I opened the Door, and he stood there, full-Dressed.

"I heard you moving abowt minutes ago so I did not hezitate to disturb you," he told me in his odd Abrupt Way. "I want to talk about your Paintings."

He had allreddy taken my Arm and was urging me into his Room.

"Sir," I said, "this is not Proper."

"Nonsense. You are not a Proper Person, and nither am I."

I was Unsertain wether or not to rezent this Remark. He gave me no Chanse.

"These are good," he said, still urging me on, "much more than good, in fact not at all the fluttering, frittering work one might expect from a female artist. These are powerful pictures, Ma'am, you paint like a man."

I was too choked with Anger to Speak but not for long.

"Do you prezume to Overjoy me with your Praize, Sir?" I cried to him, Temper a-Flame. "If so, you have Failed Singularly. What you have done is to Insult me. I am a Woman, Sir. I paint like the Woman I am. We do not all fritter and flutter, just as all men are not Strong."

He looked at me Keenly. "So I see. You must Forgive me. My experiences of your Sex has been that they fritter and flutter most Abominably—in their Conversation, in their Dress, in their Habbits."

"You have my Sympathy, Sir, for the women you have Known."

He gave me the smile that could charm even after the Sting of his Sharp Tonge. "Indeed, I begin to think I merit it. I beg your pardon, my dear, if I seemed to Belittle you, I did not mean to."

"Well, you did," I told him crossly, "and I wish you will stop calling me 'my dear.'"

He stared at me very sobberly, then put his hand out to touch my Hair, drawing some Strands of it across my showlder and against his own face.

"You have lovely Hair," he said. "That severe Knot you wear during the Day suits your fine Bones, but I like to see it Tumbelling over your Showlders as it is now . . . the color of flax, the softness of silk and the smell of fresh Hay."

I stood frozen in bewilderment at this incredible Speech. Then I became Awaire, not only of my Tumbeled Hair, which he should not see like this, but also of my Night Dress, Ill-Consealed by the Shawl. I cast him just one Horrofied look, then Skutteled back into my own Room, slamming the door shut and Leaning agenst it, Breathless and Confused.

He did not have the Look of a practised Seduser . . . why then, oh Lord help me, why then do I have the feeling I came as close as ever I have been to being Sedused?

BRYARLY

In the Afternoon

Capt. Bogardus prezented me with a Letter of Introducktion from Cornelius today. He did not chooze to say, nor I to ask, why he had not prezented it much sooner.

My Cousin also advized me that if Capt. Bogardus hired a Coach to drive to New York, I should avail myself of the Opportunity to share it with him. It meant the boys and I leaving home a few days earlier than planned but offered the Comforts and Benefit of Private Coach Travel.

Capt. Bogardus must have been aware of the Contents of my Letter; for Immediate, on my Scanning it through, he told me his hired Coach would leave from the Tavern shortly after Sunset on the morrow.

"I hope that will give you as much Time as you need for your Planning and Packing," he said with great Politeness, Therebye managing to Provoke me A-fresh, for it was Obvious his Plans would Remain the Same no matter what the Inconveenience to me.

"Thank you Kindly," I said stiffly and Hurried Away to call the Boys for an Orgy of Preparations, not forgetting a message to Mrs. Wallace's grandson Joseph bidding him come to bare her Company and do the Chores in our Absence.

Journal of Lucretia De Kuyper
9th December 1761

Annette has just left my room in a Flutter of Excitement because she is in Receipt of a note from Capt. Bogardus. He dines here on St. Nicholas Day. My dear Cousin is Painfully Obvious, for she insists that the Captain has more than a Common Interest in me and her Attemts to rowse my own Interest are laughable.

I have learned more abowt him these few days in Town. His wife died of the Fever seven years ago. The Marriage was not Happy, and wilst she lived the Captain spent more Time at Sea than he did at Home. He has been Solisited by many young Ladies of New York in the Intervening Years for he is excessively Welthy, the Owner of many fine Vessels and has his Fingers in many important Business Pies in this Town.

That Annette can think he has Seerious Intentions towards me only shows her own Loving Parshiality, for how can it be? I have

170

had pointed out to me some of the lovely Ladies who have thrown their Caps at him only to be well-snubbed for their Pains. It would take more Vanity than is mine to believe him to have Eyes for an ageing pox-marked Spinster more than ten years on the Shelf.

I believe he might have Bedded me that night had I not Run away . . . which is not to Flatter myself. Under like Circumstances, he might have Bedded any other. Yet Annette insists that he has asked Cornelius a Prodigous Number of Qwestions about me. She insists I will be a Fool if I do not try a littel to Captivate him or let such an Opportunity slip through my Fingers.

Mayhap she is in the Right of it. Why must one part of me allways be so much Wiser and more Critickal than the other Part? Mayhap this one time I should act on Instrucktions from my Heart instead of my Head.

What is the worse that can Happen? For Capt. Bogardus to Suspeckt that the new Gown Annette insists on and the Curling of my Hair are done for his sake? So be it. Let him Suspeckt . . . better that than to live with Eternal Regrett that I did not make the slitest Push to Engage his Interest when the Chanse was Offered me.

Journal of Lucretia De Kuyper
St. Nicholas Night

My fire has gone out, my fingers are Froze, but I can no more go to Bed than up to the Moon. This has been a day I shall not soon Forget. Soon? Rather, I should say, Not Ever. It began well, and the Worse that I spoke of in my Journal did not come till later.

When I dressed this noon in the new Gown Annette had ordered, I was reazonably satisfied with my Portrait in the Mirror.

My Underskirt was of Indigo blue, which Annette was pleazed to Describe as the colour of my eyes. The pannier and the Stomacker were flowered with pink and blue Rosebudds, the whole Stiffen'd with four white Petticoats. At each elbow, where the Sleeve ended, Annette's Dress Maker had Attached a fall of her mother's fine old Venecian lace.

My shoes are old, but the Maid had fresh-polished them, and Cornelius had given me to adorn them a pair of new Silver Buckels with bluepaste Jewels. I carried a lace Reticule and a Fan of Ivory Sticks, both belonging to Annette.

The one thing I had Grave Doubts about was my Hair, which a Maid, Supervised by Annette, had used Hot Irons to teaze into a mass of Ringlets. Looking into the Mirror, I felt I did not know Myself, and I wondered if he . . .

But Annette cried out that she had never·seen me Appeare more Elegante, and I became too buzy Protesting the layer of Beeswax she was coating onto my face to give the hair more attention.

"Just a littel to cover the pox marks," she cooed Deliketly. "I know how Foolishly Sensitif you are about them."

She spoke Truly, I was Sensitif, so I Submitted. From the beeswax it was but one step Further to a dusting of Rice Powder on my nose and the tinyest Reddening of my lips, so that Prezently I desended to the Parlour, furling and unfurling my Fan, feeling very much a Lady of New York.

If I had hoped to Astonish Capt. Bogardus by my Elegence, he gave no sign of it when he Bowed over my hand some Minutes later. I saw no Spechial Admiration on his Countenance nor Criticism ether. But there were other men, and I fownd myself Remembering a-new after these many years that a Fashionable Gown and Appearence are Great Givers of Confidense. Likewise, a Fan is a Veritabel Weapon of Flirtation.

I Wielded mine about my face and made Fine Play with my eyes to Mr. Courtney Smith, who Readily Engaged with me in this Delishious Game. And all the while I was Fully Awaire that across the Room, even while Engaged in Conversation with others, *his* eyes and *his* mind were Engaged with me. It was Headdy Knowledge and made me even more Flirtatious than before.

When we sat down to Dine, I was Partner'd—Trust Annette—by Capt. Bogardus. Flirting was so deliteful, I continued it with him, looking up at him from under my Lashes while I sipped my Wine and agen made Play with my Fan.

My Shock was Considerable when he reached for my wine glass between two of the Dinner Corses to rinse it in the Monteith Bowl in the center of the Dining Table and took advantage of the few Seconds of Closeness to say to me in a low but Peercingly Distinckt Voice, "I wish you will stop being so silly. It does not become you."

A Servant re-Filled my glass with the next Wine, I seezed my glass and Gulped it down, so Shamed I knew not where to Look or What to do.

Several glasses later—Seldom do I drink other than good Tavern Cider—my Confidence was Restored. I turned to my Naybor on my other Side, letting the Arrogant Captain see only my Back. A Figg for his Oppinion!

We had sat down to Dine at two-thirty and returned not to the Parlour till Four Hours later. I was feeling a bit Lite-Headed from the Wine, and I made my way to the Blazing Fire and sat down on a stool, where Mr. Courtney Smith found his Way to me. *He* did not find me Silly. We rezumed our Flirtation.

Suddenly I was Awaire of a Shadow standing over me. "Miss De Kuyper," said a Voice that made my heart jump up to my Breast as a Fish leaps high to the Bait.

"Capt. Bogardus?" I made my own Voice cold.

"Your pardon, Sir, but I think Mrs. Van Duren is trying to engage her Cousin's Attention."

He bowed to Mr. Courtney Smith, who bowed curteously in Return and withdrew. I looked across at Annette, more to avoid the Captain's Gaze than anything else. She was making Odd faces and rather Frantick-looking Jestures.

"What on Earth ails Annette?" I asked in Puzzlement.

"I think," he answered me, Cold in Turn, "she is trying to Convey a Signal to you to Remove yourself Speedily from the Visinity of this Fire."

This did cause me to bring my eyes to his Face.

"But why—" I commensed, only to have him Interrupt Rudely, "The heat of the Fire seems to be melting that Vile Stuff on your Cheeks." I could feel the Blood leave those Self-Same Cheeks as he added with eqwal Contempt, "It seems to be having just as Disasterous an Effect on those—those Curls Dansing about your shoulders."

I think—I am not sure—but I believe I gave a small Cry. I jumped up, over-turning the Stool and walked away from him out of the Room. When I Acheeved the Emptyness of the Hallway, I bolted up the Steps and into my littel Guest Bedchamber.

I closed the door and Fumbeled in the dark for my Candle and Matches. Holding the lit Chamber-stick up, I forsed myself to step over to the mahogony-framed mirror near the Window.

I bent close to the Mirror, Pityless to Myself, as I held the Candle near to my face. The curls had uncurled and hung limply about my neck. Part of the Beeswax was still Caked Hard and the other part had indeed Melted Away most unplezantly.

I rang my Bell for a maid to bring Hot Water, and when it came, I took off my Elegant gown and Scrubbed my Face clean of Vanity's Trappings! Standing in my shift and Petticoats, I brushed out my Hair, Vowing never again to make myself Ridickulous trying to be what I was not.

I hurt myself a-fresh, remembering all the Wise Maxims that could be Applied to my Conduct this day. *Mutton dressed like lamb . . . No fool like an old fool!* The Pain and Shame I felt were so great that I threw myself on the bed, sobbing aloud.

I never heard his Knock. I never heard the door Open. Or Close again. All I knew was the Giddy Wonderfull Sensation of being lifted into Strong Arms, which carried me to a chair in which he sat down holding me onto his Lap.

In one moment I was Transformed from A-cute Misery to the Exstasy of being Comforted by his Strength, and by murmured words like, "My darling, my darling, don't weep so," which caused me to Lean up Agenst him to Weep all the Harder, I knew not wether for Joy that he was here or the Angwish that had gone Before.

Prezently he said in a firm lowd Voice, "Now that will do," and I stopt weeping, restored to my Senses and Also to the Shame of my Situation. Here was I in naught but my Shift and Petticoats, sitting on this Man's Lap in my Bed chamber.

I leapt off his knees as though they had suddenly become Hot Coals.

"Sir, you should not be here," I said in shaken tones.

He looked up at me, amuzement clear on his face.

"Why should I not?" he enqwired agreeably.

"You know it is not Proper," I began primly enough and did not go on for he was laughing at me.

"I think," he said, "you had better get used to seeing me in your Bed chamber."

I stared down at him, unable to believe he meant what he seemed to be Saying.

"When we are married, my lovely Lucretia, we will share the same bedchamber and be in it alone together very often. You are going to Wed me, aren't you, Lucretia?" To my great surprize, his

Voice shook a littel as he added, "I don't think I can bear it if you Refuse me."

Refuse him! Did not he know what I have known, thow I never admitted it even in this, my Journal, that I have loved and Wanted him from the first day, almost the first Moments?

Yet there were things that must be said. "I don't understand," I said painfully. "I am one and thirty. If it is children you want, then—"

"I don't," he interrupted, "not any longer. Once I did, but I am two and forty and that time is Past. I am content with my Nephews in Rhode Island, and I am sure you will keep our Home well supplied with young Bram and the Van Duren Brats to say nothing of your Orphans. Come, Lucretia." He rose from the chair and held out his Hand to me. "Is it so hard for you to believe that I want you for yourself?"

"I—I—I am neether Young nor p-pretty; my p-pox marks . . ."

"If I wanted a Milk and Water miss or a pretty moon-faced China Doll with an empty face, no, I would not want you," he told me Forsefully. "But I do not. I was married to one like that, God help me, and Once was more than enough. You are all Woman, my dear, and I want all of you." He smiled at me with Great Tenderness, adding, "If you mention your Insignificant pox marks again, I swear I will be Tempted to shake you, my love."

Annette might not have Approved such un-Maidenlike lack of Restraint, but . . . "I have loved you," I said in my old Impettuous Way, "from the Moment that you stole my bread and cheese."

This time when he held out both his hands to me, I flew into his Waiting Arms.

Journal of Lucretia De Kuyper
2nd April 1762

Tomorrow is a Doubell Celebration. Philadelphia will have her third Birth Date and I will be Married to Captain Arend Bogardus.

We will live in my fine new-furnished House on Bowling Green, and Bram will make his Home with us as well as Arend's youngest nephew, Martinis Asher, whose Education we undertake, also Ben, who has allredy begun his training under my Captain's Chief Merchant. My one Regrett is that we lose Obidiah, but he is so happily Setteled in Philadelphia that I cannot Repine. We are a Complete Family.

After Supper tonite Cornelius gave to me as his and Annette's Wedding Gift the deed to five hundred acres of their land in the Tarrytowns, including the strip around my Beloved Island. On this Property Arend proposes to build us a farm house or Cottage so that we will spend our summers in West Chester.

I am almost Afraid, I confess it, of so much Happyness.

Tomorrow is the Day I never thowt to come . . . my Wedding Morn . . . and immediately after the Ceremony and Breakfast, I, who have never been farther from here than Poughkeepsie, depart with my husband on his finest River Vessel for a Wedding Trip to Charleston.

Journal of Lucretia Bogardus
4th April 1762

In the early dawn of this day I came fully awake all at once, which is unusual with me, usually my Awakening is Slower. I Laid very Still, immediately awaire of my Husband beside me and not Wishful to Disturb his rest. My Husband, I kept repeeting in my Mind, my Very Own Husband. Who could have believed it? Then my Busy Mind dwelled on the night just sped and the Colour flamed in my cheeks. Who could have believed *that?*

"What are you thinking?" asked a soft Voice beside me, and I realized the Man lying in Bed with me was no more Drowzy than I.

I hesitated, and he repeeted his Question.

My husband and I then had a Conversation, which as Near as I can Remember went like this:

"I was thinking," I told him, "that it's not at all the same as with the sheep and cows and pigs. The Horses, too. I used to watch them Mate. And the Rooster with the Hens. I always Fancied, except for Kissing, it was much the same with Humans. But it isn't. Not at all."

His lips twiched a littel at the Corners.

"I'm pleased to hear it," he said with the Tender Mockery in his Voice that is so much a part of the way he often Speaks to me. "At least I Assume I should be pleazed."

"Oh yes," I Hastened to Assure him. "I meant it as a Compliment. It was very—very—"

"Very very what?" he pursued after a long Pawse.

"Plezurable," I answered faintly and with some Regret. Had I said too much? Had I been too Forward? "Except just in the beginning when it was Painful," I added hastily.

He frowned a littel, and my Regrett grew. I had said too much.

Then he explained away the frown. "I am sorry I hurt you," he told me gently. "I tried not to."

"But you did not," I said, greatly Relieved, "except that least littel Bit. Truly, I liked it *Enormously.*"

He gave a great Showt of Laughter.

"Perhaps," I told him Unsertainly, "you would rather I did not Speak so Freely."

We had been Directing most of this Conversation towards the Ceiling. Now, he turned on his side, facing me, and his strong sure hands that had held me in the night turned me on my side, Facing him.

"Why should I not want that?" he enqwired.

"Annette told me," I answered Honestly, "that Women Respond to Men differently than Men do to Women. She said we have to Some Times—well, *Pretend* more than we feel—and other times, to be Lady-Like, Pretend Less."

My Husband said in what I Imaggine might well be the Voice of Capt. Bogardus on his Qwarter Deck, "If you do any Pretending with me, Lucretia, my love, I shall beat you with great Vigour."

I stared him Back, more Interested than Fearfull. "Will you really?"

He pulled me Roughly into his Arms. "No, but I promise you I will think up some other Dire Punishment. Don't you know, you Foolish Child, there is nothing more Wonderfull, than to know you found the same Pleazure in my arms that I found in Yours?"

He settled me more Comfortably in those same Arms, with his Chin resting on the top of my Head. Prezently he said, Half sleepy, half Sarcastick, "What other Pearls of Wisdom did you learn from Annette that I shall have to un-Instruct you in?"

"Oh, nothing," I said qwickly, "nothing much. Just about my Duty to you."

"Your Duty?"

"When you wish to—to—to—"

"Make love, Lucretia," he said gently. "Between two persons who love, it is called Making Love."

"Well, when you wish to do that, it is my Duty to Oblige you," I said, Some What Flurried, "even if I have not the—the Inclination."

He raised himself on one elbow to look down at me. "Making Love and Duty have nothing in Common. God Forbid that you ever give Yourself to me out of a Sense of Duty. I want you when you want me just as much. If ever you do not, you must tell me." He chuckled a Littel. "Of course, you must tell me tactfully, Sweet Heart. Most men, even yours, are a littel Sensitif about being Refused. Never the Less, I want you only when your Desire eqwals Mine, just as I would be Flattered for you Openly to Express your Desire for me."

"You would!" I could not help exclaiming, all Amazed.

There was a short Silense between us, then he asked agen the Qwestion that had begun our Conversation. "What are you thinking?"

"I am going over my Lesson," I said reddily. "I must be Allways Honest with you about my feelings, never come to your Embrase from a Sense of Duty, Refuse you if I wish but in a Way that Does not Offend you, and if I ever have the Inclination to Make Love, why then I am to tell you so."

He bent to kiss the tip of my nose. "You are a Very good Student," he praized me.

"Captain?"

"Yes?"

"Husband?"

"Wife."

"I think I—I—it is my Impression just now that I perhaps have the Inclination."

The sun was high overhead before we left our Cabbin.

CHAPTER
16

Philippa Jansen entered the room and, by repeating my name several times in an increasingly loud voice—"Mr. Ormont, Hey, Jake!"—finally managed to snatch me away from the eighteenth century.

At the same time, I was drawn back to reluctant awareness of the twentieth. The fire had died down long ago; my hands were chilled, and my feet were frozen. The room was damply cold; dark, too, for night had fallen.

"Jake, I have to dress now for dinner at some friends'. Would you like to stay on here and continue your reading after I've left?" she offered. "I've no objection; I'm not the least worried that you'll steal the pewter."

In spite of her courtesy, I knew I had been trespassing in her home for too long. Putting a curb on inclination, I refused quite firmly and was rewarded with a warm invitation to return as early as I wished the next morning.

In tearing spirits, I drove back to the motel and telephoned Bryarly. She answered on the first ring. Had she stayed around the apartment all day, I wondered, waiting —hoping for my call?

"Hello, Jake," she said before I could speak.

"How did you know it was me?"

"I just knew."

"The same way you knew I would find Cousin Lucretia and Philadelphia?"

I heard the sharp intake of her breath.

"Did you find them?"

"Yes. Answer *my* question."

"It wasn't quite the same. I've been waiting all day for your call. I was disappointed whenever the phone rang. This time I *felt* it was you. Just intuition."

"So your notion of a girl named Philadelphia wasn't simple intuition?"

"I've known for years she was out there somewhere. I wanted desperately to find her, but I didn't know where to look, or how, until I heard about your dream. It was confirmation. It also meant"—he could tell she was smiling —"that I could use you to do the leg work."

"So all along you knew that you and I had a common link—bond—past? Something?"

"Yes."

"I've got a lot of questions to ask you, young lady, but not on the phone, not now. There are more papers to go over, but no matter what, sometime tomorrow I'll come back to New York."

"Jake," she begged, "aren't you going to tell me anything you've learned?"

"Philadelphia was a colonial girl, which you already know. Cousin Lucretia was a kind of second mother to her. Mostly I've been reading about Cousin Lucretia, a jewel of a woman, incidentally. I'm not trying to be tantalizing, darling. I need a few more hours of study before I can talk fully and freely. I just wanted you to know I love you, and you weren't imagining things."

"I wasn't imagining things," Bryarly said aloud to herself after their good-bys. "But I've always known that. I just couldn't tell anyone before. I wouldn't have been believed."

She stumbled almost drunkenly to the bathroom. On the top shelf of the medicine cabinet was the pill box with its magic capsules. They brought quick oblivion to the insomniac, and later, when sleep had overtaken her body, the nightmare would overtake her mind. The patch nightmare with its piece of the past.

As she stood, hesitating, torn between the need to know and fear of the nightmare, a dim figure appeared behind her in the mirror. The head under the mobcap was gently shaking.

"Cousin Lucretia . . ."

Under the kind but unyielding stare of the blue eyes in the slightly scarred face, she put the pill box back on the shelf.

"I just wanted to see her before he comes back," she said defensively. "I wanted to be sure."

"You're sure," a soft voice echoed in her mind.

As a lightning flash of red darted across her vision, she staggered back in panic, throwing one arm across her face. The flash was gone almost instantly, but before her still-covered eyes was another picture . . . a young girl with flyaway blond hair, merry blue eyes and a laughing mouth. The laugh faded, the merriment died, and the flyaway blond hair lay all across the bowed shoulders and head. The girl was kneeling on the grass . . . no, not grass . . . grass wasn't like that. Red, so very red . . .

Stumbling, trying to get away from her mind's picture, she tripped over the bath mat. Philadelphia was gone—the flash of red was gone—but Bryarly lay sobbing on the floor.

Early the next morning, I took up *A Secret History* where I had left off the night before.

Journal of Lucretia Bogardus
River Cross Tavern
3rd April 1763

Impossibel that it is one year today since I was Wed, the time has gone so qwickly by. It has been the most Wondrously happy year of all my Life.

Flip and Filly are at the Manor House under the care of Thomasina, but Arend and I, out of Sentiment, choze to occuppy the Guest Parlour of the Tavern for Severall Days.

Mrs. Wallace, rejoyced to see me, is even now in the Cook House making my favourite Cheshire Pie. I told her Flip and Filly would joyne us for Supper and she snorted her Disdain that any Christian children should have such Heathenish sounding Names.

I exclaimed as I have innumerable times that Flip was the nearest Philadelphia could get her tongue about Philip's name when she was a Babe, and this Appellation has stuck to him ever since. As for Philadelphia, her father himself it was who so often called her "a Mettelsome Filly," that she, too, answers only to this name.

Annette stays in New York with the other children who cannot leave their Skooling, and Bram will arrive with them the end of May.

My Captain and I came on this long ahead to Attend to the Building of our House here so long Delayed. The plans are all Complete, and by summer's end the house should be, too, built Sheltering into the side of the Hill like a proper Dutch Farm House, and with the broad sweep of the Hudson below to please this Partickular Dutch Housfrau, to say nothing of my Husband, who grows Restless out of Sight of the Sea.

Journal of Lucretia Bogardus
30th July 1764

Obidiah arrives on the morrow from Philadelphia and Ben from New York to Spend the Month of August. Not since just before my Wedding have we all been Gathered, and to have it here in the Tarrytowns where we Lived and Worked Together in our Tavern Days . . . Bram is qwite wild with Exsitement. I, too. Oh Lord, what a Joyous Reunion it will be.

Journal of Lucretia Bogardus
Bogardus House, New York
3rd April 1765

I look to see my dear Husband home agen very soon now. Every day Ben brings me the news of Returning Vessels from the Indies. Never since we were Wedded have we been Parted so long, and never would I Consent to such a Parting agen. Broken Ankel or not, I should have gone with him. A Ship would have been no more Confining that the Couch to wich I have been Tied these many Weary Weeks. Thank God for Mr. Noel's Library. Annette changes my Books for me Twise Weekly or I would be in sad Case.

I must Confess I shed some silly Childish tears when I awoke alone in my Bed on this Morn. Today I am three Years married . . . and not to have Arend with me.

Late Evening of the Same Day

How Ungrateful I feel. How Rich I am. All my Loved Ones, save only that best Loved One of all, came tonite to do me Honour. We were a very Merry Party Indeed. The slitest remark set us off to laughter, be it Silly Family Jokes or Sly Mimickery of Friends and Naybors. Bram needed a Cushion for his Chair, and this provok'd as much Mirth as anything Else. It seems he had put a Mouse in the Schoolmaster's Desk and was well Rewarded with the *Roede* where he Deserved it.

Filly disregarded the conseqwences to Bram's Backside and Shreeked with Joy at his deskribing of the Dominie's Dismay when the Mouse did leap up out of the Drawer at him. I held my Peace abowt it, but well do I know my God-daughter, and I forsee that one Day in some School there will be a Mistress who meets with the same Fate.

This day that began with Tears ended with Joy, despite the Pangs of Separation that I am never free from so long as *he* is in one place and I another.

Journal of Lucretia Bogardus
Bogardus House
17th April 1765

On this Joyfull day my Husband did return to me! "Never agen!" I whispered when he Klasped me in his arms and he, who knows my Heart as I know His, did Ecko the same Vow. "Never agen. Where I go, you shall go, too."

Journal of Lucretia Bogardus
Old Amsterdam, Holland
9th August 1766

I think I shall never wish for a Letter agen!

I have been longing to hear from Home and wondering why for so long there have been no Letters, and then today there were Three at the Same Time, two of them having come from England first and been sent on to me by Mr. Worthington, my Husband's Business Agent in Great Britain.

The News of these Letters turned my Blood to Iced Water. Even before my Arend returned from his Day's Work, I set the Maids to Packing. I knew without telling what his Response would be to Cornelius' Plea.

Dear God, I go wild when I think of the Many Weeks till I can be Home agen to share the care of Annette with Cornelius, to help ease his own Grief, and to give the Comfort to the Children that they must Sorely Need.

Thank God for Thomasina. I am sure she is the one Stable Rock in a Family so Deranged, the Father Distrawt and the Mother Incapable of soothing their Infant Fears.

Thomas Hawley, STONE CUTTER
Cortlandtville, New York
August 8, 1766

Mr. Cornelius Van Duren
Pearl Street
New York City

Dear Sir:

I am in Receipt of yours of the 1st and have Modified the Specifications accordingly. I feel Certain that the Stone will meet with your Approval. It is of a large Double-Size, Rounded at the Top and Engraved in the Manner you dictated. I am Enclosing a Copy of the Design.

The Stone can be Delivered by Waggon whenever you so Desire. I shall await your Instructions pending your arrival at Van Duren Manor. Pray accept my Heartfelt Condolences on the Affliction under which you are Suffering.

Your Humble Obdt. Servant,
T. Hawley

1766

In Memory of JACOB, the son
of Cornelius and Annette Van Duren
He died July 9
Aged 10 years and 1 day
also
CARL, their son, who died the same day,
Aged 8 years, 5 months, 28 days
also
RACHEL, their first born child
Died five days later
Aged 13 years, 8 months, and 10 days.
Another daughter still-born on July 23.

Journal of Lucretia Bogardus
On Board the Sailing Ship William of Orange
18th August 1766

Arend is above Deck with Capt. Klockoff, and I have just Chozen to Torment myself by Reading a-new those Fatefull three letters and the two that arrived after them, Ben's in Partickyular, just before we Departed Holland. Between all five, I have Managed to peace together the Details of the Trageddy that has Struck my Cousin's House Hold.

By Arend's Arrangements made before we left our Country's Shores, Bram and Martinis and Pieter, those Insepperable Friends, departed the end of May for the Tarrytowns. Philip had been Unwell much of the Winter, with his uzual Consumptive Colds, which Indused Annette to send him with them under Thomasina's care. We have both Freqwently Notised that his helth allways Improoves at the Manor. He appears Inviggorated by the fresh

Country air of West Chester. When she heard the plan, nothing would do but that Philadelphia must go with the Boys. She is allways Helth itself, but her Dispozition is Happier in the Tarry-towns.

Annette and Cornelius were to Follow in a Fortnight with the other three Children and the rest of the Staff. Alas, it was not to be. Rachel fell ill of a fever first, though she was the last to Die. Jacob and Carl, the two boys, took to their beds next, Died and were Buried before her.

Three out of Six Beloved Children so qwickly Seezed, so soon Dead. Life can be a Bruttal Business. Cornelius' Grief I can well Imagine, for he was ever a Loving and Devoted Father. But Annette . . . when I think of her, I Tremble. Can her Mind and Body endurre this Trial? She is Gentil and far from Strong, not made for Sorrow. I fear she has not the Tough Fibers in her that are needed to Endurre great Tribbulations.

I weep for the three little ones, so young to Die before Ever they were given a Chanse to Live. And then, God Forgive me if it be wrong, but I cannot Help Myself, even as I pray for their dear Souls, I thank God for those that still Live. Surely it was by His Grace that Bram and Pieter and Martinis, as well as Flip and Filly, were gone from New York before the Fever Struck. By God's Mercy they were Spared, so I think he will not blame me for Rejoycing at their Deliverance.

Household Accounts Book
Van Duren House, Pearl Street
August 5, 1766

On this day I put up for sale this House of mine on Pearl Street, where I brought my Annette as a Bride, where our seven children were Born and four have so Recently Died.

It was done by Annette's Wish, the Second Wish that she has made since we have been Bereft. The First is already in Motion, and when the Summer is over, we shall Transfer the Final Resting Place of our Little Ones from Trinity Church Yard to our own land in Tarrytown.

Annette's second Plea was that we leave New York Forever. "There are 12 thousands of Souls crowded together in this City," she said to me. "How can it be otherwise than Unhealthy? Let us take those children we have left to us to live in the Country where the Air is Fresh and Clean so that they may be Spared to us."

I agreed without thinking what it would Mean. There is no Request I would not Grant her to Ease her Sorrow in the Slightest.

But now that I have time to Reflect, it seems the Best Plan. My Business here is in good hands, and I will Journey to the City from Time to Time. But in Tarrytown, I will have time to do many things I have Intended for Years, such as Treble my wheat crop and build a Shipping Dock so as to Transport Directly my Beaver Skins, grains, and other Crops. I will be able to Expand the Mill as well.

My Father, when he built the Manor House, meant for me to direct my Business Empire from there and live in it as Lord of the Manor. So now his Wish comes to Pass, though God has Afflicted me Sorely for this to Happen. His Ways are past Understanding.

Journal of Lucretia Bogardus
Cottage at the Tarrytowns
10th October 1766

A Sadder Site I never expect to see than today when the Waggon came from New York with its Sorrowful Burden of Coffins and a Mournfull Prosession of weeping Relatives wended their Way to the new-broken Ground of the Private Van Duren Cemetery to see the four littel Graves filled in and the single Large Stone raised over Them.

Tonite Arend and I talked together, and it is desided between us that we will Winter in the Tarrytowns. Annette and Cornelius are not yet in Condition to do Well without us, and so much I owe them for their many years of Kindness and Consideration that this seems but a small Return.

The Children need us even more. Pieter and Bram and Martinis are so Close, it would be Cruel to Deprive Pieter of his two good Friends when his Need has never been greater. He has become so Sobber, so sad, so unlike the playful boy he used to be. And Philadelphia, she Worries me much, alternating as she does between gusts of passionate tears and Storms of Temper. Philip sleeps Poorly, Thomasina tells me, crying oftimes in the Night with Troubled Dreams. I know what Preys on the poor Child's Mind, for

I was prezent once when he asked, "Am I going to Die, too?" Annette broke into such an Histerickal Fit of Weeping, there was no putting a Stop to it. We finally had to carry her to her Chamber and Resort to a Dosage of Laudanum to bring Sleep to her Tormented Spirit.

Journal of Lucretia Bogardus
The Tarrytowns
11th October 1766

Cornelius was Overjoyed to hear that I will be here to bear Annette Company. Sadly, I suspeckt he needs a little Relief from her Company himself, he knows not how to deal with her Exsess of Sorrow, and Allmost I begin to feel there is an Ellement of Blame in her Feelings. They dined with us at the Cottage today, and suddenly, heedless that there were Servants in the Room, she said. "You were Wize not to have Children, Lucretia. I shall not Bare any more to fill up Graves."

My heart went out to her, but even more to Cornelius, who Burried his face, grown qwite red, in a Beaker of Cider. I studyed my plate for the moment, not knowing what to say, but Arend, bless him, qwickly turned to talk, and Annette said nothing more.

Journal of Lucretia Bogardus
Bogardus Cottage
19th October 1766

Cornelius has desided to close the Tavern. I cannot help but feel a pang that this wich was a Happy Home to me should be relinqwished, but it is true, as Annette says, that the Children are constantly Lured to it. Now that the Family is in Permanent Residense here, she feels the Influence of the Tavern to be Undesirabell. I hold her Innocent of any Intent to Wound me by such Words, but I smile and sigh when I think of them, for the Annette I knew Beforetimes would have been more Thoughtfull.

The Schoolmaster arrives from New York within the Week. For the prezent time, the Front Guest Parlour of the Tavern will be the Schoolroom and the Chamber that was mine will go to him. The Overflow of Servants from the Manor House will use the Upstairs Rooms. Mrs. Wallace will come to me here.

Estate Book
Van Duren Manor
April 9, 1767

This day, 7 Years since she first entered my Household, I granted her Full Freedom to the Slave Woman known as Thomasina. She has taken the name of Free and henceforth will be known as Thomasina Free.

The three new Dependencies, which I had built on the Hill for my Servants, are now Completed. Thomasina Free, for her long and Faithful Years of Service to the Van Duren Family and her Nursing of my Daughter Philadelphia in her Infancy, shall have the Pick of these Shelters.

Journal of Lucretia Bogardus
Tarrytowns
27th April 1767

I took a long walk through the Woods today to Colleckt some Wild Herbs for Mrs. Wallace's Possets and came home Trembling with the Shock of what I Discovered. My Cousin Cornelius and Thomasina! How can it be? He such a Loyal Loving Husband and she so Despizing of Men!

When Cornelius bilt the three new Dwelling Places for his Servants and Farm Hands, we thowt it Nothing Strange that she get the Biggest and Best, even thow she is but one and the other Familied Men. Cornelius has Ever been Gratefull for her Loving Care of his Children. Annette was Satisfied, too, so long as she knew Thomasina would not leave the Manor House till after the Children were a-bed and is allways the first one Awake and Around there.

Now I know differently. I was coming down from the Hill and I slipt, as I freqwently do, my Ankel having always been week since it was Broke. I was not much Hurt, but I stayed on the Grownd for several seckonds Catching my Breath. In just those few Seckonds I saw Cornelius Emerge from Thomasina's Cabbin, first looking about in a Furtive Manner and then making a Speedy Dash for the Road. Still I did not understand, not untill Thomasina came to the Door and called after him. They met on the Road halfway, and she

Offered him Some Thing, Gloves, I think. They parted Swiftly, but not before, just for a Moment, he put his Hand to her Cheek. There was no misunderstanding this Jesture. Not Master to Servant, but Lovers! My Cousin Cornelius is Lover to his Servant and my Frend Thomasina.

Journal of Lucretia Bogardus
Bogardus House, N.Y.
15th May 1767

We are Home for just one week wilst Arend, at Ben's many Behests, attends to long-Negleckted Business. Then back to the Tarrytowns for the Summer Months.

We traveled Down River on Cornelius' new Hudson Vessel, *Sweet Annetje,* which Naming I might have fownd less Ironick a month since.

The two days on the River were a sheer Joy to me, and best was that I Finally unburdened my Heart to my Husband.

Arend surprized me Monstrously by not being Surprized nor even Critickal, being not Prepared to Condemn ither one. He pointed out to me that Annette no longer shares her Bed with Cornelius, nor has she since the Poor Littel Ones died, and that is near ten Months now.

"Cornelius is a man, not a monk," he reminded me.

I said Somewhat Weekly that Annette was Determin'd to bare no more Babes, as who could blame her.

"She could take the same Meazures to Prevent that you do," he Retorted. "No, no, Lucretia, Grief has Warped her some How, and she Seeks to Punish him. If she does not take Care, she may Destroy them both."

I cannot deny it. So I turned the Subjeck to Thomasina. How many times had she not Deklared her Hatred of Men and her Vow never agen to be Used or Abused by One!

To this Arend said Calmly that he saw no Evidense of Use or Abuse in the Case, did I not know Cornelius too well to Believe he would ever Forse himself upon any Woman, Servant or not?

He sat Beside me on our Bunk and presst my Two Hands. "Think of them as two Lonely Unhappy Persons who Seek a littel Comfort and Eaze of Heart's Pain with one another. Juge them not."

"But what should we do about it?" I Besaught him.

"Do? Why, nothing," he said firmly. "Do nothing, say nothing. Just continue to give them your Love and Understanding. Also," he added Forsefully, "your Silense."

He is so Rite, so Wise. A great Waight was lifted off my Heart by our Conversation.

Journal of Lucretia Bogardus
Bogardus House, N.Y.
28th November 1767

Two letters from Obidiah Harmer in Philadelphia, one to his Brother Ben and one to me, both Conveying the same News. He is Betrothed to his Benefactor's Youngest Girl and will turn Quaker to please her. They will wed in the Spring. What a pare of Children to be Setting up House, he will have barely made nineteen by the Time of the Wedding and his Sally is two Years Younger. How the Time goes . . . When I think of the Fearfull little Orphan'd Boy who first came to us at the Tavern, Afrayd to move out of his Brother's Shadow.

Arend is Prepared to be his usual generuss Self to one he knows I regard as part my Son . . . there will be monies to buy into Mr. Pendelton's Cabinet-making Buziness.

Journal of Lucretia Bogardus
Tarrytowns, the Cottage
1st July 1768

It grieves me Sorely to Return to West Chester after the long Winter and the Spring in Philadelphia and find that Matters between my Cousins are no Different than Before.

Annette and Cornelius are calm and Curteous with one Another, but that is a far Call from Warm and Loving as Once they were. Cornelius is very Busy about the Land and in his Estate Room, where he manages his Vast Enterprizes. Annette spends more and more time in her Chamber, freqwently days at a time in her Bed. And to be blunt, she is allways in her Bed Alone.

Thomasina Manages the Affaires of the House and Mothers the Children . . . yes, and I believe she still gives what my Arend calls "Ease and Comfort" to Cornelius when he Seeks her out.

It is the children who worry me the most. Not so much Pieter, who is as sturdy and solid and Dependable a little Dutchman as ever there was and looks after the others. But abouwt Flip and Filly, I am Sore Worried. Their Mother allternates between days of Negleckt and Fits of almost Obsessif Consern. She fusses about there Cloathing and Food, and above all, there Helth. Philadelphia laughs this off, but Philip has become overly Conserned about Himself in an Unbecoming Way. But what can be expeckted with a Mother who is known to see nothing of him one Week and weep because he Sneezes the next?

Cornelius' little Filly is the most Loving Child there ever was, but she is becoming Wild to a Fault, being allow'd to Run out of Control. Martinis, I am sorry to say, now that our Coming has browt them Together agen, encourages her Behaviour as he allways did. He has the same Touch of Wildness. But I have spoken to Bram, and he will speak to Pieter. These two will try Some What to Check the Exuberanse of the Others.

Journal of Lucretia Bogardus
Tarrytowns
3rd September 1768

Each Year we grow more and more Relucktant to tear Ourselves away from the Beauty of West Chester to return to the City. This Year we plan to stay on untill after St. Nicholas Day and Twelfth Night, returning to New York in January for the Winter Months. Then we will Hasten back here in Early Spring.

Bram and Martinis are Delighted. Little Indians that they are, they feel more at Home in the Woods of West Chester and on the Shores of the Hudson than on City Pavemints; but Ben must, of course, be much Separated from us as Arend counts on him in his Business. Mayhap it is just as well. He is more a man than a boy now, almost one and twenty and may want his own Home one day Soon.

Pieter, Flip and Filly are Overjoy'd not to Lose their Dear Companions, and they will all go to School together at the Tavern. I allways think of it thus, never as the School House. Mr. Hook is an able Instrucktor and Deals with the Children well, being Kind but

Firm, Understanding the peckulyer Problems of my Cousin's children with Regard to their Mother.

Journal of Lucretia Bogardus
Tarrytowns
2nd December 1768

The Indian man, Joseph Long Horn, has faithfully Deliver'd to us the five Indian Costooms that Arend Ordered made this Autumn past to prezent to the four boys and Filly on St. Nicholas Day. They are made of the Softest Buckskin, with the Trowsers fringged from Waist to Ankel and the Wammuses fringged all about the Bottom and the Length of the Sleeves. The boys' are all Plane, but on Filly's Wammus there is some Intrickate Beading. I can Scarcely Waite to see the Children's Pleazure in these Outfits and how they will look in them.

Journal of Lucretia Bogardus
18th December 1768

Oh, the Delight of them all when they Beheld their Indian Dress! They lined up, my five Littel Indians, in Order of their Size and Age . . . Pieter, Bram, Martinis, Philadelphia, Philip . . . Even Annette showed some Animation at the Remarkable picture of Helth and Beauty they Prezented. I long to paint them as they looked, but it is Impossible to get the five to stand still so long . . . I am doing some Charcoal Sketches, and I will try to Paint a Portrait from these Drawings.

Journal of Lucretia Bogardus
Tarrytowns
11th January 1769

Cornelius Informs me that there will be a Sixth Littel Indian soon. Mr. Hook is returning home to Connecticutt, where he will take up his Divinity Studys at Yale, and the new Dominie who will now Dwell at the Tavern is a Widower with a Son of ten or eleven. I have reqwested Cornelius to send for the boy's Meazurements that I may have another Indian Costoom made up, as I would not wish one Child to be Different from the Others.

Cornelius has not seen the Man. He hired him by Corresspondense, on the Referese of Adolph Phillips at Phillipsburg Manor. I trust he may be as Addept at Handeling our Devilish Pranksters as Mr. Hook.

Filly's Journal
Van Duren Manor
Jan. 20, 1769

Ant Lucretia gave me this Book. She sed she began her Journal wen she was Nine, and I am near enuff to that so it was Time I started Mine.

It is a Gorjuss Book with silky pages and a Lether Binding. The cover has my name in Gold Letters. Unkel Arend calls it Embosst. It ses:

Philadelphia Lucretia Van Duren
Her Journal

That's my Batismal Name, but I like it better to be just Filly. Ant Lucretia sez a Journal is like a Buzom Frend, you can tell it all your Thowts and Feelings, and she sent Karl to my room wen there was no One Arownd to Bild a Secret Plase where I can Hide it and not Wory that one of the Boys will Sneek up and Reed it.

Filly's Journal
Jan. 25, 1769

Flip is in Bed with a Swollen Knee and he cumplaned it is Boaring so Pa is letting Mr. Derwent give him Fife Lessons two times a Week. We close all the doors wen he Praktisez, it sounds Terribel, but I wud like to learn the Fife myself wen I hear Mr. Derwent. Mama sez No, it is not Genteel for a girl. She wants me to have Harpsikord Lessons. I hate the Harpsikord. Flip sez never mind, he will teach me the Fife after Mr. Derwent teaches him. Dere Darling Unkel Arend sez he will send to New York for a Fife for me if Pa is Willing. I will make him Willing.

Filly's Journal
1st Feb., 1769

I will beginn this Month by saying that I think I hate the new Skoolmaster. He is tall and skinny and Strait like a split Oke Logg, and his Fase looks like Mrs. Wallas might have Pickeled it in Brine alongg with her Pepers. Only he is all smileing wen Mama and Pa are by. He is a Hipokrit!

I hurd Pieter tell Bram he looks like he has the Parler Poker stuk up his Reer end, and they both laffed, but wen I laffed, they both skolded me for being Vulger. Boys are so unfare. All eksept Martinis. He never Preeches at me to think and Beehave lady-like.

Journal of Lucretia Bogardus
Tarrytowns
20th January 1769

It is not my Place to say so to Cornelius, but I like not his new School Master, Mr. Kerstan Bruegel. He is a grimm and Humourless appearing Man, smacking too much of Self-Rightiousness. The Truly Godly man Practises his Religion rather than Proclaimes it. Mr. Bruegel is a Proclaimer!

I have never Favoured tall men lest they be well-bilt, and this one is Tall and Spare, with flapping arms and Twiching hands. He would look Naturel, I think, with a *Plak* attached to one set of his Fingers and a *Roede* to the other. Indeed, he express'd his disappointment to Cornelius over the Rule that he was not to use the Birch.

Arend made Mock of a speech he over heard him Address to Cornelius at Supper this Nite when we were all bid to the Manor. "I am Fare and Deliberate in Meeting out Punishment, but I must Confess I am a great Believer in Dissapline for the Young and Impressionable."

Thank the Lord Cornelius merely Smiled and Noded, saying he Preferr'd to Dissapline his Children himself, but would Welcome any Report from Mr. Bruegel of their Misconduckt. From the Sowr Look on that Gentilman's Face, I would Hazzard there will be many such Reports made.

It is Arend's Oppinion, and I am of the Same Mind, that the child Dierk is Afeared of his Father, wich I cannot like. Helthy Respeckt is one thing, Fear qwite another. I know many Parents believe it to be Nessessery, but I cannot Agree. Better to Rule thru love than thru Fear, say I.

Dierk is past eleven and large for his Years. He seems a Pleazant boy, mayhap a little on the Dull side, but I am grown used to our Wild Indians. He did, However, look Gleefull on lerning that he is to have full Indian dress of buckskin Breeches and Wammus just like the Others.

7th of Feb. 1769
School House

My dear Mr. Van Duren:

I feel it to be my Duty to report to you that on more than one Occassion this week Past your Daughter Philadelphia was both Pert and Sausy, also she does not always pay as Proper Attention in Class as I would Desire. Philip is Lazy and does not Prepare his Work. When I take him to Task, he pays no Heed. He is Exceeding Careless in his Penmanship. I am more Pleased with Pieter, who is Bright and Quick in his Lessons, but a Proper Attitude of Respect to me as Master is Lacking.

Your Hmble. Obdt. Servant,
Kerstan Bruegel

7th of Feb. 1769
School House

Dear Captain Bogardus:

It grieves me to Inform you that I am most Dissatisfied with both the School Work and the Conduct of your Nephew, Martinis. He is Idle and Disrespectful, he Disrupts the Class and Indulges in Profanity Shocking for one of such Tender Years. More Over, the younger Pupils ape him, my own son not Excluded, for which he was well Whippt. The Brain is not at Fault. Martinis has as much quickness of Mind as any other in this Class but Chooses not to Exercise it. Reprimands do no good. In my oppinion, Stern Measures from you are called for.

Bram, on the other Hand, is my best Pupil but Sometimes his Manner to me is Insolent.

Your Hmble. Obdt. Servant,
Kerstan Bruegel

196

School House
3rd of March 1769

Dear Mr. Van Duren:

During Recess Play your daughter Philadelphia used a word that brought a Blush to my own Cheeks, yet she a Young Maid was Unashamed when I confronted her. I attempted to take her into the School House to Wash out her Mouth with Soap, whereupon she Kicked my Shins and Ran Away, nor did she return for the Afternoon Session. I must Urge you to Punish her, and I desire an Apologgy for her Gross Behavior when she is Returned to my School.

Your Hmble. Obdt. Servant,
Kerstan Bruegel

School House
4th of March 1769

Dear Mrs. Bogardus:

It was most Kind of you to Bestow on my Son the set of Indian clothing, and I thank you on his Behalf. I Consider this Dress very Suitable for Play but not, However, for the Class Room. I must ask that when Bram and Martinis come to the School House, they are properly Garbed, like Christian children.

Your Hmble. Obdt. Servant,
Kerstan Bruegel

School House
10th of April 1769

Dear Mr. Van Duren:

Philip's Penmanship Improves, also his Work, but he has Some Way to go before I would be entirely Satisfied that he is Performing as he Should. Pieter continues to do well, and Philadelphia has been less Sausy except on the Subjeckt of which Studies are more Fitting for those of the Female Sex. For Example, against my Express Wishes, she brings her Fife to School to play at recess with her brother. *Please exert your Authority in this matter.*

Your Hmble. Obdt. Servant,
Kerstan Bruegel

School House
19th of April 1769

Dear Capt. Bogardus:

Martinis Depicted on his Slate this Week a most Irreverent Drawing of Myself in Company with the Devil. Of the Occupation on which we were Engaged in this Drawing I prefer not to speak. The Boy maintains that your Esteemed Wife encourages him in his Artistick Endeavors, but I cannot Believe she would approve of Blasphemy and Obscenity.

Your Hmble. Obdt. Servant,
Kerstan Bruegel

School House
22nd of May 1769

My dear Mr. Van Duren:

I feel it to be my Duty to inform you that last Sabbath I was walking along the Shore and, not far from the home of Capt. Bogardus, off that Piece of Land the children call the Island, I came upon all of them Swimming in the River. The Boys had Stript down to their Small Clothes and Philadelphia had on only her Shift! Nor did she seem Aware of the Enormity of her Immodesty no matter how I Exhorted with her. Such Brazen Tendencies in her could lead, I fear, to Shame and Trouble in the Future.

Your Hmble. Obdt. Servant,
Kerstan Bruegel

Journal of Lucretia Bogardus
Tarrytowns
30th May 1769

This day I think I know how God felt when the Creation was

Complete. I have Finished my Portrait that has Absorbed me all the Winter. Dozens of Sketches I have drawn of each child Separate, and now they are all Put Together, looking as they did that day at the Island last month when the River crack'd Open and began flowing Freely.

Filly is in the Four-Front, her leggs Planted Apart, holding a Fishing Pole, and Flip Leans, Laffing, over her Shoulder, seeming to show her the Way of holding it. Except that her Hair is a more Golden colour and Clubbed with a Riband falls longer down her back, so Like they are, they might be Twins.

Bram and Pieter, just behind the Two, are Engagged in a Friendly Tussle, wilst Martinis uses a broken Tree Branch to tease Dierk, who Teeters on a Haff Submurged Logg so that Dierk looks in Imminint Danger of Falling into the Hudson.

The most Striking Feeture of the Portrait is the Identikal Garb of all of them, their Buckskin Breeches and Fringged Wammusses. Not so, said Arend. He thinks the Portrait Outstanding because the Body Proportions are so exackt and I have Executed the Faces with great Skill. Those were his Very Words, and I would not feel Prouder of Praise from John Wollaston or Jeremiah Theus than this Jugement from my own Husband who Pays me the Compliment of Considering me as great an Artist as ither of them.

The Portrait is also a Formidable Size. Framed, it will be even more so. But I care not, I am so Happy with the Finished Work. I shall call it "Six Little Indians At Play."

Oh Lord, but I am Weary. I have Painted all the daylite Hours this Entire last Month.

Arend just called me to Bed for the third Time, but I told him I was too Existed to Sleep.

"You will Sleep, my Love," he said in his calm sure Way that cannot qwite Hide from me his Passion.

I have begun to Tremble. Seven Years wed, and he can still do this to me. I must put away my Journal and Snuff the Candle. My Love awaits me.

Journal of Lucretia Bogardus
3rd June 1769

Praise the Lord, I need never agen Read and Consine to the Fire one of Mr. Bruegel's Tedjus Complaining Weekly Reports.

I went to the Estate Offise at the Manor House this morn for the very Purpose of informing Cornelius that Arend and I will reside in New York come next Winter so that Bram and Martinis may Attend Latin School to prepare Themselves for Kings Collegge. I thought that Pieter should Attend Likewise and was Prepared to Argue the Point, but Cornelius gave me no Argument. He Agreed at once. I do not Envy his Need to tell Annette, who will be Wild with Fear for the life of her Son in the Impure Air of the City. But though he Indulges her Smallest Whim, Cornelius can be Firm, not to say Stubborn when he feels in the Rite.

I also Interfered, agenst Arend's Wishes, in stating my Oppinion that Mr. Bruegel is not a Proper Person to be School Master over such Hi-Spirited Young Ones as ours. Agen, I was Surprized at his Instant Agreement. Cornelius had allreddy come to the same Conclusion.

He tells me, How Ever, that Mr. Bruegel is so Brillyent at Computing Figgures in his Head with Speed and Ackurasy, his Mathematickal skills will be of much Use in the Buziness Side of the Estate.

So it is allredy Setteled that the Estate Offises shall be Moved to the Tavern and Mr. Bruegel shall Live on there with Dierk, Keeping all Books and Reckords and Otherwize helping with the Business as he is needed. Since his Wage is Increased by Double, he is more than Happy.

The prezent Estate Offise in the Manor House shall be the School Room, and a living-in Tuttor will be hired for Flip and Filly, with Dierk sharing in the Lessons.

I feel greatly Relieved.

Filly's Journal
Sept. 12, 1769

I feel Mizzerabull! Martinis and Pieter and Bram have gone to New York with Ant Lucretia and Unkel Arend. Our new Tuttor Mr. Vorst arrives this Week and our Lessons will Beegin. If he is anything like Mr. Bruegel, I will be Awful Unhappy. But he is a frend of dere Mr. Hook, so probalee he will be Nise. I hope so.

Mr. Derwent says if I Per-Vesere I will be a real good Fifer. I intend to Per-Vesere becus I love to play the Fife.

Filly's Journal
Sept. 20, 1769

Tomasina browt my Supper Tray to my Room. I had to Eat it off the Mantel. I could Kill Dierk, it's all his Falt. Well, Maybe not all. It was me who kept saying, Don't be a Fraydy Cat, let's go Swiming. Tomasina sed it was Injun Sumer and we were Wering our Injun Close, and it was so Hot.

I was alone with Dierk becus Flip coffed twise at Brekfust and Snezd Wunce, so Mama sed he must stay in the Parler near the Fire, with Cloves to Sweetin the Air and some of Tomasina's Posits to Drink. He had a good Book so he dint Mind too much, but I did. I had no one to play with but Dierk. He's no funn without the Others. He has no Imachinashun.

So Finally I sed, well, What Ever *you* do, Cowardy Cat, I'm going Swiming. We were at the Illand, and I took off every Thing but my short Shift and went rite in, it was coldish but not too cold, and I showted to him it was Grand, so he took off his Wamos and Briches and came in, too.

Just wen we were coming out of the Water, Pa came by on his Horse. He was looking at Unkel Arend's Sheep and hurd us Splashing.

Pa sed, looking very Sad, Filly, I thowt you new you were forbid to Swim here with the boys. Of corse I new, and I only gigeld becus I was nervus. But Pa stopt looking sad and looked Mad insted, and the next thing I new he was Braking off a Willo Swich and Turning me under his Arm.

My Brothers and Cuzins wud have the Desensy to Walk Away so as not to embariss me, but Dierk just stood there, hopping up and Down, and every time Pa landed me a Lick, he let out a Yell or a Skweal, any one wud have Thot *he* was the one getting his Botum Swiched.

Pa stopt, but Dierk still kept standing there saying, Ooh don't, pleez don't, Mr. Van Duren. So finalley, I turned my head to look at him, wich wasn't eezy, Pa still had a Strangeld-Hold on me, and I sed to him, Will you pleez shut the hell up, I'm the One getting Hit.

He skwealed agen and ran away, and I had a crik in my nek, so I sed to Pa, real Polite, Pa, can I pleeze get up now?

Pa just firmed his Hold. Wat went beefor, he sed, was for the Swiming, this is for your langwich. Then he started all over agen but harder and Longer, so like I sed, tonite I ate Standing up and I gess Ill have to sleep on my Stummick.

Jan. 28, 1770

Dear Filly,

You shed enough tears on our Leaving after 12th Night to Overflow the Banks of the Hudson. If I hear of Flooding in the Tarrytowns, I will know who to blame.

Cheer up, little Coz, we will all be back Together in June, which is not that far away.

No need to Fret that your Indian dress don't fit you any more. I have Grown out of mine, too, and you may Have it. Only it has a big Ripp on the Inside Breeches legg from the Branch that time I got Caught in the Oak. Thomasina will have to Sew it for you. Aunt Lucretia says to look for it in the Bottom of the big Hall Cupboard.

One of our Fellow Students has played the Fife these five years. I give you my word he has not nearly Flip's Skill or Yours.

Your Friend,
Bram

Jan. 28, 1770

Dear Little Sister:

Martinis made a Wagger with Bram and me. He said you can't Possibley go from now untill our Return without getting into Trowbel. The Wagger is for 10 shillings, so why don't you help us win it and we will split the Take with you? All you must do is mind your Manners, your Tunge, and your Temper.

On Second Thought, it is a Fools Wagger, two Fools Wagger. You to stay out of Mischeff for an Entire Four Months! We must have been Foxed when we made it. Martinis as good as has our monies in his Pocket.

More seriously, I am glad our Parents continue Well. Do get Flip out of the House when you can. There is more to Life than reading Books or Playing on the Fife. He is too much Indoors Cossetting himself, which no one could ever Accuse you of. And also be Carefull of Yourself. I joke, but I have only the one Sister, and I do not want that One getting herself Hurt.

Your Loving Brother,
Pieter Van Duren

28 Jan. 1770

Hey Filly, all I can say is Lattin Skool isn't bad, but I wish Lattin had staid a Dead Langwage. Its all Rot too on Akount of I have no intenshun of going to Kings Colledge. I want to go to Sea Like Unkle Arend did at forteen. Ill stik this out till then, then thats it. Now dont go Blabbing this to anyone till I'm reddy. I don't want any Fuss, so its our Sekret for another Year or so.

Say, did you here about the wagger I made over you with Bram and Piet? They really are eazy Marks.

Its niser here than I thot, but I like the Tarytowns best. Stay out of Trowbel, Brat, or mebbe I shunt Wish that till my Bet is Won.

Martinis

Journal of Lucretia Bogardus
Tarrytowns
22nd August 1772

Filly came by this noon time and stayed thru dinner. She had been Fishing alone on the Island, Flip being Kept at home with a Cold. I think our little Philadelphia is Some What Forlorn about the State of Affaires here. Despite Martinis' being still away to the Indies, she is yet so Young in Mind, she thought all would be Unchang'd Once the boys came Home agen.

But Pieter spends more time helping Cornelius about the Estate than with his Fellow "Indians." Mr. Vorst is Tuttoring Bram to prepare him for Oxford, where Arend has set his Heart that he shall go the Year after this one. Even Dierk Bruegel is much away, for thru Offises of Cornelius' Friend Philip Van Cortlandt, he has been Akcepted to Study with the Evanjelist George Whitfield.

My poor little girl. She is Poysed precarriously between Childhood and being a Woman and does not care for ither State.

Filly's Journal
May 28, 1773

I am getting Buzoms. They are not very bigg, but they must be bigg enuff because I have been notising now that its Spring and I dont need a Cloke that the Farm Boys notise me. They keep staring at the Front of my Bodiss when I come by. I dont reely Mind. The only one I dont like staring at me is the Der Horst boy Tomas, the one the Indians call Tom Dumb. He cant help that he is a Simpel Simon; Pa says the Der Horsts have had a Simpel One in each Litter for three Generashuns, but the way *he* looks at my Buzoms makes me feel Sqwirmy.

I wonder if Martinis will like my having them. I spose he shud if we are going to be Wedded someday. I wudnt Mind if Martinis looked at them, but he is Different than Any One else.

Filly's Journal
July 3, 1773

I could kill Martinis. He's a Beest. He came Home yesterday just for abowt ten days and this morning we Crept out erly and went to the Island, and I aksed him abowt my Busoms. He sed where he's just been Buzoms are relly Buzoms and even in Westchester he's seen Pinn Hedds bigger than what I have. I slapt him and he just laffed, and I cry'd and ran away from him. Bram was nise when he fownd me crying. He explained to me the Ladies in the Indies are Bigg and Buxum, but that wunt be konsidered so attraktive in New York, and some Day I will be verry pritty in my own Stile.

Journal of Lucretia Bogardus
Tarrytowns
7th July 1773

My dear boys Bram and Martinis are home with us but soon to go away, Both of Them, Martinis to sea again and Bram to Oxford in England. My Heart is allreddy sore with the Pain of missing them, and yet I must be Glad, for I am Sorely Troubled by Some Thing that happened Yesterday and then agen this day. I need my Sensible Arend to tell me that I am building Mountains out of Mole Hills, but of it I have not yet Spoken to him. Later, perhaps, when they are Gone.

It seems that just after he Arriv'd, Martinis and Filly had one of there Silly Sqwabbels that the rest of us have Grown Accustommed to, but this One more Serious for she would not speak to him for Two Entire Days, and it is Unlike Filly to hold a Grudge!

She and the boys all came to Dinner with me yesterday in the Family Dining Parlour. The boys Teezed Filly, as they allways do, and she Responded to all save Martinis. When she jumped up to help Mrs. Wallace with the Cleering Up, he followed her into the Kitchen. I wached him take her by the showlders and turn her abowt to him. I did not heer their Words, but I could understand the Import. It was not there Making Up I objeckted to but rather the Manner of it.

She was barely out of Swaddeling Cloathes when she seemed to set her Heart and Mind on Martinis, and in the Family we allways Regarded this as a Prime Jest. But now she is both too old and too Young for it to be a Jest, and there was that in her Manner, in *Both* there Manners to say they were no longer Jesting, and my Heart Misgives me. I love them both so, and they are not for each other.

I sense, I have allways Sensed there is deep Passhion in our Philadelphia. She will give an Abiding Love and Loyalty to the Man she Choozes and brake her Heart if it be not Returned in the same Full Overflowing Meazure. Martinis will love Lightly and Often, it his Way. In this one Important way, they are Utterly Unlike, and in all other ways they are too much the Same . . . Impulsive . . . Impetuous . . . Reckless . . . Mischiffous . . . Hi-Spirited, Qwicksilver the both of them, qwik to Flame up in Temper and eqwally qwik to Recover. They are not for each Other. In my Heart and my Bones, I feel it, I know it.

I wached them both, arms linked, as they went out of Doors thru the Kitchen, carelessly leaving the Bottum Half of the Door open. A baby Lamb started pushing its way into the Kitchen and Thomasina went to shuve it outside agen, shutting the Door.

"You must not worry, Aunt Lucretia," said a voice beside me.

Starteled, I turned to find Bram looking at me, the Familyer Wize Old look of Concern on his Face that he has ever shown to the World.

He patted my hand gently even as Words of Denyal died on my Lips. I have allways been Honest with Bram.

"They are just playing Games now," he went on, "but the Sea is Martinis' real love and when the rite Time comes, Filly will know he is not for her."

"I hope so," I said aloud to Bram. Dear God, I hoped so, for both their Sakes.

That was Yesterday.

Today I was up at the Manor House and wilst I vizited with Thomasina in the Kitchen, they all came down begging for some of her Ginger Bred to take to the Island. Flip and Martinis and Pieter ran off with there Pockets stuff'd, but Filly stopt a bit to talk to me and Bram lingered, making as Excuse, I realized Afterwards, that he was Thirsty. Thomasina fetched him a tankard of Cider, and wilst he drank Philadelphia dansed arownd the Cooking Fires, cheking what was in the Pots for Supper.

Bram spoke up more disagreebly than I have ever Herd him Speak to her. "Take care, you Fool!" he commanded Filly. "You are too near the Fires."

Knowing the erly Traggedy of his Mother that has Haunted him all his Life, I understood. But not Filly. She cast him a Sausy Look, lifted her skirts a littel and started Dansing arownd the Open Hearth fires and jumping over the Mownds of Hot Coals where no pots swung.

Bram swore a great Oath and started to her, and as she Dansed away from the Hands that were Streching out to her, she let go her petticoats and the edgges touched the Coals and started to Smolder.

For Bram it must have been all his old Nitemares come True, saving that, Thank God and Thank *him*, this time there was no Traggedy. He had knocked her to the grownd and stamped out the smoldering ends before her skirts could flame up, even before Thomasina could Return from the Dining Parlor with the Blanket she had run fleetly to fetch.

Bram pulled Filly to her feet. She was crying noizily, more in Fright than anything else, she had Sustained no hurt. She reeched out to Bram to be Comforted and was insted gifted by him with a swinging box first on one ear and then the Other. "You bloody littel Fool!" he snarled at her. "I shud shake you Silly."

Even as Filly put both her hands over her smarting ears, shaking her head a littel, dazed by the Suddenness of his Attack, Bram slammed out of the Kitchen, Stumbling Blindly into the Storeroom. I dont think, in his Remembered Angwish, he knew what he was doing.

Filly, still holding onto her ears, began to Bleet about what a Beest Bram was, but this once I had no Patiense with her Crotchetts.

"Not only has he just saved your Life," I said Severely, "but he is perfectly Rite. You are a Fool." She looked Stricken, but I dint allow that to stop me. "Have you never heard," I asked her, "that he Watched his mother Die in just such Fashion, her skirts flaming up from the Coals of a Cooking Fire, turning her into a Torch?"

"I d-dint know. N-no B-body ever told me-me," she stammered out, Wide Eyed.

Then she turned and fled after him, and I walked near to the door to Observe them. Bram stood Motionless at the far end of the Room with his head prest agenst a Shelf on wich stood the new-made Wheels of Cheese. She came up Behind him and stood up on her Toes to put her Arms arownd him.

"Bram, dear Bram, I'm so sorry I upset you, and I thank you for saving such a Bloody Littel Fool as I am," she said in the melting Way that none in ither of our Families has ever been known to Resist.

Bram turned About slowly, facing her, his Feetures still hard and Distant.

"You can shake me silly if you Wish," Filly coaxed him. "You can even Box my ears agen if you want. It hurt, but not so much as it Hurts to have you Dislikeing me."

Her Tears had been falling for some Time, but now she began to Weep in good Ernest, and this time he was no more Proof agenst her Weeping than ever he had been.

He pulled her head agenst his Chest and comforted her like a Child, speaking half in Dutch, half in English. It was the Dutch endeerments that caused Thomasina, who had come up Behind me, to exchange Starteled Looks with me.

"Hush, hush, *mijn kleintje,* dont weep, *mijn kleine liefe.* I meant

207

not a Word of it, nor to hurt you nither, it was just that you Frightened me so, *mijn hartewensch.*"

Prezently they were both qwiet and stood there, seemingly Content, while Thomasina and I stole away, saying nothing, but both of us Understanding and Appalled.

When the two came out agen to the Kitchen, it might all never have happened, but I know in my Heart things will never be the Same agen.

She is too young, too young, our darling Philadelphia, but allreddy her Heart is given to Martinis and his to the Sea wilst now it is plane to see that it is no Cousinly or Brotherly love Bram feels for her.

When Filly ran off, Bram linger'd in the Kitchen a Moment.

"Dear Aunt," he said softly, and then, "Thomasina. Be not Affeart, ither of you. I know what a child she is yet. Why do you think I was willing to go to Oxford? She needs Time, and I can Wait. I have been waiting for her all my Life."

"Martinis?" I Reminded him hezitantly.

He smiled, Undaunted. "A child's Fancy. And to Martinis, she is a sister, a frend, not near so exsiting as the Sea or the Exottick Women he will find in Distant Ports. No, believe me, she is Mine, she has allways been Mine. One day," he said Confidently, "she will know it, as I do."

He repeeted before he left us, "Do not Worry."

But how can I help it?

Journal of Lucretia Bogardus
8th of July 1773

Arend, who is allways Cawtious about Interference, has urgged Strongly that I perswade Cornelius to send Philadelphia away to Skool.

So be it. I shall try.

Filly's Journal
July 22, 1773

Martinis is gone agen and Bram takes Sail for England next Week. It will be so dreadfull this Winter with them both far away and Pieter staying in New York with Aunt Lucretia and Unkel Arend.

Even Worst, Grate Aunt Katrina has come to stay for a Full Month. Pa sez she allways Deesends on her Family in turn, and we shud Konsider ourselfs Lucky its been five years since the last Vizit. But I dont Konsider anything abowt Grate Aunt Katrina Lucky. Unkel Arend sez shes a Wich and Pieter sed shes a Prize Bich, and I agree with Piet.

She Pokes her Nose in Every Thing that Dont Consern her and she tells us all what we shud do and Today she was down in the Kitchen ordering Tomasina abowt till it made my blud boil, saying her Receets werent good and hers were better and Critisizing her Pots and Pans that they were not Cleen and finally when Tomasina spoke up a bit Sharp abowt having to get on with her Work, Aunt Katrina hit the top of her hedd with her fan. It dint hurt, I spose, Tomasina's got so much hair piled on top, but what rite did she have to hit Tomasina? Im going to make her Sorry she did that, reel Sorry, if its the last Thing I ever do. Ill think of Some Thing, see if I dont.

Journal of Lucretia Bogardus
25th July 1773

The Preechers all tell us that God moves in misterious Ways, and indeed I beginn to believe it, having now the Evidense of my own Eyes. Who would have believed that a Field Mouse, a Chamber Pot, Grate Aunt Katrina and a Peace of Filly's Mischeff could have led to a Rekonsiliation betwixt Annette and Cornelius, resulting Further in the Separation of Flip and Filly (which Arend and I have long Considered would be best for the Two) as they attend Seperette Skools?

Aunt Katrina has resided with Annette and Cornelius these past ten days, acting the while her uzual disagreeble Self, critisizing the boys, nagging at Filly. Even Annette Objeckted to having Pointed out to her her Defishensies as a Mother. As for Cornelius, he is Livid!

My Arend, after partnering Aunt Katrina at Supper one nite, said firmly that Once is Enuff, and he will Stop at home till she Departs the Manor. Her sharp Tonge, said he, was bad enuff, but he Found it even more Painfull to sit or stand Down Wind of Some One so proud of preserving the Naturell Oils of her Body, she is utterly Averse to the use of Soap and Water!

Several days ago there was an Eppisode with Thomasina in the Manor Kitchen. Thomasina remained Tranqwil, but it threw Filly into a Temper. She can never Bear to see Thomasina slited. Piet told me the Entire Story of how Filly got Revenged. It was Reprehensibill, but I had to be Amuzed. As for Arend, he laughed untill he Cried.

Hi-Ho, I am weary and will save the rest for another day.

Letter fragment in Annette Van Duren's handwriting

My dear Joanna:

I write in haste and in hopes that this letter arrives at your Home in Red Hook before Aunt Katrina does. I know that, having decided to leave Us, she proposes to make your home what dear Arend dubbs her "next Port of Call." May God give you and your family strength, dear Joanna. She is indeed a Trial, and her Interferences in my Household Affaires has wrecked Havock among the Servants and Children and destroyed the peace of All. Happy we will be to see her Leave us even though

Van Duren Manor
25th July 1773

My Dear Bram:

How I have Envied you these past two weeks, facing nothing more fearfull than the Dangers of the deep Atlantic while we have shivered under the Frightening Onslaught of a visitation from Great-Aunt Katrina.

Happily, and thanks entirely to our Philadelphia, she took her Premature Departure yesterday morn.

Pa, though expressing himself much Mortified to have a guest abused under our Roof, was to my mind as Pleased as the rest of us though not so Honest in saying so.

It happened because Filly was greatly Incensed by

Aunt's Insolence to Thomasina and decided to pay her Back. Do you recollect a certain mouse in the school-master's desk when you were a lad? Well, our little Filly made your Escapade seem Trifling.

You know what a stubborn old Dutchwoman Aunt is. She had declined to sleep in the Four-Poster Bed in the best guest Chamber, choosing instead (to be sure no Breath of Night Air might reach her) to Install herself in the Box Bed in the small downstairs Chamber. She also insisted that the Bed Cord be Repared, which one of the estate men did while we Supp'd, so that she might have it to grasp to keep herself sitting Uprite wilst she Slept. The old Witch really Believes the Devil might come for her Soul if she lay Prone! (Perhaps, on second Thoughts, she is not so far Wrong about that.)

The Cream of the Jest, however, is that she keeps her Chamber Pot, instead of Beneath her bed, on the Cubboard Shelf Within it. This Filly learned of from the House maid Leah, and knowing Filly's Fertile Brain, can you not guess the Rest?

Joe Nease's boy Danny procurred the Mouse for her in a little Box she provided complete with a bit of Straw and a generous Portion of Cheese. In the night, just before Aunt Retired, Filly had only to Creep into her Chamber and bait the Trap—or should I say the Pot?

The House was deep in Sleep when Aunt had her Call of Nature. The Mouse, replete with sleep and cozily at rest on its Bed of Straw, was Naturally Affronted by its rude Awakening. It protested in the Livelyest Manner being Subject to such Indignity, producing such piercing shreeks from Aunt Katrina as brought the entire House-hold awake and crowding into her Bedchamber.

Pa was only a little Behindhand in Grasping the Situation. I had Comprehended a bit before him but Wisely kept my Silence. Pa restored Order and helped Capture the Mouse, which, betwixt us, was far more Frightened of Aunt Katrina than Aunt Katrina of the Mouse. He then sent away the Gaping Servants except-ing Leah to change the Bed Lininns and Thomasina, who was still in the Kitchen, to procure a Soothing Posset for the Sufferer.

Flip, Filly, and I made a discreet Withdrawal to the Second Floor and were about to go our Separate Ways when Pa came striding up the Stairs and with one Pointing Finger bade us stay where we were. You are not so long gone from us, are you, my Friend, as to have Forgot just how Pa does that, and who but he could Retain his Dignity even in A Flannel Chamber Robe, bare feet, and night cap?

"Well," he said, strait out, "which one of you was it?"

Flip and I exchanged Glances. Then we stepp'd Forward at the same Moment. We were both trying to Accept the Blame when Filly, like the Gentleman she is, spoke up Firmly. "It was me, Pa."

"Aunt Katrina is an old Lady," said Pa more in Sorrow than in Anger, "and also our Guest."

"I know, Pa," said Filly with unwonted Meekness. I noticed she didn't say she was Sorry, which Pa noticed, too, and Commented on.

Then he sighed and caught hold of her Elbow and Propelled her into her Chamber. He closed the Door, so we couldn't see but we could hear, first the Creaking of Filly's wooden Rocking Chair under Pa's great Waight, then the Crack of his Hand on her thin-clad Rump.

Fortunately, before he Delt her more than three or four smacks—did not the Schoolmaster give you six? —Mama was in our Midst. She flung open Filly's door and Stormed inside like one of the Amazon ladies we studied, calling out like an actor in a Play, "Loose her at once."

Pa did this so promptly, standing up at the same Time, that poor Filly rolled off his lap and her Bottom hit the Floor, producing the first yelp I heard from her. But she Confided to me this morning that a few licks were a small Price to pay for Aunt Katrina's Departure.

Tell me, has Oxford any Excitements to offer exceeding ours, and will not Life in England seem Dull without our Philadelphia?

I am eager to hear of the attitudes in the Mother Country to our troubles here, but be cautious of what you say when you write my Parents. I would not wish you to Offend Pa and be in his Bad Books. It seems Strange that it should never have occurred to him that we might not be the Ardent Tories he is, and I see no reason to make him Aware till the Need is Pressing. He speaks Scornfully of Kings College as a Hotbed of Sedition, but assumes I, as his Son, will be Immune to this partickular Disease.

Frankly, I chafe here, wishing the weeks away so that I may find myself in that same Hotbed, of which I will write to you in Detail when I have arrived there.

Your Devoted Friend,
Pieter Van Duren

P.S. As a Result of her latest Prank, it is now decided that Filly shall go away to School. God help the School!

Filly's Journal
July 25, 1773

I relly scairt Aunt Katrina haff to Death with the Mouse in her chamber pot. She left yesterday, promising never to return. Also I am cutt out of her Will. Unkel Arend ses I was probebley never in it.

The last time Mama dragged me along to the Van Cortlandts to hear Mr. Whitfield preech from there Front Porch, I dint pay much Heed, but I remember him saying Some Thing abowt God moving in Mistory Ways, wich seems to fit what happened, I mean Mama and Pa.

I never was so Surprized at anything as her coming into my Room, and after she told him to let me go, she ackchually Stamped her Foot at him, not wunce but twise, saying, "How dare you strike my Daughter?"

Pa and I both scrambeled uprite together, staring at her, all amazed. She wore nothing but a Night Shift, a reel short one so thin I could see her Bones thru it and with lace all over the Buzom, and I could see thru the lace, too. Her hair, her byutifull black hair (I never knew she had so much of it) streemed over her showlders and down her Back. There were even littel curling Tendrils of it heeving up and down across her Buzom. She is uzually so pale, but her Face looked all Flushed and her eyes were shiney like Coals. After the seckond Stamp, she sed, "Katrina Van der Post is a mean old Wich. What ever our Philadelphia did to her, she well Deserves and I Approove it. Will you strike me too, then, Cornelius Van Duren?" Then she drew nearer to him, while Pa stood like one struk Dumb. "Will you, Cornelius?" she asked agen.

Finelly he answered her in a strange Horse Voice. "Anetje, Anetje, my love. You shud not be out of bed in the cold nite air."

"I *am* cold, Cornelius," my mother wimpered and put out her arms to him.

In three grate Strides he was at her side. "You are Shivering. Why have you not a Shawl arownd you? Where is Bessie?"

"I dont need a Shawl. I dont need Bessie. Only you to warm me."

He swung her up in his Hefty arms like she was a babys Size. Her arms Stole arownd his Neck and her head rested on his Showlder. Both had Forgot I was Alive. Were these two Strangers with the love shining on there Faces my Mother, my Father?

When they were gone, I sank down on my Bed on my knees, carefull to keep my Bottum in the Air. The latch on the door lifted agen, and my brothers came Creeping in.

"Does it hurt much, Filly?" Flip wanted to know. Piet just Grinned.

"If thats not a silly qwestion," I snapt. "He has a Hand like a Slege Hammer."

The door opened agen. It was Thomasina this Time.

"Come on in," I yelled. "Every one come in. It's the Common Room of the Ferry Tavern. Maybe I shud serve some Ale."

"You hush, child, and lie on your Stummick." She pointed to the door. "Out!" she sed sternly to my Brothers, and out they went. She yanked up my Shift and gentelly spred one of her cool Ointmints over my flaming Beehind. "This'll take the Sting out. You'll be no more than a Littel Sore tomorrow and a good thing, too. It will Remind you the Van Durens has proper Noshuns how to treet a Gest in this House."

"How abowt the Way she treeted You?"

"I'm a Woman Grown, Child. I been a Servant all my life and a Slave most of it. I can take a Harsh word or two withouten I Flinch.

You had no call," she added shrewdly, "to make me the Excuse for you Misbeehaving."

Before I cud answeer, she tapped the top of my Hed with her Finger. "Get under that Fether Bed and go to sleep. The cocks will be Crowing soon."

I snuggled down into the warmth of my Fetherbed as Thomasina opened the door. I herd her speak to Leah, who was going by, and before the door closed agen, I herd the rich full sownd of Leah's laffeter coming all the way up from her belly.

"Oh Lord, Oh Lord, what a to-do there was, with the Chamber pot upside-down on her Bolster and that scairt littel Mouse jumping over the bed and Miz Katrina swinging from the top of the bed post screeching like the Devil was after her. Laff. I aint seen Mrs. Van Duren laff so harty these last five yers . . . and then carrying on like a girl with the Master and him toting her back to bed."

The door closed before Thomasina could answer, but I am not Stoopid, and I understand. Ive known for Years that Pa sleeps on the Trundell Bed in the Schooll Room that used to be his Estate Offise and Mama sleeps alone in her Bigg Bed, not together like Cuzzin Lucretia and Unkel Arend. And now they are sleeping together. I wonder does that mean theyll get a Baby. I think I'll ask Thomasina.

Journal of Lucretia Bogardus
29th July 1773

Annette and Cornelius are so wrapt up in there new Discovery of one Another, it proved surprizingly Easy to perswade them that Filly must not spend the next Severall winters running all abowt the Hudson Valley like an untamed Boy or the Indian she so long pretended to be. It is Desided. She is to go away to School. Annette wishes it to be a Quaker School, so she has sent Instrucktions to one of her Du Bois Cousins in Philadelphia.

From there it was but one step further for them to See that Flip would be Sad and Alone here, so he is now to winter in New York with Arend and me and attend Lattin School, as the other Boys did.

This leeves one problem only—Thomasina. For years, while Annette deny'd him her Bed, Cornelius turned to my dear Friend.

Not often perhaps but ofttn enough to make this new State of Affaires Painfull for her and an Embarrassment to him.

I think I will propoze an Exchange this Winter—Mrs. Wallace here, where she Prefers to be, Thomasina in New York to look after young Philip. His mother is so conserned with his physickal welfare, she will Heed me, and Cornelius is bownd to Encouragge her. I think it a Cunning Skeme.

Next day at noon

It was. It worked. Thomasina comes with Us.

Filly's Journal
Aug. 1, 1773

Damn and Blast and Hell and all the Horribelest Words I know. I am being sent away to School in Philadelphia. Pa sez its for my own Sake and not a Punishment, but Im the one whoze going, and it feels like a Punishment.

> Philadelphia
> The one in Pennsilvania
> Sept. 18, 1773

Dear Couzin Lucretia:

The girls here are mostly all Quakers and the Staff, too. Never have I heard so much theeing and thouing. Some of them come in by the Day and some live here like me. Mostly they come from Philadelphia and Germantown and other Towns nereby. They think that our Hudson Valley is a wild wilderness airea with only logg Cabbins to live in and Indians popping out of every Tree. They were more than ever sure of it when I put on Bram's Indian wammus and Brittches and mockassins. It was Funn to see them oohing and talking like I came from the wild west Ohio. And their eyes popped when I played my Fife.

Philadelphia (the city, not me) is niser than I

exspeckted, but I miss our River and the trees and the Hills. Its so flat here and so full of tall Bildings.

And I miss the Boys. Its all girls girls girls here. But the Boys are all Away anyhow, so I gess I would miss them even if I was at home.

Please tell Thomasina I miss her Cooking and think of her a lot. Thee (ha, ha!) and Unkel Arend, too.

Your Loving Filly

Anthony Benezet School for Girls
Philadelphia
29 Sept. 1773

To Mr. Cornelius Van Duren
Van Duren Manor
Tarrytown, New York

My Dear Sir,

I have allowed a full Month to go by since we received thy daughter here so that I might Form and Render to thee a fitting Judgement. My estimate of her in all these weeks remains Unchanged and should set thy Apprehensions to rest. Thy Philadelphia, or Philly, as she prefers to be called, is a lovely child and possessed of great Charm. She has also, despite certain Gaps in her education, something more of quickness than most girls. The Gaps may—and assuredly I shall strive to have them —be Filled In, but the Quickness will serve her all her life.

During her first week here, I turned a Blind Eye, though knowing that among the girls at night she Peacocked around in her Indian male attire, striving to Shock and Impress. At first she accomplished her Object, but that same natural quickness rather than any hints of mine soon made her aware that the Sentiments she excited came from those whose admiration was not a Desirable Distinction.

The Indian garb soon disappeared, and she commenced cultivating worthier Friendships. I am pleased to report that her particular Intimates include two of my most outstanding Pupils, Deborah Norris, whose deceased father I believe to have been distant kin of Mrs. Van Duren, and Deborah's dear friend Sally Wister. Both girls come from two of our fine Quaker families and are young ladies of Intelligence and Refinement, particularly suited to be Philly's Companions. Sally exerts a quieting Influence and Deborah matches her in Spirit. They form the heart of a group that study and read and chat together, challenging one another.

I would not wish to suppress the Life and Vivacity that are so much a part of Philadelphia, and if I have been several times perplexed how to curb that great spirit of mischief within her, I may say that at least I never appealed in vain to her Sense of Honour. This I do consider more important than Needle Wisdom or Sampler Stitching. At these I doubt if she will ever excell, but she is Diligent in her other studies and making remarkable strides in Latin. (I believe her excellence in the latter is less than Saintly, however. She wishes, I heard her say, to show up Flip. One of her brothers, I deduce.)

My dear Mr. Van Duren, thee may rest easy in thy Mind. I have no more doubts of Philadelphia's Disposition and Moral Tone than I do of her ardent Nature. She needs a little polishing up and toning down, to be sure, but these may be attained by Education and contact with Cultivated Minds as well as the inevitable Progress of Time.

Thee may be assured she will one day take her proper place in New York Society as a young Woman of Culture and Accomplishment, one her parents may well be proud of, as I will be proud to have played my small part.

Your Humble Obdt. Servant,
Anthony Benezet

Benezet School, Phila.
Jan. 2, 1774

My dear Couzin Lucretia and Uncle Arend:
I dreded the Hollidays in prospect, but they turned out

Joyous. Obidiah's Sally had studied so well how to please me, we had a Truly Dutch St. Nicholas Day and Twelfth Night. Was it you she wrote to for the Receipts? Her Loaf covered in Egg White was near as good as Thomasina's. (Don't tell Thomasina I said so.) We also had minse Tarts, Gingerbred cookys, oranj peel, and cranberries, and for 12th Night, she had Remembered to Fashion the Bell out of greens and Fruit with a Clapper of Misseltoe. We had lots of Musick. Sally played the Harp and I the Fife and the others sang. All were so Kind it was Impossibel for me to feel sad.

It is so hard to think of Obidiah grown a Man with children of his own, but Sally is allreddy big with thir Second, so big that I expect, as I once heard you say of Fanny Nease, she will Probably Drop it any time.

I like Sally. She is a Rownd Dumpling of a Girl with Cheeks red as Roses and a Smile Always on her face. All four Sisters were there with their children, eleven Littel Ones in all! She—I am back to Sally—makes Obidiah very Happy, you will be pleazed to know she told me with great Simplicity that, if the child is a girl, it will be named Lucretia after "the only Mother dear Obidiah has ever known."

Sally was Likewise eagger to know, had Mrs. Wallace receeved the Shawl she knit for her. She hopes some day they may meet, as Mrs. Wallace, too, was so good to Obidiah. Indeed, she is full of Good Will to Anyone who ever extended the hand of Friendship or Kindness to her Husband. It is Impossibel not to love Someone who is so full herself of Love and Good Will.

I send you Greetings of this New Year in hopes that 1774 will answer the Heart's Desire of all of us.

Your loving Filly

P.S. I have not Heard any word from Martinis these many Months here. Have you? Is he well?

Benezet School, Phila.
March 10, 1774

Dear Cousin Lucretia,

Just a few lines to Inform you that Mr. Benezet Kindly arranged for one of the Teachers to take me to Obidiah's Cabinet-Making Shop that I might Tell him of the Death of Mrs. Wallace. He was much Greeved. Coming on topp of their Child's being Stillborn, to lose another of the Objects of his Love was a Severe Blow. However, I believe that he has Akwired Something of the Quaker Habbit of Acceptance, and it stood him in good Sted. He was very much aware of the Greef you must be feeling and talked much and Feelingly of the years when you and Mrs. Wallace and he and Ben worked at the Tavern and were All in All to one Another. Dear Cousin Lucretia, I know you are Indeed Sad, and you are much in my Thoughts and Love at this Sorrowfull Time.

Your loving cousin,
Philadelphia

P.S. I appreciate the Messages from Martinis but could Wish he would take up his Pen and Deliver them to me in his own Person.

Benezet School, Phila.
April 3, 1774

Dear, dear dear Bram:

I am the Envy of the Entire School. It was Melancoly to be away from Home today. Never have I been from my Family on my Birth Date. But just as I was Feeling Exceeding Sorry for myself, Sitting in my Chamber, Staring out the Window, and Sqweezing out a few Tears, than the Summons came from Mr. Benezet. And there was your Box, taking up near his full desk space! He even gave to me the Covering Letter, which had come with it Weeks Before. How Good of you, dear Bram, to send my Gift so much Beforehand rather than run the Risk it might be Late.

It needed the man of all work to carry the Box to my Chamber. I followed him, dansing with Eagerness, and *a whole Prosession of Girls trailed after me. If I had wanted Privasy, I was Beside my Luck, for it was Impossible to Shut them Out.*

So now let me Ennumerate my Riches. First came Tumbeling out the Bolt of Silk, which you say matches my Eyes, but to me it is the Colour of our River, and No Where is there a Colour to Compare to our Hudson Blue. I shall save it to have made up for a very Speshal Occasion.

The Books were next, and you may believe me when I say there is such Hunger in this place for good Poems and Novels, I will be in Luck or very Clever and Sellfish if I manage to get the first Reading of them for myself. But what a wonderful Supply, and especially Pamela, *which I have been longing to read even if Debby says she is quite silly. And thank you, my darling Cousin, for paying me the Compliment of Realizing a few Chapters of such reading as is to be found in* Moll Flanders *will not Corrupt my Mind. It is my Observation, acqwired here, that the Mind that can be Corrupted by Books is Allreddy Corrupted—or Corruptibel.*

Your Pardon, Coz. I did not mean to Leckture you, I am sure Oxford affords you enough Such. To go on with the Inventorry of your Gifts. The Musickal Box is Indeed lovely, and a few tears Returned when I heard the Tinkeling Notes of Greensleeves. *I closed my eyes, and I was back in our Parlour, with Mama at the Pianoforte, Flip and I at our Fifes, and all the rest singing lustily this Favourite of ours.*

As to the Fan of Ivory Sticks, all painted in Dresden Shepherdesses, I have never had anything so Elegent, and since I am now Fifteen, I must think in Terms of Elegence. I have Desided . . . I shall carry it on my Wedding Day and hand it down to my oldest Daughter. Speaking of Wedding Days, has Cousin Lucretia Informed you that dear old stick-in-the-mud Ben is caught at last, and by a Mere Girl not much Older than me.

Getting back to your Gifts . . . Dear Bram, how utterly Bram-like this has been of you. How thoughtful! I cannot find enough words in either English or Dutch to thank you, and my French, even my Latin, are inadequate to the task. You are the dearest Cousin a girl ever had. In truth, you are more than that, you have always been as much and dear a Brother to me as ither Flip or Piet. But in Kindness and Consideration, you are Unique. None can compare to Bram De Kuyper, say I,

His Devoted Loving Cousin, Sister and Friend
Filly

P.S. Do you hear from Martinis at all? I would think from the lack of Communication, he had broken both his Hands, but he could hardly be a Sailor if that were the case. Uncle Arend says he has left Holland for Spain.

Benezet School, Phila.
May 2, 1774

Dear Cousin Lucretia,
What great good Fortune that Sally's Brother-In-Law has Business in New York and can carry the Blue Silk for me. I have enclosed with it my Meazurements, which you may note are a little changed, but not I regret to say in the Buzom, which Defies the Laws of Nature by Remaining the same Size while the Rest of me grows. Thankfully, my Waist is also small, even as my other Contours take on a more Pleasing Plumpness.

The silk will make up into a Marvelously Lovely Gown for Ben's Wedding, Tell him I thank him again and again for Delaying it till I am come Home. Nay, never mind, I shall write to him and tell him Myself.

How I long to see you all now that the time is no Near.
Your loving Excited Filly

P.S. 1—In reply to Uncle's questions, I regret I have no more to tell you about the Congress meeting in

Phila. than may be found in any newspaper. Thee forgets I am in Quaker surroundings, and talk of Dissension in our Colonies is much Discourraged. I have allready been Reprimanded, though Gently, for teaching some of the Younger Girls the song *Revolutionary Tea.* Has it come your way? 'Tis great good fun to sing in a group. I append the first Verses.

> There was an old lady lived over the sea,
> And she was an Island Queen;
> And her daughter lived off in a new country,
> With an ocean of water between.
> The old lady's pockets were full of gold,
> But never contented was she
> So she called on her daughter to pay her a tax
> Of three pence a pound on her tea.

> Now mother, dear mother, the daughter replied
> I shan't do the thing that you ax;
> I'm willing to pay a fair price for the tea,
> But never the threepenny tax.

And so on. I shall bring the *Musick* home with me.
P.S. 2—Is there any Prospect that Martinis may be Home for the Wedding?

> Benezet School, Phila.
> Oct. 11, 1774

My Dear Martinis:

The Spanish Shawl, which you tell me is called a Mantilla, and the set of Jeweled Combs arrived here by Post from off Uncle Arend's Vessel, though the Box and Wrappings showed the signs of its long Travel. The Mantilla is a lovely Exotick thing and the Combs so Splendid, allmost I am tempted when I go home to beg a Black Walnut Dye of Thomasina so that I may colur my Tresses black like Mama's, which is more suited to the Combs than my Dutch fair hair.

I have one Problem. Your letter—all three lines of it—tells me these Delicious Offerings are in Honour of my Birth Date, and that leaves me at a Loss. Do I thank you Belatedly for my Fifteenth Birth Date gift this April past or my Sixteenth Birth Date this April coming? Since it may be another two and twenty Months before I hear from you in any way at all, mayhap I should make my thanks Double!

As for School, it is not so Bad as you seem to think. I enjoy the Course of Study and have many dear friends, and if Some Times the Longing overcomes me to put on my Buckskin Suit and roam the Woods of Westchester, I force myself to remember that even at Home now I am more Restrained than I was used to be. It distresses Mama if I act the Boy or play the Indian. Once that did not Hinder me, but perhaps I am growing up for I find myself more Reluctant than formerly to give her Pain.

But I promise you I am not so much changed that you need Fear to come Home to me. Try to make it this Summer, and indeed the Indians will hunt the Woods again and go fishing on our Island.

I can never forget the Wonderfull times we all had together. I hope that may be as True of you, too.

Yours, Devotedly,
Filly

Benezet School, Phila.
Jan. 24, 1775

Dearest Cousin Lucretia:
How eagerly I seized on Piet's letter when the Post came this morning and how swiftly my Joy in a letter from him was turned to Tears. Indeed, I have wept untill I had no tears left in me. I cannot believe that I will never see dear Uncle again. I know that he was well past his fifties, but I have seen men half his age who had not his Youthful Air and Vigor. Mr. Benezet said I should find Consolation in the Nobility of his Death, for he saved a Young Mother and several of her children in

that runaway carriage. But they were Strangers to me, and Uncle Arend was close and dear, so dear I know not how we are to go on without him. Particularly you. There was such Love between you. I could not but be aware of it, and looking about me, not be aware also that it is not given to many Men and Women on this Earth to share such Love.

Dear Cousin Lucretia, I meant to offer you Sympathy for your Grief and instead I seem to have indulged Myself in Selfish Lamentation. What can I say? What can I do? I want so much to help you. If only I could come Home and be with You.

Your loving Filly

Oxford, England
Feb. 18, 1775

My Beloved Aunt:

If you had not been so Firm in Anticipating my Intent and Urging me against it, I would be on my way Home to you now. I might have even made good enough Time so that you would be receiving me instead of the cold Comfort of a sheet of paper. But since it is so strongly your Wish, I shall finish out the term and be home by the Summer, but not to Return to England. This I insist. Two years at Oxford will do me. If he is still willing, come Autumn, I can go straight into Mr. John Jay's offices to read Law under him.

Dearest of Aunts, more than my Aunt, the Moeder you have been to me all these years since I lost my own, please let me have my Way in this without any Protest. Let me, for my own Sake, have the Satisfaction of doing this little thing for you as just the smallest possible Return of the many many things you have all your Life done for me.

It is true what you say, Uncle Arend did want me to complete my Education at Oxford, but when he sent me, he did not anticipate that you would be left without him. And who but I or Martinis, with whom you both

225

generously shared your Lives, can know what that Void means to you?

I believe what I am intending is Right. I believe it is what he would want and expect me to do.

Dear Aunt, you know how much I loved him. Like my own father he was. Many times when I was younger, I wished I had no other, and that he and I were tied by Blood as he was to Martinis. Did you know that I once spoke of this to him, and he just put his hand on my head and said in an unusually Gentle Manner, "Be satisfied, Bram. You are the son of my heart." Then he clapped me about the shoulder, more in his usual style, and growled in what you always called his Quarterdeck Voice, "Come along, enough of such Sentiment." But I noted that often after that he would take pains to address me as "Mijn Zoon."

May my own Life be over before ever I forget what I owe to him. I know that I will think of him and miss him always. Your loss is mine, your grief I share. I shall be thinking of you constantly in the months till my Return.

> *With Love and Sorrow,*
> *Bram, Your Son*

Filly's Journal
Bogardus House, New York
June 27, 1775

Last night Cousin Lucretia and I sat, very Cozy, sipping a little Wine, which she said in quite her old Twinkling Fashion would be good to elevate the flow of our Spirits. I do not know about my Spirits, but it certainly elevated my Tongue. I cannot think what else could have made me question her with such Familiarity about her new Condition.

Cousin Lucretia did not seem to Mind. Rather, she seemed almost Glad to speak Freely.

"Never again say you are Sorry for me, Filly," she admonished me at one point in our Converse. "If it is true, as you once told me, that Arend and I shared such Love as is given to few Men and

Women, what have I to Weep about? Only that I was not granted twice the 12 years and 9 months we had together. I wish it, certainly, but there is no use Crying out against what cannot Be. What I had with him in those Years, I will have all my Life."

She gave me an Ironick Smile. "I have been far more Unhappy than this in my past, Filly, before I worked at the Tavern for your Father. Believe me, 'tis far better to be a Welthy Widow."

She poured out more Wine for us. "I have borne no children, yet I have Many," she continued. "I have my Business Affaires, my Painting . . . There is still much to attach me to Life even if the Heart of it is gone."

In these twenty-four hours since, I have been thinking of all she Divulged to me, and I do see that, with all her Present Sorrow, she is a Fortunate Woman. Uncle Arend was the Rock on which was formed the Foundation of her Happiness. Could Martinis ever be such a Rock to me? I perceeve him more as a Rolling Stone. It Troubles me about the Future I once planned so Blithely.

Filly's Journal, N.Y.C.
July 5, 1775

Martinis is Home. And Bram, too. They came together from England. Our Joy is as deep as it is Unexpected.

Ben rushed into the House this morning with the first news of a Ship's Arrival, and we hurried to the Harbour, hoping, yet afraid to Hope. Imagine our Supreme Happiness when not one but two came down the Plank.

Almost I was shy with them after the first Embrases, for they are not the Boys I grew up and played with. They are become Men. How handsome Martinis. And what Comfort I find in Bram's Presence!

Filly's Journal
Van Duren Manor
July 12, 1775

Is there never Joy without a Tinge of Sorrow? Is there never Happiness unmarred by Trouble? Or Peace by Strife?

Here we all are in our beloved Home again, and allready the Quarreling and Disputes have begun.

My Father and Mr. Philip Van Cortlandt, who went to School together and have been Friends all their Lives, are now great Unfriends.

Everywhere other Friends are turning against Friends, and Neighbors against Neighbors. With Mr. Frederick Phillips of Phillipsburg Manor, of whom he was allways somewhat Disdainfull, my father is now drawn into a Close Allianse because their Politicks are the same.

Our greatest Trouble, however, is that Pa and Pieter are at Swords' Points with one another, for Pa stands by the King and he was Shocked and Horrorfied to discover that with Piet it is otherwise. They quarrel constantly. I am greatly in Fear of what will be.

Filly's Journal
July 29, 1775

What I have dreaded all along has come to Pass. My father and Pieter have had an Irrevockable Quarrel, and Piet has been Banished from our House. Rather, I should say, his leaving was by his own Choice, because he was Determined to throw in his Lot with his Countrymen. If this meant fighting, he told Pa, then he would Fight.

Pa answered that if Piet took up Arms against the King, he was no Son of his.

"I am sorry, Pa," Pieter told him, white-faced but calm, "but I have allready writ to Mr. Van Cortlandt who commands the Second New York Regiment and offered him my Services."

Pa had gone very white, too. "You would fight against your own People?" he thundered, smiting his desk with a mighty Fist.

"For my own People, Pa," Piet retorted. *"For* them. Good God, what is the King of England to me? Or the English? On your side I am pure Dutch, and the closest we came to England was in the fighting years ago under William of Orange. On my Mother's side I come of Swiss Quaker stock and the Du Bois French Huguenots who fled here from religious persecution and found refuge with our

Dutch forbears. We have been British subjects, yes, colonials under British rule, subject to British taxes and Tyranny, never accorded the full rights of free-born Englishmen!"

"We have grown rich and prosperous under English Rule."

"Only a rare few of us."

Pa tried a new Tack. "Will you break your Mother's heart?"

"I do not mean to," Pieter said softly, "but I must do what I must do."

They parted in such Anger and Bitterness that Pieter did not even stay the Night under our Roof. He packed up the few things he might need and took Refuge with Cousin Lucretia at the Cottage.

Filly's Journal
Aug. 3, 1775

All is Gloom and Sorrow and Desolation in our House. My beloved brother Pieter received a Letter from Col. Van Cortlandt today, and within hours of my taking it to him at Cousin Lucretia's, he was gone to be a Soldier. This Evening my Father made a solemn Ceremony before Flip and me of writing his name out of the Family Bible. Our Mother would not attend but took to her Bed instead, as she was used to do when Life became too Difficult. I fear she will never forgive Pa. I do not find it easy in my Heart to forgive him myself. A Son is no less a Son because you mislike the Road he takes for his Journey! Cousin Lucretia even has his anger because she sheltered my Brother for four nights, and I tremble to think what he will say when he Discovers that Bram and Martinis, too, have chosen the American side. That I have Chosen it as well he will not care; he does not take seriously female Oppinions on Politicking.

Filly's Journal
Aug. 5, 1775

Martinis kissed me today, not the brotherly Smack on the cheek I have allways had from him, but a Kiss from Mouth to Mouth, which he did so well, I knew that what was New and Exciting to me was, however Exciting, to him an old old Story.

But it pleasured me to see that I could stir him so!

"Well, well, well," he said, "the little Indian's grown up a Lady, and who has been giving you Lessons?"

I flashed him a demure Smile but said Nothing. Not for Worlds would I confess it was the very first time for me. It seems I have a Natural Skill in the Art if I can Fool him. So much the Better. Martinis ever Strives Harder to Obtain the Object more out of Reach.

He goes down River to New York tomorrow on Business for Cousin Lucretia. I think I am glad . . . I need a little Thinking Time.

Filly's Journal
Aug. 8, 1775

Martinis is gone. Flip is a-bed with a cold and Mama with her Sorrow. Pieter is God knows where.

I was as happy as could be when Bram suggested he and I take Lunch and go to the Island. I put on my—no, *his* Indian clothes, and we were so happy and merry together, putting out of our minds the Strife and Sadness of this last year.

We sat and talked of many things, Heart-felt things. There is no one I can do that with so Readily as Bram. This has been True all my Life.

When he told me that he, too, was going to serve under Col. Van Cortlandt, I felt as though my entire World was crumbeling to bits Beneath me, and I wept bitterly for the Sorrows of the past and the present and the ones I feared were to Come.

Bram put his arms about me and held me; he rocked me to and fro and Comforted me. He spoke with such great Tenderness, I wept all the more for Wanting him to Stay. But when I spoke my need of him, he asked gravely, "Philadelphia, would you have me stay safe here in the Tarrytowns wilst others—your Brother!—fight my Battles for me?"

I turned in his arms, crying out passionately, "Yes and yes and yes, I surely would. Don't talk to me of your Duty, Bram. It is for your Safety I am concerned."

"And my Honour?"

"A Plague on men's honour, if it means fighting and dying. For Honour my father disowned Pieter and is destroying my mother.

For Honour Piet may die. For Honour Martinis, if I know him, will plunge recklessly into whatever is the most Dangerous Enterprize that offers."

He laughed suddenly, and I was so enraged at this, I gave him a quick hard slap. The next moment I was in his arms, not as I had been before, but Differently. He was holding me close, not tenderly at all, not at all like Brother or a Father. For the second time in three days I was kissed by a man as a man kisses, and I kissed back with as much enthusiasm as I had showed before and—I must Confess it—a deal more of Energy and Passion, I know not why unless it were the aftermath of Anger and Great Emotion, but I kissed Bram, who has been my Brother, with far more Fervor and Fierceness than Martinis who I have Intended for Years to be my Lover. Bram, the calm, the steady, the Dependable, was none of theese things when he Kissed me. A veritable Tiger he was, and in his arms I became Someone I did not know.

It is past my understanding that I could love one Man and Revel so much in the arms and Kisses of Another.

After a while, when we tore our mouths apart from one another to gulp in some air, what I saw on his tight face and in his blazing Eyes made me give a little cry and hide my Face against his Shoulder. In that one moment, wilst my face stayed Hidden, I had a Moment's Revelation. For some fortunate girl, Bram might well be her Rock!

When I turned my face to his once more, he was quite himself again and looking Thoughtfull. He suggested quietly that we eat; and though it was the farthest thing from my Mind at the Moment, when he spread out the food, I fell to with good Appetite.

To my Regret, he did not attempt any more Kissing. Indeed once, just before we Departed the Island, when I put my face close to his, laughing up at him, Deliberately tempting him, he put me gently away from him, saying, "Don't play games with me, Filly."

My face burned. In Truth, I had been trying to.

"You are only sixteen," he said. "And I am going off to War. Martinis, too, I think, even if his plans may be different than Mine." He smiled into my indignant face. "You will not be able to do anything silly untill we both come Home again, which is one Worry off my Mind."

I would have quarreled with him then, but not when he was going away to be a Soldier. I will not be so Foolish as Pa, who has created his own Misery.

But why did I have such pleasure from Martinis' kisses one day and Bram's only three days later? Surely it is Wanton to enjoy more than one Man's Kisses. I never knew before that I could be Wanton.

Filly's Journal
Aug. 11, 1775

I had barely time to feel the Desolation of Bram's going before Martinis was back, saying all of Cousin Lucretia's Business was Attended to. His face was full of the Mischiff I know so well. Business is not all that he Concerned himself with. I know it. Coax and Cajole him though I would, however, I could not get more from him. Mayhap Cousin Lucretia has had better Luck, but I doubt it. There is a tight-lipped look about her that does not bespeak Knowledge, only Worry.

Filly's Journal
Aug. 14, 1775

Now Martinis, too, is gone, and without a word to indicate that there will be anything between us in the Future. Several Times we were alone together, and he snatched a few more Kisses, but they were Casual, almost Careless, and nothing in his Manner or Speech said to me, These Kisses mean Something. So I have to face the Truth I have long been Avoiding—his Kisses mean Nothing more than the Pleasure of the Moment. He does not Love where he Kisses; certainly, he does not Mean to Marry.

I cannot blame him. It was I, not he, who tried to build Bricks without Straw. Martinis cares for me, only not as I Fancied he did. I am his sister, his cousin, his friend, but not his Love. Bram saw this long before I did and tried to Hint to me. I see now that his little speech, at the Island that so angered me was really meant to Spare me Pain.

Well, there is less Pain than I thought, just a vast Emptyness where Pain should be. And Love as well. I had thought my Life laid out in such a Strait Line, all Nice and Neat; now my World is turned Upside Down.

Bram need not fear. I will not now have the chance to do

anything Silly. When I receive a Direction from him, I must write and tell him so.

Filly's Journal
Dec. 16, 1775

I woke up this morning with the Notion it was to be a Momentous Day. And so it was . . . a rare Letter from Martinis arrived!

Filly's Journal
Jan. 10, 1776

Cousin Lucretia will not return to Tarrytown before Summer, if at all, because she plans to be active in Uncle Arend's Shipping Business. It is a Blow, though not an Unexpected one. I am afraid I shall be very Intimate with Solitude this Winter, and Dullness will be a more than Frequent Guest.

Here I am in my own Beloved Home, and I find myself wishing I were any other place . . . Back with Sally and Debby and my other Friends at School . . . Or in New York with Cousin Lucretia, who ernestly besought me to bare her Company this Winter.

How Guilty I feel because I so wanted to accept her Invitation. I am loath to face the Truth, that I find more enjoyment in Cousin Lucretia's company than that of my own Mother. Yet I cannot go to her, because I feel Mama's need is the greater. Poor Mama. She hardly leaves the House now, except to visit our little Cemetery. When she feels unwell, I cut greens or flowering berry branches and take them to her room for her to see before I put them on the graves of Rachel and my brothers.

When I sit with Mama she talks endlessly of our Dead or of Piet, whom she has given up to Death allready. Our Talk together is one long endless Lamentation, so unbearable to me, I sometimes want to Scream and Run Away.

Flip has little time for me these days because Pa keeps him close by him, determined his last remaining Son shall not choose the American side. Please God he will never go to be a Soldier. I think it would kill Mama.

My one Comfort these days is Thomasina. In the Kitchen, helping her Prepare the meals, listening to her Homely Wisdom, I am sometimes Content.

I have read this day's writing over and feel ashamed. If I do not take care, I will become like Mama. Perhaps it were better that I hang up my Pen till something offers worth Relating.

Filly's Journal
July 26, 1776

A rare letter from dear Debby Norris in Philadelphia relating how she clambered upon the garden fence behind her house in order to hear the Declaration of our Independence read from the State House steps in the adjoining square. Oh, that I had been there!

Here I dare not even mention the Noble Document (it so rouses Pa's Ire) except with Flip, who confided in me this day, he believes in the Cause of our Independence, too. Only what to do? I cautioned him that to speak of it to Pa is pointless until such Time as . . . my Voice faded away, then I made myself go on. "You are barely sixteen," I pointed out.

"Boys my age are serving under Washington. One need be only sixteen or as Tall as his Musket. By seventeen," said my brother with Resolution, "I mean to join up. I would like to be in a Military Band. I have read there is great need for Fifers as well as Drummers in the Army."

I was forced to realize that despite Flip's being my *Younger* Brother, he is no longer my *Little* Brother, to be pushed and prodded by me.

But please God let the War be finished with before he Decides to go!

Filly's Journal
Aug. 10, 1776

Even here in Westchester we have heard of the amazing feat of Bravery and Resource by which half a dozen Americans captured a British supply ship lying at anchor in the East River of New York under the very guns of a British man-of-war named the *Asia*. All this without a single shot's being Fired!

By letter from Cousin Lucretia, received today, I have just learned that Martinis was one of the Six. In Truth, it was he who pointed out to their Leader, Capt. Nathan Hale, the School master with whom he Recruited last year, that by the way the sloop lay in the Water it was heavily loaded. They both speculated on the probability that it carried Food, a Commodity the American Army is much distressed for.

Without permission from any Higher Authority, they got together Kindred Spirits, rowed out to the Sloop, Overpowered the single Guard and daringly boarded the Vessel while the Crew slept on below. It was then the work of moments to cut the supply Ship loose and bring it back to Shore.

Cousin Lucretia told me that when Martinis related the whole to her with great good Spirits, his main Source of Enjoyment seemed to be in the dazed astonishment of the sleeping British crew on awakening to find themselves Prisoners on the American side!

How like him, both in the daring and the Humour!

Filly's Journal
Oct. 9, 1776

Oh God, oh God, I am so Frightened.

I was glancing through one of the New York newspapers that lay open on my Father's Desk, and I read that an American named as Nathan Hale was captured out of Uniform behind the British Lines on Long Island and hung as a Spy.

Can there be *two* Nathan Hales? Martinis, Martinis, can this be what you are engaged in? It would be just like you—reckless, daring and dangerous!

Filly's Journal
Oct. 19, 1776

Cousin Lucretia arrived here yesterday. God be praised, she had heard directly from Martinis less than a week ago. Also, we have to be Thankfull that her House was saved in the Fire that Devestated New York.

She will be staying with us at the Manor House after tomorrow because her Business here is to Strip the Cottage of all her Household Furnishings and Possessions and send everything North to a house she has rented for that purpose near to West Point. It is her Firm Conviction that no matter what the Politicks of the Home

Owner here in Westchester, none of our Property will be safe in the Years ahead.

She and Pa argued fiercely about their differing Convictions at the Dinner Table today. The theme of her Argument is that we shall stand squarely between both Armies here and are like to be preyed on by the Riff-Raff from ither side. Pa pounded the table with his Fist in his usual Stile and ranted that British Soldiery were incapable of such Acts. There was no moving him. He considers it an act of Loyalty and Patriotism to show his faith not only in the British Army but their Ability to protect us from "those damned Rebbels."

Cousin Lucretia, knowing well when argument with him is Fruitless, gave it up and Ventured to speak on another Flammatory Topick.

"You will be pleased to know," she said quite cooly, "that I received word from both Pieter and Bram in the last two weeks, and they are in good health and good spirits."

Mama shed tears of Relief, and I saw Pa's shoulders sag, as though a Burden had been lifted from them, but he would not acknowledge it. Stubborn, stubborn man.

Filly's Journal
Oct. 23, 1776

Save for a few old Trundel beds and cupboards Cousin Lucretia said were not worth the taking, the Cottage is stript bare.

Seven Waggon Loads of goods started off for West Point today, and if Pa but knew, one waggon load of goods was ours. Mama and I had determined between us after that first night that some of our things should be saved, so we sent all the Du Bois Silver and Plate and Pewter, the portraits of the boys and the Miniature of Rachel and my Du Bois grand-parents. Mama included a coffer of her jewels, her great grandfather's sword, some books, and three leather trunks of Household Furnishings and Linens. All that Pa would not notise we sent, and Cousin Lucretia drew up a signed Inventory which I have hidden Away.

I would not be surprised if Pa never notised. He is so busy with his Politickal activity, he is almost unaware of anything going on about the House.

Flip has not changed his Convictions, but he does not mind going about with Pa so much since he received the gift of his new Mare, Jenny. She is a lovely creature, to be sure, and when I hinted to Pa that such a gift would not be amiss for me, too, he said it were better in these Troubled Times that I stick Safely to Home.

I longed to give Pert Answer that this was not how he had spoken to Cousin Lucretia about our Safety here, but he looks so Tired and Worn down by his Cares, I had not the heart to be this Saucy. Hard as it is for me to do, I held my Tongue.

Filly's Journal
Oct. 27, 1776

Cousin Lucretia has gone back to New York and Life has resumed the same dreary Round as before she arrived. She wanted me to go with her, and again I had to resist my Selfish Longings in order to do what I think right and stay on here with Mama.

I had hoped that Cousin Lucretia would spend the Winter now that Ben is living in the Indies, managing the Business from there; but she feels in New York she can be in closer touch with Bram and Martinis and Pieter.

I am so Lonely. All the laughter seems gone from our Lives.

Filly's Journal
Nov. 10, 1776

Dierk Bruegel is home on a visit to his father. He has not Changed the least bit, not in my eyes. He looks and acts exactly the Same, which is to say a bit of a Strutting Peacock when he is alone with me and a Cringing Boy in the presence of his father. I should not blame him. Mr. Bruegel was ever a cold cruel father, but Dierk is a man now . . . or should be . . . and halfway to being a Preecher.

I think he still has a Fancy for me. Since he will be here for only a Week, perhaps I may Flirt with him a Little.

Filly's Journal
Nov. 13, 1776

We walked to the Island today, where I allowed Dierk to Kiss me. No, if I am to be honest, *allowed* is not the Word. Out of loneliness and longing for Others than him to be there with me and anger that they were not, I invited his Kiss.

It was a strange Sensation. His hands on my arms holding me Clumsily against him were rather Moist, while by contrast his lips, pressing heavily onto mine, were not only dry but flaky, just like the Skin of a Snake. This, after some awkward maneuvering to keep our noses from Bumping together, by which I judge his Experiense in such matters to be not much more than mine.

I felt Nothing. Nothing at all. Except Relief that it was over.

I am ashamed of myself for toying with Dierk, who seems not to know the way of it. No more Flirtation, Filly, till a more Equal Partner offers himself.

I think . . . yes, I am convinced that my Mother will not be well and will need my Constant Attention till his Visit is over.

Filly's Journal
Nov. 16, 1776

Oh dear, oh dear, Dierk is staying on for the Winter. His father is in poor Health, and he will work at my Father's Accounts and put money by to go to the Divinity School at Yale next year. Now how do I avoid him the rest of *this* year?

Filly's Journal
Nov. 21, 1776

My first Proposal of Marriage, and an unromantickal affair it was, not at all the way Debby and Sally and I used to picture back at the dear Benezet School.

He actually bent one knee to me, and since we were in the Herb Garden off the Long Walk, I was fearfull any moment to see someone come along. What with trying to tug my hand out of his, get him up on his feet and Refuse him without wounding his Sensibilities, I was well-nigh Distracted.

Someone did come along, Tom Dumb, and Dierk leapt up at once, scowling at the Simple Simon who, for the first time in my Life, I was glad to see.

My smile must have encouraged the Poor Fool, for he said, "Pretty, Pretty," and reached out and touched my Breast. I shrank back, and Dierk shouted at him to Begone, which he did, fleeing fleetly as an Indian. But then I had Dierk to deal with, and in the end the only way to Save his Feelings was to tell him that he was and always would be my dear Friend, but I cared more for someone else, indeed—I thought the Lie had better be a Convincing One—I was secretly Betrothed to another Lover.

He scowled fiercely, guessing at once, "Martinis?" Then he added, almost savagely, "I could stand it's being anyone but Martinis Asher; I've allways Hated him."

I was more grateful than I could say when Thomasina came down the Long Walk and into the garden for some herbs. Eagerly I went to help her fill her apron with those she needed, and Dierk departed with just a word of angry resentfull Farewell.

I think he is as much afflicted by Hurt Pride as disappointed Hopes, which means his Sufferings will be of Short Duration. Nor can I conseal from myself, however unwellcome to my Vanity, that there may have been a large Consideration of thwarted Ambition in his Demeanor. Was it Filly Van Duren he wanted for Wife or the Daughter of the Lord of the Manor? His anger Furnishes me the less flattering Response.

Filly's Journal
Nov. 25, 1776

This day has been the most Incredible in all my life. Firstly, I have been with Martinis and under Circumstances so strange that from this day forward I must keep my Journal well hid as I used to Years ago when I feared the boys might Find it and use my Private Thoughts to make sport of me. The false floor of the old Cupboard is as Safe as it ever was, and henceforth I shall put my Scribblings there for Safe Keeping. I use the words Safe Keeping advisedly. My own Safety, as much as his, depends on it!

It all began early of this morn when I went down to the gardens to get some sweet herbs for the pot-pourri bowls in Mama's Chamber. One of the lambs had somehow strayed and got himself all tangled up in the Vines climbing over the grape Arbor. I went to set him Free, and at the same moment a Shepherd, so I thought, came from the opposite Direction. As I turned to leave the job to him, a whisper floated across to me. *Silly Filly, she's a dilly.*

It was what Martinis used to say to Enrage me, he and only he! I whirled around. Farmer's rough homespun clothes and shabby tricorn, scrubby farmer's Boots, but no mistaking that Bronzed Face with its devilishly laughing mouth and snapping black Eyes.

"Martinis," I breathed, hurrying to him.

"Hush," he said softly. "No names. Help me free the Lamb."

Dumbly I obeyed, and as our hands met in this Homely Task, my shaking ones received a quick warm Clasp. "None of that. I need your Help."

"Why?" I asked desperately. "What? Was Nathan Hale—"

"Shh. Keep it low. Poor Nathan. His own Cousin is said to have turned him in. You're not going to do that to me, are you, Filly, my Love?" And he smiled at me as calmly as though we were discussing wether he would stay to Sup.

"Of course not. But God help me, I can't speak for Pa any Longer. You know him and his Duty. And some British Officers are coming to drink Tea with us today. We have them all the time. And . . . oh my God . . ."

"What is it?"

"Dierk. He's coming this way. Dierk Bruegel."

"The sixth Indian. Good old Dierk. It's Donkey's Years since I've seen him."

"You had better Hope it's a lot more years than that," I snapt on the Verge of Hysteria. "Good old Dierk is not only a Tory, he has a deep and Personal Hate for you. Pay heed now, he's coming Close. Keep your head turned to me, for God's sake, and listen to what I say."

The Lamb was free and ran away, and as Dierk came within Hearing Distance, I said quite loudly, "My mother is extremely upset that the Graves are so Over-Grown. Please cut all the Vines back and stack the Evergreens. I'll be there in a few Moments to see to the placing of them."

"Aye, Mum. I'll see to it." He touched the Brim of his Tricorn and dipped in an awkward Bow, then walked off at a slow Ambling Gait.

Dierk came up two minutes later and would have passed me by with a Civil Bow and a cool Greeting, but, fearfull he would catch up with Martinis, I detained him with a prolonged Inquiry into his father's Health. He had no choice but to Linger and answer me, though he made it plain his Preference was to be elsewhere. When I saw that Martinis was well past the Estate Office in the old Tavern, I let Dierk go. Then I hurried to the Cemetery.

We were Safer there. Kneeling together, pretending to be at Work on Jacob's Grave, we could risk a whispered Exchange.

"It's dangerous for you to come here, Martinis."

"I had to. I got picked up once and Bribed my way out. Not likely I'd be twice that Lucky. I had to get off the road. I'm carrying Papers that have to be delivered Today."

"Where? To who?"

"A man Fishing. Down at the Ferry Tavern."

"You can't go there. It's Crawling with British." I looked up in Alarm at the sound of Horses. "Oh, my God, the Soldiers are coming now."

"Never Fear," he said quite calmly. "They're headed for the House."

"Where are your Papers?"

"Inside my hat."

"Take it off."

He removed his Tricorn, as though to wipe his Brow, and let it drop to the grave, seemingly carelessly. I felt around inside it till my fingers touched paper. Bending closer over the Grave, I worked them slowly out, dug up a square Patch of Earth and Grass with my nails, laid the papers into the small hole, then replaced the patch to cover them. Then I piled a Heap of Evergreens over the Whole.

"How were you to know the man?" I asked Martinis, rising.

"When I ask him how the Fishing is, he'll say he's trying to get some Lobsters." He grinned Cheekily at this little Jab to the British. Then his eyes narrowed in sudden Understanding. "Oh no, not you, Filly, you're—"

"Is it Important that the Papers be delivered, Cousin?"

He set his teeth. "Yes."

"Well, there's not a Chance in Hell that you could do it," I told him calmly. "The Ferry is well guarded. Papers or not, you'll be Lucky to get away with a Whole Skin. Fill your arms with Evergreens."

He obeyed me rather meekly for Martinis.

"Now head for Cousin Lucretia's Cottage. It's mostly Boarded up, but you can get through one of the Windows if you have to. Wait there for me. I'll come by in the evening. Go up the Hill and the long way round, but if you meet Any One, play the simple Shepherd."

I turned back to my grave-tending wilst he made his way up the Hill. When he had disappeared from View, I got up on my feet and made for the House.

I seldom joyned my Father, except at his express Command, when he entertained the British Officers. It seemed the least Loyalty I could show to Piet and Bram and Martinis. But this day was different from other days. I told Thomasina I would serve the Tea, then dressed in my newest Chinz and went down to the Parlour, prepared to be Affable.

If Pa was surprised, he did not convey it, and the gentlemen, all Six of them, showed much Pleasure in receiving my Company. I used the word Gentlemen because their behavior and manners contributed to this Character. They were all well made, except for Major Stone-Leigh, who was monstrously tall and brown, a cross and proud man. But their coats were Scarlet, and that I cannot ever forget!

Two of the Officers, Lieut. Huntley and Lieut. Rice, were Young, so when I proposed to walk after we had drank our Tea and ate Thomasina's Cakes, both eagerly urged themselves on me as Escort. I hesitated prettily before accepting, then ran upstairs for a Cloak and a Basket, which I hurriedly stuffed full of dried flowers.

"If you gentlemen will be so kind as to Delay a Moment," I told them, "I must just stop at the cemetery and put these flowers on my brothers' Graves. My Mother likes them changed each day."

Naturally, they could not Demur, especially with my giving them the flirtatious kind of smile which, in the old days, would have got me dipped in the Horse Trough if the Indians had seen me putting on such a Parade of Insincere Charm!

Thus it was, that with an escort of two British Officers, I was able, under cover of Decorating the Graves, to slip a slim sheaf of papers into the flower basket over my arm. Then, laughing and prattling merrily, I led those two poor hapless Young Men down to the River and along the path that led to the Ferry Crossing.

Sure enough there was a shabby Fisherman on the banks of the River. As we passed by him, I asked casually, "Is the fishing good today? Have you caught any sturgeon?"

He doffed his cap. "No sturgeon, Ma'am, but some Shad. I'm hoping to take out a boat later and get some Lobsters."

"Have you seen our Hudson Shad, gentlemen? They're the finest anywhere," I said, thankful they were too ignorant of our River to know the Shad would never run in November.

While they politely disclaimed, I dropped my basket at the Fisherman's feet. We both stooped together. "Allow me, ma'am," he said, and as he restored it to me, I slipped the papers from the bottom of the Basket into his waiting Palm, my Cloak as I swung around concealing all this action, which took not more than ten Seconds.

I smiled radiantly at the fisherman as the three of us went on our way. His face remained otherwise Sober, but one eye closed in a Wicked Wink.

When the Officers were gone, I descended belowstairs to the Kitchen to fill my basket with bread and meat and a Wedge of pie, also a small jug of cider.

Then I went to the stables and had Will saddle old Granny, the one Horse left to us that Pa wouldn't notise was gone, if he should come by.

By horse, even on old Granny, using the Back Trail, it was just fifteen minutes to Cousin Lucretia's Cottage. I turned the Key in the front door and lifted the Iron Latch, which allready showed the signs of Neglect in a house Unused. Most of the Nails studding the top half of the Door had been yanked out.

I closed both halves behind me, whispering, "Martinis?"

"In the parlour."

I flew towards the sound of his voice and he towards mine. We Hurteled against one another, but he held me off for a moment, Gripping my shoulders almost painfully. "The papers?"

"Delivered. I like your fisherman. He Winked at me."

He fetched a deep Sigh. "Oh Filly, there's no one like you."

Then we were Kissing each other, madly, Hungrily, breathlessly, and we didn't stop until Martinis remembered that his most overwhelming Hunger was for food and I remembered I had brought a Basket of it for him.

We sat on the floor together while he ate, breaking off pieces of bread and tearing the meat apart with his teeth.

He kissed me once more before he sent me away, saying he

wanted me Safely Home before Nightfall, when he planned to set out himself.

"How will I know you got Safe Away?" I wailed just at the last, and he smiled in his old reckless way. "I've only to cross the River, and thanks to you, I carry nothing Dangerous. I'm just a simple Farm Boy." He jerked me back into his arms. "I'll get word to you somehow," he said roughly. "Filly, did you know I love you?"

"No," I answered faintly.

"Silly Filly." His voice might have been another Kiss. "We all loved you. Bram and Dierk and me. Is that why Dierk hates me, has he spoken for you?"

"Yes," I said more faintly still.

"Well, I'm not worried about *him,* poor stick, but mind you wait for me."

Supremely sure, he said it as a Command, not a question. Then he kissed not my lips but my Hands, looking at me the while with eyes so Glowing, my stomach churned with a host of new Sensations. Speechless still, I found myself turned about; one cautious Look he cast about, then I was sent out of the house with a brotherly Pat on the Bottom.

Twenty minutes later I led old Granny into his stall and then ran to the House. No one appeared to have noticed I was gone, and though Thomasina looked at me sharply when I returned the empty basket to the kitchen, she said Nothing.

I'm alone in my Bedchamber now, and Martinis must be crossing the River. Look after him, please God, keep him Safe. Come to think of it, he probably had to Steal one of our Boats.

But he said it. How many years have I not Waited to hear him say it? He loves me. And the look in his Eyes before he pushed me out of the House. It heated me more even than his Kisses. And brotherly or not, I can still feel his Hand on my Bottom . . . Oh Martinis . . . Martinis . . .

I was right about something else. He and Nathan Hale . . . It allways seemed a Dishonourable way to act, but if it's on Behalf of one's Country . . . ? It's no less dangerous than soldiering; indeed, the Risk of an Ignoble Death is greater.

Great God, I have just realized another thing! *I* took the Papers and delivered them for Martinis, and right under the noses of two British Officers. It seemed to my mind at the time the safest possible way to get the job done. Who would suspect a silly girl Flirting with a Pair of Redcoats?

At the very thought that now occurs to me, I am so mightily scared that even as I pen these words my teeth rattel in my mouth and my hands shake like Aspen Leaves, and I must call Reason to my Aid to keep from running downstairs and howling my fears aloud. Instead, I must call Fortitude to my Aid and never speak to any Being of anything that happened this day.

Only in my Journal, now to be Hid away, may I confide that this day *I*, too, have acted the Spy!

Filly's Journal
April 3, 1777

I am eighteen today and feel years older. There is no Celebrating the Occasion, how can there be? I do not write much these days. Somehow I feel Unsafe when my Journal is out of Hiding . . . Moreover there are not many pages left to this Volume, and the Scarsity of paper begins to be so great, I know not if there will be another Book for my Scribblings when this one is finished with. It seems as though I should write only of Important things, the last of which occurred very many Months ago, the Joyous Tidings conveyed—I know not how—in the slip of paper left among the flowers on Rachel's Grave. It said that the one I was Concerned about was Safe Away. And afterwards, by letter long delay'd from Cousin Lucretia, came word that Martinis was a soldier fighting in Uniform, for which many a night I have fervently thanked God, preferring that he risk the enemy's bullets in preference to a Hangman's Rope.

Since then we have known much of Gloom and Misery in these parts, for all that Cousin Lucretia foretold has come to pass.

This part of Westchester stands between the Americans and the British, so that they call it the Neutral Ground, which has a Grim Irony about it, for a less Neutral Area it would be hard to find in these new States of America.

What has happened is that we are preyed on here not only by both the Upper and Lower Parties, but even as Cousin Lucretia said (would that she had been wrong!), the Riff-Raff that attatch themselves to both Armies and even private groups that claim allegance to one Side or the Other though it is plain to all their only allegance is to themselves. But one durst not say this aloud for fear of even greater Reprisals, though what more they can take from us I know not.

Our livestock is mostly gone, all our Cattle, half the Sheep, most of the Horses, stolen by the cowardly Tory Ruffians who are styled the Cowboys because it is their Habbit to take up the cattle and empty the stables of Friend and Foe alike and drive this plundered Livestock to New York, where the Profitts from sale are greater. They ask not the Politicks of either Horse or Cow they steal and more than that of the Owner, and when my father has protested his loyalty to the Crown, they demanded he prove it by allowing himself to be robbed. The first time, a daylight Raid, having no other choice than Consent, he Consented; and we were all only thankfull that Flip was out on his mare Jenny for I think it would break his heart to lose her. Our good Fortune it was, too, that a half dozen of the horses were in use on the Farm and not found.

Since the first Raid we have learned to be Cunning, and we try to hide what we can, but it is not always possible for they Swoop down on us by day and night, and the armies are in no way willing to exert themselves to protect the Unfortunate Inhabitants of this Land.

A group called the Skinners are professedly patriotic to the American cause, which is not the case at all, for which I am gratefull because I would blush for our Cause to think it represented by such as these. They are, if possible, even worse than the Cowboys, robbing, even killing those that Oppose them. One of their wretched Victims was our Farmer Jacob Vorst, who, because he protested their emptying his Barns, they hung up by his arms from the Barn Doors, to punish, they said, his lack of Patriotism. His sufferings till he was Extracted from this position I can hardly describe.

As for the British, they encourage the acts of their Partisans and make no difference between Tories like Pa or the most ardent Americans. To them we are all Provincial Rebbels!

Our Storehouses and Smoke Houses are empty, the very cheeses, still unripened, are taken from us. They march through our House, helping themselves to any Triffels that take their Fancy from our spider cooking pots to fine China Cups, and if they are in the mood, they smash our Possessions and Axe our Furnishings for the sheer pleasure of Destruction. Thank God for the Waggon Load of goods Mama and I sent to West Point along with Cousin Lucretia's. It may well be all that is Salvaged intact by the time this War is over.

Just yesterday two sad old black mares were in front of the House when a Foraging Party rode up.

"I see, Sir," the Leader said to Pa, "you have two black mares there."

"Yes," said my father, "but no mind to Dispose of them."

"No need to trouble yourself, Sir," said the Leader. "We'll do that for you."

And the Horses were run off and the House ransacked again.

Pa did not like the way the Leader looked at me. He wants me to hide in my Chamber when Raiders come. Flip too. But Flip allways rushes off to Cousin Lucretia's, where we keep Jenny hidden. Pa's Horse, too, and the milk cow Gretchen. Poor Cousin Lucretia. She may not be House Proud, but even her Stout Heart would be daunted by the sight of a Cow in her Kitchen and Horses in her Store Room.

Mama is the only one who seems to be not affected by the Ravages of this War. She keeps to her Chamber, mostly to her Bed, and we all protect her as best we can. How strange a thing is the Human Mind. I think her dead are more real to her than her Living Children.

I wish it were summer and Flip and I could go Swimming off the Island. I wish it were Years ago, and we were Six Indians playing there together, fishing, fighting, laughing, singing.

How many more years will it be untill we do those things again?

Filly's Journal
April 8, 1777

Four days since, in the name of King and Country, a cowardly lot of Cowboys drove off the last of our oxen. Last evening a ruffian band of Skinners, making jests and likewise proclaiming it our Patriotic Duty, absconded with the last of our Sheep, all but a few stray Lambs.

So now our farmers are without their Beasts to plough, and we are like Shorn Sheep ourselves, robbed of the flocks of which my father was so proud. (His experiments in Breeding were but last year writ up in the Agricultural Journal.) From where will come the Wool for this winter's Spinning? And where the Mutton to salt and store against the freezing months when we cannot take fish from the River? And how wild and ragged our Lawns will be without the Sheep to Crop the Grass.

Even if we could secure more Livestock, what use, Pa asks? We would only be buying them for one or another of our Enemies. A Pox on Men and their Wars!

Filly's Journal
April 15, 1777

Though I never thought to hear myself say it, God be praised, the Pigeons have returned in great numbers as they do every Year at this time. For a week now they have formed an endless track Overhead and the Men with their Weapons literally reach up and Pluck them from the Skies like so much Manna from the Heavens. We have Pigeon Pies and Pigeon Soups and Pigeons dressed and roasted as only Thomasina can prepare them, but above all, plenty of Pigeons to salt and store away. We will dig underground store rooms this time, Pa says. This will make Food for us and Ours, not for our Oppressors, be they Tory or American.

Estate Book
Van Duren Manor
July 30, 1777

On this day my Beloved Wife Annetje was gathered to her Maker. These past six weeks since Philip's slain body was brought Home, she has lain in her bed as one already Dead, silent, motionless, except for her shallow Breaths, but this day at Dawn her Frale Heart gave up the Struggle, she breathed her last. Too much she Endured. Too much we have Endured together. Three of our dear ones taken from us in their Infancy, miscarried of one child and one dead at Birth. Her heart broke anew when I struck Pieter's name from the Van Duren Bible, but a Vow is a Vow, and he ceased to be my son when he joined with the Rebells and took up arms against our King and Country. When my Annetje lost Philip, it was the final bitter Stroke. A Pox on doctors and ministers with their Pompuss Pronouncements. She died of not wanting to Live. She is at Peace at last. I would not bring her back if I could for her own Sweet Sake. What is there left to me? My God, my God, why hast Thou forsaken me?

Estate Book
Van Duren Manor
Aug. 1, 1777

We buried my dear Wife this noon time. She lies alongside Philip and near to all her Other Dear Infants. As I dropped the first handful of earth onto her Coffin, I had this one thing to be thankful for, that my Dear Wife expired without knowledge of our daughter's disgrace. God's Goodness extended so far—she Departed life unknowing the name of Philadelphia Van Duren is become a By-Word and a Scandel through all of Westchester County.

As much as I am able in my Grief, I have given Thought to this Matter and can see only one Remmedy, which is to hide Philadelphia's Name Beneath Another. My acres are in Jeopardy until this Rebbellion is ended, but I still have good Dutch gold, and English, too, to buy Dierk Bruegel's name for my girl. He and his father have both Signified their Willingness. And why not? Before, they could not have Aspired so High.

Just a few moments since when the Funeral Guests had departed, I summoned Philadelphia to the Estate Office and told her of my Arrangements. She paled but uttered no word of Protest and soon afterwards Sought her bed. Adversity has made her more Amenable. She knows she has no other Choice.

I have reached another Decision, as yet Unknown to any other. My last tie to this place was my Wife; she would not leave the Graves of her Beloved Dead. But graves mean nothing to me; I carry my dead with me in my heart wheresoever I may be. My Properties are eaten away Bit by Bit by the Skinners and the Cowboys. It is only a Matter of Time untill my lands are all taken from me by the Rebbels. I would not be Here when that day arrives. There is the small Estate my father bought in Suffolk all those years ago. To England then I will go untill these warring Colonies are brought to their knees.

Let me but get Philadelphia Wedded, the final Duty I owe to her, and then I will be gone from this Hellish Land of Unhappiness.

Estate Book
Van Duren Manor
Aug. 20, 1777

The Carts are lined up in the driveway with a half-score of my Tenants and Servants, full-armed to guard us into New York City. Philadelphia has just come from the Graveyard and gone to join Lucretia in the carriage. I could not see her face clearly, but she held her Head high. I Misdoubt that she was crying; her Pride Protects her even now.

I Ship for England within the week, which does not allow enough time for the Banns to be read and Philadelphia and Dierk to be Wedded. But I will leave all in Lucretia's hands, and Philadelphia understands my Desire to be quickly gone from these Shores. Indeed she was the one who urged that I not wait for the next Ship.

"Mijn Vader"—I recalled afterwards that it is only when she is much moved that she uses the Dutch form of Address to me—"let us not Pretend that your Trip to England or my Marriage are ordinary Events. They are both things to be gotten over with quickly and with as little Fuss as Possible. Please take the first Ship out, as you are longing to, and Cousin Lucretia will attend to my Affairs."

For the First Time since I cast my eyes on Philip's crushed and Bleeding Head, I softened towards my Daughter. God forgive me if I have been Unjust, but it is True that I have blamed her Recklessness for All.

"Philadelphia," I said more gently than I have spoken to her in many Weeks, "it is not too late, if you wish to come with me. No one in England will know of you. I can give Bruegel some small Monies to compensate him and we can say you are Widowed in one of the Battles."

Even before I finished Speaking, she was shaking her head. "I hate the British, God damn their Souls to Hell," she said in her old Passionate Way. "I will not live among them. Even Dierk would be Preferable."

God forgive me, but when she rushed away again, I was Gratefull that she had not accepted the Offer made in my Momentary Weakness. She was once dearer to me than all save Annetje; she is my last surviving child if Pieter be not Alive, and of him I try not to think. Still, the Terrible Truth is I do not want her with me. I want all Ties Severed, so that I can take up my Life in the Old World without Memories of the Bitter Past.

A knock just sounded on the door, and when I called out, Tom Nease's voice answered gruffly, "Master, we be all ready."

"I will be with you in two minutes," I answered him calmly.

Two minutes. Aye, two minutes to end a Way of Life.

This will be my last Entry in this Book for many years, perhaps For Ever if the Rebbels are not put to Rout. I shall not take this Logg and the others with me. They belong to Van Duren Manor. My last Act before I Exit this room shall be to hide them Behind the Wainscoting back of the Book Shelves. One day perhaps I shall Retrieve them.

My Father Dreamt, when he bought these Acres, that we would be Lords of the Manor here on the Hudson for Hundreds of Years to come. Farewell this Dream. Farewell Annetje, my love, my life.

CHAPTER
17

Within twenty minutes of arriving at my motel, I was on my way home to New York and Bryarly. I still had her set of extra keys, but rather than use them and come on her unaware, I had the doorman announce me.

When the elevator stopped at the fourteenth floor, Bryarly stood right opposite it waiting for me. She wore a long, pink flannel house coat and her face was scrubbed clean of makeup. The door of her apartment yawned wide and welcoming.

I dropped my suitcase when I got to her, and she came into my arms as naturally as a flower lifts its face to the sun. She did not raise her face for the kiss I coveted, though; I had to content myself with pressing my lips to her cheek and the tip of one ear.

In the living room we sat on opposite ends of the couch. Bryarly sat very upright with her ankles crossed and her hands clasped tightly on her lap.

"Relax, sweetheart," I said softly, and bent forward to separate the hands before she could cut off her circulation.

"Jake, *please,*" she implored.

So I told her briefly about Philippa Jansen, who was a descendant of the colonial Van Duren family, and her Hudson Valley Dutch Art Historic Society . . . about the house and pictures . . . and the secret history of the Van Durens as it had unfolded to me in the journals and correspondence of Lucretia De Kuyper and the Estate Book of Cornelius Van Duren, then later the letters of the next generation . . . the boys who became the Indians, Pieter Van Duren, Bram De Kuyper, Martinis Asher, and of Philadelphia, the heart of them all.

She listened with head bent and face slightly turned away. Her concentration was focused so fiercely on every word I spoke that the atmosphere about us fairly sizzled with emotion.

"What became of her?" she asked in a strained, colorless voice, greatly at odds with the high-voltage intensity of her attention.

"I don't really know—not yet. I read only as far as her growing-up years. Philippa Jansen sorted the family papers and appears to have divided everything in different sections. This was Part One. Philippa made me comfortable by the fire to read it," I laughed, "but I wasn't allowed to take notes."

"So that's all there is to it?" Bryarly asked with a curious fatalistic little shrug, finally turning her face toward me.

"Not at all. Philippa invited me back, and you, too. She is completely willing to show us both more of the story."

"You told her about me, too?"

"I told her enough about my nightmare to justify my own curiosity. I brought you in," I continued carefully, "by mentioning a Cousin Lucretia in your life and the feeling you have that Philadelphia poses some sort of barrier between *us.*"

"What did she say?"

I grinned reminiscently. "Well, at first she thought I was making the whole thing up to get at family records that have been kept secret a long time. When she began to believe me, she decided I, *we,* had a right to know. She's also curious. She really wants to meet you."

Bryarly sat silent for a long time. When she finally brought her face around to me, my heart turned over, a little in pity and in pain. The old lost look was back in her eyes. She moved a bit away, unconsciously setting the same distance between us physically as she was mentally.

The tip of her tongue flicked lightly over her lips. "Was she—Philadelphia—was her life good?" she asked hesitantly.

"Very good, I would say, for the most part. She was a happy, beloved child and a happy, beloved girl. A bright, appealing little tomboy who became a warm, lovely, intelligent young lady."

"You mean no inhibitions, repressions, or neuroses?" she asked me mockingly.

"Delightfully few." I realized too late that, however accurate, my answer showed a stupendously stupid lack of tact.

"You really liked her?"

"I really liked her."

I was tired and hungry, I think, or I wouldn't have made my second blunder. "If I weren't so in love with you, Bryarly, I think I might be a little in love with her."

She gave me the remote stare and chilly smile of our earlier meetings. "How interesting. I wonder that you could tear yourself away from her to come ho—here."

She had started to say *to come home,* and it gave me fresh heart, that, and the incredible suspicion I was beginning to nourish. *She was jealous of my interest in Philadelphia.*

I began a cautious retreat. "In 1777—that's when the part of her life I read ended—Philadelphia was eighteen. If she lived to be a very old lady by the standards of those days, let's say till 1827 when she was sixty-eight, then she's been dead exactly one hundred and fifty years." I seized the hands, which had been clasping and unclasping in her lap again. "So, however charming and delightful she might have been—and she was both—I can only be interested *in* her, my love, not enamored *of* her."

Her cheeks reddened; she jumped hastily to her feet. "Are you hungry? Would you like something to eat?"

"Something to eat would just about save my life."

"I wasn't expecting you. It will have to be just leftovers." She was edging toward the kitchen as she spoke.

"Leftovers will be fine. Give me a few minutes to wash and unpack, and I'll come help you."

"You don't have to bother."

"It's no bother." I took three long steps. My hands reached out for her shoulders, detaining her. The blush, which had begun to ebb, flowed over her face like the tide as I turned her around. "Bryarly, I missed you," I whispered against her hair.

She gave an unnatural high-pitched laugh, trying to make a joke of it. "Likewise, I'm sure."

"I love you."

She gave the same nervous laugh again but this time didn't speak.

"Can't you say, 'likewise' to that, too?" I teased gently.

The words almost exploded from her. "Jake, whatever it is you want of me, I don't have to give."

I let go of her shoulders. "Tell me," I said casually, "why has talk of Philadelphia upset you so? I thought it would help you to find out she and Cousin Lucretia did exist."

"That's because . . ." She bit back whatever else she had started to say and asked me wearily, "Can't we let it go for now? We'll talk while we eat."

We didn't, though, because the telephone rang just as we started on our grapefruit, and all during the pick-up meal, Bryarly stayed on the phone, talking and listening and revealing more to me than she would ever know.

"Joe, I know it hurts when she locks you out of the bedroom, but think how she's hurting. It has nothing to do with how she feels about you. She's testing you; she wants to know if you still care . . . and if you do, my God, now's your time to show it in ways that are important to her . . .

"No, never tell her to forget it happened. First of all, she can't. It would be damaging to her to think she should and not much use in court when the son of a bitch comes to trial.

"So let her talk, Joe, at midnight, at two in the morning, wherever and whenever she wants. Let her know it's all right with you.

"You've got to understand. She accepted guilt in the beginning because our society imposes that guilt. She didn't understand, as she does now, that she damn well has the right not to be raped!

"That's okay, all you're supposed to do is sympathize, not wallow in pity.

"Right. Just don't set time limits. Remember, when you think she should be over the worst of it is not necessarily when it will happen.

"You may find it hard to believe, but your marriage can wind up better and stronger than before.

"Don't ever think that. It's what I'm here for. Call any time you need me. Yes, I'll set up a date with Rita any time she wants.

"*De nada* . . . You're very welcome . . . Good night, Joe . . . Yes, any time . . . I'm very glad . . . Yes . . . Yes . . . Of course . . . Good night."

On the first "good night" I had gotten up and removed her plate from the oven and set it down before her. She pushed the now dried chicken and limp vegetables around with her fork and took a few unenthusiastic bites.

"I'm not very hungry," she murmured, putting the fork down.

"I don't wonder. It's a bit overdone. Eating has revived me quite a bit. Shall we go out and get something fit to eat for you?"

"No, I really mean it, I'm not hungry. Later, if I am, I'll have some fruit and cheese."

I sat quietly for a while, watching her set mouth and frowning abstraction.

"I understand your compulsion to do this work," I said quietly, "but should you if it upsets you so?"

She looked up in surprise. "It doesn't upset me. It's very satisfying. Did you know—it's a noteworthy fact for the book—that almost eighty percent of marriages, when a wife has been known to be raped, end up in divorce? But if the couple comes to a crisis center or advisory group of any kind, the way Rita and Joe did, they almost never break up. Joe's a really good guy. He cares about *her,* not what people say. He's angry that it happened, but his anger takes a proper direction. It's not pointed, as it so often is, at his wife, the victim. Also, which helps, he's willing to vocalize what he feels and let her do the same."

"I thought you handled him well. Personal interviews of that sort would add enormously to your research material. Will I be able to sit in on some of the counseling sessions?"

"I'll arrange it with anyone willing," she said a bit absentmindedly and lapsed into her own somber thoughts again.

When I started to do the dishes, she woke up and came over to help me. Afterward we went back to the living room, and I patiently endured two half-hour television shows chosen, I felt sure, to keep us from talking. When she went to switch the channel for the third time, I put my hand over hers and firmly switched off the TV.

"If it's not Rita and Joe, tell me what's upset you."

She curled up on a big hassock with her legs crossed under her, yoga style. "Not what," she corrected, *"who."* She looked away from me and then looked back a bit shame-facedly. "It's Philadelphia," she muttered.

"What about her?" I asked patiently.

"That's my question," she burst out. "There has to be more to her story than you told me."

"There is. I told you I only got as far as when she was eighteen."

"And all was sweetness and light until then? I don't believe it."

"I didn't exactly say that. After all, I was condensing twenty years of records into a short résumé. There were family troubles . . . deaths . . . marriage problems with her parents . . . and the War of Independence had come to Westchester and disrupted all their lives. In the very last two pages she gave definite hints of big trouble. Her father's Estate Book told of her mother's death and her young brother's; he seemed to hold her responsible. There was some kind of estrangement between them . . . he considered she had disgraced the family name."

"Ahhh." The one word came out of her as a deep prolonged sigh. It was almost as though she'd been expecting me to say it and was all set to pounce when I did.

"What had she done?" Bryarly demanded.

"It wasn't made clear. I expect it will be in the next section. I've got my suspicions, of course."

"Which were?"

"Bram De Kuyper was in love with Philadelphia from early childhood, but she had a king-size crush on Lucretia's nephew by marriage, Martinis Asher. Even after he joined the army, there were secret meetings between them—he seems to have done some spying, by the way. She was terrified he would wind up like Nathan Hale. I have a feeling perhaps she got pregnant by him, and he wasn't available for a shotgun wedding. Her father arranged a marriage with Dierk Bruegel, the only one of the six Indians who wasn't part of the family."

Bryarly unfolded her legs from beneath her and stretched them out. She held out her hands, studying her dragon-lady fingernails as though she had never seen them before. "Are you a betting man, Jake?" she asked me softly.

"Not really."

"I'll make you a big bet or a little one or any kind you want. Philadelphia may have gotten pregnant, but if she did it wasn't by this Martinis or Bram or any one of the Indians."

"I don't get it."

"I know you don't, and you should if you're going to make a success of our book. You've got to get inside the heads of a girl's loving menfolk. Why would a father—not to mention a husband or lover—consider a girl had disgraced the family name?" A touch of hysteria shrilled in her voice. "She was *raped,* Jake. Your darling Philadelphia was *raped.*"

"That's preposterous," I thundered at her. "It doesn't fit the facts at all."

"You're so wrong," she riposted bitterly. "It fits them all too well. Make your bet, Jake, if you don't believe I'm right. I'll bet you anything."

"Anything?"

"Anything."

"That you'll sleep with me? No sex, just share my bed one night. Would you bet that?"

"I'd bet that!" she flung back at me with a spit-in-your-eye kind of thrust to her chin. "That's how sure I am."

"Will you drive up to Tarrytown with me tomorrow? I could phone Philippa and arrange it right now."

"Arrange it for yourself, Jake. I'll come the next time."

"Why not this one?"

"Because I want you to tell this Mrs. Jansen—Philippa—what I just said. After she's given you the next section to read, I want you to show her what I'm writing down now. Not before . . ." She had opened her desk and was scribbling on a piece of paper. Judging from the speed with which she wrote and sealed her note in an envelope, it couldn't have been much more than a dozen words. "Promise me," she insisted, licking the envelope and pounding it closed with her fist, "promise me neither of you will read it until after you've read more about Philadelphia."

"I promise," I said, equaling her in solemnity. "Do you mind telling me why?"

"You'll understand then . . . maybe you'll understand," she amended in some doubt. "And Mrs. Jansen can decide after that," she added almost wistfully, "if she still wants to meet with me."

When I left for Tarrytown shortly after breakfast the next morning, she asked if I had her note. I patted my inside breast pocket and kissed her cheek.

Philippa Jansen greeted me on my arrival like an old friend and seemed genuinely sorry I had come alone. I told her about Bryarly's note.

"I'm curious to read it," she commented. "Let's get to work."

This time the manuscript she gave me was much slimmer.

A Secret History of the Van Duren Family, the file cover said, just like the first one. Then I turned the page, and a wild, frantic pounding sounded inside my head.... I felt as though it were suddenly encased in some kind of pressurized band.... My heart plunged all the way down to my boots and then soared sickeningly back where it belonged.

Part II: A Case of Rape in the Tarrytowns, 1777, I read aloud.

The words sort of staggered before my eyes for a minute. Then gradually the line of typing straightened out, and I turned the page again to let the past speak for itself.

A Secret History of the Van Duren Family
Part II: A Case of Rape in the Tarrytowns, 1777

Journal of Lucretia Bogardus
New York
3rd Nov. 1777

On the highest Rise of our land here in the City, at the point where the lawns slope downward to the banks of the River, the year before his death, my Arend caused to be bilt a special Stone Bench. It has a wide Seat just right for two, side Arms and a High Back to brake the East Wind.

"When we are old and gray and Unfit for greater Exercize," he said to me wunce, the Familyer Twinkel of Fun in his Eyes, "we will Totter Together to our Bench each morning and sit Holding Hands whilst we gaze at the River."

I have avoided Arend's Bench ever since. It brings me Memories too Painfull. But now every Morning after we Breakfast, except that it be Wet, it has daily use, for Philadelphia wraps herself in a cloke and with dragging feet makes her Way to it. She sits on the Bench for Hours, looking out, but I fear me she does not see the beauty of our River. Her eyes look inward, and when I have Approched her sometimes with a warm Afghan to put over her—for she is Regardless of cold and wind—I have seen the Despaire writ large on her Face.

She prefers to be alone. I note that now she carries an Afghan with her. This is not so much for the Warmth of it as that I may not feel Obliged to bring it to her. The very need to Greet me, to Smile, to say a few Words is an Effort that reqwires her to Gird up her Strenth.

I have been Content these last Weeks to Leave her to her Brooding. She needed time for Healing. But now I Wonder. Must I be Cruel to do what is Right for her and bring her back amongst the Living?

She is my dearest Objeckt in Life save only Bram. These two, Martinis and Pieter I now live for. Dear God in Heaven, Help me to Help her.

Philadelphia Van Duren, Her Journal
New York
Nov. 17, 1777

I never thought to write in my Journal again. Even as I pen these Words I am not sure I will be able to go on with it, but I must make the Effort.

Cousin Lucretia came to me last week as I was sitting in her Orchard on the Qwaint Stone Bench with its curiously carved arms and comfortable Broad Back. For some reason or other, she does not care for the Bench, which is Surprising, since it was built for Uncle Arend.

I am afraid I was not very Welcoming, for of a Truth, I am grown accustommed to Sweet Solitude, and I resent almost any Intrusion upon it. Cousin Lucretia has been most Kind to my Moods these past two Months, but not on this Occassion.

"It is time we Talked, Filly," she said to me.

A Spasm of Pain clutched at my heart, for Filly was a silly innocent *ignorant* child who died in her folly some five months gone.

"Do you know, Cousin Lucretia," I said, moving aside to give her room as she sat down beside me, "I have a Fancy to be called Philadelphia now. It is, after all, my name, and I am no longer a child."

"No, my dear, you are not," she said with some Compassion, "and it is of that we must Speak."

Heat and Wetness broke out all over my Body, as though I had the Sweating Sickness. A Voice as unlike my own as could be came from me. "I cannot. If I could speak to anyone, it would be to you . . . or Thomasina . . . but . . ."

I put my two hands to my face and cried out again in Agony from behind their Frail Shelter. "I cannot. I cannot."

"Philadelphia, *mijn lieve, mijn dochter,*" she said and Rocked me in her arms, which she has Seldom done, though I have always Felt her love like a Warm Garment about me. "I know you cannot. Yet talk you must. Thomasina agrees with me. No wound ever Heals unless first the Poisons are purged from the body. Write it down, Philadelphia, in a letter to someone you Love, or, if not that, then in your Journal."

I recoiled in Horror. "Never in a letter to—to—"

"Then your Journal," she said placidly, putting me from her. "Vomit it up as the Fish did Jonah."

"There are no Pages left in my Journal. Even were there, I don't think—"

"I will give you one of Arend's Business Ledgers to start a new One, I have a-plenty," she told me in that same calm way.

"Cousin Lucretia," I began pleadingly, only to be interrupted once more.

"You have never been a Coward, Philadelphia."

I reminded her quietly, "Many things about me have changed, Cousin Lucretia, none for the Better."

"I refuse to accept that." Her hand rested against my Cheek for a moment. "I will not pretend to believe with the Preachers that all things Happen for the Best. What I do believe is that your Courage will Revive and your Strength Suffices to carry you through this Crisis. Happiness is in your Grasp . . . perhaps not now . . . but Later."

Happiness in my Grasp? I have ever thought Cousin Lucretia to be one of the wisest Women I know, but that is a Truly Laughable Notion.

Her other notion, though . . . that I should write it out and purge myself of the Poison. At first I thought I could not contemplate it . . . to live again that Terror, bring back the Foule Memories.

Then Cousin Lucretia, without another word to me on the Subject, laid the Ledger on the desk in my Chamber. I found myself again and again Reverting to this empty Accounting Book as though some Charm of Prose or Poetry lay within it instead of Blank Pages. Again and again I turned those selfsame pages, their virgin whiteness acting on my Brain like a Hypnotick. Almost I was soothed by the thought of Sullying that whiteness . . . as I . . .

God above, if You are there, do I ask too much . . . not to be free of the Memories . . . I know that to be Impossible! But to be Clean of them? God, let me be clean.

In the Morning of the Next Day

I had to stop writing last night and seize the Bowl I keep by me, for Cousin Lucretia is more Right than she knows. If there be Poisons in the Body, they must come out. Her Comparison with Jonah and the Fish was all too Apt. Nightly these many weeks I have Vomited up my Poisons. No wonder I grow Rail Thin and see the Bones poke out from between my Ribs. In Vain it would seem, since the more I Vomit, the more are the Poisons Retained; it is the Nourishment I am Ridden of.

The maids are aghast at the number of Baths I take. They think I am Scrubbing away my skin and eating into my Flesh. They Whisper that it is no wonder I am grown so Thin and Pale.

And so I am Resolved to try Cousin Lucretia's Remedy, being Unable or Unwilling any Longer to go on as I have Done. God help me if she be not right for I am like to lose my Mind as well as my Health.

Philadelphia's Journal
Nov. 20, 1777

It was one thing to Resolve. It has taken me another two days to Bring me to the Point where I can act on my Resolution.

I have tried this Hour past to think of ways to begin. There are none. I must Begin at the Beginning and go on till I am done.

In the middle of this June past a Squad of British Soldiers were encamped on our land, some Officers quartered within our House who every Day took their meals with us.

My Father was pleased because no Cowboys or Skinners dared come while even this small Might of the British Army protected us;

Headquarters added to our Food Supply and gave him written Garantee of Payment for his Services. Above all, they replaced some of the Horses and Live-Stock he has lost.

Withal I felt great Guilt to sit and sup with them when I thought of Martinis and Pieter and Bram serving in the Continental Army, which opposes this one. The very men I sit laughing with over Table might Some Day meet my three Dear Indians on the Battle-Field.

Flip was Affected by the same Qwalms.

"Let's get away from the damn British," he proposed to me early of one Morning. "It seems forever since our last time on the Island."

I made Eager agreement and Thomasina packed Lunch for us in a Basket. Flip mounted his dear mare Jenny, I took one of the new Work Horses, and we Stole off as we used to when we played Truant from Mr. Bruegel's Class.

We lay on the Banks of the River, fishing idely and talking. Flip told me his plans to leave at summer's end to Join the Army, which came as no great Surprise to me. Then we ate and talked some more. We played our Fifes in concert, which we have not done in many Months, sad songs and merry ones, and Flip played alone a Tune that he had Compozed for me, *Song of Philadelphia*. There were nine Verses, I think. I can remember but the first, which he recited for me Several Times.

All in all, we had three Hours of greater Peace and Contentment than I have known since coming home to Westchester from Philadelphia and am ever Like to Know again.

Then the Soldiers came, British redcoats. Deserters at a Guess. And with them the Simple Simon of the Der Horst Family, he the boys call Tom Dumb.

Like a child of five, Tom Dumb jumped up and down in Glee. "See. Tom told you there were Horses. See the Horses. Tom's a good boy."

"Tom's a right good boy," agreed one of the soldiers, a fox-faced creature with sharp eyes and a thin pale mouth.

The Other, a great overgrown Lout with reddish hair, said in an Insinuating way I much Misliked, "Tom's a very good boy; he found us more than Horses."

Flip and I had both jumped to our feet. Now he sprang in front of me.

"Don't dare to touch our Horses! There's a British troop at our House. I'll see you both strung up if you Try."

They both carried Muskets and Knives.

"Flip, let them do as they want," I told him low and urgently. "The soldiers will go after them later."

"Well, you see, Sonny," drawled out Ferret-Face, "we're trying to make Tracks between us and the Army, being allreddy in enough Trouble, so your Threats don't make us never No Mind."

As the Lout lifted a foot to Jenny's stirrups, Flip flung himself at him, dragging at his legs. The two grappeled together for a minute while I reached out for a Stout Tree Branch.

I had one in both hands, Ready to Swing, when Ferret-Face brought his Musket down on my wrist. With a shrill cry of Pain, my Hand opened up, and the Branch fell to the ground. As it did, the Musket flashed in the Sun again and came down with a much more resounding thud on my brother's uncovered Head.

With just the Slightest grunt, Flip crumbeled to the Ground. I would have dropped to my knees Beside him, but Ferret-Face had me by the wrist, the same one he had almost Paralized with his Musket. It caused me a most Wrenching Pain.

"Take the horses and go!" I cried. "You'll be Safe if you hurry. I won't try to stop you."

"Fancy that now, Georgie," the Lout said mockingly, "the Lady won't try to stop us."

"The Lady's stopping me, Bill Boy," said Ferret-Face, grinning awfully. "I can't ride in my Condition. How about you?"

"I could do with a spot of Relief, George. Do we have the Time?"

"I say we make the Time, Bill Boy."

My head was jerking back and forth between the Two of them. Though not quite understanding the meaning of this Dialogue, I knew enough to fear it.

Ferret-Face pressed down on my wrist to bring me to my Knees before him while the Lout drew nearer. There was something Cruel and Feline about their Smiles. A deep Instinct of Revulsion told me what was Intended.

I pleaded with them. God, when I remember how I Begged, how I Abased myself, I, who always held my head so High. I brought my Pride low without cause; I Humbled myself for naught—they had no Pity.

After kicking away the remains of our lunch, they stretched me out on the Grassy Mound where Flip and I had eaten. Then they plucked Blades of Grass and determined by their Length which one would go first with me.

George, the Ferret-Face, won and the Lout went to my head and held both my Hands pinioned above it in one of his great horny paws while his other hand tore at my lacings and made rough play with my Breasts.

The pull to my arms was so agonizing I felt I was being Stretched upon the Rack; the fire of Pain from my wrist was such I feared it might be Broke. Added to this was the lothsome touch of those Fingers inside my Bodice . . .

Then these which seemed such Horrors became nothing by Compare, for my overskirt and petticoats were bunched about my waist, my shift torn away, and I lay there bared before him, staring with incredulous Horror at what was disclosed when he Loosened his Breeches.

"Spread your legs," he growled, at which, mad with fear, I brought them tighter together.

Swearing a great ugly oath, he seized my ankels and stretched out my legs, jumping nimbly between them. Then he fell a-top me so that the Breath was knocked out of me and only Recovered in time for me to Scream and Scream and Scream as that Monstrous Instrument thrust violently into the Innermost Recess of my Body and all but Tore me Assunder. It Emerged only to Thrust forcibly Inside once More.

Then he Battered me Again and Again till I was bloody and Bruised and in a Twilight World of pain that Redused me to a poor whimpering thing crying for its Mother; a poor prideless thing crying for an end to Torment.

Suddenly Ferret-Face seemed overcome by a spasm of Pain himself. I stared up at him, Numb and Dumb as he cried out, with his face Contorted. Then he suddenly Slumped over me, and I felt his Breath fanning my face and turned away, for this was a final Intimasy more than I could bear.

Whatever had overcome him was soon finished. He slid away from me, and there was the Slightest Easing of the Burning Pain that Afflicted me between the legs.

"Damn me, if we didn't get ourselves a Virgin, Bill," said

Ferret-Face, buttoning his breeches. I closed my eyes against the Sight while the Lout protested that he had been cheated.

"Once she's been Swived," he said sullenly, "she's no more Virgin."

There was a whispered exchange between them during which my hands were freed, and I turned on my side, I know not why, to curl up like a Babe in its mother's Womb, gulping in deep breaths of air while the tears rained ceaselessly down my cheeks.

When I felt rather than saw them return to me, I gave a dry Sob of Despair and turned over on my stomach, determined to make more of a fight of it.

This time it was George, the Ferret-Face, who grabbed at my wrists, his fingers banding them cruelly tight while his face came right up against Mine.

There was no fight possible; all I could do was Flap helplessly around on my stomach, like a landed Fish; and the more I struggled, the more he laughed, so that I was staring down his throat and at his rotted teeth, or, if I lowered my Eyes, at the blinding Red of his uniform.

Then the Lout knelt over my legs and once again my skirts were lifted and my body bared. Even now to think of it . . . to write it down . . . Among the beasts of the field who act thus, there is willingness on the part of both. Sometimes the Female is skittish and plays with the Male. She may tease him; but if she is really reluctant, she butts him away or runs off herself.

Only men are lower than the animals. Only Men Force themselves on the Unwilling and take Delight in Inflicting Pain. Forced to Endure the Unendurable, I screamed out my Anguish till I had no Voice left to me and all the while I cursed my brother in my heart that he should be Unconscious and I not.

They were done with me. I was on my knees, dully watching, as they got set to mount the Horses. Suddenly Tom was in their way, crying like a petulant child, "Me, too. Me, too, ride the pretty Lady."

They laughed so hard that tears stood in their eyes. They slapped one another on the Back. They Wiped their Faces, and the Lout choked out, "Sure, Tom boy, you get a Ride on the Lady, too."

I was sure that I could handle Tom, and perhaps I might have, had we been alone, but there were the Redcoats to encourage him. I found myself seized again and thrust beneath a Male Body, which straddled me awkwardly. Hands tugged at me uncertainly.

"She's a Filly, Tom," Ferret-Face called out. "Plunge in like a proper Stallion. Ride her High, boy, ride her High!"

Thus encouraged, Tom plunged in, spearing me so fast and furiously that it was less than a minute till his seed filled me, spilling out down my legs and onto the ground. In the selfsame moment, the Lout rose up in his Stirrups as Tom had just risen up in me, and he shot the Simple Simon between the eyes. Tom slumped down upon me, his head against my Breast.

They galloped off, their laughter floating back to me, as I scrambled from beneath the inert Body, desperately swiping with the edges of my skirt at the blood upon my Breast.

I know not why they killed Tom Dumb any more than why they Spared me. What I remember next is kneeling on our Island, swaying to and fro in the wildness of my shame and Confoundment. Then I crawled slowly and painfully to where Flip lay so still to examine his Hurts.

I knew the instant I saw his head, with the skull caved in. Sobbing harshly, I turned him over. He lay looking up at me, white and peaceful and quite dead.

I held his head against my bloodied breast. I rocked back and forth with him held to me like an Infant. I begged his Forgiveness for having cursed him. I begged him to speak to me. I begged him not to be Dead.

The Dead do not Reply.

Presently I laid him down and looked about me. My lifeless brother lay before me; the lifeless mad boy behind me. There was only me to go for help.

I staggered to my feet, and the pain was so excruciating when I tried to walk that I achieved my Dearest Wish of the Moment. I fell over on the Ground in a Faint.

I awoke God knows how much later in a Nightmarish Confusion of Pain and Remembrance. There was a Crushing Weight on my Chest. It seemed I had Died and was being Buried. They were putting the Stones on top of me.

My eyes opened, flutteringly at first, and then all the way, and I screamed out in piercing Terror for there was a red-faced animal sitting on my chest. As I heaved up to free myself, the animal turned to stare at me with the grey-green eyes of Ferret-Face. I screamed again, and as it flicked its tail in my face and skittered away, I saw that it was just an old cat, a big striped Tabby, and its face was Red with Tom Dumb's Blood. It stood over his body even now, Delicately lapping at the gaping wound in the middle of his forehead, its face growing ever Redder.

My groping fingers found a Stone, which I Hurled at him. The Tail clicked indignantly again; the grey-green eyes gave me a Chilling Stare, and then he ran away.

I crawled back close to Flip, and I put my arms around him; and all the rest of that day I lay there with him, holding him Close to me while I drifted in and out of consciousness.

Some time after dark, the British Patrol, alerted by Thomasina where to look for us, arrived at the Island.

I came awake to hear a kind voice with a soft Scots Burr saying, "puir lassie, puir puir lassie."

But when I opened my eyes all I saw was the Red Coat on his back, on all their backs; and I screamed and cried and fought them like a Bedlamite untill the Scotsman said, "Puir Wild Creatir, we must"; and I felt a fearful Tap on my Jaw and sank back into the Welcoming Darkness.

Philadelphia's Journal
Nov. 21, 1777

I do not pretend to understand why. I thought I would do myself Immeasurable Harm by opening old Wounds. Instead, after writing late on into the Night, I suddenly realized that for the first time in Many Weeks my food had stayed Down, there had been no Need to Resort to the Bowl.

I snuffed my Candle and I had the first full night's Sleep I have known these many months. It is Plain that Cousin Lucretia's Remedy was well-advised.

And so I must continue.

My brother had been most cruelly Murdered and I most cruelly Raped. I thought I knew the Worst that could come to me. I did not yet know the World looks with Scorn and Suspicion at a Woman who has been Ravaged. This I discovered at my Brother's Funeral.

Thomasina, who had tended me lovingly as any Mother, did not want me to be present at the Burial. I thought she deemed my physickal Condition still too Precarious, but I was Determined that my darling Flip should not go to his Grave without me to Bid him Farewell. Who else was there save my Father, for my Mother had taken to her Bed in the Agony of her Grief and Cousin Lucretia, though sent for, had not yet arrived from the city? Pieter and Bram and Martinis were away serving their Country.

Neighbors came, our Farmers and Tenants, the work men, people from the town, my Father's Friends. Even before the Service in the Cemetery, the whispering began. They stood in little groups and Whispered, then eyed me and whispered some more. None met my eyes. None of that Congregation who came to offer Condolences to my Father Offered any to me.

I stood alone save for Thomasina, not understanding; and Thomasina, who had known how it would be, kept her arm about me and proudly stared the Starers down while my Head drooped lower and lower in Guilty Confusion. Why was I shamed? What had I done? Even the Preecher would not meet my eyes.

I saw Dierk Bruegel and his father come down the Long Walk towards the Cemetery, and my Spirits revived just for a Moment. The sixth Indian. He alone of all there had shared some of the Good Times with Flip and me. As they came through the Gate, I took a timid step Forward, smiled a Timid smile in his direction. Not quite knowing what I did, my hand went out to him.

I think if my Smile had been Returned, if my Hand had been Taken, I might have come to love him.

Nither thing happened. He averted his eyes from me and skirted a group of Mourners, Intent it would seem on getting as far from me as he could. My hand fell down to my side, to be tightly held by Thomasina; and I watched Dierk go quickly to the side of Farmer Brassem's daughter and engage with her in Spritely Conversation.

The Service began.

Across the Grave I met my Father's Look, and in it I saw a Jugement no different than any other in that Crowd. Indeed Worse, for there was not only Blame but also a kind of Suppressed Anger.

He wept once, "My son, my last son"; and the words seemed to be Flung at me, as though they had a different meaning . . . *Why he and not you?*

Food was served at our House afterwards, and I could not but be

Conscious how he Avoided me . . . as though . . . as though . . . I were a soiled garment he had cast aside.

It came to me gradually that I had become exactly so to him. I had been his Princess, his Darling, his Plaything to exhibit to the World because it had such a Pretty Face and Precocity of Spirit. I had been but was no longer a Source of Pride and Satisfaction.

Cornelius Van Duren, Lord of his Manor in Tarry Town, could take no Pride in a Daughter whom the whole World knew to have been Tumbeled on the Ground like any cheap Harlot by the Dreggs of the British Army and the Town Idiot, too.

And the Whispers grew . . . and the Gossip extended . . . and there were plenty to murmur that where there had been Smoke, there must be Fire, and who was to say Philadelphia Van Duren had been so Chaste? Among the Torries there were Rumors of Wild Picnicking on the Island, Myself with all those young men who were in the Rebbel Army . . . The Patriots shook their Heads over stories of bathing in the River, Myself as Nakked as any New-Born, and the Boys right there with me . . .

My only Comfort other than Thomasina's Tender Care was the Arrival of Cousin Lucretia. The gardener's boy brought the news that a Sloop had arrived from Down River with Miz Bogardus on it.

I flew out the house and along the Long Walk, through the Gardens and down the Hill to the Dock, meeting her halfway.

I hesitated a moment, almost fearing to look in her face and see a Sign that she, too, had turned against me. But when I Gained the Courage to look, all I saw was love.

"Cousin Lucretia," I choked out and hurled myself into her willing arms.

"Why does my father hate me so?" I wept to her that night. "I did not Sin, I was Sinned against. I did nothing shameful; shameful things were Done to Me."

I didn't really expect an answer, I was merely Unburdening my Sorrow.

"He blames me for Flip's death," I told her, though she must have known it. "It isn't fair. We went to the Island together as we have Done Hundreds of Times."

"I'll speak to Cornelius," she promised.

Whether she did or not . . . whatever got said . . . it did no good.

Cousin Lucretia shared the nursing of my mother with Thomasina and me. It was not very difficult. She lay there Still and Silent most of the time, with her eyes closed, or they were Open and Staring off into Space. Sometimes, like a Litany, she murmured over and over the names of her children who were gone from her ... Jacob ... Karl ... Rachel ... Philip ... Pieter ...

I was Alive, and I was there, but she never once said Philadelphia.

Philadelphia's Journal
Nov. 22, 1777

In the days before she died, whenever my father came to my Mother's room wilst I was there, I would rise from my chair in the Corner and leave them alone together. When Cousin Lucretia was with her, I would sit alone in my Chamber or with Thomasina in the Kitchen.

Thomasina had treated me with Herbs and Remedies in those first terrible days after the British brought me back from the Island. Herbs to prevent Infection ... Herbs to heal my bruised Tissue and Torn Muscles ... Herbs that I gathered were for other Possibilities she would prefer not to speak of, except that Soldiers were not allways too Clean, and we must take care. When Cousin Lucretia arrived, I overheard the two of them discussing the Remedies together. I heard the words "lest they were diseased," and I went quickly out of hearing, unwilling to Hear more.

There were Herbs that helped all but one thing.

I missed my monthly flow. I began to give up my breakfast in the morning. The bosoms that Martinis had once teased me into Tears by calling smaller than Pin Heads swelled up like overripe Tomatoes.

There was a morning in the Kitchen when realization dawned. I grew sick and dizzy and clung to the back of the big Hutch chair, while the very Blood seemed to Drain from my Body.

"Filly, what is it, child?" Cousin Lucretia asked.

I said dully, "I am to bear Tom Dumb's child." Then, as her own face whitened, I cried out in wild appeal, "Oh God, help me,

Cousin Lucretia, help me, I cannot. That—not what happened to me—would be the Fate worse than Death."

We told my Father on the day before my Mother died. On the evening of her Burying, he acqwainted me with his Decision. As many another Father before him, he thought to Hide my Shame in the Respectability of Marriage. Dierk Bruegel averted his eyes from me and publickly disdained my Hand at my brother's Funeral. But now he would take that selfsame Hand in Marriage for the sake of my Father's monies, and I was Presumed to be Graetfull for the sake of the Creature in my Belly. But I was not Greatefull. I could never forgive Dierk, so I told Cousin Lucretia, his Abandonment.

"Could you not bring yourself to marry him?" she asked me hesitantly when I sought her out after the Interview with my Father. "You were once good Friends."

"We were so," I said fiercely, "which is why I Disdain him the more. He would have nothing to do with me when I needed friends and kindness. Now he will Marry me for my Father's Money and make me do Penance the rest of our lives, even as he lives on our Bounty. Have I deserved such Penance? What Crime did I Commit?"

She made me no answer, so I spoke again softly, savagely, "Besides, I need no husband because I will bear no child. This is no baby in my Belly but rather a Monster. Tom Dumb may have planted the seed of the Der Horst madness in me, but I will not bring it to Harvest. I have no Wish to Die—God knows there has been enough of Dying in this House—but I promise you I will do so before I give life to this—this evil thing inside me."

"Filly, what are you saying?"

"I have heard there are ways to put an end to Undesired Pregnancies," I told her steadily.

"Why are you so sure the Simpleton fathered it?"

"I know. Don't ask me how—I just know. But even if it were Otherwise, do you think I want to bring to life a child of any one of them? At least Tom Dumb had the excuse of a Sick Brain."

She thought deeply. "I know of no one here."

"But in New York?"

"I am acquainted with a number of Mid-Wives who might help me to Contrive it . . . but how do we get you to New York?"

As it turned out, my Father made all easy for us. He anticipated that Van Duren Manor would soon be lost to us and decided that he would go to England to live until this war is over. My grandfather bought an estate in Suffolk more than forty years ago, which has allways brought in a good Income. With the Owner's foot on the Land, said my Father, it should Pay even better and be a good place to live until the Strife here ended.

I have begun to be more clearly acquainted with my Father's Charackter than in the days when I was his Adored and Petted daughter. Despite his present grief for my Mother, by the time the war is over, he will have a new young English wife and possibly one or even two new young English children. I feel positive he will never come Home again to Tarry Town. Nor did he offer to take me with him. I was the last Encumbrance to be swept from his Past neatly and tidily by a marriage to Dierk.

His very Decision, as it Happened, paved the Way for Cousin Lucretia and me. The Ship he desired to Travel on was leaving New York Harbour before the Banns could be read. I persuaded him all too Easily to take it and leave all Arrangements in Cousin Lucretia's Hands.

Papers were signed with the Attorneys in New York and a Considerable sum of hard money transferred at the Bank. Once my Father was gone, Cousin Lucretia summoned Dierk to inform him there would be no Wedding, but there would be a reasonable Compensating sum of money which would permit him Independence.

He took the Monies and fled his Father to give up Preeching and buy a Farm in the Jerseys. When this was known, I received a Blistering letter from Mr. Bruegel on my Broken Pledge, which I tossed, uncaring, into the fire where it belonged.

So another Indian Departed my Life!

Philadelphia's Journal
Nov. 23, 1777

I woke up screaming with Nightmares every night my first two weeks with Cousin Lucretia. Allways it was the same Dream. There was a Tree growing inside me; its trunk riddled with rot and its Branches spreading out like Tentacles, crushing and destroying all the Organs in their path. I was being eaten alive from inside by this Monstrous growth.

One day early in the third week Cousin Lucretia sent all Servants from the house save Thomasina. A physician came and with him a Mid-Wife. I was given a Dosage of Laudanum, whether to put me to Sleep or eaze me from the Pain, I do not know.

I only know that when I came out of my Languorous State, Cousin Lucretia was bending over me, one of my hands squeezed tightly between hers. "All is well, Filly," she told me, and a Great Weight fell from my Shoulders. The Incubus was gone from me. I could begin to live again.

If one can call it living. True, there are no more nightmares. Still, am I haunted by the Past, not only in Dreams but in all my Waking Hours, too. I keep remembering *them,* I see their faces, their voices, feel their hands on me, their bodies in me. I see my brother Philip's poor crushed head and Tom Dumb's face with the hole between his Eyes.

I keep seeing their damned Red Coats and that damned cat with its blood-smeared face . . .

Blood everywhere . . . on my breasts and bodice . . . my legs and skirts . . . on my brother and the Idiot . . .

Oh God, will the memories ever grow Dim so that I may be clean again? May I nevermore see their Red Coats . . . the Red Cat . . .

CHAPTER
18

The pages of Philadelphia's story shook visibly in my hands as I came to the end.

Red Coats. Red Cat.

I remembered Bryarly whispering in her nightmare, whispering about them both. Bryarly, who before I started poking into the lives of the Van Durens, had never even heard of *A Secret History.*

Red Coats. Red Cat. And she had erythrophobia . . . morbid fear of the color red . . . ailurophobia . . . morbid fear of cats.

I put *A Case of Rape in the Tarrytowns* down on the end table next to my chair and made a grab at my inside pocket for the envelope Bryarly had given me. My hands were shaking as I slit it open.

The words Bryarly had written leaped out at me, incredible, yet somehow no longer unexpected.

"Now do you understand, Jake? I'm Philadelphia."

As I went dashing into the elevator, I called back over my shoulder for the doorman to ring Mrs. Allerton and tell her that I was on my way up. It was early afternoon. I had spent two hours in earnest heart-to-heart conversation with Philippa Jansen before breaking highway speed records to get home to Bryarly.

Somehow I was sure she would be standing there opposite the elevator waiting for me as she had the day before, wearing the long, pink house coat. We would walk inside together, our hands entwined; and all the distance between us would vanish, the barriers would crumble, and she would tell me all the things she had never told anyone before.

I was wrong.

There was no Bryarly waiting for me. The door of her apartment stood symbolically closed to me. I rang the bell and wound up using the key. Then I walked through the empty rooms, calling her name, knowing there would be no answer.

In the kitchen I found a big sheet of paper with a very few words on it taped to the refrigerator door.

Dear Jake:
Out for the evening. Some spaghetti sauce in green casserole dish if you want to eat in.

I didn't.

As I snatched the note down, tore it into bits and dumped it into the garbage, I swore at length and with extensive earthiness. I was wishing all the while it was Bryarly's long, slim neck on the receiving end of this manhandling. She *knew,* goddamn it, she *had* to know how crazy I was to talk to her, how much we both had to say. Damnation, she had done it on purpose. She was deliberately avoiding me—or a confrontation between us, which amounted to the same thing. She was playing games, which I liked even less.

Neuroses I was willing to cope with, but not dancing to any tune she chose to play.

I marched resolutely into the office and worked over Bryarly's files for the next few hours. Then I telephoned through my address book till I found the first New York friend who was free for the evening, Jeff Martell, from City College.

We went to an Italian restaurant, where the food was mediocre, but not more so than the conversation. Jeff was having wife trouble, and after three martinis, his sad story lacked all interest as well as coherence.

I breathed a sigh of relief to find myself back in Bryarly's apartment even though it was still empty.

She arrived home about an hour after I did, and I was waiting for her like an angry parent for a truant child.

"Aren't you going to invite me in for a nightcap?" I heard a deep male voice say as I marched out to the hallway, switching on all the lights in my path. That way, when I came stomping up to them, he couldn't miss the full glory—not to say intimacy—of the terry pajamas and robe I had modestly bought just before Bryarly came home from the hospital.

He was tall and handsome and about six years younger than me. The only thing I had more of was hair . . . that, I suddenly told myself with renewed confidence, seeing his mouth drop open, that and the nine-tenths of the law that count—possession. I was here in my girl's apartment in pajamas and Mr. Glamorous was on his way out!

"Hi." I stuck out my hand. "Jake Ormont."

His hand responded reflexively, and I gripped hard, smiling to see him wince. "Brian Halliday," he said in a strained voice.

I beamed at the two of them. "Did you have a good evening?"

"Very," Bryarly answered for both, eyeing me nervously. She knew I was up to something, but she wasn't quite sure what. "We went to dinner and the ballet."

Handsome Halliday cleared his throat. "Er—very fine performance."

"Delightful." My smile stretched even wider, and I continued to stand there, barring their way to the living room.

"D-did you have a pleasant evening?" Bryarly babbled.

"Oh, very. Met an old friend. Talked over auld lang syne. Just got in a few minutes ago myself." I yawned widely. "It's late, you two must be mighty tired." I yawned again. "I know I am."

"Then why," said Bryarly, unclenching her teeth just enough to get the words through, "don't you go to bed?"

"Without you?" I told her reproachfully. "You know I can't sleep till I know you're tucked in, too."

Poor Brian's eyes popped out, then back in again. "Thanks for a great evening, Bryarly." His voice rang with false and fulsome heartiness.

She said quickly, "I'll call you," then gave me a glance of quick loathing as I chuckled. "What's so funny?"

I moved in for the rabbit punch. "In my day," I explained gently, "he would have said that to you instead of vice versa."

While we were still glaring at one another, Handsome Halliday made his escape. As soon as the door closed behind him and I turned from attaching the chain and fastening the locks, my cool, poised, remote, aloof Bryarly turned all too wonderfully human.

"You bastard!" she snarled and started swinging. I allowed her one clop on my chops to let off steam, then I caught both her hands in mine and pulled her to me. She landed up against my chest, with my hands holding her wrists behind her. I could feel the wild thumping of her heart against my chest and see the pulse fluttering in her throat as she slowly raised her face to me. Then her lips moved slightly, ever so slightly to meet my kiss.

She would have broken away from me quickly, but helped by the clumsiness of her cast, I kept a firm hold on her, moving and molding our mouths together till she gasped for breath. Then I freed her mouth and stroked her with my hands, massaging her shoulders and back, and using my fingertips to kiss the sides of her jaw and her closed eyes.

She stood quivering to receive these attentions, neither participating nor withdrawing.

But her mouth, her thumping heartbeats, her gasping breaths, and the trembling of her thighs against mine had already told me all that I needed to know. Her senses had been in a long deep-freeze, her mind in deep panic. She was frozen perhaps, frightened definitely, but frigid never.

She gave a deep unconscious sigh as I put her from me. It was a child's sigh of longing, even regret, and I couldn't help smiling slightly, despite my far more poignant, not to say painful, longing and regret.

"I hope you're not too tired," I told her sternly, marching her toward the living room. "You've got a lot of explaining to do."

"I thought you couldn't wait to get to bed," she jeered.

"No, merely for your Brian to go off to his."

"He's not my Brian—just a friend. Now I'll have to make him all kinds of apologies and explanations tomorrow," she added crossly.

"Not on my account. That's a lovely dress," I said, eyeing her black sheath. "Why don't you take it off? I mean," I grinned, as she jumped nervously back from me, "go make yourself comfortable for our little chat, while I fix whatever you want—coffee, tea, or something stronger?"

"A white Russian, please. Lots of Kahlua, easy on the vodka, and a dash of milk."

I raised my eyebrows. "Building up your courage?" But she had gone without answering.

I had two white Russians ready when she came back in the pink housecoat. I took both glasses from the tray on the sideboard and handed one to her.

She sank down in the big armchair near the fireplace and gulped her drink as though it were lemonade. I raised my glass to her. "To you," I said, "whoever you are."

"I *am* Philadelphia."

"I believe you believe it."

"Tell me, Jake, was I right? Was she raped?"

"She was raped."

She finished her drink and set the glass down on the arm

of her chair. She stared straight up at me but without seeming to see me. Her eyes were fixed on something outside our vision; her face and body were rigid. "By men in red coats, two of them, British Redcoats and a farmer boy," she said to me in the singsong voice of a child reciting a lesson. "And there was a cat. A big ugly red-faced cat. And a horse. The horse was frightened of the blood. There was blood. On the ground. On my long petticoats. Lots of blood. And death. And shooting. I—she lay on the grass with the body, then more Redcoats came. They were all around her. Redcoats. But the red-faced cat ran away."

She was speaking in deep, shuddering gasps, and by the time she got done she was shaking all over. A sweep of her hands sent her glass to the carpet, unheeded.

I moved swiftly to kneel beside her chair and shelter the shuddering body within my arms. I rocked her and stroked her and murmured words of comfort till she lay quiet against me, ghastly pale and with a look of horror in her eyes. I wanted it to go away, yet I had to ask, "How did you know about Philadelphia, Bryarly?"

"I lived it over in a hundred nightmares," she whispered, "not *my* rape, but hers. After it happened to me, I kept reliving it happening to *her* whenever I was drugged. The first time was in the hospital where they—they . . . I was torn, they had to patch me up. Under the anesthetic, the first bit of it came to me. And the next day when I was upset—my stepmother came to visit, and she was angry because I'd reported it to the police—I guess I got a bit hysterical, and they gave me something to calm me down. Instead, I started living over another bit. That's the way it's been ever since when I take strong drugs, even gas at the dentist's. Or if I'm very upset. I live over *her* rape, not *mine.*"

"But what made you feel that you were Philadelphia and it was happening to you?"

"I didn't," she said simply. "Cousin Lucretia told me."

I'd been on my knees in front of her chair the better to hold her. Now I pulled away and stood up slowly, staring down at her disbelievingly.

"You think I'm crazy, don't you, Jake?" She smiled pitifully. "Why do you think I've kept this secret for thirteen years? It's why, even with you knowing as much as you do, I've gone the long way round to tell you. After I heard about your nightmare, *I* pushed you into finding Philadelphia for yourself. I made you find out the truth, hoping there was a slim chance that if you did, you wouldn't think when I told you that I'd gone completely round the bend. But I was wrong, wasn't I? You don't believe me? You think I'm—unstable?"

"Stop that!" I ordered roughly, hearing the tinge of hysteria in her voice. "Don't tell me what *I* think." I pulled a small wicker chair over and sat in it so close to her our knees touched. Hers were trembling, but not with passion as they had a half hour before. "You're emotionally scarred, Bryarly, which you have every reason to be. That's a far cry from crazy. All I'm trying to do is unravel the mystery. Tell me about Cousin Lucretia."

"It was in the hospital—in Atlanta—I was kind of weak and weepy and upset, and there was this one really nice resident doctor—I'll always remember how kind he was. He despised my family. He asked me one day if I didn't have anyone else to give me some TLC—tender loving care."

She looked at me and said plaintively, like a child. "I'm thirsty."

"Here." I handed my drink over to her and curbed my impatience while she slowly sipped it.

"What happened then?" I asked after a while.

"I went to sleep and when I opened my eyes, she was there. Cousin Lucretia."

"How did you know?"

"I asked her." She gave me the ghost of a smile. "Well, wouldn't you have? There was this lady in colonial dress and buckled shoes with a sort of frilly white cap on her head, wouldn't you have said, 'Who are you?'"

"So you asked, and she said . . . what?"

"She said, 'I'm Cousin Lucretia. The doctor is right. You must find someone else to turn to. Someone who loves you.' She seemed to bend toward me then, and it was the strangest sensation because she didn't touch me, yet I felt as though her hands were on my forehead . . . I felt an aura of warmth and love and protection so powerfully about me that it was unbelievable. I hadn't had anything like it since the day my mother and Benjy died."

She was quiet for several minutes, and when she turned back to me, she was no longer trembling. Her hands lay quiet in her lap, and her eyes were serene.

"I thought immediately of Aunt Lucy and Joel. We'd been apart so many years, but I was quite sure they were the ones I was meant to turn to. The young doctor helped me call Boston. I went home with Aunt Lucy two days later."

"And Cousin Lucretia?" I asked her.

"I began to think I'd just dreamed her. But she came again . . . and again . . . whenever I had nightmares. Usually, she calmed me down . . . Often she gave me strength or a push in a different direction than the one I was going in. She spoke very few words; mostly it was the feeling of love that came from her that guided and strengthened me. Just once she said—it was just after Terry Ramundo came to stay with me—'Philadelphia, this time some good can come out of it. Women are fighting back now.' It was after that I started my work for MART."

She leaned back in her chair with a tired sigh and tilted her head sideways. "Well, Jake. Have you nothing to say?"

I told her slowly, "I thought meeting you was a miracle, the miracle of a chance at love and happiness I no longer expected to come my way. Now it seems as though all our lives, we've been moving in a direction that was predestined —toward each other. I have never believed in what I can't rationally explain, but if you are Philadelphia . . . It's true I dreamed of you long before we met, just as you dreamed of red coats and a red cat and the things that happened to Philadelphia before you ever heard of the *Secret History* of the Van Durens. My God, Bryarly! It's beyond belief. If someone else had told me this . . ."

"You're still plagued by doubts, aren't you?" she asked me rather sadly. "Jake, do you remember in *your* nightmare that there's a song the six Indians chant. Always the same one. You said you can't recall it when you wake up, but you would know it if you heard it."

"Yes."

She got up and stood over the fireplace, then turned and faced me from there. "Listen to me, Jake. Listen very carefully."

Her eyes never left my face; her voice was not much above a whisper, but it echoed in my ears like a battle charge.

> *Six little Indians, all of them alive,*
> *One got his head caved in, and then there were five.*
>
> *Five little Indians, where once there were more,*
> *One ran away, and then there were four.*
>
> *Four little Indians, wanting to be free,*
> *One got himself hung up, and then there were three.*
>
> *Three little Indians, to their country true,*
> *One stopped a bullet, and then there were two.*
>
> *Two little Indians, warring side by side,*
> *One in the Army was said to have died.*
>
> *One little Indian, who suddenly knew*
> *A dead little Indian was left alive, too.*

With barely any change in voice, she said, "Well, Jake, have you heard it before?"

"Christ, yes!" It was my turn to shudder. "That's it. How did you know?"

"It's been in *my* nightmares, too, for years. She is standing over a grave—that song is going through her head over and over. The only difference between you and me, Jake, is that I've remembered it. Sometimes I even hear the thread of a melody, as though it's being sung."

I got up, went to her, and took one of her hands. "If we're Jake and Bryarly, struggling all our lives to find one another, and you're Philadelphia—then who am I? I have to be one of them because we're talking reincarnation, aren't we?"

She shook her head. "You can find out if you go back, but you may not want to know."

"Of course I want to know. Do you realize what this means to us, in terms of each other?"

"I think *I* do. I think *you* don't. We loved in our past, Jake, but we didn't find happiness. I think the pattern's meant to be repeated. Everything else seems to be."

"Like hell it is!" I roared so suddenly she gave a little jump backward. Her mouth was set stubbornly, but I could be mulish, too; and I was all set to prove it when I saw the lines of tiredness around her eyes.

I took her by the shoulders and kissed her lightly on the forehead. "Go to bed, Bryarly. You look bone-weary, and tomorrow's going to be a busy day."

"It is?"

"We're going back to Tarrytown. You made a bet with me; now I'll make one with you."

"Yes?"

She looked at me with her mouth a little open like a baby bird expecting a crumb. I couldn't help laughing.

"'Journeys end in lovers' meetings,'" I assured her tenderly. "I'm not saying she had it easy, any more than you, but I'm betting on Philadelphia and the last Indian, just as I'm betting on you and me. The same bet, by the way. One night of chaste bundling."

She smiled weakly, gestured good night and left me.

CHAPTER
19

Half an hour later I was lying wide awake on her convertible when the door to her office opened.

"Are you asleep?" came Bryarly's whispery voice as she lowered herself down awkwardly onto the edge of the couch.

I sat up. "Of course. Asleep and dreaming that a lovely lady just came and sat on my bed."

There was a short pause. It was too dark for me to see her, but the struggle she was having with herself was so intense, the atmosphere around us sizzled with emotion. It was almost powerful enough to be touched and tasted.

"May I stay with you tonight, Jake?" Bryarly asked me in a voice of quiet desperation.

"Bryarly," I reminded her gently, "you won the first bet."

"I don't care about that. I'm so tired of being—odd. Neuter. I'm so tired of looking on at other people's lives. I want to know once and for all if I ever could—never could—"

She drew one sobbing breath as my arms went around her and subsided on my shoulder, quietly weeping.

"You're quite simply tired, darling," I said. "Lie down with me."

I eased her down, making sure even as I drew her snugly against me that there was a blanket between us. I was nude, and she would be scared as hell if she felt physical contact without that frail barrier between. No matter what she said, she wasn't quite ready. I wanted her in longing, not in desperation.

She sighed deeply, relaxed in my arms against my swathed body. After a while she said sleepily, "Will you make love to me, Jake—just a little?"

I grinned in the darkness. "That sounds like the girl who's just a little bit pregnant," I told her. "There's no such animal. Unless you're talking about a few mild kisses? I admit I prefer passionate ones myself."

"I've never been kissed passionately—I don't think," she said consideringly. "Boys of twenty kiss greedily, not passionately. And it's been thirteen years . . ." Her voice trailed away. "Till you, and you've kissed me like a—a father, or kindly uncle."

"Thanks a lot."

She giggled softly. "You know what I mean."

"Only too well. Believe me, it's not the way I want to kiss you, love. Shall we try it for real?"

"Yes," she said in the same tone of grim determination she might have used if I had asked if she was ready to get her tooth pulled.

I turned her a little in my arms. I caressed her face and then her mouth, tracing the outline of her lips with the tips of my fingers, parting them as I did. Then suddenly, swiftly, I lowered my face to hers; and whatever *she* may or may not have felt, it was damned passionate kissing on my part.

When I finally released her mouth and lifted my head to gulp in a fresh supply of oxygen, she said, "Oh, Jake!" on a sighing breath and put both arms around my neck. She didn't sound frightened at all. It was a rare sweet moment in my life.

"May I touch you a little, Bryarly?"

"I—I don't know." But I was lowering the blanket to my

waist even as I spoke, drawing her against me so that only the silky stuff of her pajamas was between us. I slipped one hand under her pajama top, stroking her side for a long while before I moved slowly frontward. I was cautious, taking my time—but obviously not enough.

She reared back all at once, dashing my hand away. "Don't. Don't do that." Her voice was suffocated, panicked.

"I'm sorry," I said quietly. "I didn't mean to hurt you."

"You didn't hurt me. It's just—I don't like my—my —being pinched *there*."

I said deliberately, knowing she would find my out-spokenness a shock, "I didn't pinch your breasts, Bryarly. I caressed them. They're very lovely, just as I expected them to be, very caressable."

There was a strained silence. "I'm sorry," she said in turn. "I didn't—please don't be insulted. It's just that —that—"

"For God's sake," I told her, "stop sounding humble. You've a right to express your feelings, and you might credit me with some understanding. I did read the report, you know. I remember what was done to you. But you also might remember I have the patience as well as the love to deal with a virgin."

"A virgin!" she repeated incredulously. "God Almighty, *me*, a virgin!"

"Did you think otherwise?"

"Untouched by human hands?" she jeered with the bitterness of self-hatred.

"Exactly. Did you really think you qualified as a lady of the evening because you spent an hour or two in bed a dozen or so years ago with an insensitive boor with so little experience or ability to please a woman he thought physical evidence the only proof of virginity?"

"You're not by any chance overlooking the night that followed?"

"No, my darling." I moved my lips against her neck. "I'm not overlooking anything where you're concerned. Four rotten, bastardly, woman-hating thugs criminally savaged you. They may have damaged you, but they didn't in any way sully you." It was what she hammered at to others in her MART work, yet never seemed to have accepted about herself. "What they did has nothing to do with what you are," I added firmly.

"What am I?"

"A sexy, loving woman afraid to come out of the deep-freeze. I think you want me, Bryarly, maybe not quite as much as I do you—not yet—but you're afraid to try. You're afraid I'll hurt you, which I won't. Afraid you won't like it, which is possible—it will take time for you to come to full enjoyment. Most of all, you're afraid you'll find out once and for all that you're never going to lose your fears; and this one has you so damn petrified, you'd almost rather live in perpetual doubt in your never-never land than put it to the test."

"In other words," she said huffily, "I'm a coward?"

"Yes, darling, I think you are a bit," I said calmly. "Not that I blame you, but . . . after all . . . thirteen years in retreat from life."

"Kiss me again!" she ordered furiously.

I kissed her once gently; I kissed her again hard. Then I kissed her in the valley between her softly crested hills.

"Do something else!" she ordered presently, her voice still quivering with rage, and I smothered a laugh as I obeyed.

Presently she quivered with something other than anger . . . but then, just as I thought—I must have gone too fast. She cried out in fear, struggling as wildly as though I held her against her will, which I did not. Her body grew rigid, and she hit out at me wildly, not even knowing, I think, what she was doing.

I reacted in what seemed to me the best way. I rolled away, freeing her. She was sobbing, but I resisted the yearning to comfort her physically.

"My dear girl, why all the boo-hooing?"

"I told you," she gulped. "I said I wouldn't be any good."

"You're crazy. You did fine."

"You're crazy. I was awful. I couldn't let you—"

"Well, naturally, you couldn't. I didn't expect you to.

We've got years of inhibitions to break down. Did you expect to do it all in one night? That's asking a bit too much of *me*. I'm Jake Ormont, not Don Juan. Hell!" I complained. "You're certainly making me feel like a failure."

This got the expected laugh, albeit a feeble one. She stopped crying, blew her nose hard—I hoped not in my sheet—and said with sniffs between each word, "Was I really all right?"

"Word of honor."

I knew she was fairly restored when she asked, stammering a little, "H-how do you know?" Then, "Jake, have you had many women?"

"Bryarly, for God's sake, I'm forty-three years old."

"That means yes," she said wisely. Then, more hesitantly, "Jake, has there been—you know—anyone—since you've lived here?"

"Bryarly, I told you once before I have a tiresomely monogamous nature. There's been no one but you since the day we had breakfast at the Waldorf. There will be no one but you for the rest of my life."

"Jake, I do love you, did you know?" Her voice sounded sleepy and far away.

"I had begun to suspect."

"And I've never been married."

"I suspected that, too."

"You did? But how—when—"

"You're a pretty prolific liar, Bryarly, but not a particularly efficient one. Your having taken a husband didn't fit the picture. I checked as thoroughly as I could and didn't find any record of a marriage . . . or of an Allerton who had died in Viet Nam. I would say a husband was the weapon you used to keep men away. But why Viet Nam?"

"When I started at Hunter, I had to have a reason for not dating," she told me drowsily. "So I invented a soldier husband . . . then I had to put him in Viet Nam to account for why he never came home. When the war ended, I made him a prisoner for the same reason. It kind of got out of hand," she added on a yawn. "Finally, the prisoners came home, so I was able to make myself a widow." Her voice faded away. "It was a bit of a relief, being a widow."

When her quiet breathing told me she was asleep, I removed my hand from her disturbing grip, and myself from the couch, making a quiet transfer to the bed in Bryarly's room. I had to get the hell away from her, since, tired or not, I wasn't quite the man of steel I pretended.

The next morning, immediately after breakfast, we headed up to Tarrytown.

Bryarly was armored in full war paint, meaning Oriental dress, Oriental face mask, and the deceptive, defensive sheathing of a cool, aloof, and decidedly off-putting manner. In other words, it was the shell of Bryarly I presented to Philippa, not the real and vulnerable Bryarly I loved.

I needn't have worried. Philippa, even in a man's flannel shirt and jeans, could more than hold her own with the pseudosophisticated worldling who greeted her with a reserved, "How do you do, Mrs. Jansen?"

"How do *you* do, Cousin Bryarly?" Philippa riposted.

And first point to *you*, Cousin Philippa, I thought admiringly.

Bryarly's apricot cheeks took on a slightly red tinge. "Oh, Jake's told you all that nonsense," she murmured.

Philippa flashed her a look of wide-eyed innocence. "But I understand you don't think it's nonsense at all?"

Bryarly swiveled her head around, biting down on her lower lip. After a few seconds, when she turned back, she had recovered her dignity and also, I was pleased to see, her naturalness.

"No," she said, "I don't think it's nonsense. I've lived with Cousin Lucretia in my life for a good many years now, and I've accepted, as she seems to do, that I'm—I was Philadelphia. I take that very seriously."

"Come along with me."

Philippa led us both to the formal dining parlor, where I had not been before. On the wall opposite the doorway was a huge portrait of a woman sitting at a small table, teapot in hand.

Bryarly's face was transfigured.

"Oh, Jake, look," she sang out joyfully, clasping one of my hands in both hers, "it's Cousin Lucretia. She really did exist." She let go of my hands and went to examine the portrait more minutely. "She's much older here," she said over her shoulder, this time to Philippa. "I'm not used to seeing her with gray hair and those lines in her face. Otherwise, it's just like her."

"You see, I wasn't being sarcastic when I welcomed you, Cousin Bryarly," Philippa said gravely. "The only problem is, I'm at least twice your age in the present, but as Philadelphia, you'd be my ancestress. It's going to make family relations a bit complicated."

Bryarly laughed shyly.

"Jake's been telling me about *A Secret History*. I've been almost afraid to see it until this moment. Now I can hardly wait—if you're willing."

In the small dining parlor, where I had sat the first time . . . same chair . . . same blazing fire . . . *Part I* lay ready on the small table. We left Bryarly completely absorbed in it, and I went with Philippa to the kitchen, watching while she filled the coffeepot.

"Nothing for me this time?" I quizzed her.

"Oh, plenty. Months of material. Years even. But, if you mean have I something that's of particular interest to you this very moment, the answer is yes." She stopped cutting bread for toast and tapped her knife on the counter. I had a very definite feeling she had a surprise up her sleeve for me. The question was, what kind?

I felt my way cautiously. "What would be of particular interest to me?"

"The Revolutionary War journals of Philip Van Duren, starting in 1778. Three out of four of them survived."

"Philip Van Duren. But Philip died—he was killed in 1777 when Philadelphia was . . . Could there have been another Philip Van Duren in the family, an uncle or cousin I haven't come across yet?"

"No."

"But then, why would Philadelphia have invented . . ."

No, it didn't add up. I had read that account of hers; there was no way she had fantasized that. I would bet my next year's royalties that the account of their last day on the island came straight from her guts!

"Look," I told Philippa, "give it to me more slowly. Revolutionary journals, you said. You mean, Philip joined the army?"

"As a fifer . . . a musician."

"They both played the fife," I said slowly. "They—well, I'll be damned. Of course, it's the only way it fits." I smiled broadly at Philippa. "That devil! Now I've got to see them. Well, are there any conditions?"

She answered, if answer you could call it, rather obliquely. "I've been working on these files by myself for the past couple of years and trying all that while to find just the right person to write this book—or books. I think I've found him."

"Me?"

"Yes, you. I've read one or two of your books since our first meeting. I've had you checked out by reliable people. In my own judgment, and theirs, you are right for the job, and you do have one unique qualification most other writers lack."

"Which is?" I asked her politely.

"You're in love with Philadelphia."

"I'm in love with Bryarly."

She gave me a smile of friendly malice. "That qualifies you just as much."

"I'll be busy with the rape book the rest of the winter."

"I'm not in any hurry," she said equably. "After a few hundred years, what do a few more months matter?"

"History and biography aren't my line."

"You can rise to the challenge."

"And if I don't wish to?"

She shook her head mournfully. "It's *such* interesting material."

"Blackmail, Mrs. Jansen?"

"Let us rather say pressure, Mr. Ormont. Of the *most* delicate kind and in the *most* positive cause."

"Do you want me to put it in writing?"

Sarcasm didn't faze her. "Certainly not," she said, shocked. "That's among the things I found out about you, Jake. You're tough, but honest. Your word can be counted on. It's going to be nice to have you in the family."

"I wish I could be as sure of it as you seem to be."

"Aren't you?"

"Bryarly's got this fool idea that Philadelphia never married or found happiness, and that we're destined to follow the same pattern."

"And you?"

"I don't exactly see myself in the role of star-crossed lover. I hope Filly found happiness. If she didn't, I'm damned sorry, but I don't intend to follow suit."

"Will you write the book?"

"You twisted my arm." I relented and grinned across at her. "Of course I will. I decided to the first time I came here."

I received a damp dishcloth in my face as she went to get the journals. There were three of them, as she had said, with cracked, falling-to-bits leather covers, each in a separate small box. Philippa gave me the first slim volume, and I handled it with the same tender care she had displayed.

The ink had faded even more than in most of the stuff I'd seen, but the writing was clear and firm, and I knew it now as well as I knew my own. There were some loose papers inserted inside the cover. I glanced at them first.

My final entry in Philadelphia's Journal
till . . . I know not . . .

Philadelphia, Pa.
January 19, 1778

Little did I think ever to write again from Philadelphia. Under these circumstances, God forfend that I ever had to.

I arrived at Obidiah's home a se'ennight ago, and the first news that greeted me was the worst that there could be. My dearest brother Pieter, last of my brothers, had not survived his wounds.

No longer am I a Stranger to Evil Tidings. Out of need I have grown intimate with Death and Disaster.

Except for Bram, with Washington's Army not far from here, I am alone now. Truly alone. They are all gone from me. Philip . . . Martinis . . . Piet. . . . Victims of the accursed British, even as I. My Mother, too, in a different way. My Father has fled; but I lost him long before. Cousin Lucretia and Thomasina are in a distant Land.

Most lovingly Obidiah and his Sally have Urged me to make my Home with them until Cousin Lucretia's Return. I cannot bring Myself to do so. I cannot warm Myself at the Fires of their happiness or Feast on the Crumbs from their Table.

It is not my way to accept second-Best any more than it is my Way passively to bear Oppression. I am no patient Sufferer. Wrong was done to me and mine, and I am on Fire to do Wrong back. I long to inflict Hurt for Hurt, Death for Death. I remembered my vow against the British: *Now I will make a very bitter enemy.*

The Ways and the Means to do so and also to give some Purpose to my Life came to me in the Morn Yesterday as I entertained the Children by playing on the new Fife that Obidiah, in his Kindness, had bought for me.

It must have been all the thoughts of my brothers churning through my head, but all at once I found myself playing the Musick of Flip's Song to me that he had Fifed our last day on the Island. Afterwards I sang softly the Words of the one Verse I Remembered.

> *I sing of Philadelphia*
> *Who fears not man nor gun.*
> *If my sister was my brother*
> *She would be with Washington.*

As the last note died away, the Plan blossomming in my Mind had reached Full Flower. Since then scarce else has Occupied my Thoughts.

The will to carry out my Plan is not lacking. If my mind moved cautiously at first, it was because I wanted to Assure myself I would not Fail.

Flip and I are . . . that is to say, we were, as like in our Faces as two peas in a pod. When we were very small Martinis often redused him to Tears by teasing, "Put a dress on you, and they'd mistake you for Filly."

As we got Older, Flip learned to tease back. "Put breeches on her, and she becomes me," he used to retort.

If I became him then, I asked myself, why cannot I now?

My hair is already cut short and dyed to the Color of his. I have made casual Inquiry about the American uniforms. They appear, for the most part, to be sufficiently Bulky above the Waist for my Purpose. Besides which, though I wept the time Martinis described my Bosoms as less than the size of Pin Heads, how I rejoyce now that I am not handsomely endowed on top.

The only remaining question is—Bram.

Even in men's clothes, with my hair cut short and dyed to a darker Shade, will I be able to Fool him?

At first, when I thought of this, my Heart failed me, and I was sure my Plan could not be. Now I have Pondered much and I feel more Confident. The girl Bram said good-by to when he went for a soldier was a happy creature with a healthy Bloom and Plumpness and a skin colored by the sun.

I am thin and Bony now with a pale Wasted Look that was always more like Philip's than mine!

Flip grew taller, but Bram was not there to see him. His voice deepened, but how is Bram to know?

If it is Philip he expects, Philip he sees, he will think only that Philip has not changed at all.

If he knows that his little playmate Filly is gone forever, he will cease to look for her.

Journal of Philip Van Duren
A Fifer in the War for Independence
Book I—Valley Forge & Monmouth
January 28, 1778
Valley Forge in Pennsylvania

On this day I took up my new life.

Having given much consideration as to wether I should keep a Journal at all, it finally appeared to me that an Accownt of a Soldier's mundane Dailey Life in our Struggle for Freedom from

Britain's Tyranny might prove of interest to Future Generations. Besides, old Habbits die hard.

Other than this one Consession to the Past, I shall not think again on what has Been but live my life from Day to Day as best I am able.

Thus, in the Event that years Hence the pages of this Account may come under the Scrutiny of someone Unknown, let me begin by stating the Facts as they now Exist.

I am called Philip Stephanus Van Duren, youngest and only surviving son of Cornelius and Annette Van Duren, late of Van Duren Manor of Tarrytown on the Hudson, fairest of all the Fair Spots in the County of West Chester. My Mother died of her sorrows this summer past, and my Father, an Avowed Tory, has sought refuge in England. Others of my family have died in the American Cause . . . My brother Pieter . . . Martinis, my cousin by marriage . . . there was a sister, too, of whom I prefer not to speak.

At yesterday's noon I entered this Encampment, where Genl. Washington's Forces are quartered for the winter. Long before the sun was set I was enrolled as a Fifer in Col. Philip Van Cortlandt's 2nd New York Regiment. I am to be a member of his eight-man Military Band, of which there are but seven such in the entire Continental Army, and for this Privilige, I have Pledged myself to learn to play also upon the Flute.

It is not Boastfull of me to say that I could have taken my pick of any Band or Regiment, for they are so Hungry for Musicians that they Raid upon each other, offer all Manner of Indusements, and even go so far as to use some of those who are captured in Battle.

Col. Van Cortlandt, as do the weltheir Officers, pays his Band out of his own Pocket. He was no less eager than any other to Secure my Services. When I was at first brought to him, he consoled with me on the loss of Pieter, and I tried to express myself fittingly as a Soldier. Since his family had moved away from Croton before all our Tragedys happened, they had not come to his ears, for which I thank God fervently, for had he heard them, then all my Plans would have been Overset.

When I told the Colonel that I was a Fifer, he Expressed himself Highly Elated and at once begged of me a Tune. So I played Greensleeves and won a Hearty round of Applause from his Aides. He was disappointed that I played no other Instrument, but on

Hearing that I am mightily Quick to learn, which I assured him without any False Modesty I was, he proposed that I take lessons of his Fife Major on the Flute.

Later on I discovered that the last Flutist they had was invalided to Home, having been Wounded in Battle. Our Drum Major subseqwently assured me that he must have been hit by Accident, for the wounding of a Musician in Battle is no common thing, it being considered atroshus bad manners to fire upon Fifer or Drummer. It was an effort to conseal my Smiles at his Innocent Belief that it would Console me, were I wounded, to know the Bullet had found its way to my Body by accident rather than Designe!

Col. Van Cortlandt agreed to pay for my training, instruments, and extra cloathing and Rations, which is no small Consideration in the Army, I am told. A Fifer gets paid seven and one-third dollars to the Month, which has created much Jeloussy in the Ranks, since a Private's Pay is less, only six and two-thirds dollars Monthly, I believe.

The Hut in which I will live the rest of this winter is made of rough logs set Crosswise and chinked between with Clay. It is next to the one Habited by the Drum Major and the Fife Major. I share it with five others, which is Considered Vastly Luxurrious by Some, as the lower ranks have as many as twelve men to the Hut.

The other five here are all Fifers or Drummers, two play the serpent, one the horn, and another the trombone. They are all between nineteen and twenty-two years of age, which makes me the youngest, for I was born, as was set down in my enlistment Record by Col. Van Cortlandt's Adjutant, on May 17, 1760.

I made the acqwaintance of one of the Harsher sides of army life on the Moment of my entering into my new home. As the Drum Major pushed me ahead of him, four steps down from the En-tranceway, into the Darkness and Dankness of this rude Shelter, one of its Inhabitants was standing facing a corner of the room, quite obviously Relieving Himself.

Reminding myself I must become accustomed to such crudities, I averted my eyes, but evidently it is against Custom, for the Drum Major gave a howl of rage, and a wicked looking strip of leather seemed to appear in his hands almost by Magick. He took the

Culprit by the Collar at the back of his neck and hurled him onto a wooden Bunk, with his face down in a mattress made of Straw.

The Drum Major then looked about him Fiercely. "You know what Genl. Washington's orders are about using your Hut or the Company Street as a Necessary.* Only pigs muddy their own Streams. No wonder Disease is so Rife in this Camp."

The unfortunate Victim's shirt was pulled up, and three sharp quick Strokes applied to his Shrinking back.

"Next time," said the Drum Major, rolling up his strap, "it will be the cat. I've brought you a new Fifer, Philip Van Duren. Philip lad, these ugly specimens are Enoch Jones, Jan Koos, and Cady Talmage. Andrew Davis is over by the fireplace, and the pig lying in the Bunk is Gulich Ver Loop."

To my surprise the "pig" sat up, moaning slightly, pulled down his shirt and grinned at the Drum Major without Apparent Hostility.

"Ah, Sir, you know my shoes are full of holes, and I got so many Tears in my Britches, there's a draft up my Ass the minute I got out this door. It's a cold walk to the Necessary."

"It's a colder walk to your Grave; and if we can't get this Camp cleaned up, that's the Walk you'll all be taking. Any more pissing where you eat and sleep, and I'll have you Dancing to the Rogues' March."

"What's the Rogues' March?" I inquired civilly when he'd stalked out.

Three fifes were whipped out, and they played it for me. A merry derisive little Tune, which they explained afterwards was used to Parade a guilty man through the Camp to the Place of his Punishment or to Drum a truly great Offender out of the Camp entirely.

Andrew Davis wrinkled his nose suddenly. "I knew this Place would make a Lunatick of me. Here I stand stirring beans, and I could Swear I smell roast Chicken. I'm going mad." he groaned.

"No fear," I reassured him, and before their wondering eyes, pulled out of my sack the two chickens I had brought with me. Long

---

*It was actually in April 1778 that Washington issued the order for 5 strokes to be given on the spot to anyone guilty of this offense.

before they were reduced to stripped bones, which Cady disposed of in the fireplace, my Popularity with my new "Family" was assured!

Jan. 30, 1778

The moment I have been dreading most was the one in which I would Confront Bram and tell him what had to be told. My Ordeal came on me suddenly last Evening.

I had been Informed that he was on Duty out of Camp and not expected back for Several Days, so my Heart rose to my throat when I turned to see that dear-loved Figure bending to come through the door. I knew him on the instant even with the unfamiliar growth of Beard and the grime and his eyes red-rimmed with Fatigue. It was hard to stand still, man like, to receive his hearty hand shake.

"Flip boy," he said, "it's good to see you." He grinned. "I never dreamed you would be able to get here; I didn't think Filly would let you get away. How is she?"

I blurted it out, not meaning to be Cruel, only knowing it had to be said and not knowing how.

"She's dead."

He blinked a few times. He said in a sort of stupid way: "What did you say?"

My throat clogged up. "Filly," I said and then stopped. I couldn't get the words out.

We stood there, staring at One Another. The Others in the Hut had all gone silent.

"Our Philadelphia's dead?" Bram said finally.

I bowed my head, not meeting his eyes. I couldn't bear his Pain. Even less could I bear giving up my means of Revenge.

After another long while he said in a dull flat voice, "When did she Sicken?"

"She—she didn't exactly," I said lamely. "It wasn't like that. It got rough back Home . . . the Cowboys and the Skinners and . . . she got—hurt."

I saw his eyes blink again and then shutter over, trying to absorb it.

"Who hurt her?" the same lifeless voice asked me.

"British deserters . . . two of them, and . . . and . . ."

I stopped myself in time from adding Tom Dumb. At least that Much I could Spare him.

"Come outside with me," Bram said. The way he said it Reminded me for the first time, as his Draggled Uniform didn't, that he was an Officer. When he said Jump, I would have to Jump. I went outside with him.

"Now tell me the truth, every bit of it," Bram ordered.

"You'd be better off not knowing."

"You damn fool." But he said it without heat or Emotion. "If *she* had to bear its happening to her, then I can bear hearing of it."

So I told him of how we had gone to the Island together, she and I; we had talked and eaten, fished and fifed and been Happy and at Peace till the Deserters came, led by Tom Dumb. They had knocked me down and tied me up while they abused her. I had come to only to find her Dead.

He listened in Stillness so long as I Spoke. Then he turned his Back to me and stood for a long while, making no Movement, not so much as a Twitch of his Shoulders. Just as I began to fear Grief had turned him to a Pillar of Stone, he wheeled back to me.

"Why did your Father or my Aunt never send word to me? I had a right to Know."

I moistened my dry cracked lips with my tongue, Seeking my Words carefully.

"Cousin Lucretia *did* write to you . . . not right away, there was too much . . . Confusion. My Mother was gravely ill and in July she, too, died. In August my father took Ship for England, and I went to stay with Cousin Lucretia. I know she wrote to you then."

"I never received it. It's not surprising. In the Army more letters than not go Astray. I'm sorry, Flip, about your Mother, I mean. I was allways fond of Aunt Annette."

I said Straight Out, "It was a Grief to me but not to her. She no longer wished to Live."

"After losing Filly, you mean? Yes," he agreed huskily, "that would be her Finishing Blow."

I opened my mouth, remembering with a pang how little Philadelphia had been in our Mother's heart as she lay dying. Then I closed it. What use to add even one wisp of Straw to the Burden of his Sorrow?

We were silent together till he presently asked me, "How did Martinis take it?"

"Martinis was Captivated." I found myself whispering the Words. "He never knew."

"Sweet Jesus, what more!" He put his hand on my shoulder. "Poor lad. No Wonder you looked like a Lost Soul when I came into your Hut this evening. When was this?"

"We think after the fighting on Long Island, but we can't be sure. He was Imprisoned in the Provost in New York."

He had allways been Quick off the Mark. "Was?" he repeated sharply.

"One of his friends escaped later and told us . . . months after it was over . . . Have you heard of Beast Cunningham?"

He nodded, dawning horror in his eyes.

"He starved them and he Froze them, and Those that showed any Fight—you wouldn't expect Martinis not to Fight Back, would you?—one fine night he had him taken out with his hands tied behind his Back and a Gag in his mouth and they strung him up and Hanged him till he was Dead."

Two slow tears Ploughed their way down his cheeks, and then several more, leaving a Crooked Trail in the dust and grime of his face. "Poor lad," he said. "Poor Martinis. We used to jest, remember, that he was born to be hanged . . . but this . . . God! I'm glad he didn't know about Filly."

"It wouldn't have made any Difference to him," I muttered defensively. "He wouldn't have thought the Worst of her."

He stared at me, seemingly Perplexed.

"Of course, he wouldn't have. But this way he was Spared the pain of knowing."

"*You* didn't want to be Spared!" I burst out.

"I'm alive. And I," he added, "am different. If he had lived, Martinis would have gone back to sea. I would have stayed with her, wedded her."

"She would have wedded no one after what they did to her!" I said vehemently.

"Do you think I would have cared . . . or held it against her? I would have helped her, healed her. You don't understand. She was mine; she allways was Mine, from the first tottering Steps she took towards *me,* not mother or father or brother. I looked over her and loved her and set my Heart on her when you were still in your Cradle."

"It's you who don't understand," I said quietly. "Those men did terrible things to her, ugly vicious things. She would have been terrified of the Marriage Bed, of any man's touch. The girl you loved, even had she Lived, would have been gone Forever. It's better that she's Dead."

I thought he would strike me. He half raised a clenched fist, then slowly let it Fall.

"Never say that!" His voice was like the Crack of a Whip. "By God, never say that again. You didn't know her as I do. I would have brought her to Life again . . . *my* Philadelphia." As he said her name, his Voice became a Caress. "*Mijn kleintje, mijn hartewensch, I would have brought her to love.*"

What was there I could say to him. I gestured Helplessly, and he gave me a strange Unfathomable look, almost . . . my lips twisted bitterly. Ironic! Was this Another wondering why *I* should be the one to survive? Then he suddenly ran from me, staggering almost Drunkenly down a dirt path in the direction of a Wooded Area. I heard him retching and sobbing, and I returned to my Hut feeling like the lowest crawlingest creature that ever Crept the Earth.

Feb. 5, 1778

I am completely Uniformed, which is more than can be said of most men in this Army, for we are glad to Obtain any cloathes that are Obtainable. It is the Rule that musicians wear the Reverse of the Regiment's colors, so that if its colors be grey with blue facings, then the Musicians wear blue with grey. But where there is a Lack, the rule must give way to Expediencies; and the men here wear whatever will cover them, even captured British Uniforms, which I will go Naked before ever I shall do.

My jacket for Parade is of blue with buff facings, but for common use I have a Homespun Hunting Shirt dyed brown. These were provided me by Col. Van Cortlandt, along with a complete set of white woolen small cloathes and an extra pair of lether Breeches.

Cady and Andrew roared with Laughter when I admired the Breeches.

"They'll strangel you," Gulich warned me. "After a couple of hours, you'll need a pail of snow for the fire in your Crotch."

I refrained just in time from asking why, but even in the dim light of our smoked-up hut, they saw my hightened Colour.

"Look, it blushes like a girl," Enoch jested.

I blushed more furiously.

"Let the lad be," Jan Koos admonished. "You're barely shaving yourself, Enoch Jones."

But in this short time I had learned the Way of Army Talk.

"Gulich's just trying to let us know he's got something to fill his own Britches," I said calmly, so that the laughter turned on Gulich.

A moment later Cady Begged me, "Say, Phil, lend me your shoes, will you, I got to go on Duty with the Sentry."

But when I handed them over, he couldn't get his feet into them.

"Jeez," he complained, "just our Luck you have the only shoes without Holes and the smallest Feet in the Army."

"We Van Durens are known for our short Feet and tall Stories," I said, causing them to laugh again.

With such dangerous Moments is my Life here punctuated!

Feb. 10, 1778

I had never dreamed to be kept so Busy. I thought in Winter Quarters much time would pass in Idelness. But I have had so many pieces of Musick to learn . . . *Peas Upon A Trencher* to signal to breakfast; *Roast Beef,* which signals dinner time musickally if not in fact. Then there is Reveille and Taptoe,* the *Rogue's March* and varied Military Marches.

We are called to practise every afternoon at the same hour, which time is known to the entire Camp, so that none may interpret our Signals wrong and take alarm, as did Happen, I understand, in the fighting at Germantown, where a drum beating Parley was mistaken for Retreat, and some troops panicked.

Every day I have Lessons on the Flute from the Fife Major, who is an exceeding fine Musician. I feel myself fortunate to have his Training.

---

*Tattoo, or taps.

Sometimes I go on Duty with a Sentry, though more often a Drummer is reqwired. Then frequently the Band is called upon to play at an Officers' Gathering or even around the Camp if the Spirits of the men need cheering.

There are my Cloathes to keep in order and our Rations to be cooked, and the Hut, which I clean out so fiercely every day and force my "Family" to clean, too, so that they call me "Misstress Philip."

But there is less Sickness since Gulich got his three Strokes and my Broom sweeps clean, I point out, so that they Grumbel but Yield to me, partickularly as I bribe them with my Rum Ration. I try, but I cannot like Rum. I am fonder of Whiskey, not so much as to taste but for Keeping out the Cold.

How Strange is Life. I came here thinking to do Battle with the British, longing to ease my own Hurt by inflicting Savage Hurt on as many of them as I was able.

Instead, what do I do Battle with, in the midst of an Army, but Dirt and Disease and Disorder? Just like any proper Dutch *Hausfrau*.

At first it all seemed pointless. I began to Regret that I came. But now I am at home here. I have schooled myself to Patience. The ways of Men and War are strange, and I must learn them. My Revenge will not be less sweet for the Waiting.

Also, I am easier in my mind regarding the Possibility of Trouble with Bram. Although we are in the same Regiment, such is the Life in the Army, we seldom meet. The lives of Officers and the common Soldiers lie far apart. Moreover, our food is in such short supply, and so Coarse withal, I am not like to lose the wan sickly looks he must ever associate with Philip in Ill Health. What a thing to have to be Thankfull for!

Feb. 19, 1778

Yesterday I saw the Great Man himself, Genl. Washington. Capt. Hallet sent me with a message to one of the General's Aides, who resides with him, as do all his Military Family, in the Potts Farm House, which he rented.

It was a long Tramp from our Eminence high on the hill, with its clear Fields of Fire, to the banks of the Valley Creek, where the

Potts House is located, but I was warmly dressed, with two pairs of woolen Stockings tucked in my shoes and Leggings over them, and I enjoyed the brisk Walk.

Some laundresses were washing out cloathes in the Creek, despite the chill air. A marvelous Smell came from the Dewee House nearby, where the Baking for the Officers is done. It had me nigh Faint with Hunger for we have been a week without Bread.

Two of the Life Guards admitted me to the House and brought me to the office where Col. Tilghman awated my message. It was as I left that I glimpsed Genl. Washington as he came down the stairs, He is an incredibley Tall Man, that was my most overwhelming Impression, his Hight and Breadth and the sternness of his expression. Then the Life Guards hurried me away, and I saw him no more.

As I passed again by the Bakehouse, I made my way to the Kitchen, where the Baking was going on, and Prevailed upon a motherly looking Soul, who took pity on the six successive days I have been eating only Fire Cakes, to give me a crusty roll. Whereupon I played her a Tune upon my Fife, which so pleased her she smuggeled me a whole Loaf meant for the Officers' Table. Tonight my Family and I shall Feast all the more finely for wondering which Officers we have Deprived.

Just the same . . . this life is passing strange. I enlisted to fight for my Country, not go hungry.

Feb. 28, 1778

The Camp is full of Rumors about the Prussian Baron who arrived today to Drill us into more Military Ways. Von Stubbin or Stauben or some such name.

March 3, 1778

The name is Von Steuben, and I have heard some Jests among the Officers about whether the title is his by Birth or Adoption. He is to drill Washington's Life Guards first, all 42 or 44 of them. As the General's personnl Body Guard, this is Deemed Appropriate. They are some fine specimens of Manhood, as why should they not be, with the amusing Reqwirements for Entry into this august Body? As well as native-born Americans of five feet eight to ten inches in Hight, they are reqwired to be Handsome, Sturdy, and Well-Dressed. I wonder who passes Judgement on their handsomeness. Mrs. Martha Washington, perhaps? And does it please the General to Oblige her in her Choices?

March 10, 1778

Von Steuben continues to drill the Men daily, and I do declaire it is as good as a Fair come to Town. I am not the only one to think so. The Drill Field is the gathering Place every day for all the Farmers and Camp Followers and indeed any one of us who has the Free Time.

Yesterday we all fell down laughing for you never saw so many Men, each intent on going in his own direction while our Drill Master, on the Verge of Apoplexy, tried to make them go in Unison. There were face-to-face encounters, some going forwards while others at the same time retreated back, not to say sideways. Their Weapons tangled together; they fell over one another, rich curses mingled with Apologies. I swear it was as good as the Play, and Von Steuben kept getting more Purple in the Face by the Moment, pouring forth a rich vocabulary of Obscenity, most of it in German and French, but the little English he has acqwired Appears to be a String of Curses.

German being not too unlike Dutch, I can understand some of his Prussian swearing as well and am eagerly appealed to translate it for anyone near to me. Von Steuben's tame Frenchman and Capt. Walker of one of our New York Regts. translate on the Field for the men.

Fighting men we may be in the Continental Army, but it would take a more Optimistick mind than Mine is to believe we can be drilled into the Presision of European trained Soldiers!

March 12, 1778

God must be smiling a little more on us these days. Two days in a Row this week we have had our Proper Ration of meat. But I mistake to speak lightly of God's goodness because it does not extend to the health of our men here at Valley Forge. Disease continues to Dessimate our Numbers most Horribly . . . though we do not know how many Succumb for the sick are sent, willing or not, to the Regimental Hospitals, and if they be considered in a Bad Way, are Bundelled off in open wagons to Bethlehem or Yellow Springs for Recovery or to Die there. Few return.

My Hut Family has taken note that, under the Rules of Strict Cleanliness I have Enforsed, we are in better Condition than most. We neether Cough nor Itch. There is not so much teasing these days about "Mistress Philip." No more remnants of Food and Bones are thrown on the floors or Bedding. No spitting on the Grownd. Regular trips to the Necessary. Cloathes kept Clean as is Possible. I have even hung Crude Pomanders filled with Pine to sweeten the air within the Hut, and if not Sweet, nither is it so Foule as it was before.

My confidence grows for it is six weeks now, and none suspect me. The rules of Helth protect my Disguise . . . if I am just carefull not to let my Mask slip.

Sunday, March 15, 1778
at Valley Forge

Today, for the first time, I would have wished to be anywhere else than here. All the drummers and fifers in the Army were summoned by His Excellency the Commander-in-Chief himself to attend on the Grand Parade at guard mounting for the Sole Purpose of drumming out of the Camp Lieut. Frederick Enslin of Col. Malcolm's Additional Regt.

The Charges of which he had been found Guilty, and thus dismissed from the Service with Infamy, were two: attempting sodomy with a soldier and Perjury, in swearing falsely about it.

His Crimes, which had already been Trumpeted all about the Camp, were read aloud to Shame him further. It was Moreover announced that there would be publication of his Offense abroad as well as here at Valley Forge, which means that he will be Forever Disgraced and may never go home again to New York.

With his coat turned about, the High Criminal—who looked more the frightened lad—was marched to the end of the Parade

Ground. The Musick was loud and merry, but I played no part of it, though I kept my Fife to my mouth. Just at the end, when he was to be turned out of our Camp, a young drummer lad—from one of the Pennsylvania Regts., I believe—dashed out of the ranks and aimed a well-placed kick at the Unfortunate's backside to send him staggering. He regained his Balance and proceeded on his Way, but there was a look of Shame and Suffering on his face which Haunts me strangely.

I looked to see the Drummer boy Reprimanded, but instead there was Laughter and cheers for him, and Jeers for the Objeckt of his Unkindness. It seems this Final Kick to a Guilty Man's Backside is accepted practise.

I do not understand the Lieut.'s—*former* Lieut.'s—nature, but he only *attempted* . . . he did not *force* himself on anyone. Yet he is a Villain and the soldier, who suffered no Injury at his hands, is the Hero. Why are the Rules for Men and for Women so differing? So unfair?

In this period at Valley Forge I have suffered Insufficient Food, Ill Housing, lack of Warm Cloathing, the Possibility of Disease and Various minor Ills without any great Distress of Mind, happier than I have been for a long Time before, Convinced I was where I belonged.

Today, witnessing Petty but Cruel Persecution of the Hapless man—whose greatest Crime, if Talk I have heard is True, is that he got Found out—the Nobel Cause we serve seems slightly Tarnished.

Besides, what harm do we do against the British roosting here? Soldiers are supposed to Stand and Fight, not sit on their Backsides.

April 3, 1778

Bram sought me out today after Musickal Practise and asked me to walk with him a little. We wandered in the Direction of an Eminence, still plentifull with fine Oaks to be torn down for construction of Huts or our Firewood. There was a fine view of the Schuylkill River, which provides one side of our Defense here and, I am told, will soon be rich with the "finest shad in the world." Of course, those who say this have never tasted our Hudson shad!

I perched upon a rock, with my hands clasped about my knees, in a way that my brother was used to do, as surely Bram would note. Bram himself stood Tall and Strong against a big Oak.

"I have been avoiding you," he said without any Preliminaries.

I nodded, it being too obvious a Truth to need Acknowledging.

"I ask your Forgiveness, Flip. It was not well done of me considering our past Friendship and the Family Relationship in which we stand. But I needed time to—" His voice faded away for a moment, then he stood even Taller and sounded Firmer. "I needed time to come to Terms with a World in which I lived and *she* did not."

I told him hardily, "I understand. You have nothing to reproach yourself with."

"You are generous. I do reproach myself. You were Suffering greatly, too. Our Sorrow could have been Shared."

I licked my lips, wishing to be finished with this dangerous Subject once and for All.

"I had many months before you to become Accustomed. There is no further need to castigate Yourself. I beg you will not."

This time it was he who nodded in Acknowledgement.

There was a slight pause. Then he looked towards the distant Schuylkill, his eyes glazed over with Pain.

"Do you remember what day this is?"

"Aye."

"She would have been nineteen. Do you know the first time ever I celebrated her Birth Date she was not there with us? It was seventeen Years ago today. Your family was yet living in New York; Cousin Lucretia and I worked at the Tavern with Ben and Obidiah and Mrs. Wallace . . . Still, we made ourselves a Fine Feast that night because Our Philadelphia was two years of age."

I knew not what to reply, and he came out of his Reverie to say to me briskly, "I ask you to Remember from this moment on that we are Friends as well as Cousins and you can count on me Allways."

I said with overdone Solemnity, "I will remember. Thank you kindly, Cousin Bram," and he laughed and came and took me by the shoulders and Shook me with gentle Affection.

"None of your Impertinence, Boy. Remember I'm an Officer."

"Aye, aye, Sir," I said in mock fear and got rapped on my head for my pains. One hand was still on my shoulder. I slipped out from under it and walked away from him, Facing the River. Closeness is a danger to Disguise.

"It's beautiful, isn't it?" I asked him over that same shoulder, which seemed to Burn where he had Touched it.

"But not the Hudson, that's what you were thinking."

"Yes, beautiful, but not the Hudson."

We walked back together to our Company Street in thoughtful but Friendly Silence.

April 19, 1778

The Shad Run has been a marvelous sight to Behold. I managed to sneak off once to Partake in the Fishing, and our netting was Magnificent. Our diet has improved greatly with the addition of this Fish and more or less regular Rations of Meat. I must Confess I am now unable to Judge if this Shad is inferior to ours at Home. I only know that None has ever tasted Better to me than here at Valley Forge.

May 7, 1778

Yesterday was one of glorious Rejoicing throughout all the Army that we have a Treaty of Alliance with France.

There was rather too much Preaching and Discoursing by the Chaplains in the Morning and then a grand Parade Inspection and all manner of thirteen-gun Salutes from the Hights where a dozen or more six-Pounders had been drove.

There was a vast amount of cheering, which we had been directed to do but came from the Heart nevertheless. Feasting and Drinking and Revelry continued all the day.

And one other thing occurred, thank God. The General, in Honor of this day, pardoned three of the men who were previously sentenced to Death for their Desertion.

May 10, 1778

We now have a strong Ally to give us Strength and Importance in the eyes of the World. No longer does the Weather hold us in this

Place like Prisoners. Yet still we linger on, surely the Do-Nothingest Army that ever was.

I Chafe continually at the Delay, and I growled about it to Bram, who I Chansed to meet on our Company Street today.

He laughed and slapped me Heartily on the back, advising that a soldier does more Waiting than he does Fighting. More soberly he added, "Be grateful you will be in the Rear, doing no fighting at all. When the battle begins"—this time his laugh was grim "you will learn all too soon, lad, there is no Glory to be found in War."

"I seek not Glory," I told him, "only Vengeance."

At his look of Amazement, I Recolleckted myself. "I have a score or two to settle with the Redcoats," I muttered and hurried away.

It is Unsettling to be with him. The Part I play is allways harder than with Strangers.

May 15, 1778

Orders have been issued that each Hut shall have no less than two Windows. Since most Huts are like ours and have None, and I have been lamenting this lack since the first day of my Enlistment, Gulich and Enoch have made a fine jest of the Notion that I have the General's ear and this Order has come through me. To which I retort that the General and I may both be Visited by the same Attack of Common Sense. Now that the Weather improves, a fine Breeze coming through the Huts may well rid us of the Noxious Odors that Remain, even though our Hut is one of the Best. Of the some few others I have entered, I had to rush right out again. I have never seen a Dungeon Cell, but I Misdoubt one could be less dirty, dank, stinking, or cheerless!

May 17, 1778

Bram remembered that this was the Eighteenth Birth Date of Philip Stephanus Van Duren. He Bestowed on me three presents, the first of which was a Haversack of goatskin, far Superior to any I have seen here. Secondly, he gave to me a captured British Fife case, which Differs from our own in having a small compartment with a Lock and Hasp. This makes it usefull in Battle for carrying messages, which is another part of a Fifer's Duty. My third Gift, which I am told will be of the most Important Usage when we are on the March, is a Tin Canteen, also of British origin and Capture. For this I am much envied by my Family, Jan and Gulich having only Wood ones and Andy and Cady, not even that, but only glass flasks sewn into lether, which are highly Damageable.

I did not ask where my Gifts came from, which is the Hight of Tactlessness in the Army, where one takes what one can Obtain with no Embarrassing Questions asked.

In the evening Bram came by again. By what Miracle I know not, he had Obtained from the Bakehouse a plain cake filled up with Marmalade. He stayed to share it with us.

May 29, 1778

A most amuzing thing has Occurred. There is a young Camp Follower here, I judge about fifteen years of age. She is daughter to one of the Corporals in the 3rd New Hampshire, who, like we of the New York 2nd, are in Poor's Brigade.

Well, the Truth of it is that this sweet Creature has become Enamoured of me and Follows me about whenever possible with the Devotion of a small Puppy and brings me small Treats, which I am loath to eat—I fear they may come from her own Ration—but she is so cast down when I Refuse, I generally Yield.

She is a pretty thing, though not overly Clean, with Hair that might be Golden did she wash it and great eyes of Brown, like a young Fawn's. However, I fear my taste runs not in this Direction.

June 3, 1778

I was sitting outside today, a little removed from my Hut, playing on the Fife for my Young Inamorata, Prudence. She was partickularly fond of the tune I must take credit for having composed myself and Vastly Impressed that I should be able to make up Musick. I will be very Puffed up in my own Conceit if I deal with her for long.

She wanted to know if it had any words, so I sang the one verse which I remembered from one year ago this very month.

Even as I did so I noted with some surprise that there was far less Pain than Formerly. Time truly is the Great Healer.

Softly I repeated the verse:

> *I sing of Philadelphia*
> *Who fears not man nor gun.*
> *If my sister was my brother*
> *She would be with Washington.*

When I looked up Bram was standing over me and Prudence had run away, much frightened of the yellow cockade in his hat. Officers do not much come her way.

I said to him, "Some day it will not hurt so much as it still does, Bram."

"I know that," he replied, "but the Time has not come yet; and I will miss her all my life long."

He put one hand across his eyes and stood there motionless for what seemed to me—itching to get away—a long, long Time.

"Seeing you like this," he muttered, his eyes still covered, "sitting there—just so—one leg crossed over the other . . . hearing her name on your lips . . . I was reminded so of—"

He never finished his sentence, just turned abruptly and made off from me.

My Heart, which had given one quick Leap of Terror, still Fluttered Fearfully within my Bosom. Slowly I uncrossed my Leggs.

Months of Success had made me over-Confident. I had grown Careless, forgetting I must never Cease to be on my Guard.

Unknown perhaps even to himself, a tiny Seed of Suspicion has been planted in Bram's mind. He would be more Watchful now and the Seed might grow. Either I must uproot it quickly or my life as a Fifer in the Continental Army could be in Jepardy.

June 4, 1778

The Deserter who came here two days past to Spy for the British was hanged this morning. I know I should Despize him and be glad, but I cannot be. To kill in the heat and Turmoil of Battle is what we are here for, and I am no less Eager than other Soldiers to do it; but to determine Beforehand in cold Blood that a living man shall be Hanged . . . that is something I cannot accept. When I think of Martinis, gagged and dangling from a rope till the Breath was entirely Choked out of him . . . God, it will haunt me forever!

I did not know wether I should be able to Steel myself to be able to Parade the Offender to his End, but gladly was I spared this Ordeal. Capt. Wright, who I know to be good Friends with Bram, came by as we were lining up, Plucked me from the Ranks, and sent me to General Varnum's Quarters with a message. I knew it must be at Bram's Behest, and it is Favoritism, but I care not. Never did I Speed on my way to any Place more Thankfully.

June 5, 1778

There had been a General Order from Von Steuben Complaining about the Quality of the Army Musick. Drum and Fife Majors are to be Redused if it does not improve. So our practise time has been Doubeled.

In any spare time that is mine, I have formed the Custom of sitting up on the Hill to practise by myself. The little Prudence, whenever Possible, sits near to me to listen to my Musick and gaze at me Adoringly.

This afternoon we were together Thus and I had paused to Rest, closing my eyes. When I opened them, it was to find that Prudence had removed from her former place and was now sitting so close to me that our shoulders almost touched.

As I turned my head in surprise, she raised her face to mine.

Why, the little Minx, I thought, she is asking to be Kissed.

A hand stroked my sleeve. An arm stole about my waist.

By damn, she wasn't just asking, she was inviting. My first Impulse to push her away died down. A spirit of the old Indian Mischief bade me wait to see how far she would go.

Quite Far.

So far that I was just prepared to Spin her about for a boot in the Rear, followed by a stern lecture on the Troubles that could come to a Maid so free and easy with her Person.

Even as my hand was on her shoulder, I saw Bram walking in our Direction. He had not Notised us yet but soon was Bound to. The Perfect Plan for allaying his Suspicions popped full-Grown into my Head.

Instead of using my Hand to turn Prudence around, I employed it to bring her into my Embrase. A rather Stand-Offish Embrase it was, since I dared not let her Bosom press against Mine, even though I have been binding mine flat since we put on our summer uniforms.

As I stroked and caressed her cheeks and rather dirty hair, part of the time staring Fondly into her eyes and wishing I knew more about how men made love, I could see that Bram's Gaze was now on us.

With my hand on the back of her neck, I brought her closer and planted a Kiss on her forehead and one on her chin and finally, gritting my teeth, a last quick Kiss on her Lips.

"Oh Philip! Oh Sir!" she gasped, sighing so hard in her ecstasy that her Bosom near heaved up out of her Bodice.

I got my hand on whatever Part of it was exposed, pretended to have just Notised Bram standing by and gave a Violent Start, pulling my hand free from Prudence and jumping up.

The little Minx blushed violently, as well she should, and once again ran away.

Bram grinned across at me. "So the boy is reaching for the man?" he said.

I gave him what I hoped was a man-like Wink.

As we walked down the Hill together, I felt reasonably sure the Kernel of Doubt in his mind had withered and died.

June 12, 1778

I have been avoiding little Prudence this past week, and whenever we meet, her glance Reproaches me for my Neglect. Sometimes her eyes on me are those of a wounded deer, sometimes of a lovesick Cow.

My Conscience Reproaches me as much as her eyes. It was not Kind of me to make use of her for my own Purposes and then Cast her out of my life.

But what choice have I? I cannot Continue to make love to her, even love of the mildest sort.

June 15, 1778

My Problem has been Solved for me. I thank God. Young Prudence came to me today, weeping and red-eyed, to Bid me good by. She and her mother are going home before the Summer Campaign.

Quickly I made a Trade with Enoch, the chain he wears for my Canteen.

Kissing her tears away, I made the poor child a present of the Chain and promised never in this Life to forget her.

She Embrased me warmly again and ran to show her Mother the Chain. Her excessive Grief seemed forgotten.

June 18, 1778

Great excitement Prevails. The British left Philadelphia during last night and one of our Divisions is already on the Move.

We leave Valley Forge tomorrow, exactly six months to the day from when the Army arrived.

Soon we shall meet the British on the Open Field. Soon I shall see them cut down . . . *their* lives ruined . . .

I would be lying if I said I did not Experience great Trepidation. Yet I have less to fear than most. In the Fighting I will be behind the lines, Fifing, Delivering messages, helping with the Wounded. My Life will hardly be in Danger. But War is new to me and so I fear it. What helps is my Instinct that the sight of a British redcoat will always be enough to make my Hate rise high enough so that the Fear is second.

I said so to Bram when he came by to offer me Encouragement.

"Are you afraid, Philip?" he asked me.

"A little," said I, "but I hate them more than I fear them."

"Amen," said he.

To myself I repeated the same vow I had made the day I stood over the dying boy's bedside and heard about Martinis. *Now will I make a very bitter enemy.*

June 23, 1778

We have crossed the Delaware and are now in New Jersey, where it becomes obvious . . .

[two pages smudged out with water marks]

Monmouth County Court House
June 28, 1778

Today I performed wonderfully calm considering I was in my first Military Engagement. Now night has fallen and I lie here on the Ground with a blanket for my Mattress and a Cooking fire for my light, my Insides all a-Quiver like a Custard Pudding.

The first fighting began in the morning when the enemy began its march out of here. My Regiment was held back, and I had nothing to do for the first Several hours but to Swallow my Bile and speculate on weather I would disgrace myself by Giving up my Breakfast if the Worst came to the Worst.

Then there began to be Wounded in the Rear and I was assigned to Help bring them to where Medickal Aid would be provided.

This was Gruesome Work, for I have never before seen Men Wounded in Battle, and the first Wish of my Heart is that I nevermore Will again. The sights and sounds of the Suffering are not to be Described this side of Hell. Indeed the day had another Aspect of Hell, for the sun shined down on us without Mercy, and I have stood at the Mouth of our Bee Hive Oven in Van Duren Manor when it was at full Blaze, and reached inside to remove the new-Baked loaves, yet not felt such scorching Blast of Heat as we Experienced today.

The situation did not look good for us in the Beginning because Genl. Lee, who is second in Command to Washington, led an early Retreat. Tonight there is much talk among the Soldiery here of a Confrontation between Generals Washington and Lee that Presumes to have taken place right on the Field, where the Commander-in-Chief, in a passion of anger, damned Genl. Lee for the Retreat and for Cowardly Behaviour.

This may be mere Soldiers' Gossip, greatly Exaggerated—and for Gossipping, I would any time match a Regiment against a

Woman's Quilting Bee. Still all of us take much pleasure in the notion of a String of Oaths issuing from the Mouth of our Commander-in-Chief, who frequently issues pious Genl. Orders about the unsoldier-like, ungentleman-like Conduct of Cursing. I Confess the Orders allways before had me in a Puzzle. There is nothing so much soldier-like, as far as I can perceive, as Swearing.

Late in the day an Enemy Force crossed Weamaconk Creek, attempting to get on Stirling's Flank—Major General Lord Stirling, that is, the only British Lord in the American Army. Our Brigade was sent to Prevent them; and during this Period I was used as a Messenger, shutteling back and forth between my own regimental Commander and Stirling's Forces, who were stationed on an Elevation where they could fire down upon the Enemy. I continued in this Duty even when Stirling sent a part of our Brigade to drive the British back across the Creek, where our Americans persued them until we gained possession of the Field of Battle.

Monmouth
June 29, 1778

I was interrupted last night when some of our officers came among us to offer their Commendations to the Regiment on our Conduct yesterday.

We expected to resume the fighting this Morning but came awake at dawn only to find the Enemy had crept away in the night in such silence that, though they passed right near to our Brigade, we heard them not.

So the enemy is Routed and the Field is ours, which should mean Victory, but I have been listening to some Heated Discussions among the Officers and I am perplexed about wether we achieved One. Capt. Hallet argued that the British left their dead or wounded on the Field, three to one of ours; so he feels we won. Ensign Herring maintains it is no such thing, since Clinton did not want the Field but only to Get Away. I fear me I will never understand Military Matters.

To me the most remarkable Occurrence about yesterday's Battle was the Cool-Headed Conduct of the woman that the Pennsylvania troops call Capt. Molly. She is Wife to an Artillery man and, when she was not beside him at his Cannon during all the Heat and

Danger of the Engagement, she was drawing water from the well about four hundred yards in back of Stirling's Forces to refresh the soldiers suffering from heat and Thirst. I several times saw her at both Tasks as I scuttled about delivering my Messages.

Today the Pa. men are Boasting Fondly of an incident that took place when she tended her husband's gun after he fell Wounded. Her feet, happening to be firmly planted apart as she was in the Act of reaching for a Cartridge, a British cannon ball shot midway between her legs and carried off her lower skirt and petticoat. She is said to have looked down at her Sorry garments and Observed without undue Concern that she was lucky the shot had not passed a little Higher or it might have carried away Something Else.

I can appreciate her Bravery the more since I was out of Fire Range myself, only once happening to go through the Lines instead of Behind them. Bram saw me from the Firing Line, and shouted at me in a Fury to get back to a Safe Position.

I did so, and all the rest of that Long Day I was numb with fear for him, for he was in the midst of the Fighting. When the long Day was over, I sought him out and, not finding him anywhere, went out on the Field to look among the Dead and Wounded.

As I bent over a wounded American in a buff and blue uniform, out of the Corner of my eye I saw a Flash of red off to my Right. I never dreamed I could act so quickly, but I snatched the Bayonet, which lay in the Continental's hand, and whirled around, ready to strike.

He was a young British soldier, and the movement he had made was just the slight raising of his Body; but as I saw that red uniform come at me and remembered the last time I had knelt on the earth and witnessed Such, my bitterness rose within me and I raised the Bayonet—only to have it struck down so hard by a musket dashing against it, that my Wrist Pained me for hours afterwards.

Bram's shocked face was above me, his Musket, now that he had disarmed me, swinging back at his side.

"Good Christ, Philip!" he swore at me. "He's just a lad."

"He wears a British redcoat!" I spat back at him.

"He's wounded and disarmed."

"I—so was Philadelphia—on our Island—when they came."

"Because some of them are Barbarians, must we be?"

Even as he said it, a Spasm of Pain crossed his Face; and I

320

Rejoiced to see it. Let him Suffer, too, if he must be Nobel. As for me . . .

"He is our enemy," I argued heatedly. "Now and forever any man who wears the British Uniform becomes my enemy. I cannot understand these fine distinctions of when it is and is not proper to strike at the enemy."

His voice became the voice of my Regimental Captain—cold, hard, commanding. "Not when the Battle is over and he lies Helpless at your feet, Fifer Van Duren."

"Even if, Unwounded, *he* would not be nearly so nice in his Notions?"

"Even then."

"I wonder if Philadelphia would say so, given the Chance," I demanded of him bitterly. "Or Martinis. And Piet."

He put out his hand to my shoulder. "Flip, lad," he said huskily, "I do understand that—"

I tore away from his hold. "No, by God, you don't understand! You weren't there . . . you didn't . . . Damnation! I enlisted in the Army to get my—to be—to rid the Earth of as many British redcoats as I might."

A childish Whimper sounded in our ears, and we both turned at the same moment to look down at the red-coated Creature lying on the ground. The Bloody Stain on his jacket had grown much larger. His eyes were fixed on us in a Glassy Stare.

As we stood looking, the eyes blinked twice and then glazed over with Pain. The Whimper sounded again. This time we could distinguish his Words. "Mama . . . need . . . Mama."

A Lump of Pain invaded my Breast even as Bram's eyes accused me.

"I'll see if I can find help," he told me curtly.

Left to myself, I sank to my Knees.

"Mama!" the soldier cried again as I gently pulled a Handkerchief from about his Throat and used it to wipe his sweated Face.

"Oh God!" I cried in my Heart. "I'm so Confused. I want Retribution from them for all I've lost, but not like this."

I continued to kneel by him, shading him from the Heat, my eyes averted from the red of his jacket. I kept asking myself over and over, Would I have done it? If Bram had not come to the Field, probably looking for me as I had been for him, would I have struck with that Bayonet? God of Mercy, would what Bram said be True? Had I joined with the Barbarians?

The whimpering ceased. The British soldier looked up, quite clear-eyed. He whispered to me, "My thanks to you"; his eyes rolled over Briefly. Then he died.

Revenge? All I had left was a Leaden Weight in my stomach, a Foule Taste in my mouth.

Revenge? No . . . only dust and ashes . . .

End of the First Book

Continental Village
Peekskill, New York
Oct. 10, 1778

After several months I resume my Journal.

There were many causes why I ceased my regular Jottings, the Scarcity of Time and Paper not the least of these. I was Fatigued by the constant Marching and Ill Food that was our Lot till we reached Danbury in Conn., and my Spirits were greatly Depressed by what happened between Bram and me on the Field at Monmouth.

For many weeks he seemed to Avoid me as he had when I first came to Valley Forge. Sorely missing his Friendly and Familial Support, I seized my first Opportunity to tax him with his Neglect. I freely Blamed myself for the loss of his Esteem.

He denied it. When I pressed him further, he grew almost Sullen, Bram, who allways had the pleasantest Temper of all the Indians. In the end he gave in to my Entreaties to Explain, though doing so in the most DisJointed Manner.

"You had such a look of her, standing there with that Bayonet raised . . . upbraiding me . . . Sometimes there is an expression on your face, just fleetingly . . . and I feel as though I am going mad. You were allways like, you two, but now that *she* is not here, you remind me so Painfully . . ."

For the first time in all these months I felt a vast Compunction for what I have done, and for one Terrifying moment I even thought to Speak the Truth and put an end to the Agonized longing in his Voice.

But it cannot be.

This life of mine is the one I sought and wish to Preserve till the British are driven from our Shores.

Even without this War, what Bram wants he can never have. The Philadelphia he loved is gone Forever.

I Preserved my Silence.

Peekskill
Oct. 13, 1778

I swear the Army has not its equal for acting Nonsensical. Its actions decide the Fate of our Country and all its Citizens. Every day it deals with Matters of Life and Death or, at the very least, of great Conseqwence. What then was the Main Concern of the last Court Martial, with our own Colonel presiding . . . why, the charge brought against a private in Col. Van Schaick's 1st N.Y. Regt. for the theft of one John Babcock's Britches? The Court acquited him of the Theft but Adjudged the britches to Babcock! On such a decision, might Rome have fallen? Did anyone steal, I wonder, the Toga of one of great Ceasar's Legionnaires?

Continental Village
Oct. 21, 1778

This town, midway between Fish Kill and West Point (where Cousin Lucretia rented the House to store all her Furnishings from Bogardus Cottage), was picked three years ago as one of the Sites of Ship Building for the Continental Navy, also as a Storing Space for Military Supplies. The shipbuilders and store keepers have made it into a very likely Settlement.

It is a pleasant place and one which I will be sorry to Leave, but I think the time of leaving is soon to be for all Officers and Men on Furlough have been Recalled and the Word has gone out that no further Furloughs will be granted on any Pretext whatsoever.

Oct. 22, 1778

I do well as a Prophet. Our Brigade is ordered to Hold itself in Readiness to March at any time.

BRYARLY

Peekskill
Nov. 4, 1778

We are in Readiness to March but have no Marching Orders yet. In the Mean While the local Inhabitants Complain severely about the Soldierly practise of Stealing their Sheep, Poultry, and Cabbages, and our Commanders castigate us in Writing for these Depredations and whenever Possible, Catch the Thieves, Try them at Court Martial, and March them out to the Merry Sound of our Fifes and Drums for the usual physical castigation—one hundred lashes each, well laid on the bare back.

By God, I grow weary of the sound of the lash and the screams of the Victims, but never do I grow Accustomed.

To death Sentences freely handed out to Deserters, I have likewise not grown Stoickal, though as often as not, there are Reprieves granted, sometimes so near the End as to be given at the Place of Execution. This seems to me a Veritabel Species of Torture. I think we all die a little with each Victim.

Why cannot we be content to kill the British—not each other?

Peekskill
Nov. 5, 1778

Our first new Cloathes received at last, and we are asked by the Genl. Order "to give Pertickuler Attention to their Preservation." The Army, oh the Army. If we wear naught else, how can we?

Continental Village
Peekskill
Nov. 12, 1778

I have never writ, lately being my first opportunity, that while we still lay at Danbury a letter from Cousin Lucretia that had been long on its Way at last caught up with me. It was dated this April past and came from the West Indies by way of Obidiah in Philadelphia, enclosed no doubt in one to him and then sent on to Bram.

"I wonder why Aunt Lucretia enclosed yours to me," Bram puzzled when he brought it to me. "I had three of my own from her after all these months with none."

I sighed, believing I knew. I do not think Cousin Lucretia, having a shade of Dutch superstition, could bring herself to direct her letter to Philip Van Duren of the Continental Army.

My letter contained no reproaches. That is not Cousin Lucretia's way. I append her letter here:

My dear Cousin,

I cannot approve of what you have done, Wich I am sure comes as no Surprize to you. Even less do I think it Coreckt of you to have Forsed your Will on Obidiah in the Manner in wich you did, to gain entry into the Army. Still, you were ever Head Strong and Wud have your way, and there is no Use in my Weeping over what cannot be Altered.

I have the news you have been Waiting for, which is that I will soon be returning to my Home in New York with your dear Nurse Thomasina, who is in the same good Health and Spirits as myself. With us you will be Surprized to Know we are bringing an infant Daughter of my late husband's Nephew, Martinis Asher, the Bereaved Mother having died in Childbed shortly after her dear Husband met his end on the Battlefield. As she was unhappily without close Kin, it Behooves me as the nearest member of Martinis' Family to Rear the Child as my Own.

We expect to be in New York before summer's end, if the Child is well enough for Travel. I know you cannot come to an Occupied City, but I have given instrucktions to the Heidens, man and wife, who Care-Take my West Point home that Any One who gives the name Van Duren is to be treated as an Honoured Guest. Make use of the Contents of my home At any Time in whatever way you find Needfull.

Untill we meet agen, I remain, as Allways,

Your Affectnt. Cousin,
Lucretia Bogardus

"Summer's End!" I exclaimed aloud to Bram. "So they may be Home even now."

Since the Contents of his letters duplicated Mine, his Amazement knew no Bounds. I saw his Brows Knit, and his Eyes Narrow . . . but in Spite of the Pain of the Things I was Reckollecting and must now tell him, I could not Help laughing when he fell to Counting on his Fingers.

"Yes, Bram," I laughed at him, "it takes nine Months to get a Child."

"Then how can this be? If Martinis was captured in the Fighting on Long Island, as you told me, and Imprisoned in the Provost untill—"

"The child has nothing to do with Martinis," I told him simply. "She is my sister—half-sister. My father got her on Thomasina while my Mother lay dying."

"Holy God!" Bram said and then gave a low, long whistle. "But then, Philip, why this Charade?"

"We all agreed on it Beforehand. If Thomasina raised her own Babe, no matter who the Father was, no matter how pale the color, the Child could never rise Higher than a Servant. Thomasina wanted more for it . . . her. She is a Van Duren, as much a Van Duren by blood as I am. We cannot, for her own Sake, claim her by name, but as Martinis' child and Lucretia's grand-niece, she will have a Proper Place in the World. Martinis would not grudge his name to an Innocent," I added as he looked at me. Doubtfully. "Rather, I warrant, wherever he has got to, he is laughing Heartily at this Fine Jest played on Society. You know his way."

"I do," he said soberly. And then, more soberly still, "I'm sorry about your father, Lad. I see it Galls you that so shortly after Philadelphia . . . and your Mother in such sad Case . . . I never would have believed . . ."

I returned somewhat Mockingly, "And Philadelphia and I thinking you so all-knowing. We Suspeckted years ago, though at that time we did not Blame him, seeing my Mother in her Sick Grief barred him from her Bed so long. But he wasted no Time while her Life slipped away, just Weeks after we lost my—my Sister. Such is a man's Deathless Love."

"Sorrow takes many strange Twists and Turns," he suggested Gently. "Perhaps he just sought Comfort."

"Perhaps he just did." I spoke from the Depths of a Bitterness never Recovered from. "But the rest of us had no such Comfort.

And he owed much to Thomasina. He might have considered her Well-Being."

"Nay, I am sure my Cousin Cornelius never Acted against her Will."

"He was the only Man in her Life ever to be Kind to her. How was there any resisting that? The Lord of the Manor condescending to his Servant—what Proof had she against such Blandishment?"

"Do not Torment yourself, Philip. What is done is done. And the little one, your sister, when we come home, mayhap she will be a Comfort to *you*."

"Mayhap, she will be," I agreed dully, "when we go home."

Before he left me, I reminded him, "Bram, your Word you will never mention this to any Living Soul. It is a Family Secret that must be Buried with us."

Solemnly, seeing how Important it was to me, he gave his Word.

Continental Village
Nov. 18, 1778

We bid Farewell to this Place Tomorrow. The General will beat at eight o'clock in the Morning, at which time the Waggons are to be Loaded with the Tents and Baggage, but our Camp Kettles we are directed to Carry.

Our Destination is the Indian Country in the Western part of this State, where Tribes of the Six Nations have joined with the British, making Depredations on our Settlements. We go to Guard our Frontiers against them.

This is not the kind of War I had in mind when I Enlisted at Valley Forge, but where the N.Y. 2nd goes, so go I. Even though I am a Fifer and Flutist in Col. Van Cortlandt's Band of Musick rather than a Fighting Soldier, still I am part of the Continental Line. I travel where I am Ordered, and my Musick gives Comfort to the Soldiery.

I only hope it will, as the Saying goes, Soothe the Savage as well as the Soldier's Breast. Because it is one thing to play the Indian but another to face in Uncivilized Areas one who may be after my Scalp. I have the Unsettling Notion that, Contrary to the British, our Indian Enemies are Unlikely to Observe the Military Decency of not Firing upon Musicians. Cady and Gulich, all that are left with me of our Original Valley Forge Family, share equally in this Dismal Conviction.

Albany, N.Y.
Dec. 3, 1778

Before I left the Continental Village, I sealed up my Journal papers and posted them in Cousin Lucretia's name to her House at West Point to be kept there in Safe Keeping.

On this Journey I have but a small Quantity of Paper, and Ink is hard to come by on the March, so my writings must of a Necessity be Short and not too Frequent. Moreover, we are so much on the March, it is Difficult to Write nor am I allways sure what Day it may be. If I ask, an Argument is likely to Ensue; most seem no more sure than I.

Five Deserters were punished tonight at Retreat Beating with the usual one-hundred; I stuffed my ears with Spruce Gum against their Screams. There were to be six, but one had his Sentence remitted. Of the Five, one is also to be Executed. He is sentenced to be shot to death at the head of the Brigade tomorrow Morning before the Troops March for Fort Plank. To Flog a man due to die on the morrow is a Cruelty I would Expect from the British, not in the American Army. I gave up praying long ago, but tonight I shall pray that, in the usual last-minute way, this man may be Reprieved.

Jan. 22, 1779

We have arrived at Fort Plank near Fort Plain in Montgomery County, New York, and since we are to stay here for a Period, Garrison Orders are that we shall keep some Plasier to Clean our Under-Cloathes against next Sunday. Be damned to next Sunday; pray all will clean theirs Immediately. Never did Troops smell so All-Together Ripe!

Lahawack
March 27, 1779

Here I have spent most of the Winter in Col. Van Cortlandt's own Block House, thus my fears of the Indians have been Needless. I have seen no Iroquois, though they are all around not far from here, nor any Rattel Snakes, of which I must Confess I had Previously been Eqwally Afraid. They Abound a-Plenty in this Area, I am told, but Mercifully I have Encountered none.

My time has been given to Musick, and I have Composed some of my own, the Chief of which is the *Lament of the Six Indians*. The Words I had Made up out of my own Sorrow; and then one day I set them to Musick, the Melody seemed to come to me almost as a Gift from Heaven, for it appeared to spring to being all at once inside my Head and I had very little work of Composition. The words of my *Lament* are these:

> *Six little Indians, all of them alive,*
> *One got his head caved in and then there were five.*

> *Five little Indians, where once there were more,*
> *One ran away and then there were four.*

> *Four little Indians, wanting to be free,*
> *One got himself hung up, and then there were three.*

> *Three little Indians, to their Country true,*
> *One stopped a Bullet and then there were two.*

> *Two little Indians, warring side by side,*
> *One in the Army was said to have died.*

> *One little Indian, who suddenly knew*
> *A dead little Indian was left alive, too.*

For many weeks I played it softly to myself, for my own Pleasure only, a curious Pleasure, I admit, for it is a soft sad Tune. Then others heard me and asked for it, and when one of the poor fellows in our Regt. was Scalped while on Patrol, our Drum Major ordered the *Lament* at his Services instead of the sombre *Roslin Castle*.

From there it was but another Step to reciting the words on Request, and now Cady and Gulich have learned them, Likewise some Others. I feel a little Uneasy, wondering if I have been incautious; but Bram has been on duty away from the Block House all the Winter. The Musick, if he heard it, would mean nothing; the words . . . It is foolish to Fret. I think I disturb myself Needlessly. I have been in the Army 14 months now, and his suspicions have been laid to rest.

Lake Otsego
July 30, 1779

We are ordered to hold ourselves in readiness to March. Under the leadership of Genl. Sullivan, we are about to move more Strongly against our Indian enemies.

Aug. 2, 1779

The women of our Corps who can ride are to quit the Boats and go by land as there will be a Sufficient Quantity of Horses. I think I am cravenly glad to be a man in this Case, for I feel safer in the Bateau than I do on a land march through Indian Territory.

Aug. 3, 1779

Reveille to beat tomorrow at Day break. The General will beat at five o'clock, Assembly one half hour later, and the March to Commense at six Precisely, with our Regt. forming the Rear Guard.

On the Susquehanna River
Aug. 7, 1779

We are ordered to make our Marches by land and water as Silent as possible, which gives rise to Fearsome Speculations about Indians lurking behind bushes and Watchful Enemy Eyes upon us as we Proceed.

Many soldiers—Alas, I could not be one of them, as even in this Heat I must keep my coat buttoned against Betraying myself —Frolicked and Refreshed themselves in the Susquehanna, but we are all now Forbid to do so on Account of having to take our Cooking and Drinking water from the River.

In recompense we each received a gill of Rum; and Officers having been ordered one quart, Bram called me to his Tent in the evening to share his with me. To think I now look forward to the Wretched Stuff!

Tioga
Aug. 14, 1779

An Indian or perhaps a Painted Tory lurking outside our Encampment yesterday created Havock among us with only a Single Shot. There was so much panicked Firing of Musketry, without direction or aim, some of our own men were Wounded.

Aug. 21, 1779

We lack the great Number of Baggs needed to carry Flour for the Army. Since there is no other way of Procuring them, our Tents are being cut up and then stitched to Fashion these Necessities.

Aug. 22, 1779

A Sgt. in one of the N. Jersey Rgts. was reduced to the Ranks for Robbing the State Store of some Liquors. He was Paraded at the head of his Rgt., his Drum Major having first turned his coat wrong side outwards and tied a Canteen about his Neck. Then he was returned to the Ranks. This Childish Punishment, though Humiliating, was Preferable to the Brutal Sentence carried out on three others, who had to Run the Gantlope* through Maxwell's Brigade, a Brutal Business more Befitting the Enemy that *we* call Barbrous.

I do not understand this Venture that is so taken up with burning crops of corn and Indian settlements, the building of Roads and Punishing our own Men. I enlisted in my private Fight against Red Coats, not Red Men.

What kind of War for Liberty is this?

---

*Gauntlet

Sept. 3, 1779

Cousin Lucretia used to chide me, "If you ask a foolish question, you may expect a foolish reply." I could have Wished *my* perhaps foolish question in my Entry a week ago had been answered Otherwise.

A large Indian-Tory Force took their stand against us at the Indian Village of Newton, and we had our first Major Battle of this Campaign, defeating the Foe so decisively that they ran off and left their Dead, which is not a usual Custom with them. Three of our men only were killed, but not a single one of the New York Brigade.

As at Monmouth, I took extreme Fright when the Fighting was ended.

Sept. 10, 1779

The King of Spain has proclaimed himself our new Ally. He has announced the Independency of America and declared War against England. There have been Several days of Celebrating this Happy Event. Extra Rum and Whiskey were Ordered us, leading to Consequent Carowsing and Merriment.

Wyoming, N.Y.
Oct. 8, 1779

I have been Subject to much jesting among all the Members of our Band of Musick for having found the Nest of Camp Kettles, Coffee Pot, and Sundry other things belonging to Genl. Poor and having been advertised as Lost beneath this day's General Orders. On the same sheet a Money Reward was offered for the return of a Parchment Pocket Book with Valued Papers inside it. A New Hampshire Sgt. was so lucky as to find the Pocket Book and receive the Money. My Reward, offered in writing by his Adjutant, was the "Cincere Thanks" of the Genl. Gulich thinks he could at least have offered me an extra Gill of Rum. Amen to that; the nights grow cold.

Oct. 17, 1779

From West Point have come Congratulations from our Commander-in-Chief as well as from Congress, both Rejoicing at the Success of what is called the Sullivan Expedition. Washington enumerated that 40 enemy Indian towns were Reduced to Ashes, their crops all destroyed, and whole Communities Obliged to flee to the British Fortress at Niagra, so that they no longer Pose a Threat to our Settlements. Since the whole of this has been Accomplished with the loss of less than Forty men on our part, including Killed, Wounded, and Captured, as well as those who died Natural Deaths, it would seem we scored a Master Victory.

I confess this somewhat eased the Doubts with which I have been sorely Troubled about the Usefullness of our Expedition.

Easton, Pa.
Oct. 19, 1779

We have received word that the official Uniforms of all the Regiments are Determined on. New York's are to be Blue faced with Buff, with white Linings and Buttons. It pleases me no touch of Red will adorn them. I will ever consider Red the colour of the British.

Of course, Congress and the Commissaries being what they are, wether or not we shall ever get these Uniforms remains a Question in Doubt. God alone knows the Answer!

More important right now, a Consinement of new Shoes has arrived, 667 pairs of These being Appropriated to our Brigade. My Boots are so worn down I can Verily feel a single Blade of Grass through the Souls. Heaven send one of the 667 Pairs finds its way to me.

Easton
Oct. 22, 1779

There is Great Rejoycing here amongst the Officers as well as in the Ranks over the Outcome of the Court Martial of Lieut. Col. Pierre Regnier de Roussi of our Rgt. He had been accused of Unsoldierlike and Ungentlemanlike Behaviour in Wantonly Abusing Doctor Moss and Maliciously attempting the Life of Dr. Moss and Commissary Pratt.

Having found him Guilty of the first charge and Acqwitted of all others, the Court Sentenced him to be Dismissed from the Service. Genl. Poor, who was President of the Court Martial, approved—I do him the Justice to believe that, however Reluctant, he had no other Choice.

However, all was Saved by the Intervention of the Commander-in-Chief, who promptly sent Notice that in consideration of Col. Regnier's long and Faithful Service he is Restored to his Rank. I do not doubt Genl. Poor had informed the Great Man there is no more popular man in the New York Brigade than de Roussi and if the Sentence stood, half the Officers in the 2nd would Resine with him, and as many of our men whose Enlistments were up would follow them.

Many are chuckling over Washington's strongly added *Hint* that Regnier guard against the "Sallies of Passion which can only Serve to involve him in Disagreeable Difficulties." It is these very "Sallies" of his which cause the Men to love him. We know that they are Induced by his Concern for us. He will not only lead us to War against our Enemies; he will also Fight Sturdily against the Butchers in our own Medical Division and the Commissary Thieves who would Rob us of our Just Rights and few Comforts.

We are to receive extra Whiskey and Rum, though mention was carefully not made that this is for a Special Celebration in the New York 2nd.

Oct. 23, 1779

The Overthrow of Col. Regnier's conviction has Served to Overset *me*. What I have dreaded these one-and-twenty Months has come to Pass. I am un-Masked.

It happened in this Manner.

I was sitting at our Fire with Gulich and Cady and Tom Williams, and we had finished our Gill each of Rum and were playing Merry Musick for our own Entertainment and that of anyone who chose to stop by.

Bram came along, seemingly without Purpose and stayed to Listen.

After a Waltz tune and three Marches, we had Gathered an Audience. It was at this point Bram called out, "Give us *The Lament of the Six Indians.*"

My Heart plunged down to the Souls of my new shoes. Someone called out that the *Lament* was too gloomy and a few murmured agreement, but Bram was, after all, an Officer. Perforce, we played him the *Lament*. Some of the men wiped their Eyes upon their Sleeves, greatly Affected. Bram, staring strait at me, said, "Give us the words." 'Twas Gulich, not I, who sang them. My throat was too dry with Fright to Speak, let alone to Sing.

When the last note died away, Bram said in a Casual Manner, "Fifer Van Duren—to my Tent."

He did not look back, carelessly Sure I must Follow, which I did, my Fife in my Hand and Sick with Apprehension.

We lowered our Heads to enter Bram's Tent, where a Jug of Whiskey stood on a Tray placed upon one of the two Camp Beds. There was no one else there.

Bram Clapped me on the Shoulder so Heartily I Staggered from his Strength.

"Take your ease, Philip lad. In the Privacy of my Tent, I'm your Cousin, not your Captain. Here, let's have a Drink."

He poured out two generous Tots of Whiskey and handed one to me. "Here's to Regnier," he proposed. "Confusion to all Sawbones and Commissaries."

In my Excess of Relief about the Purpose of my Summoning, I drank . . . and drank . . . and drank . . .

Presently he lay sprawled out on his Camp Bed while I lay sprawled upon Capt. Vanderburgh's. We were still Drinking, I Believe, as nearly as I can Recolleckt now, and talking about Other Things. I no longer had Fears for the Safety of my Secret. Bram told me of his past few Weeks, when he had been sent to West Point, and inqwired for news of our Encampment while he had been gone.

Then he introduced the Subject of *The Lament of the Six Indians,* but I was too far gone in Drink to be Conserned.

"You wrote it, I understand," said he.

"I did," said I.

"It's about us," said he.

"It is," said I and wept a few Drunken Tears.

He stood up over me. He said, "Philadelphia got her head caved in, Dierk ran away. Martinis got himself strung up. Piet stopped a Bullet. That leaves you **and** me, Philip, only you and me. But if *one in the army was said to have died* . . . that leaves only me because I know who I am, Philip. Who then are you?"

"Me," I hiccupped stupidly, waving my half-full Cup. "I'm Ph—Ph—Philip."

"Then take off your coat, Philip, for my sanity's sake, and let me see for myself."

I stared up at him, making no Move, and he Seized me with Savage Impatience and Ripped my Hunting Shirt violently over my Head; then he tore at the Buttons of my coat. I wrestled him for it, but Needless to say, he was the Stronger and soon had it off my Back. I lay Still, knowing the Struggle was in Vain now, as he tugged at my Small Cloathes. He Rid me of my Under Shirt and at once Saw all he needed to, for it was only in Summer, with the Scant Protection of a Light Uniform, that I had to bind my Breasts. Now it was October, and there was no need. Even in the Dim light of his Camp Tent, he could see the Clear Proof that I was a Woman.

"Oh God!" he said in a Strangled Voice and Rushed out of the Tent. I could hear him Retching. It seemed Strange to me that he should Vomit as much to find out I lived as he did to learn I had Died.

When presently he returned, I was fully Cloathed again, standing and Waiting for him.

"What will you do?" I asked him.

"Why?" he asked me. "Why?"

"I wanted to Serve in the Army, to be a Fifer as Flip intended. There was no other way."

"I loved you," he said slowly. "I have loved you the whole of your Life and most of my Own. All this time you were Serving with me, I have been Faithful to your Memory. Your Memory was more real to me than any Live Woman. I would have given my arms—my legs—my Life to have you Restored to me. And now I find you alive, and I could Strangle you with my Bare Hands. You knew —who knows better?—what I Suffered. With a word you could have taken the Burden from me, and you chose not to."

"I was afraid you would have me Dismissed from the Service."

"That, of course, you will be once I have given my Report to Col. Van Cortlandt. It must be Obvious that, for her own Safety, we cannot let a woman Serve in the Line."

"This woman," I told him Ironickally, "has served in the Army nearly two years, without so much as a scratch. I was at Valley Forge, Monmouth, and all through the Indian Campaigns. You are not Conserned about my Safety, Capt. De Kuyper; you want to be Revenged on me for the Sufferings you Fancy I have inflicted on you. Perhaps I have, but if you will Forgive such Selfishness, I was far more Conserned with my own Sufferings than I was with yours. As for your Report, make it if you Must, it will not Affect my Safety or my Service. Fifers are still in Demand. I can enlist in another Regiment under Another name."

While he stood Dumbfounded by my Outburst, I walked out of his Tent and Returned to my Own. Now, all I can do is Await the Outcome. The next Move is his.

Oct. 24, 1779

God knows how much I drank last night of Rum and Whiskey both. I woke before Day Break with such great pains in my Head that I felt as though it were being split in twain with a Tomahawk. It was all I could do for the Upheaval in my Stomach to Stagger out to the Woods. Betwixt Head and Belly, I felt myself to be Dying, and such was my State, I could not care. I Remember thinking with great Self-Pity as I heaved that Bram would be Sorry for his Cruelty when I was no More. However, after I Tottered back to my Tent and drank down a Vile Mixture Cady made for me from one of Thomasina's Receipts, which has been Invaluable in the Army, I began to think I might not Regret that I went on Living.

Shortly after Assembly a Private summoned me to go to Bram's Tent. He was there with Capt. Vanderburgh, who walked out as I walked in. I Saluted him and after a moment's Hesitation, Saluted Bram, too, and stood strait before the chair on which he sat.

He eyed me Coldly and in Silence for a short time before Speaking.

"I have not yet made my Report to Col. Van Cortlandt," he said Finally, and my Heart gave a great Leap of Hope.

"Whether I do or not depends on . . ." He did not Conclude what it Depended on. "Did you mean what you said last night?" he Demanded in a very Different Voice. "If you are Dismissed from the 2nd, will you Enlist elsewhere?"

"So much I mean it that I swear on—on the heads of my Dead Brothers—that is what I shall do."

He gave a weary Shrug. "I never Doubted it for a Moment,

337

knowing what a Stubborn a—Mule you are. I Suppose I wanted to hear you say it Aloud to Justify to myself the Breach of Duty I am about to Commit. I will not Report you to Col. Van Cortlandt."

"Thank you," I said softly.

"Don't thank me!" he Rapped out. "It's against my Reason, against my Judgement, against my Duty as an Officer. But I would rather have you here where I can keep my Eye on you than in some Regiment in another part of the Country, where you could get yourself in all Kinds of Trouble."

There was another Silence so Prolonged that, after Shifting about on my Feet for several minutes, I Ventured to ask him, "Is that all, Sir?"

"No!" he snapped, then got up from his seat and turned his Back to me. Speaking in a more calm manner, he asked me almost Humbly, "Why? I am still trying to understand why. Last night you said it was because you wanted to be in the Army, a Fifer like Flip. But what would make a girl—even a willfull Hoyden like you —choose the Army, away from Everyone you love?"

"Everyone I love!" I repeated in a Passion of both Anger and Despair. "Everyone I loved left me! *Who* had I left? *What* was there left? Can't you understand? My Mother was dead and my home gone. My Father had left, ashamed of me, not wanting me with him."

He wheeled back to face me. "Ashamed of you! What nonsense is this? He adored you."

"Not after Flip was killed. Not after the Redcoats and Tom Dumb enjoyed my Body. I was Soiled then, Damaged goods, not something the Lord of the Manor could point to with Pride."

He half-raised his hand as though to Ward off the Pain of what I was Saying, but I rushed on as the Philadelphia of old would have done, having no mind to Spare him.

"Do you know what it means to a Woman to be Raped, Cousin? I was Virgin, you know, and they were not exactly Gentle. The Pain was quite Incredible, to speak nothing of the Degredation together with the Terror of not knowing what else they would do to me. After the first one took me from Before, the second one attempted me Behind. I think he enjoyed hearing me Scream."

I fetched a deep Breath, filling up my Lungs so as to Continue.

"So there I was, no Mother, no Father, the Brother I had been closest to dead, the ones I could have looked to for Protection—you and Martinis and Piet—all gone to the Soldiers in the Army, an Outcast where I had lived all my Life for Something that was None of my Doing. I had only Cousin Lucretia and Thomasina. Only they didn't turn from me in Disgust; only they gave me Love and Comfort. They stood by me when there was a Tangible Result of what I had Endured."

"Result?" It was barely a Whisper.

"Surely you know such things happen. Evil compounds Evil . . . I had one of the Bastard's Bastards sprouting inside me."

"Ah, Christ!" he said and sat down again with his head in his hands.

"Never Fear," I addressed the bowed Head mockingly. "Cousin Lucretia got Help for me. I was rid of the Incubus."

He raised his ravaged Face to my View, but I had no Pity for him. I was living it all over . . . the bleak November day when the Farm Pedlar came to our door with fresh eggs and chickens and a whispered message about an Escaped Soldier on his Farm outside the City who had important information for Cousin Lucretia.

We were on our way in Minutes, sure that it was Martinis, from whom nothing had been heard in So Long. We were Wrong. The dying boy in the Barn was not Martinis, but he had been Prisoner with him in that Hell-Hole, the Provost Prison in New York, where Beast Cunningham Starved and Froze and Tortured his Prisoners, Denying them Common Humanity let alone Food and Comfort. When Martinis led those who Fought against Cunningham, Reviled him and Rebelled, he was made an example of. There was no Trial, just Cunningham's Will. In the dead of Night they came for him, bound him and gagged him, then took him out and Hanged him by the Neck. He had time only to leave a Message of Love and Farewell for me and for Cousin Lucretia.

"I knelt by the straw mattress in their old Barn," I told Bram now nearly two years later, "and listened to a dying boy deliver that message as he had vowed to do. I made vow of my own then, directed against the British. *Now will I make a very bitter enemy.*"

Unknown to me then, as I also told Bram, was that in that selfsame week Thomasina had unburdened herself to Cousin Lucretia of the news that she was with child by my Father. They had decided to go to the Dutch Indies, where Thomasina could have the child Secretly, so that when they returned the baby could be passed off as a Member of the Family.

When I was admitted to the Secret, I had the notion to name Martinis the father, knowing he would not Grudge it.

At first I had no other thought than to go to the Indies with them, but even as we Prepared, Obidiah came to bring the news of Pieter's lying ill from his wounds received at Germantown. He meant at first to bring my Father back; he even had a British pass for him.

We all decided quickly. Cousin Lucretia must go with Thomasina, so I would go to Piet in my Father's place, using the Pass. I dressed in Bram's Wammus and Breeches; I cut my hair. When I came out dressed, with my hair clubbed at my neck, they all wept a little, I had so much the look of Flip.

"Can't you see?" I knelt suddenly before Bram's chair, not knowing why it was so important to me for him to Understand when up to now I had Desired nothing more than to Wound him with my words. "When I arrived too late—Piet had died of his Hurts and been Buried three days before—it seemed to follow as the Night the Day. Philip had wanted to be a Fifer, and I was Philip now. I had vowed to be a bitter enemy, and where could I be so but in the Army? There was no one for me to go to but *you*, and where had you gone? So I stained my hair darker with a dye of Onion skins to make it the shade of Flip's, and I used my Pass through the British Lines and came to Valley Forge."

"But to tell no one!" he said, raising me to my feet and himself, too.

"I told Obidiah!" I admitted ashamedly. "I thought *one* should know in case—in case—"

"And *he* consented?"

"I said I would run away and do it somewhere else."

"The same Blackmail as with me."

"I meant it."

"I know you did. Ah, Filly, Philadelphia, don't weep, don't weep so, my love."

His arms went around me, a Veritable Haven of Strength. It felt so wondrously good, I stayed within them, wanting never to be let go. Presently, though, I heard Footsteps outside and pushed away from him quickly. The Footsteps faded away, but I did not Return to the Safe Harbour I knew now I had been aching for. I said to him in a Voice of Mischief, even as I wiped away my Tears, "If someone had come in and found us a Moment since, we could have been both Court-Martialed."

"Fifer Van Duren," said Bram between tears and laughter of his own, "I think you had better get the Hell out of here."

I got.

Camp at Morris Town, New Jersey
Dec. 15, 1779

I think that Hell has all Froze over, and we have been Sent to Dwell in it. Our Camp has been made here in an area called Jockey Hollow, and we are in Tents wilst we build our Huts in the manner that was done at Valley Forge, except that they must be 14 Feet to the Width and 15 Feet long, 6 and one-half Feet High. Some poor Souls down the Company Street fell short of these Specifications and had to tear down two days Gruelling Work and start Over again. There are to be 12 men to a Hut with Wooden Bunks for our Accommodation, not so Cosy and Private as we were in Winter Quarters at the Forge.

I have been more Fortunate than most who, for these past Several Days, have been forced to Lodge on the Frozen Ground, because I am on Temporary Assignment to the Surgeon Genl. He Dwells in a Comfortable House in the Town. I have slept these last four Nights on a straw pallet next the Kitchen Ovens and been employed helping the Sick instead of out Building our Hut in the Cold and Wind that cuts at the Skin like a Knife. Also, I have had Sufficient Food and of decent Quality, which is more than can be said for most of our Company.

I know, of course, who I have to thank for these Mercies. Though he seldom shows himself, I feel myself now to be allways in Bram's thoughts and in his Care.

Jockey Hollow
Jan. 5, 1780

There was a great Blizzard two days ago which covered the Hills and Roads, even men and Tents, six feet deep in Snow.

Two privates in a Yankee Rgmnt. nearly Killed one another over a pet dog Belonging to one, the Other having Strangled it for Food.

The cold Saps at our Strength and Will. We are Hungry. Yet our Day begins at Sunrise with Assembly on the Parade Ground and the day's Assinements; and the Discipline makes no Allowance for our Ordeal.

Camp Morris Town
The first week in Feb. 1779

Our entire Brigade is due to march out for two weeks of Outpost Duty in a town near the Enemy Lines, Brunswick, perhaps.
It cannot be Worse than here.

March 4, 1779

I no longer feel Guilty that I hide behind my Fife and Flute from the Dangers that must Confront others. I verily believe we could not have Survived these Months here without Musick. We are Exhausted with Drill and Training for future Fighting, also Inspections, Guard Duty, and Work Details. The Struggle to find Food and keep Warm Occupies us otherwise. The men risk Punishment to Divert themselves with Gambling, which Harmless Past Time we are not Allowed. Therefore, Musick is the only Solace of us all. It eases Suffering, Oftimes Soothes away Sorrow, and brings Precious Moments of Forgetfullness of where we are and what we are . . . Men forgot by Congress while we Sacrifice all for our Country.

March 1779

A soldier in the New York 4th came to me yesterday, shyly presenting a Paper on which was a Poem he had wrote. He wanted to know if I could set it to Musick. Slowly I read it out:

Come on my Hearts of Tempered Steale
And leave your girls and Farms
Your Sports and plays and Hollidays and hark away to
*   arms.*

A Soldier is a Gentleman his honour is his Life
And he that won't stand by his post will Ne'er stand by
*   his wife.*

*The rising world shall sing of us a thousand years to
come
And tell our Children's Children the Wonders we have
done.*

*So honest Fellows here's my hand and heart and very
Soul
With all the Joys of Liberty good Fortune and a Bowl.*

I looked at the Patriot Poet in his Ragged Breeches and with
Moccasins for Shoes fashioned out of Walnut Bark, naked of shirt
and Coat, so that he wore a Skimpy Blanket about his Torso over
his Under Shirt. His hands clutching the Blanket in Front were raw
and red and Blistered; the bones stood out in his face with the Skin
stretched tight over them.

"I'll set it to finer Musick than the *Essex March*," I promised
recklessly.

As he turned to go, a wide smile of Pleasure Splitting his Face, I
said, "Hold on," and burrowed Surreptitiously into my Haversack
for the half-Loaf Bram had brought me late the night before. It was
Hard and took two hands to break it in Two. I consealed one Half
inside my Shirt and walked with the Soldier outside my Hut. There
I removed the Chunk of Bread and placed it in his hands.

He stared down Reverently, clutching the Bread to his Bosom,
then began to Stammer out Thanks.

"Thank *you*," I said, "for Restoring my Faith." Then I went back
into the Hut to Huddle about the Fire with my Friends.

*Still the Cold Dreary Month of March
in the Year 1779 at Morris Town*

'Fore God, I think that Boredom is our greater Enemy than the
British. Yesterday when I came into the Hut, greatly elevated by my
few minutes with the Soldier from the 4th, I found Nathan Jones, a
Drummer, Scuffeling on the Frozen Ground with the new Fifer
while the other seven men in the Hut looked on Apathetickally.

The cause of their Dispute? Why, the Merits of the Cure each one
espoused for the Venereal Disorder.

343

At my Urging, the Combatants were Separated, but Nathan continued to argue the Efficacy of his Cure with me later while we cooked our Scant Ration.

"Firstly, you take the sulphur of Brimstone for 3 or 4 mornings, that's by way of Preparation," he told me Eagerly. "Then you Boil a Generous handful each of the Roots of Upland Shumake and Mullin in 4 qts. of Spring Water, Strain it, then Dissolve in it half a Gill of Gun Powder. Dose yourself with half a Gill 3 or 4 times a day, and you'll be Cured in no time."

"The Cure sounds worse than the Disease."

"What do you use?" he challenged me.

"I've never needed One," I admitted Incautiously.

Nine pairs of eyes fastened on me.

The new Fifer spat at my feet, which is strictly against Hut Rules. "Hell!" he said contemptuously. "I'll bet this Twit has never Swived a Woman."

The rest looked at me Expectantly. I shrugged. "Not much Opportunity here," I drawled out, Un-Ruffled. "Come warm Weather, I think—I'm Reasonable Sure I'll remember how it's Done."

That Raised a Laugh, which was all I wanted. I have become Adept at turning away the Danger to my Imposture of such Moments.

After 26 months in the Army I neether Shock nor Shrink from the Vulgar. I can Dish it out in Equal Measure.

I am One of Them.

Jockey Hollow
April 5, 1780

Bram procured me a Mutton Bone and the full Breast of a Chicken today, so my Belly is Full even if my Spirits are low. There has been another in the endless Series of Court Martials that take place in the building erected between our lines and the Pennsylvanians. Tomorrow or the next day and the next after that, I will have to Fife some of my Unfortunate Comrades to their lashing. Even the Pillory and the Branding Iron have been used here.

Bram explained to me that Washington enforces Harsh Discipline to hold the Army together; if we do not stand United, our

Cause will have been lost right here. But I listen to the Screams and see the Bloodied backs of men who have drank and gambled and plundered and neglected their Duty only because they were Tested beyond Endurance, yes, even to the Point of Mutiny and Desertion. Last week one almost choked to Death swallowing the Bullet on which he had Bitten down so as not to Cry Out during Punishment.

The Fire is Bright, but I cannot get Warm. This Cough racks me. I am weary, ah God, how Weary I am. Only the last Vestige of Pride keeps me from doing what I made Bram promise *he* would not, Reveal myself to Col. Van Cortlandt and be free to leave this Hole of Hell.

Morris Town
April 30, 1780

The weather improves so that we almost feel like human Beings again rather than Icickles striving to get Warm. Now that the Roads are Passable once more, Transports of Food arrive, also of Cloathing. To Receive the Latter now, when this desperate Winter is over, is somewhat Ironickal, considering our Need is hardly what it was.

Gulich growled today on the Receipt of a new Blanket, "Sweet Jesus, next thing you know we'll be getting our Five Months back pay."

I tried not to laugh with the Rest. Laughing causes me to Cough and brings with it that Stabbing Pain in my Side.

I have not the Breath to Fife, but I must Drag myself out to the Parade Ground. Heaven forfend I not get ill; the last thing I want is to be put in the Pest-Hole they call Hospital.

May 3, 1780

I saw Bram for the first time in Several Weeks . . . he has been out of Camp . . . and we had a final Irrevockable Quarrel. It sprang up so Suddenly, I am still in a Daze for I hardly know how it began.

I remember his Accosting me on the Parade Grounds with a Scowling Greeting, "You look like Hell. Have you been ill?"

I denied it, but he looked Unconvinced and told me to come to his Hut in about an Hour for some Whiskey and extra Food. When

I did so, we were alone in his hut, which I think he had Planned; for he Launched at once into a Vigorous Appeal to me to let him get my Discharge from the Army from Col. Van Cortlandt.

I wanted to say yes. In this one place I Allow myself to admit how Desperately I wanted it. Which is the very Reason why my Pride forced me to Refuse with more Vehemence than I would Ordinarily have Employed. I will not take Advantage of a Way Out my Comrades have not.

We Fell to Bickering in Silly Childish Fashion, as in the days when we were part of the Six Indians, until he Flung up his hands in Exasperation and said, "God, I should have married you out of hand last year when I first found you out. Then I'd have Something to say about what you do now."

"You seem to be having plenty to Say," I pointed out coldly. "And what makes you think I would have married you?"

"You're going to when this damned War is over; it might just as well be Sooner as Later."

"It's going to be Never."

He towered over me, blue eyes in his still wind-burned face shooting off sparks of Electric Anger. "What the hell are you talking about?"

"Not marrying," I returned with Equal Spirit. "After what was done to me, do you think I would marry Any Man—ever?"

He said more Quietly, "I'm not any man."

I said, still stubbornly, "I don't wish to marry."

He used my name, which we had agreed Never to Do, also several Endearments. "Philadelphia, I will never Frighten you, my dear one. I will be Gentle until you—I will help Heal you. You don't understand, Sweetheart. Love has nothing in Common with—with what those wild Beasts did to you."

The Endearments caused Quick Tears to Sting my eyes and made me all the more Determined to fight against such Weakness.

"It's you who don't understand," I said sullenly, the Pain stabbing at my Rib Cage as I coughed. "I'm not afraid of Men any more; I've played one too long. It's Disgust I feel at the Prospect of being Touched or Held by one or"—I shuddered—"or Bedded."

Even Wind-burn couldn't account for the Deepening Redness of his cheeks. "In a tent . . . on the Susquehanna . . . last October . . . I seem to Recall you showed no *Disgust* of being held in my Arms."

I spoke wildly, not knowing really what I was saying, "I thought of you as I would of Pieter or Philip . . . one of my Brothers." Then I did know what I was saying, for it was Unkind of me, I admit, to add, "Or Martinis."

"You mean," he Qweried me softly, too softly, "it would not have Disgusted you to be Bedded by Martinis?"

I hunched my shoulders impatiently. "How can I know now? He's Dead."

"But seemingly still Alive to you. And I, who have loved you and lived for you, might as well be dead for all you care."

I was gathering my thoughts together to Deny this. An Apology of Sorts was forming in my Mind, but before I could say a word more, he was standing before me, rigid and distant; his icy Voice was my Captain's Dismissing me from his Presence.

"Go back to your Tent, Fifer Van Duren. I shall not trouble you again or allow you to Trouble me. Play the man; Stay the man. It has nothing to do with me any Longer. Go, and be damned to You."

May 23, 1780

We are on the March again, bound once more for New York. My own dear Land. My River . . . I shall see them again, if only passing through.

Bram has Kept his Word. He comes not near me. If I see him at a Distance, he Inclines his head formally.

May 27, 1780

Gulich pesters me to Report to the Sawbones, but I refuse. I trust them not. I made up one of Thomasina's Possets with some Herbs I gathered myself. It relieved the Soreness of my Throat from Coughing.

I Encountered Bram today, and his eyes went over and through me. I might not have Existed. I never dreamed he could be so Hard. I thought Bram was unlike all other Men, but I was wrong. Now I know Truly that all Men are Ruthless, given the Opportunity to Exercise their Power. I never meant to give him the Power to hurt me. I didn't know till his Loving Care no longer Wrapt me round that I had done so. "Stay the man!" he told me, but now it is he who has Unmanned me.

BRYARLY

Fort Edward on the North River
June 1780

Bram goes to West Point tomorrow on a special Detail for Col. Van Cortlandt, with not a word to me, not a gesture. Perhaps it is as well. If we cannot be more than Friends, we may be better off Enemies.

My store of paper Dwindles, but what Matter? What is there to write of except the same Dreary Round? Thank God I have acqwired one of a Soldier's Chief Talents, which is to get through each Day in its Seqwence, never worrying Beforetime about the Next.

There is . . .

[Several lines of writing effaced by a faded spill of ink]

End of Book II

CHAPTER
20

Philippa carefully slid Book II back into its box. I stopped her as she reached for another folder.

"Is that the third book of her Revolutionary adventures?"

She nodded. "Third and last."

"I don't want to see it now."

Her brows soared up over eyes rounded with surprise. "How come? I thought you would be panting to get your hot little reporter's hands on it."

I grinned across at her. "I am, but I intend to restrain myself. What's more, I'd be grateful if you would restrain yourself, too. I don't want Bryarly to get any further in her reading than I did."

"It might help if you gave me a reason."

"You know it already," I explained. "It has to do with that cockeyed notion she has that Philadelphia and her love were ill-fated, therefore she and I are, too. I hope she was wrong about Filly and Bram. Bram seems to be the one . . . but whether she was or not, I'm damned if I'm going to let my fate—*our* fate—be decided by something that happened two hundred years ago. Bryarly and I will work out our problems right here in the present."

After she agreed, Philippa made just me a tuna fish sandwich for lunch, Bryarly having adamantly refused all nourishment. She was lost in the past and seemed reluctant, not to say annoyed, to be brought out of it even for a moment.

So I sat with her in the parlor, my feet on an eighteenth-century coal warmer, and I maintained perfect silence as I read a falling-apart first edition of *The Scarlet Letter* that I had found casually stacked on a shelf between two pewter tankards.

I disturbed the quiet of the parlor only twice. Once to make a phone call and again to beg a cup of tea for Bryarly, which I placed on an end table near her elbow.

She sighed an impatient "Thanks," but after a while she lifted the cup and, carefully holding it away from the precious pages in her lap, drank from it thirstily.

When she came to the end of Book II, she looked at Philippa expectantly. "Didn't you say there were three books to this part?"

Philippa's eyes flicked over in my direction and then away.

"Book Three isn't quite ready yet," she lied smoothly, then as Bryarly gave a cry of disappointment, added, "Don't worry. It will be soon."

"Oh, but I—" Bryarly sighed, bit her lip, and then smiled like a well-brought-up child. "You've been very kind," she told Philippa formally. "And we've intruded shamelessly on you all day. We really should—"

"We'll make it up to her," I interrupted cheerfully. "I called in a reservation for three at Gasho's—that's a Japanese restaurant down the road a piece. I ate there several times when I was conducting my woman-hunt for Philadelphia and Cousin Lucretia."

Philippa said, "Marvelous," and Bryarly said in an indulgent maternal way, "You and your Japanese restaurants," after which she lapsed into silence again.

We arrived there early, so there were only the three of us seated around one of the large tables for eight with a hibachi burner in the middle. Philippa interrupted her conversation with me several times to glance at Bryarly worriedly.

"Pay her no mind," I advised kindly. "She's still in the eighteenth century."

Philippa smothered a laugh and took a hearty swallow of her plum wine. Bryarly sipped hers daintily, with glazed eyes, staring into the past. The chef played with his knives and forks and artistically flipped vegetables and bits of lobster over and about the sizzling surface.

"You'll observe," I said to Philippa, indicating Bryarly, "that it's alive. See how it opens its mouth to eat even if it doesn't talk."

Even Bryarly, expertly wielding her chopsticks, heard this remark and laughed. Then, shaking herself like a dog after a swim, she made a conscious effort to remain with us.

By the time we dropped Philippa off after dinner, promising to stay in touch, it was almost nine. Bryarly yawned and stretched as I started the motor.

"Lord, but I'm tired. I'd like to go to sleep right now."

"You see how much on the same track our minds are. I thought of that in the restaurant when I realized how very reluctant I was to drive back to New York tonight. I think it was the plum wine you ladies ordered. I wound up drinking most of the bottle, and in quantity it's more potent than it seems. I reserved two rooms for us at my old motel. Any objections?"

"None," said Bryarly with unwonted meekness. "Except for toothbrushes, it's a grand idea."

"The newsstand will have some."

It did, and I bought two as well as two small tubes of toothpaste, solemnly presenting one of each to her, after the bellboy had opened the connecting door to our rooms for us.

I reduced the size of his tip in proportion to the size of his smirk, said good night to Bryarly, and carefully closed the door. I didn't bother to lock it; that was up to her. I heard it click, smiled ruefully, and went to shower.

Ten minutes after I had gotten into bed with an Agatha Christie some kind soul had left in the desk drawer, there was a timid tap on the connecting door. So timid that at first I thought I was hearing things and didn't answer. When it came again, I shouted, "Door's unlocked. Come on in."

She opened the door, and my reporter's mind registered that she must have unlocked it from her side while I was showering. She had taken off her dress and hose; she wore a sheer black bra and a black half-slip edged in lace. Her bare toes dug childishly into the thick carpet.

"I can't sleep."

She said it like a confession. With a rush of dizzying joy that transcended all tiredness, I realized what it was—a confession, not of sleeplessness but of the desire to share my bed.

I lifted the edge of the sheet and blanket a discreet few inches. "Be my guest," I invited and then held my breath.

Placing one foot before the other, one slow step at a time, she reached the bed and stood there, hesitating.

"Darling, you can just stay here with me if you want. I won't touch you unless you're willing."

She stared at me solemnly for a minute, then slipped into the open space between the mattress and the sheet and lay on her side, as far away from me as she could get. I moved even farther away to ease her mind.

After a while I spoke softly to the tense shoulder hunched in my direction. "I think you'd be more comfortable without the bra."

"Yes." It was a gasp more than an acknowledgment.

"Shall I?"

I took the head motions I saw to signify "Yes" and inched forward carefully until my hands could reach the hooks. Then I slipped the straps down, saying tentatively, "Bryarly?"

She turned swiftly to face me, her eyes wide and frightened, but her lips set in a grin-and-bear-it kind of grimace.

My hands went round her like the cups of the bra, gentling the softness but exerting no restraint. I watched her face, seeing her eyes grow wider and wider and the frightened look leave them. I don't think she realized at first that she was the one rubbing against my hands, seeking more contact, greater pressure. She gave a deep, satisfied sigh as I obeyed her silent urging.

After a while I gathered her into my arms, giving her time to get over her first panicked withdrawal when she felt nothing between my flesh and hers except the silly, skimpy little half-slip.

She lay tensely against me, her head stiff on my shoulder. One of my hands lay in quiet contentment on one curve of her cute little rump; the other swept lightly up and down between her neck and her waist.

"Are you going to make love to me, Jake?" she asked me, showing no great enthusiasm at the prospect.

I smiled to myself. "Only if you ask me nicely," I said promptly.

She pulled away from me suddenly to sit up and turn off the bed lamp, then eased herself back down again.

"I'm asking you nicely," she said in the darkness. "Please," she said. "Oh, please."

"Bryarly, I want to," I told her. "I want to love you and to help you, too, but you can't take me like medicine. I'm not some kind of miracle drug for what ails you."

She began to sob. "Yes, you are, you are!" she insisted. "If you weren't, would I be here with you like this after all the years and all the men I couldn't even let touch me? Would there be the song of the six Indians and the dreams, even the nightmares that bind us together? Oh, Jake, you can't do this to me. You have to help me. No one can help me but you."

I held her close, and she snuggled against me like a puppy. The sobs subsided to whimpers and then faded away altogether. Far from protesting when my hand slipped inside the elastic band of her slip, she helped me by wriggling out of it, kicking it with one foot to the bottom of the bed.

We were doing fine until I positioned myself over her. Then she suddenly turned from a warm, eager woman into a fighting wildcat, pushing at me, scratching and hitting.

We lay far apart again, while my hands moved over her back in slow, steady strokes.

She was sobbing again. "I'm sorry. I'm sorry. It's just that—everything was fine till—I get frightened when someone hovers over me like that. I feel suffocated."

"Is that all, my darling? No problem. Just strike the good old missionary position. Would you have any objection to—what was that rather interesting word you used, *hover?* Would you mind hovering over *me?* I assure you, *I* won't feel suffocated."

"You mean . . ."

"It's quite simple . . . just . . . like this. . . ."

"This," said Bryarly in her most formal voice a moment later, "is damned undignified."

The darkness hid my grin. "Dignity," I said, my splayed fingers nipping her waist and lifting her high, "isn't what we're aiming at."

Then I was swept up in the wonder and joy of her, and she was swept right along with me. Everything about her, including her sexy whisper, aroused me. "More, more, more," she moaned, till there could be no more.

We lay in each other's arms, breathless, still oven-hot.

"Oh, my God!" she said over and over. Then, "Oh, Jake, I never knew." Then she began to cry again. "Oh, Jake, I never knew. Only you could—Only you—"

Only me. I believed it now. I believed everything of the most unbelievable. For in those final out-of-the-mind, out-of-the-body seconds, after we had climbed the mountain together, it was Bram, not me Bryarly called on. First she cried piercingly, "Bram, don't leave me!" then right afterward, "Bram, I need you."

She was still calling him as we reached the top of the mountain and came crashing down together.

CHAPTER
21

The New York Times, March 20, 1978

The Frickman Foundation has announced that River Cross Tavern in Tarrytown on the Hudson, formerly part of the old Van Duren Manor estate and an operating tavern in the 1760s, has been incorporated into its Hudson Valley Restoration project.

After extensive alterations to restore the tavern to its original construction and appearance, it will be open to the public as a museum and art gallery early in 1981.

Sculptor Philippa Jansen, the last known living descendant of the Van Duren family, will have a life tenancy in the tavern and act as curator for the museum.

The New York Times
Sunday Book Review, April 16, 1978

Between The Book Shelves by Mercy Lachine

In quite a change of pace from his latest best seller, *And a Walnut Tree,* which deals with battered wives, Jake Ormont has signed a joint agreement with Lorrimer Press and Hudson Valley Restorations, Inc., to write the history of a powerful old Dutch patroon family, the Van Durens, who settled in New York in the 1600s, fought through the Revolution and five or six other wars (not always on the same side) and managed to retain a foothold on their property into the 20th century. Publisher Mark Lorrimer has thrown out strong hints that it's all a lot racier than it sounds. It had better be, if Jake wants another best seller.

Special to *The Washington Post* . . .
London April 24, 1978

The marriage of Bryarly Allerton, Secretary of the National Men Against Rape Too organization and a vice-chairwoman of the New York branch, to Gerard E. Ormont, investigative reporter and best-selling writer under the name of Jake Ormont, took place yesterday at Lakenheath Air Force Base in Lakenheath, Suffolk, England. Capt. David Samuel Malino, an Air Force chaplain and son-in-law of the bridegroom, performed the ceremony in the nonsectarian Air Force chapel.

The bride, who will retain her own name, was attended by Terry Ramundo, secretary of the New York MART and Nancy Ormont, her stepdaughter. Dr. Joel Raphael of Boston served as best man.

Mrs. Allerton, who is an alumna of Hunter College and received her M.S. degree in Library Science from Columbia University, is a cataloguer of estate libraries and rare books. She is the daughter of the late Caroline Heston of Boston and the late Wayne William Allen of Ambruster, Georgia. She is also the stepdaughter of the late Benjamin Heston, well-known Cape Cod artist and portrait painter.

Mr. Ormont, who was graduated from City College in New York, has had four books on the best-seller list: *The Criminal Class; Promise Them Anything, But—; An American Myth: We Love Our Children;* and currently, *And a Walnut Tree.* His parents were the late Eleanor and Edward Ormont of Brooklyn, New York.

During the wedding luncheon which followed the ceremony, the bridegroom's adopted daughter, Mrs. Sue Lin Malino, was taken to the Lakenheath Air Force Hospital, where she gave birth to an eight-pound son.

April 23, 1978

My dear Bryarly and Jake:

I can think of no more appropriate wedding gift for the two of you than this . . . on loan for the long and happy life I hope you will share together. Then it should come back to River Cross Tavern where it belongs.

> *Your loving cousin*
> *across the Incarnations,*
> *Philippa*

The rich brown leather cover was lettered in gold:

A Fifer in the War for Independence

Book III

Nov. 11, 1780
near West Point, NY

I have been very ill.

Cousin Lucretia says that Saint Peter's gates stood open for me several times, but with my usual stubborness, I chose not to enter through.

Nov. 15, 1780

It was Bram who brought me here, I have discovered, taking me off a hospital waggon and putting me into one he had *borrowed* to bring me to this house near West Point, which Cousin Lucretia rented for her furnishings. The Housekeeper, Mrs. Heiden, nursed me until Cousin Lucretia answered Bram's summons.

After many months in the Valley of the Shadow, I opened my eyes—they tell me it was the third day in Sept.—to find two beloved faces bending over me ... Cousin Lucretia and Thomasina.

"Am I home?" I asked them feebly but with joy, forgetting our Manor House was gone.

"You are home, dear child," Cousin Lucretia answered firmly, meaning I was home with my own Family. When I was stronger, the full Truth was told to me.

Nov. 26, 1780

I have been promoted to a chair by the Fire in my Bed chamber. Two hours a day I am to be allowed from my Bed, providing it does not Weary me. I am ashamed of how easily I Tire; the Fever sapped all of my Strength.

This morning I was allowed to make the acqwaintance of my little cousin Martine Asher. She is a beautiful child, with the Creamiest of Skins and lustrous Black Hair as well as the Sunniest of Natures. I verily believe she will Dance and Sing her way through Life. Just Like Martinis. How Strange.

She seems an Imp of Mischief, too, perhaps too much of one for Thomasina and Cousin Lucretia ... or, perhaps, the Distance of Years we were apart Permits me to see them more Clearly. They are Growing Old.

Dec. 4, 1780

Today I offered to be Foster Mother to Martine after the War is over, as Thomasina was Foster Mother to me. I could see the same Thought had been in Both their Minds.

"Why after the War?" asked Cousin Lucretia.

"I must return to my Regiment when I am well," I said, steeling myself against Objecktion. They both cried out in Dismay, but then Cousin Lucretia made a slight sign with her hand, and to my Relief, they turned the Subject. When I am ready, I will go. Whatever my Reasons when I started, this is something I must Finish.

BRYARLY

Dec. 4, 1780

This day I walked down the Stairs to the Parlour and up again an hour later without any Shortness of Breath . . . well, not very much.

Dec. 8, 1780

I am Confined to my bed for Some Days. Thomasina said that, as allways, I did too Much too Soon.

St. Nicholas Day, 1780

Like a child I received my wooden shoe overflowing with Gifts in bed this morning . . . pins and combs and ribbons for my hair, a painted Oriental fan.

Delicious smells are floating up to me now from the Kitchen; just lately my Appetite has returned a little. I am Determined to go down to Supper. I shall practise my Walking.

St. Nicholas Night, 1780

There was a knock on my Chamber door this afternoon, and I called, "Come in," waiting guiltily for the scolding from Cousin Lucretia or Thomasina, whichever one of them it was to find me out of my Bed.

It was Nither.

I stared across at Bram, who closed the Door quietly and walked towards me.

"They told me you must Stay in your Bed."

I began to Stammer, so Surprised I was . . . and Something Else . . . "I w-wanted to p-practise m-my w-walking."

"Insubordinate, as allways," he murmured below his Breath, but Loud enough for me to hear.

I said shyly, Aware of my flannel Nightdress and Bare Feet, very aware of his Nearness, "Thank you for bringing me here. They said you saved my Life."

"After almost throwing it away. I should have known . . . I should have seen . . . you were not well." He went down on one Knee suddenly and pressed my Hand to his Lips. "Forgive me, Filly," he said huskily.

Burning Tears dimmed my Eyes. I stammered again, "I wanted to say that to you . . . if ever . . . I said things I . . ."

He rose up from his knee and took me into his Arms, gently, tenderly Rocking me, Loving me.

"B-but nothing has changed," I snuffled against his Shoulder. "I can't be a—a woman . . ."

"Hush." He went on Rocking me. "I love you, and you are Alive. That Suffices me now."

So I went downstairs to St. Nicholas Supper after all. In his arms, Bram carried me to the Parlour.

What Joy it was to be together, the small number of us that is Left.

Twelfth Night

Bram came again today, and for the first time I heard how close our Country came to the Brink of Disaster only three miles from here, last Sept., when Discovery was made of Arnold's Plot to deliver West Point into the Hands of the British.

We reminded each other, he and I, how Col. Van Cortlandt always Mistrusted Arnold. It is no great Secret that he wanted him Cashiered for his Profiteering Practises in the Army. This awfull Event has Proven him right. Ironickal that if he had been listened to and Arnold Dismissed from the American Army, that poor young British Spy might be alive now.

Of another Matter I am vastly Skeptickal. Bram spoke of the great Distress experienced over her husband's Treason by Arnold's Bride, Peggy Shippen that was. When the Plot was Discovered at West Point, Washington was sent for from Hartford. Mrs. Arnold, hearing of his Return, Begged his Presence.

She Greeted him carrying her new-born Child in her Arms and Speaking in Such Mad Frenzy of Grief and Shame and Despair that all Present feared for her Reason if not for her Life. She is held to be completely Innocent of any Complisity and greatly Pitied.

Perhaps I am Uncharitable, but well do I remember my many visits to the Shippens with Deborah and Sally when I attended the Benezet School. There was none so Fervently Tory in those days as proud, pretty, popular Peggy, and none so Set on Having Allways her own Way.

Did Benedict Arnold make a Whig of her? Perhaps, and then perhaps not. For what I also remember is what a fine little actress she was! When we acted the scenes from Shakespeare, how convincingly she played Ophelia. "A mad Frenzy of Grief and Shame and Despair" is exactly what she conveyed to us ... I think that perhaps Genl. Washington is a man like any other man, just as Vulnerable to having poor pretty grief-stricken Peggy Wrap him about her Finger!

Jan. 27, 1781

Bram has just been here and is allready Away. He does not expect to be back soon, having assinement to go Northwards.

I grow stronger each day.

Perhaps next time he comes, I may be Ready to return with him to the Army.

Feb. 8, 1781

I am in the Best of Health now and must Confess that time Hangs Heavily upon my Hands. If it were not for the Hours I devote to little Martine, I know not how I would live with myself.

It is Incredibel that I am here Surrounded by Every Comfort as well as with my Dear Ones, yet I am Fretful and feel more Deprived than when I was with my Rgmnt. I miss making Musick with the Band. I miss the daily Friendship of the Men, dear Cady, Gulich, Tom Williams, all the others.

I pace in my Room at night, Worrying for the Safety of the one I miss most of all. My Sixth Indian. My Safe Harbour. Bram. Bram. Bram.

March 10, 1781

The Doctor we hastily summoned to attend Bram is gone. I think we could have done without his Services. He spent more of his time Qwacking me than Bram, Cousin Lucretia and Thomasina having allready attended him well.

I am still Sick Inside from the Shock of the Door's opening up and Bram's standing or rather leaning in the Entranceway.

I cried out his name, as did Cousin Lucretia, and jumped to my Feet, feeling Joy, Overwhelming Joy.

As he whispered my name, not "Filly" but "Our Philadelphia," I saw the paleness of his face. Then a Bolt of Fear shot through me as he slid in a Heap at my Feet.

We got him into Bed in the Downstairs Chamber. As soon as we Removed his Hunting Shirt and the Wadded Bindings on his shoulder, we saw the Putrid Wound and Thomasina hurried to the Kitchen to make up a Poultice and Herbal Brew.

His eyes opened while I was tugging off his tight Breeches, swearing aloud at what hard work it was. He smiled Painfully and said a few Words in a Voice so Low I had to bend forward and ask him to Repeat them.

"Fifer Van Duren," Bram whispered again, "have you Forgotten the General Orders regarding Profanity?"

I whispered back what he could do with the General Orders, ready to Weep with Pleasure that he was enough himself to Jest. Then I started Ripping off his Smalls, at which he did have a sudden Fit of Modesty and Protested, trying to Stay my Hands.

I told him with the Utmost Coolness, "Capt. De Kuyper, You have Nothing concealed in these different than any other Soldier I have seen, and I have seen a-Plenty these three years I have been in the Continental Army."

Cousin Lucretia Chuckeled, Bram grinned Weakly and Gave up Resisting. I continued to Undress him and got him between the Sheets while Cousin Lucretia Bustled off to the Kitchen to Aid Thomasina.

I sat beside Bram while we Waited. His one Hand traced a Restless Pattern across the Coverlet. I captured it and Held it Still in my Own.

"What happened?" I asked him.

He answered in a series of gasps. "Patrol. Surprised by big Party . . . Indians and Rangers . . . Poor Johnson fell . . . Scalped . . . Arrow in my Shoulder as we got Away . . . Had to alarm Country below . . ."

"Hush. That's enough. Don't speak any more. Rest now," I said to him, pressing his hand for Comfort. Surprisingly, he did Sleep till Thomasina returned with her Poultice and Barley Water.

March 13, 1781

I relieved Cousin Lucretia just before Midnight of Yesterday. Bram lay quietly Asleep but within the Hour seemed Fevrish and Restless. He Tossed about so in the Bed, I sat beside him and Pinned him Gently with my two Hands, talking to him in a Soothing Voice that seemed to help.

He started calling for me, first Loudly and then Low, moaning a Little. He Repeated my name many Times. *Filly. Filly. Filly.*

I couldn't bear it and tried to penetrate the Fogged Mind, bending over him to offer Assurance. "I'm here, Bram, right beside you. Look at me, listen to me. I'm here with you."

He stared at me, his Eyes opened wide, but it was Plain he did not see me . . . not as I was.

In an angwished Whisper he addressed me, "She couldn't be Dead and I not know." Then, begging, "Could she?"

"Of course not, Bram." I almost shouted it at him. "Philadelphia's alive, Alive, and she loves you."

Until I said it, I didn't know. All these years, I didn't know. Allways, he was my Rock, my Safe Harbour, and I didn't know he was my love, too, my Only Love. I thought the crazy Wild Infatuation I felt for Martinis was Real and Exciting when it was no more the Stuff of which a True Enduring Love is Formed than a rolag of flax is the stuff from which a Silk Dress is Fashioned.

What a Blind Bungling Fool I have been. Everything Else I may have Lost through no Fault of mine, but Bram's offer of Love I threw away with my own two Hands and my own two Lips.

The words I used to him . . . oh God, what had I said? *Disgust* . . . that was the shattering Word I had uttered . . . Disgust of being Touched or Held or Bedded . . .

Oh God, if I had it to do over. To have his arms in the full Strength of Health about me, Holding me . . .

What Disgust had I felt undressing him, performing small Intimate services about his Body? None. It had seemed the most natural thing in the World to me.

I let go of him as he Qwieted and Resumed my chair to Bury my Face in my Hands. The Beastliness I had once Endured was completely at Odds with the overwhelming Rush of Love and

Desire I now felt for Bram. 'Fore God—I faced the Stabbing Truth—I would Crawl into his Bed this very Minute if he Willed it.

March 14, 1781

Bram's Fever mounted during the Night, Alarming me so I went to the Chamber she shared with Martine to A-wake Thomasina.

The drinks she poured down his Throat soon sent him into a Stupor, and presently I consented to take some Rest.

Towards night when I was again on Duty he became Restless again, moaning for me.

By the light of a single Candle, I discarded my blue underskirt, then my flowered Pannier and Stomacker, my under petticoat and shift. Then I snuffed the Candle. For what was to be, the Fire light Sufficed.

Naked as my Birthing Day, I climbed into Bram's Bed, feeling nothing but Fierce Joy as he turned to me, eagerly, hungrily, as a Babe seeks its Mother's breast. He stopped moaning, his head nuzzling against me, nestling between my breasts. Eyes closed, his hands traveled over me, tentatively, as though puzzled, and then with Gathering Assurance those same hands became strong and sure and Purveyors of such Pleasure as I had never Dreamed could exist this Side of Heaven.

The embers glowed bright in the fire place and its light cast Dancing Shadows on the ceiling above as my Love took me for his own. Then he slumbered in my arms, a deep Profound Slumber while I held him hard in my Protective Embrace.

Long before daylight, before his eyes could Open, I was up and Dressed and away from his Bed into my chair.

When his eyes opened, resting on me, clear and aware, I rose swiftly and went to him. I put my hand to his Forehead, which was cool and damp.

"Your fever has Broken," I said on a sob of Thanksgiving.

His brow unknit. "Fever," he said wonderingly. "That's why I dreamed."

"That's why you dreamed," I told him firmly.

March 20, 1781

Bram is up and getting about. His Wound is Healing perfectly. He spoke today of Returning soon to the Army.

Cousin Lucretia, with a quick look at me, said, "Give yourself time to Heal, dear Boy; no use Courting a Relapse."

He nodded at the Good Sense of this, and then as they do so often this last Week, his Eyes traveled over to rest on mine, Puzzlement in their Blue Depths.

March 24, 1781

Bram told me today he plans to return to his Duties the last day of this Month.

I nodded Briefly. "That gives me enough Time to see to my Uniform," I told him.

Cousin Lucretia said Nothing; she is Reckonciled, having allready heard of my Intentions. Bram's lips Tightened, but he waited till we were alone to Speak.

"Can nothing I say stop you from going back?" he asked me then.

"Nothing. I must finish what I started. Besides . . ."

"Yes?"

"I could not bear for *you* to go and for me to stay Behind, in a woman's usual role . . . waiting . . . wondering . . ."

"I had not thought my Fate mattered so much to you," he told me with unwonted Bitterness.

"It matters greatly."

"Yet still you would Blackmail me if I tried to Prevent your Return?"

"Not Blackmail this time. Bribery."

"Bribery?"

"I'll marry you when the war is over if—if you still want me."

"If I—" He took two qwick steps towards me, his face Alight, then checked himself. "I seem to recall a very different Attitude the last time we Talked of Marriage."

"I love you, Bram. What happened to me is something that will be with me all my Life. If you can accept that, then we—it is Possible we can be Happy."

He enfolded me in his arms. It was Wonderful to have it happening again with his eyes wide Open. "I have been able allways

Removing my cap and then my pins, so that my Hair tumbled to accept anything about you, Philadelphia. We will be Happy, my Dear Love. I promise you," he Pledged me as solemnly as a man ever made his Marriage Vows, "we will be Happy."

March 29, 1781

Yesterday in the morning Bram and I were Wed.

The Arrival of the Chaplain from West Point took me completely by Surprize. It had all been arranged by my *Husband* without a Word to me. Cousin Lucretia and Thomasina had Conspired with him, of course.

The Breakfast dishes were barely Swept from the Table when I was being Offered a few Minutes to Change my Dress, and Tidy my Hair and make my Vows.

Seeing me set to Argue, Bram pushed me into the small Parlour, where we could do it in Decent Privasy.

I folded my Arms and Pretended to Glare at him. I demanded, "Is this an Example of the Type of Husband you will be . . . Arrogant . . . Domineering . . . Tirranical?"

He grinned at me. "God help the Man who tries to Domineer over you, my Love. As for Arrogant, how could I be, when I am Humbled by the very Fact you Love me? Now what was that last . . . ah, yes, Tirranical. The Boot is on the other Foot, Dear Girl. If there is to be a Domestick Tyrant in our Household, it is far Likelyer to be You than I!"

"Bastard," I told him Lovingly.

"My darling." He looked at me, his smile Qwenched, but a light in his Blue Eyes that made my Knees Tremble so that my Legs could Scarce hold me up. "I don't want to Wait until the War is over to Wed you. I have waited too many Years allready."

My lips Quivered so I could not Speak.

"My dear love, my Heart's Desire, this one Time let me have my Way with you," he said in a Voice of Tenderness and Love such as I had never heard him Use before.

"Our Way," I whispered.

The Flame in his Eyes burned Brighter. He came Forward, but not to Kiss me. His hands Busied themselves about my Hair, first about my Shoulders, loose, uncovered, like a young Maid's.

And so we were Wed.

March 30, 1781

Bram came to my Chamber on our Wedding night wearing a Dressing Gown of Uncle Arend's over his Night Shirt. He set down his pewter Chamber Stick on my small Wardrobe.

"Don't be Fearfull, Filly," he said Softly as he came to the Bed where I sat waiting. "I do not Intend to Stay the Night, just to Spend a little Time with you, to talk, perhaps to Hold you. I will do Nothing to Hurt or Frighten you. My only Wish is to Make you Happy."

He had sat down on the Edge of the Bed as he spoke, eyeing me Warily to make sure I did not take Fright. On those Final Words he lifted the nearest of my hands and Brought it to his Lips, pressing a Kiss within my Palm.

I smiled mistily on the Bent Head.

"If you want to make me Happy," I told him, "please get into this Bed. I'm half Froze."

He Raised shocked Eyes to mine for about ten seconds, then Speedily Divested himself of his Dressing Gown, Sped to Snuff out the Candle, Returned, Stumbling in the Darkness, and was soon in Bed beside me.

A moment later I felt him Recoil from me. "You're Naked!" he accused.

I stifled a Giggle. "You didn't seem to Mind it in *your* bed," I pointed out Plaintively.

Two Hands seized me with none of the Gentleness I had been Promised. Mischiefously I pointed this out to him and got well Shaken for my Teasing.

"Never mind that. Tell me what you are Talking about."

"About the Night in your Room when you kept calling for me and . . ."

"And? Finish, you Contrary Wench, or I swear I'll smack your Bottom."

Obedient, pretending to be Cowed, I told him, "And I Obliged you by getting into your Bed—Qwite Naked—and Qwieting you as

Best I could. It seemed to Work; your Fever broke by Morning Light."

"I thought I Dreamed it. I thought it was the Fever. I nearly went Mad for two Days after, thinking . . . why didn't you tell me?"

I said, Demure as a Schoolroom Miss, "I Intended to . . . when the Time was Right . . . and I can't think of a Righter Time than Now, can you?"

He said something Genl. Washington would have Taken Great Exception to, some of the more Objecktionable Words muffled as he Tugged the Night Shirt over his Head. Then He pulled me into his Arms, saying just once, like a question, "Philadelphia?"

"Make me Happy," I answered him.

March 31, 1781

I write my last Entry in this third Portion of my Journal. I am leaving it here with the other papers, sealed, awaiting my Return.

Martine has wept the entire Morning, a little Consoled by my Promise that when I come Home again, she will live with me Forever. Cousin Lucretia and Thomasina, I know, will save their Tears till I am Gone.

My Husband just called out my name from below Stairs. It is Time we were on our Way.

Before we can take up our own Lives again, there is a War to be Won.

End of Book III

Williamsburg
Capitol of Virginia
Sept. 25, 1781

My Very Dear Cousin Lucretia,
 This letter to you will be Sped on its Way by the Army Post if I can Keep it Brief enough so as to have it in the hands of Col. Van Cortlandt's Adjutant within the Hour. Firstly, I must give you Assurance that Bram and I are well and in good Spirits, though Intensely Wearied by the long March through the Jerseys, even with the stay at

Baltimore while the Transports were Prepared that brought us Here. Secondly, I give you News I know you will Rejoice at. Fifer Van Duren is Discharged with all Honours from his Service in the Continental Army. Philadelphia Van Duren De Kuyper is Residing here in the Boarding Home of one Mrs. Hallam, recommended to Bram by Jeremy Stuart, his friend in the Virginia Light Horse. Capt. Stuart's Wife Boarded here before their Marriage when she helped run a Newspaper here in Town. You see, dear Cousin and former Tavern Keeper, there are Women like us Everywhere! As for the Reason I have embraced the Civilian Life . . . Recolleckt that before my Departure from your West Point home you Furnished me with Useful Advice and the Instruments Whereof, for which I was Most Gratefull. It so happens, though, that the Opportunities for my Husband and myself to be Alone were not very Many, and when Such Times came, I was not allways Prepared with those Instruments on Hand. When still at Fort Schuyler in July, he and I lost Ourselves from a Foraging Party and stayed on in an Old Deserted Barn one afternoon. In short, dearest of Cousins, you are about to become a Great-Aunt . . . I felt so Alltogether well, I did not realize it for some Time, the Knowledge striking at me like a Flash of Lightning when we were floating down the Chesapeake and the slight motion made me Qweasy! I, who have Sailed the Hudson in a Violent Storm! The Thought of going into Battle with my Child inside me Struck such Terror to my Heart I had to Confide it to Bram, not about the child but about my Mortal Fear. He said only "God be Praised. Wait here," then Ran from me. I stood at the Ship's Rail till he Returned in half an hour, saying Col. Van Cortlandt would arrange All . . . Pray save all my past letters. Since my Journal pages of this year were all Lost in the Haversack that fell into the River, the Letters will Remind me of these last Months of my War . . . Tell Thomasina I shall Count on her to help me Raise my Child, all my Children, including

*Martine. I hope Martine has not forgot us Alltogether,
and that this finds you—I must stop. The Messenger for
my letter is here.*

Your loving Cousin,
Philadelphia De Kuyper

Williamsburg, Va.
April 15, 1782

Dearest Aunt Lucretia:

*I write with great Relief and Joy that all is well with
Philadelphia, and she is delivered of a fine healthy Boy.
He is to be Philip after both her dear brother and our
Col., who has kindly agreed to Stand as God-father. By
the Time the two are well enough to Travel, I will be
through with my Service in the Army.*

*I was Happy to learn that you had received all the
Affidavits I sent and that Mr. Jay was Preparing them
for Presentation to the Congress. I can think of no
Greater Gift to my Darling than the Return of her
Home.*

*Our son is a lusty baby with powerful Lungs and
Appetite, so prepare Martine for a very Demanding
Brother.*

*Pray give my Respects to Thomasina. Now that we are
finally coming Home to stay, the months between till we
see you will seem Over-Long.*

Your loving Son and Nephew,
Bram

New York City
April 15, 1782

Dear Mrs. Bogardus:

*It is my great Joy to inform you that the Honourable
Congress has been pleased to Grant the Restoration of
the Van Duren Manor Properties to the rightful Heir,
your niece Philadelphia, the Affidavits from Genl. Washington, Genl. Lafayette, and Genl. Van Cortlandt having
worked so Powerfully upon the Body as to make them
aware of the Unfairness of visiting the Sin of the Father*

on the Sons who Served their Country well. All lands and Buildings on the Property known as *Van Duren Manor,* formerly belonging to *Cornelius Van Duren,* with the exception of the Southerly portion appearing on our Map as the South Acre, which was bought by *Van Duren* Tenants in 1780 and which has been Voluntarily Relinqwished by your Niece, will now Revert back to her, becoming through her Marriage the Property of your Nephew. I was Enabled because of the Service Records of *Bram De Kuyper, Pieter Van Duren,* and *Martinis Asher*—and the Awfull Sacrifices made by the Two latter, especially—to Achieve the Desired End according to the Wishes of All without any mention of the Service of one *Fifer Van Duren.*

I offer you, dear Madame, my Sincere Felicitations on this Happy Outcome and remain,

Your Obdt. and Humble Servant,
John Jay, Attorney

CHAPTER
22

Dear Bryarly and Jake:

As you can see, Bryarly's fears were groundless. Judging from later letters and diaries, they lived long and happily after. The marriage endured for forty-two years, and there were two more sons and a daughter.

Interestingly enough, Martine Asher's youngest granddaughter married Philadelphia's oldest grandson. I am directly descended from these two. The truth about Martine was never learned, Lucretia having given all her papers into Philadelphia's keeping some years before her death.

Philadelphia turned everything over to their lawyers, with strict instructions that it be kept safeguarded and sealed for another two generations.

The boxes lay stored away in some basement far beyond that time, not surfacing till 1929, when they were presented to my father, Peter De Kuyper. That was the year he lost our money and most of what was left of

*the Van Duren Property. The original Manor House had
burned down in the 1850's; we used River Cross as a
Summer Cottage.*

*My father was more interested in going after family
money than family memoirs, and my brother died in
World War II, so eventually all the manuscripts came to
me.*

*I look forward to unraveling the history of them all
with the two of you. Happy Honeymoon.*

Philippa

Bryarly bounced up and down on the bed where we both
sat reading.

"It's so wonderful!" she crowed ecstatically. "They married and were happy. Aren't you pleased, Jake?"

"Extremely pleased."

"Do you suppose—" she began, at which point I closed
her lips with a no-nonsense kiss.

"Whatever we suppose," I told her firmly, "can be dis-
cussed in detail on our way to Greece tomorrow."

"Tomorrow. But—"

"Bryarly," I explained patiently, "it was traumatic
enough becoming a grandfather on my wedding day. I don't
propose to devote my wedding night to historical research.
Not to any research at all. Unless," I amended my Declaration of Intention, "you have a sex manual we can study."

She came into my arms with a rush. "You're my sex
manual, Jake," she whispered, rubbing against me with such
loving enthusiasm the wedding night was in jeopardy there
and then.

"In that case, my dear *wife,*" I suggested practically,
though no teen-ager's heart ever pounded harder, "let us
start studying."

I removed her arms, then, with careful control, her
nightgown. She trembled, but she made no move to hide
from me.

"Yes, let's, my dear, *dear* husband," said Bryarly.